MAGDALENA'S

DEDICATION: For Tina – Christine and Stephen

CREDITS

I would like to thank Jenny Hewitt who edited the original draft of this novel and Michael Glanister who advised on the final proofs. Also Doctor Elizabeth Smiley who checked some of the medical details, Jo Smith who once again typeset the final version, and veterinary surgeon Colin Baxter. I must also offer profound thanks to the Petersfield and Forest Writers' Groups, whose members listened so patiently to my reading aloud and offered good critical advice. Last but by no means least, my thanks to Tim and *One Tree Bookshop* in Petersfield. Previously I have written two novels based on the world of sailing and both in locations that were important to me. This time, apart from an excursion to the West Coast of the United States, I have set my book in a rural farming village and its nearby market town. Taraton is an amalgam of two such places that I know well and the village of Crossfield is based on three villages in East Hampshire. If a few people recognise themselves among the nicer characters I cannot say if they are deluded. In truth no character in this novel bears any relation to anyone in the real world. All spring from my warped imagination. Finally may I thank the many friends who supported and encouraged me when I was the recipient of rejection letters, plus the sarcastic comments of a bank manager who refused to advance a penny towards this project. Yes, Madam, farmers can and do write books.

AUTHOR

After retiring from forty years in farming and forestry Jim Morley turned to writing and freelance journalism. He has written two previous novels including the highly acclaimed *Nemesis File* and *Rocastle's Vengeance,* a mystery thriller set on Dorset's Jurassic coast. Both books were based around his love of boats and sailing. With *Magdalena's Redemption*, Jim has returned to his home ground of rural Hampshire.

COVER: The shoreline in Chapter 1 at Dell Quay near Chichester

James Morley
September 2007

MAGDALENA'S REDEMPTION

James Morley

Magdalena's Redemption

First published 2007

Published by Benhams Books, 1 Fir Cottage, Greatham, Liss, Hampshire GU33 6BB

Typeset by John Owen Smith

ISBN 978-0-9548880-2-2

Printed and bound by CPI Antony Rowe, Eastbourne

CHAPTER 1

April 1999

She lay on the shoreline basking in the warm April sun, her slender body curled in a ball, her face asleep and at peace. Tom, gazing down at her knew it was a cruel deception. She would never know warmth again: she was dead.

He squatted beside her on the shingle and gently brushed aside the loose brown hair from her forehead. Then on impulse he moved his fingers down her face and closed the eyes. Her head looked so comfortable lying on the folded green jumper. The face bore an odd enigmatic expression that was also relaxed and at peace. Nothing was striking about her clothing: a plain white T-shirt, faded blue jeans and scuffed white trainers.

Tom stood up. The incoming tide was lapping within inches of the girl. He knew he was not supposed to move the body, but if he did not do so at once the tide would carry her away. He looked for help, but the footpath along the sea wall was deserted. To his right he could see the forest of yacht masts in the boatyard. Looking the other way, his view was obscured by the old wartime pillbox: a lichen-encrusted relic half-engulfed in thorn bushes. Two curlews pecking along the foreshore were the sole sign of life.

Tom came to a decision. He focused the camera he carried and quickly shot two frames. She was a pretty girl, mid to late twenties: maybe no older than his own daughter. Whatever the cause of this tragedy it was a cruel waste. Very gently he bent down and lifted her under the armpits – she was still warm. Even lifeless the girl seemed as light as a child and it was no work to drag her the thirty yards to the high-water line. As he laid her down he saw the name bracelet on her left wrist, the one distinctive object she possessed. He read the engraved name, *Magda*. Something else was troubling him.

'You're beautiful, Magda,' he muttered. 'I've seen you before. I know your face, but where – I don't know – such a bloody waste.'

The tide was washing within a few feet of Tom and the girl when the police found them. Three officers unrolled tape around the scene, grumbling as they snagged their uniforms on the thorn bushes along the footpath. Tom was ordered, none too politely, to stay where he was. Two more police arrived, this time dressed from head to foot in white overalls. They examined the body and then quartered the ground to either side. When Tom tried to explain that this was not where the body had been found he was ignored. One of the forensic men picked up an object from the grass, showed it to his colleague, and then dropped it into a sealed plastic envelope. Last to arrive was the photographer. Tom pointed to his own camera, saying that he had already photographed the girl at the original site. No one seemed to be listening.

'Now, sir, I understand that you are the person who reported this matter.'

The police station smelt of floor polish and disinfectant while the personnel seemed to be distracted by some other emergency. Tom was left alone in the reception area for a full half-hour. It was dark outside and cold now the sun was down. Probably a frost tonight, he speculated.

The interviewing officer was young, cocky, and overbearingly self-assured. Tom regarded him with narrowing eyes but decided against a confrontation; it was nothing to him, he only wanted to go home.

'Name and ID, please?'

Tom slid his bankcard across the table. 'The name's O'Malley.'

'That sounds Irish,' replied the PC with a curl of the lip.

Tom's grandfather had been born in the Forest of Dean. How he'd come by a name like O'Malley, God alone knew and Tom was fed up with years of explaining. No doubt his paint-spattered overalls made him look the part and his West Country accent was sometimes mistaken for Irish.

'You got a permanent address?'

'Boxtree Farm, Crossfield – that's near Taraton.'

'Occupation?'

'Estate manager,' Tom grated the words.

'You mean you're a builder?' The officer frowned.

'No, I'm a farm manager.'

'Status – that means are you married?'

'No, I'm a widower. I lost my wife last year.'

'Careless of you.' The lip curled again.

Tom knew his face was reddening. This insensitive racist jerk had no idea he was dealing with a senior magistrate, nor that he would shortly be the subject of a complaint to his Chief Constable. The man's sneering reference to Tricia was more than Tom was prepared to take. Fortunately the tension was broken by the entry of another policeman and this time Tom knew him. Sergeant Storey had sometimes given evidence when Tom had been on the bench and the recognition was mutual.

'Your colleague is convinced I'm a builder from the Emerald Isle,' said Tom. 'I think he's working up to accuse me of something.'

'Never said that.' The PC looked wary now.

'Mr O'Malley, it's a small world,' Storey looked at the constable. 'See here, lad. Mr O'Malley is a JP, Mid-Hants Bench. He's also the business manager for Gustav Fjortoft.'

'Fjortoft?' The PC's mouth fell open.

'Business manager is a bit strong,' said Tom, smiling now. 'I run his farms.'

'Christ,' said the young policeman, as well he might. Everyone in the land knew of Gustav Fjortoft. The tall blond film director was a massive celebrity, never out of the public eye for long. His lifestyle and huge fortune was a staple of the tabloid press. No wonder the little copper looked chastened.

Storey turned back to Tom. 'That girl by the water – there's no suspicious circumstances that we can see. Our officers found a used syringe on the footpath. We're having it checked for residues and prints,' he sighed wearily. 'The thing is, the casualty doesn't look like a regular druggie to me. We're postulating a suicide as the most likely outcome.'

Tom nodded. 'It was pure chance I came along when I did. I've been painting my boat in the yard there. I was taking a walk along the shoreline for some fresh air when I saw her – poor kid.'

'I understand you moved the body. Normally we would regard that as irregular but in this case…'

Tom was annoyed. 'I couldn't help it. The tide would've floated her away if I hadn't.'

'I know, and fortunately for us, your credentials should satisfy the coroner. Now, sir, a statement – let's get this all down on paper and in proper form, eh?'

Tom drove the twenty-five miles to home in a daze. The image of the dead woman was fixed in his mind and he couldn't have shaken it free if he'd tried. Who was she – where had he seen that face before? He imagined the police knocking on a door. The white-faced woman police constable and her nervous male colleague: just as it had been that evening seven months ago.

'I'm afraid your wife was dead on arrival at hospital, Mr O'Malley. It was a head injury. There was nothing the doctors could do. We're very sorry.'

Farmer's wife killed in riding fall shouted the headline in the local paper. *Mrs Patricia O'Malley, noted trainer of endurance horses, was killed in a fall from her mount Desert Hero... Coroner's Court questions lack of protective headgear.*

The national press were even more effusive. *Gina's kiss for dying friend. Gina Fjortoft, thirty-eight-year old former model and wife of millionaire Gustav Fjortoft, fought to save the life of her friend Trish... "I knelt beside her to give her the kiss of life..."*

'You OK, Dad?' Tom's daughter, Lucy, was tapping on the side window.

Tom looked up, startled. He was sitting in his car, parked in the stable yard of Boxtree Farm. Somehow he must have driven home on autopilot.

'Yeah, I'm fine – I was thinking.'

'How was the boat?'

'She's in good shape – we'll put her in the water again in a couple of weeks.'

Tom liked horses but had never shared his wife's passion for riding. Sitting on a horse gave him vertigo. His interest was sailing, a skill taught him by his father. Lucy had been encouraging him to work on the boat. He guessed that she knew it was the one place where her mother's memory would not intrude. Tom was immensely proud of Lucy. At twenty-eight, a fully qualified doctor, she was experiencing her first taste of general practice in nearby Taraton.

'What kept you? I thought you'd be back hours ago, your supper's in the oven'

'Something happened. I found this girl near the boatyard.' He told her the whole story.

'Oh, Dad, I'm sorry. What rotten luck – will you have to be a witness?'

'Probably. I wonder who her family are?'

Memories of the last coroner's court were surfacing and Tom felt sick. He turned abruptly and strode across the yard to the first of the loose boxes. The horse craned his neck over the half-door.

'Poor old Hero,' said Lucy. She stroked the muzzle. 'You miss your mum don't you.'

'I wonder if we'll ever know what really happened,' Tom sighed.

'Hero knows, don't you old fellow – you were there and you can't tell us.'

'Please,' Lucy put an arm around him. 'This doesn't do any good. It won't bring her back.'

Tom grunted. 'Charlie says Gina's flying in tomorrow.'

Lucy looked at her father. 'You don't like her.' It was more a statement than a question.

'No I don't, but then I've good reason not to.' He quickly changed the subject. 'You know, I've seen that girl on the beach before somewhere and try as I will I've no idea when. Tell you something else…' He hesitated.

'Go on.'

'The police seem convinced it was suicide.'

'That seems logical – you say they found a syringe.'

'I saw them pick it up, that's the thing that's wrong. If only they'd listened to me at the scene.'

CHAPTER 2.

'I can see what you mean, she's a pretty girl.' Lucy was peering over Tom's shoulder.

On the desk lay the two photographs of the dead woman. Tom's father ran a photographic shop in Taraton and he had asked him to process the pictures. Tom did not want their existence to be common knowledge, let alone risk the furore of taking the film to Boots. He had collected the prints the following day and had been studying them obsessively ever since.

'These can go to the police, but I've asked your grandfather to copy two more full-plate.'

'For God's sake, why?'

'I don't know, but there's something about her that fascinates me. I wish I knew the full story.'

'Are the police sure it's suicide?'

'Apparently.'

'That's odd.' Lucy bent over the pictures. 'I would say there's a flaw in that diagnosis.'

'In what way?'

'Look at her hair – what do you notice?'

'I thought it was attractive, chestnut colour, very like your mother's.'

Lucy's mouth puckered in a despairing grimace. 'Is this what it's about, Dad? It's because she reminds you of Mum?'

'No, not really, but she's got something about her, or she did.' He rotated the desk chair to face her. 'Come on, what is it about her hair?'

'It's the look of it. I would say it's been styled that day. Maybe only an hour or so before she died, and those hair-extensions would set her back a hundred quid – more probably.'

'So what?'

'If I was set on killing myself, I doubt if I'd sit down in the hairdresser's, pay all that dosh, and then walk out and do myself in.'

'You're not everybody. Maybe it was to impress some young man and he didn't appreciate it.'

'Since when have you been into female psychology, Dad?'

'Well it's as good an explanation as…' His voice faltered as the phone rang.

Tom picked up the receiver, listened, and made a wry face. He jabbed a thumb towards the extension on the other desk. Lucy picked up the handset, looked across at her father and grimaced.

'Hi, Gina, heard you were home – good trip?'

'Tom, darling, please help me –Spider's gone.'

'Gone where?'

It was his employer's wife on the phone. Spider was Gina's horse; her own little cob that Trish had chosen for her.

'He's been stolen. The stable door's open and the yard gate.' In her distress Gina's affected Southern States accent was breaking up into pure Brooklyn.

'Have you told the police?'

'Not yet – please, Tom, sweetheart, come down and look – please.'

Tom groaned, it was a filthy night, he could hear the rain battering the windows, and neither he nor Lucy had eaten.

'OK, I'll come and look.'

The floodlights under the trees were on full power and the old manor house stood out in the driving rain and sleet. Tom brought the Land Rover to a halt by the front door. Gina, blonde hair awry, was waving frantically from the porch.

'Climb in, Gina,' Tom called. 'We'll give you a lift round to the stables.'

The slender figure in the Barbour coat sprinted across the gravel and clutched the passenger door. 'It'll be a bit of a squeeze, I've got Lucy with me,' he added.

Gina's wan face appeared at the window and for a split second it registered a frisson of anger. Lucy moved to the centre of the cab while Gina climbed elegantly into the vacant seat. Tom put the vehicle in gear and drove round to the rear of the house. Ahead of them was the gaunt Victorian stable block, with its rococo style clock tower.

'I thought you said the gate was open?' He was looking at the entrance to the yard. The big security gate that led onto the road was shut.

'Not that gate,' Gina snapped. 'The other one, onto the gallops.'

Tom swung the Land Rover into the pasture and switched to four-wheel drive. The rain pounded in noisy combat with the windscreen wipers. The soft grass beneath the wheels sagged and squelched. He drove round to the rear gate. It was open, swinging wildly in the rising gale.

'We'd better shut that one or it'll rip off its hinges,' Tom grunted.

'Oh sod to the bloody gate – come and look!' Gina's savoir faire had completely forsaken her.

Tom stopped by the empty stable. The bright halogen yard lights revealed an open door and the softer glow within showed a fresh straw bed and a rack of hay.

'You checked the others?' Tom shouted.

'No,' Gina looked woeful as she wiped the rain from her eyes.

Tom ignored her and strode along the line of boxes. 'Which one's Solar Light?' he yelled into the wind.

'Number four.' Gina had finally come to her senses at the awful possibility. Solar Light was Gustav Fjortoft's most valuable horse. The two-year-old mare was due to go to Lambourne in a couple of weeks for training. She was worth as much as every other horse on the place. Thank God she was there. Solar Light stared at Tom with an aristocratic sneer and then resumed munching hay.

Tom ran back to where Gina and Lucy were huddled. 'Who locked up tonight?'

'One of the grooms I suppose.' She looked defensively at him. 'It's not my fault.' The phoney Virginian drawl was back again.

'Well, somebody's messed things up. Come on, Lucy, we'll go and look. He won't get far on a night like this.'

They left Gina standing in the rain as Tom swung the Land Rover out of the yard and headed for the hills. 'Stupid cow,' he muttered. 'If anyone was seriously rustling horses they'd have sneaked up to the proper gate with a wagon. Dead easy with her away and the house empty. I told Gus his security's lousy.'

'Why can't she look for herself?' asked Lucy.

'For two pins that's what I'd make her do. No this is for your mother – she was fond of Spider.'

'Likeliest place is down here,' said Tom as he turned into Button's Lane. A good tarmac road ran as far as the grain drier before it turned into a dirt track running gently downhill into the hangers: the old copses of ash and beech. Gravel and mud spattered in the wheel arches as the vehicle crabbed on the slippery track. On either side the trees dripped as the branches swayed in the wind. Everywhere was a swirl of hill mist and stinging rain.

Halfway down, Tom stopped. 'Sorry, but it's legging it and torches from here on. You call the old boy – he'll come for you better than for me.' He groped in the back of the truck and threw Lucy an old waterproof. It smelt distantly of silage. She sniffed it, made a face, and put it on. Suddenly she laughed.

Tom wiped the rain from his eyes and shivered. 'I don't see anything bloody funny.'

'Sorry,' she laughed again. 'I was just wondering if this whole charade is a ploy to get you into Gina's bed. Did you see that look she gave me?'

'Well she's out of luck tonight. It's too cold, too wet and all I want is a hot bath and something to eat.'

They walked on in silence, splashing through puddles that were rapidly turning into a moving stream. Tom stopped.

'Garlic,' he called.

'What?' Lucy looked at her father as if he'd gone mad.

'Sorry, I mean smell it. Wild garlic – something's trampling the leaves over there.' He ran into the wood on their right and began to play the torch. The beam picked out two luminous eyes. Standing wet, bedraggled and miserable was Spider.

Tom clipped the bridle rope onto the head collar. 'I suppose we'll have to lead this silly sod two miles home,' he muttered.

'No way – give me a bump up and I'll ride him,' said Lucy.

'Will you be safe with just a rope?'

'Sure – Spider knows his way home as well as we do.'

Tom drove the Land Rover slowly down the track. The road was becoming steeper, while the flash water was building into a torrent eroding deep grooves into the road surface. It would be white water rafting soon, he thought. He looked anxiously in the mirror, but horse and girl were picking their way down the slope carefully enough. Tom turned the cab heater to maximum. Lucy had been right; Spider was far more adept in these conditions than they were.

He breathed a sigh of relief as the Land Rover slid down the last ten yards towards the hard surface of the Crossfield road. Another quarter of a mile and they would have made it. His lights glinted on metal: a sleek Volvo was parked on the verge directly opposite. One of the business set, Tom speculated, out for an evening of untamed passion with a girl he shouldn't be with. Most likely he'd drowned his engine and wanted a tow. It would cost him forty quid, take it or leave it.

Tom grinned as his headlamps illuminated the whole of the other car's interior. His expression changed; it wasn't the scene he had expected. Only one person sat in the Volvo, a woman sitting hunched at the steering wheel. She turned her face to him, shading her eyes and blinking in the glare. She was strikingly beautiful, young and dark-haired; the kind of face that remained imprinted on the memory. In his surprise Tom stamped on the brake pedal and the Land Rover slithered the last few feet, hitting the tarmac road with a bump. The girl in the Volvo stared again into the dazzling lights before starting her engine and driving off, wheels spinning wildly, heading away from the village towards the junction with the A3.

Tom felt unsettled, he wondered who this beautiful mysterious woman might be. Why should she be driving the back lanes alone on a night like this? Lucy and Spider had appeared beside him. Tom told Lucy to go on ahead while he protected the rear with the motor. Lit in the glare of the lights, horse and rider braved wind and rain in front of him. Spider must have sensed warmth, food and shelter, as he broke into an ungainly trot. Tom marvelled how Lucy could sit so nonchalantly on the slippery bare back holding only a single bridle.

The stable yard at the Manor House was deserted with no sign of Gina; Tom presumed she had gone back indoors. Lucy had dismounted in front of Spider's box and was pulling at the door, which seemingly had blown shut. She turned and shouted something that he couldn't catch. He left the truck and went to her. 'What's up?' he asked.

'This door's been locked. What the hell does Gina think she's playing at?' Lucy kicked at the door, while she clung onto the increasingly sullen horse with the other. The stable was securely locked with a hasp and padlock.

'We've got to get him into the warm and give him a rub,' said Lucy. She yelled Gina's name, her voice lost as another icy squall swept across the yard.

'Shut up a minute,' Tom called. He was standing by the door listening. Inside came a high-pitched wail followed by a loud hammering. 'It's Gina, the silly bitch has got locked in.' He examined the padlock. It was a solid looking affair and there was nothing with which he could pick it open, even if he had the expertise.

'Stay here,' he said. 'Tell her I'll get some tools.'

He ran across to the workshop. He had the key for this one on the ring in his pocket. Two minutes later he was back with a massive set of bolt cutters. 'Steady the end of the hasp,' he ordered.

'How? I can't let go of the frigging horse!' Lucy yelled. She was shivering convulsively and the rain was turning to hail.

With difficulty he managed to steady the jaws of the cutters and shear enough metal to snap the padlock.

Lucy was clutching Tom's elbow. 'Dad d'you realise, she can't have locked herself in – it's impossible.'

'That much is bloody obvious. Come on – let's get her out of there. I want an explanation for tonight's fiasco and it'd better be good.'

Gina pushed hard against the door nearly falling as it opened. She flung herself on each of them in turn gibbering incoherently, while the horse forced his way through the middle and into his place in the stable. Lucy found a towel and a rug from an adjacent stall and began to rub the sodden animal with vigour. Spider seemed to have no interest in anything beyond his hayrack.

Lucy finished and joined Tom who had already put Gina in the Land Rover. She started to cry, loud heart rending sobs that Tom knew were likely to last for a long time.

'Who did it – who?' he asked over and over again.

'I dunno, I heard them – they pushed me.'

'We'd better get round to the house,' he told Lucy. 'If she's left it open someone could be ransacking the place.'

The heavy oak door of the Manor House was wide open. Tom walked into the great hall, stopped, and listened. He could hear nothing but the sound of wind and the rain beating on the windows.

He returned to the Land Rover. 'Lucy, I don't know if there's anyone in there or not but I'm going to check – you stay here with Gina.'

'No, Dad, I'll bring her in, and I don't think you ought to be prowling around this stupid great house on your own. We'll ring the police…'

'No, no police!' Gina's hysterics had evaporated. 'Gus wouldn't like it.'

'Don't be stupid,' said Tom. 'There could be someone in there right now doing the place over. Look, were you alone? – where's Otford?' Otford was Gina's shadow; the minder that Gustav Fjortoft paid to protect her in exactly this kind of situation.

'He was upstairs – unpacking.'

'Right, let's find him.' He thought of shouting, but with the noise of the gale, his voice would be lost. Crossfield Manor was a vast pile. They stood in the old part, the fourteenth century half-timbered house with its great hall and oak stair leading to the gallery above. The passages to either side were a labyrinth that led to a Georgian wing to the right and a Victorian Gothic extravaganza to the left. The whole complex covered the best part of an acre.

'Where was Otford when you last saw him?' Tom seized Gina by the shoulders. She was unresponsive: her blonde hair was bedraggled, hanging in her eyes and makeup was running down her cheeks in ugly smears. Tom sighed; the woman had become a traumatised zombie.

As he ran up the grand stair to the gallery he vaguely recalled that the guestrooms were in the Victorian wing, while the Fjortofts lived in the Georgian part. He set off running down a long corridor, trying some of the doors to either side, but they were locked. He noticed his wellingtons were leaving a wet trail on the polished floor. Somebody had been this way because the lights were on. He reached the far end of the passage and stopped.

'Hi, anyone around?' he called.

The rain and wind could still be heard, but the surrounding walls muffled the sounds. Above the background noise was a faint splashing of running water. The noise came from the half-open door on his left, a bedroom with all pink décor and a massive four-poster bed. A shower was running in the en-suite bathroom. He walked across and looked inside the half-open door of the shower cubicle. Lying on the floor, half inside and half out was the grotesque naked body of Alan Otford. He was alive, thank God. The horrible obese form was breathing and the eyes were open. Seconds later Tom was racing back to the stairs yelling for Lucy. At least by lucky chance there was a doctor here.

'This man's a diabetic, isn't he?' Lucy spoke with urgency as she knelt beside the unconscious body.

'Yes, but he doesn't like people to know that – spoils his tough guy image.'

'We need an ambulance, have you got a phone?' Tom fumbled in his pocket, found his mobile and called 999.

'We've got to move fast,' said Lucy. 'He looks hypoglycaemic – he's in a coma. Is there a syringe and a bottle anywhere?' She jumped to her feet and began rummaging around the bathroom shelves. 'Yes,' she yelled, 'here it is – pre-set syringe used and a phial. It's probably an overdose.'

Tom replaced the phone in his pocket. 'Ambulance is on its way now.'

'Good, in the meantime I'll need your help, Dad. Gina's no bloody use. I left her swilling vodka and all my gear's at home.'

'Tell me what I can do.'

'Go and find anything sugary. Energy drink, glucose, something like that. Make Gina co-operate – OK?'

Tom didn't wait for more. He knew the man Otford flush with too much insulin was living on borrowed time. Gina was in the drawing room slumped on a sofa, a bottle by her side. Tom didn't stand on ceremony; he lifted the woman and shook her. 'Gina, the kitchen! Where is the bloody kitchen?'

She opened her eyes and gaped at him. 'Down the stairs … hall – left hand side,' she mumbled.

Tom knew where she meant. In fact he'd seen the house staff use that door enough times. He ran down the stone steps to a corridor with a scrubbed tile floor. At the far end was a heavy oak door. It had no latch or knob so he made a desperate heave with his shoulder and nearly fell into the room. The spring-loaded door swung quietly shut behind him; a faint glimmer filtered through the window from the floodlighting outside. Tom fumbled along the wall for a light switch. Then he froze. He could feel a presence and a slight scent of body-wash perfume. Another person was close by.

'Hello, who's there?' He tried to make his tone firm and challenging, but he knew he was scared and the timbre of his voice must have shown it.

Next a faint scratching noise, soft footsteps, the sound of a door shutting and the turning of a key in the lock. From ten feet he saw the silhouette of a man pass outside the window. At that moment his fingers brushed the light switch. Instinctively he closed his eyes against the glare. Tom could see the outside door through the archway into a storeroom. He ran to it and pulled the handle, but of course it was locked. He peered through the window into a concrete unloading bay; no sign of life – only the teeming rain. He stood still and forced himself to be rational. He wanted to ring the police, but he had another priority. Upstairs was a dying man.

Now he ransacked cupboards and shelves. The best he could find was a bottle of cola from a crate in the storeroom and a bag of white sugar. He put both in a plastic bag then sprinted back to the hall to see Lucy leaning over the balcony above, her face white with concern.

'Bring that stuff and get Gina up here; carry her if you have to. She's got to help me find something!' There was a crackle in Lucy's voice that startled Tom. For the first time he failed to recognise his own daughter.

Gina was still on the sofa, lying full length. He picked the woman up, pitched her over his shoulder in an ungainly fireman's lift, then grabbed the sugar and ran up the stairs. A minute later he was with Lucy in the room. He dropped Gina none too gently on the bed and stood back breathing heavily. Lucy seized Gina by the hair, pulled her upright and delivered a stinging slap to the face. She opened her eyes and whimpered.

'Gina,' said Lucy in a tone that was irresistible. 'I want Al's overnight bag. Which is it?'

'Why?' Gina's voice was slurred.

'He's dying. I'll lose him in the next few minutes unless I find something. He should have it in his bag!'

'It's the black grip – that one in the corner,' Gina mumbled and lay back on the bed.

Lucy was already ripping open the bag, up-ending it on the floor. She scrabbled among the contents and gasped with relief as she lifted a transparent plastic envelope. She ripped it open, removed a syringe, and ran into the bathroom. Tom followed her.

'Glucagon,' she said without looking up. 'Sorry about all that drama but I had to make her co-operate. If I can get this into him now he'll probably be OK.' She probed for a vein, emptied the contents of the syringe and sat back on her haunches.

The ambulance men carried the now conscious Al Otford down the grand stair and out onto the gravel.

Lucy looked utterly drained. 'He should be all right now,' she said. 'They're keeping him in hospital for a day or two to stabilise him.'

'Professional triumph for you, my girl.' Tom put an arm around her.

'Not really, Dad – I was scared stiff. I can't tell you how relieved I am to see these paramedics. They know a damned sight more about this sort of emergency than I do.'

'Don't sell yourself short, love. I was proud of you tonight. You took command of the situation, made us do the right things and saved a man's life. They used to call it leadership when I was your age.'

The police had arrived at last. Two constables in a car and one was the local beat bobby, PC Ross. Ross was a good local copper. He knew every inch of the ground in three villages and almost every inhabitant by first name. More important, from Tom's point of view, Ross knew both of the Fjortofts and their foibles and eccentricities. Everybody trooped into the house. Gina had sobered enough to make a statement. Not that it was much of one. Yes, somebody had pushed her so roughly that she had tumbled inside the stable and the door had been locked. This had happened within five minutes of Tom and Lucy driving off to search for her horse. Tom reported sighting the intruder in the kitchen. All this had been noted down and the police had made Gina take them on a tour of the house. Nothing was missing.

'We'll have some officers check the outside in the morning,' said Ross.

'There definitely was a man in the kitchen,' Tom insisted. 'But the lights were out and I never had a proper look at him.'

'He'll have run a mile by now, and let's face it, nothing's missing, the lady's quite sure of it.'

Tom was still not satisfied. 'Remember she's Gus Fjortoft's wife. Have you considered this might be a kidnap attempt?'

'If so, the kidnappers would have grabbed her and vanished,' Ross was dismissive. 'My advice is go in the house, reset the alarms, and then find Mrs Fjortoft somewhere safe for tonight. We'll keep a discreet watch and review matters in the morning.'

'Don't you worry about me, Officer,' Gina intervened. 'I'll be just fine. Tom'll put me up for the night, won't you, darling?'

They took Gina back to Boxtree Farm. Tom insisted that Lucy have first turn with the bathroom. She was wet through and shivering, both from cold and from reaction to her fight for Otford's life.

'I'll ring Mike and tell him I'm staying over,' she said.

'You needn't bother, I'll be all right.'

'Dad,' Lucy sounded menacing. 'I am not leaving you alone with that woman. Absolutely no way!'

'You're being overprotective – I can look after myself.'

'I doubt it.' Suddenly she smiled. 'I think I'll do something really unethical. When I've had a bath, I'll put her to bed in the spare room and I'll mix her a micky.'

'A what?'

'I thought two crushed temazapan tablets in some hot milk. That'll fix her – she won't molest any man for ten hours.'

'Is that safe after all that vodka?'

'In her case, yes. She'll just feel lousy in the morning.'

Tom had a change of clothes before going to the kitchen to cook them both a pasta dish. Lucy came down from the bath to report that Gina was in bed asleep. She stood beside him, dressed in her mother's favourite blue bathrobe. She looked so like Tricia that momentarily Tom was immersed in regret and self-pity. Halfway through their meal the telephone shrilled. Lucy went into the study to answer it. Tom was puzzled. At half-past eleven at night – who on earth? Lucy returned and sat down at the table. She picked at her food for a moment and had a troubled expression on her face.

'Who was that?' he asked.

'It was the ward-sister at the hospital.'

'About Al?' If, after all their efforts the man had died… It didn't bear thinking about.

'He's fine; they've just had the police in.'

'What's happened?'

'It seems he's demanded to make a statement. Wouldn't stop nagging until they gave in and fetched the law.'

'Why do they want you and how did they know this number?'

'I rang them earlier. You see there are several things about his case that don't make sense. The hospital say Al's way over the limit with his insulin, but he says he never injected himself and it was the wrong time of day for his shot.'

'Is this what he's telling the police?'

'Yes, but there's more. He says someone attacked him while he was undressing for the shower. After that he doesn't remember a thing until he came to with us staring at him.'

CHAPTER 3

From downstairs came a murmur of voices. Tom looked at his bedside clock: it was six thirty. He knew that anyway; a lifetime in farming gave one a mental clock of astonishing accuracy. He was puzzled by the sounds clearly coming from the kitchen below. Then every recollection of last night came flooding back. The wet, the cold, the escaped horse – no accident that – then the helpless feeling watching a dying man, and Lucy's triumph in saving him. And he hadn't imagined that figure in the darkened room. He'd felt the presence all right and seen the figure silhouetted against the window. He was wide-awake now, striving to bring these events into focus. It was stupid but his thoughts kept drifting back to that woman in the Volvo. One didn't forget a face like that. She had lustre, a dark natural beauty, very different from the contrived elegance of a model girl like Gina. Oh God, what was he going to do to control that woman who was now ensconced under his roof? There was enough talk around the village already.

It had been hot that July evening by the pool and Gina's orgasmic screams had been loud enough to echo from the hills. Both Lucy and her boyfriend, Mike, had heard rumours during their medical rounds; the sort of whispers, nudges and winks that village gossips delight in.

He dressed and went downstairs. Lucy was in the kitchen cooking breakfast. Sitting at the table was the owner of the other voice, Charlie Marrington. Charlie was the Manor House gardener, handy-man and, when called upon, chauffeur. Tom was surprised to see that Charlie was wearing his driving blazer while his chauffeur's peaked cap was on the table. Through the window he could see the silver-grey Mercedes parked in the yard. Charlie was a sixty two-year-old, lugubrious and doom-laden country character. The man was not a bundle of joy at the best of times and Tom was not sure he wanted to face him at breakfast.

'I gave Charlie a call,' said Lucy. 'He's going to run Gina home.'

'Why?' Tom was annoyed. 'She doesn't need the Merc for that. I'll take her in the Land Rover, or make her walk – do her good.'

'The car's for the airport,' said Charlie. 'Guvnor's due at Heathrow – eleven o'clock or thereabouts.'

'I've told Charlie what happened last night,' said Lucy meaningfully. 'I've asked him to be discreet.'

'Thanks Charlie,' said Tom. 'The village will be buzzing when the police come back. I'd rather nobody knew Gina was here.'

'Oh aah,' Charlie's sniffed. 'Wives,' he grumbled. 'I don't like my own one, let alone other people's.'

'You're a misogynist,' Lucy looked at Charlie accusingly.

'No he's not.' Tom grinned. 'The miserable old bugger hates everyone and he doesn't see why he should make an exception for women.'

Gina came shakily downstairs and they plied her with black coffee. Shortly afterwards Charlie drove her away. The house staff would be arriving to open up the Manor and Gina would have enough on her plate.

Lucy climbed into her car and wound down the window. 'Dad, I'll be finished with surgery by lunchtime. How say we both go and see Al Otford?'

'What about the police?'

'We can go when they've finished. He'll be in hospital for another twenty-four hours so we've all day.'

Tom followed Lucy as she swept through the familiar hospital corridors. Otford sat in a wheelchair wearing only a shabby dressing gown. His face lit with delight as Tom held out the plastic bag with a fresh set of clothes. They waited while he changed and Lucy appropriated an empty office for them to talk in undisturbed.

Big Al was not happy. The fifteen stone professional bodyguard had lost kudos and the feeling was evidently painful. Lucy had learned from the ward sister that the diabetes was stable and the patient would be discharged following further tests in the morning.

'I never did it,' Otford growled. His voice was a deep Mid-West drawl, which combined with his heavy build frightened some people. In reality Al was a teetotal practising Mormon and something of a charmer.

'What happened?' asked Lucy.

'I was running the shower when the bastard got me.'

'Any idea who?' asked Tom.

'Told the police I never saw nuthin but a shadow; the fella must've been crouched behind the curtain.' Al took a large gulp of water from a plastic cup.

'What curtain?'

'In the corner – covers the medicine shelves.'

‘What did he do?’

‘Stuck me with a needle. I was reaching to turn the faucet and he came at me.’

‘And you still didn’t see him?’ Lucy was sceptical.

‘True, lady, he came over my right shoulder, quick and silent.’ Al’s face registered embarrassed dignity. ‘He stuck me in the butt – don’t remember nuthin’ else.’

‘They’re extending the tests on your blood sample right now,’ she said. ‘Couldn’t have been straight insulin if it pole-axed you like that.’

‘How long after you arrived did all this happen?’ asked Tom.

‘Not long, half an hour I guess. We’d been travelling all day – the flight from New York and the drive from the airport. I wanted a shower – thought it’d be OK – never expected trouble.’ Al looked worried. ‘Guess I let my guard down – dereliction of duty.’

‘Where was Mrs Fjortoft?’

‘Told me she was goin’ to see her horses. Didn’t seem no harm in that. Guess I screwed up this time – don’t know what the boss’ll say.’

‘Oh, he’ll be all right,’ said Tom. ‘But it’s a worry; nothing like this has ever happened in Crossfield. Is there anyone in these parts who might have it in for you personally?’

Al shook his head. ‘I don’t go outa’ my way to make enemies.’

‘Whoever attacked you came prepared, and he must have known about your condition.’

Lucy did not add the obvious, thought Tom. But for her intervention they would have had a murder on their hands.

Tom let Lucy drive home. He was preoccupied with his own thoughts and for half an hour he said nothing. He had been in a few perilous situations, but never before had he stood in a darkened room within feet of a potential murderer. Did he believe Al’s story? The man’s religion always made him transparently truthful. Integrity was one of the reasons Gus gave for hiring Mormons. Al did not lie, but he hadn’t told them everything, of that much Tom was sure.

Gustav Fjortoft had arrived. The full house staff had engulfed the Manor, while packing cases stood in serried ranks on the driveway. Gina was in the middle, supervising the surrounding chaos with majestic calm. For all her faults Gina was superb at such moments. She could organise and run this kind of establishment like the captain of a tight ship. Like the said captain, the staff adored her and when the occasion demanded she would be the perfect hostess. Tom caught her attention and left a message for Gus. Could his employer find time tomorrow to discuss the farm plan? Gina graciously promised to see that he did so.

Tom drove back to Boxtree. Tomorrow was going to be no mere routine business discussion. The crisis gripping the whole of UK farming was no less here in Crossfield. Only the organic vegetable growing was profitable and that, with the garden centre, was keeping the whole enterprise afloat. Billionaire he might be, but Tom doubted if Gustav Fjortoft would subsidise a loss-making business for long. He switched on the computer and began for the hundredth time to play with the budget figures. A knock on the window interrupted his thoughts. Tom looked up to see Charlie peering through the glass.

'Good trip?' Tom asked as he ushered him inside.

'Good trip,' Charlie grumbled. 'Motorways and all them townies – what's good about it?'

'I thought you enjoyed a spin with the Merc.' Tom smiled – enjoy was not one of Charlie's words.

The man never answered – he was staring at the two photographs on the desk. 'Who took them pictures?'

'Actually I did.' Tom was annoyed with himself for leaving the prints in full view. They were a secret between him and the dead girl. If Lucy didn't understand, there would be no point in explaining to Charlie.

'Aha, the sleeping beauty, eh – catch 'er in the act? They was an idle bunch, they furriners.'

'What are you on about, Charlie?' Tom was baffled. 'And she's not sleeping, she's dead.' Now he was going to have to explain.

'All right, keep your hair on – I knows her that's all. My missus used to make 'em cups o' tea – the idle sluts.' He looked sharply at Tom. 'What d'you mean she's dead?'

'I found her last Sunday on the foreshore by Chichester Harbour. She was dead. I had to move the body before the tide carried her away. That picture's for police evidence.' He stared at Charlie. 'What do you know about her?'

Charlie looked at the photograph. 'Magda they called her. She were one o' they furrin girls what worked on the sprout picking – remember?'

Tom found Steve Le Blanc watering in the greenhouses and dragged the man protesting into the main estate office. Steve had sole management of the vegetable growing and the booming garden centre. It was he who hired and fired the army of students and migrant workers who kept the operation on course through the year. The young Channel Islander was an honours graduate in horticulture. Tom liked him and generally left him alone to run his expanding empire.

'Steve, last year, late summer.' Tom didn't waste words. 'Is there any record of those foreign girls? The ones who were around when you finished onions and moved on to the sprouts.'

'Muriel in Accounts will have some sort of list,' Steve replied. 'Why – are immigration on our backs?' He looked worried.

'No, it's not that.' Tom told him about the dead girl.

'Yes, Charlie's right, one of them was called Magda. We had six of them in that group she was with – all East Europeans of some sort. They seemed honest and they worked well – that's all I cared frankly.'

'Charlie says they were a lazy bunch of sluts. His words – not mine.'

'Don't take notice of what he says. It's none of his business anyway – miserable old git.'

'He never was a ray of sunshine,' Tom agreed.

'But as I've said they were good workers. Pretty girls too, all of them,' Steve smiled. 'Used to work in their bikinis when it was sunny. Nice to have around.'

'What did Gina think of that?' Tom couldn't help asking.

'Not a lot,'

'Is that her?' Tom handed over the original prints.

'Her hair's been styled, but that's Magda.' He paused for a second clearly distressed. 'How did she die?'

'The police say suicide.'

'That's awful – I'd never have believed it.'

'Why not?'

'I don't know, but I'd have thought it unlikely. She wasn't a loner. I mean; that entire group were very supportive of each other. Much closer bonding than most of the little student cliques we get.'

Tom sighed. 'I suppose these things happen. When did they finish here?'

'End of October, but where they went to after that I couldn't say.'

Tom was uneasy. The full implications of what he'd heard were disturbing. He would have to tell the police about this. Of course he had a perfectly clear conscience, but he could imagine how the official mind might work. It would look odd that he had failed to recognise one of his own employees, even though the girl was a mere casual worker. He now had a traceable connection with Magda that he had failed to declare. That little policeman he had humiliated might like to make something of it. Who, that afternoon, had seen him in the boatyard? The yard staff were absent on a Sunday, but John the yard manager had called to collect something from his office and Tom had spoken to him briefly. There had been other people around, none of whom he really knew. No doubt he could establish a credible alibi but it was still a worry.

Last night's incident was out of his hands, and for that at least he could be thankful. The police had walked all round the Manor House and taken fingerprints within. Apparently they were satisfied with his statement, but would be returning to discuss the situation with the Fjortofts in the morning.

A surprise awaited him at Boxtree. Parked by the front door was that distinctive customised Jeep, and standing beside it was the man the world called the Bear: Gustav Fjortoft.

The Bear was Fjortoft's great film. He had acted, directed and partly financed this early 1960s feature. Shot in Northern Canada, and beautifully photographed in black and white the epic had made Gus's name and immediately propelled him to Hollywood. Tom was not normally a film buff and had seen little of Gus's later output, but *The Bear* had genuinely impressed him. He had watched the video at home twice. It was a bleak story, without humour, but it had heroism, pathos and a touch of cruelty. Tom admitted to being moved by the film's finale, while Tricia and Lucy had openly sniffed and dabbed their eyes with tissues. None of it seemed to square with the character of his employer as he saw him day to day. Tricia had said something about creativity and that the really great artists could be quite normal on the surface. Tom was not sure he would describe Gus as normal. Sometimes he detected a dark and brooding quality in the man. Not today though: Gus was at home and in the place he loved best.

Truly he had something of the bear about him, if one could imagine a bear dressed in jeans, green wellingtons and a checked logger shirt. He was a huge man; not obese, but tall, large framed, with short stubble hair still blond though tinged with grey. He exuded fitness amazing for a man in his mid-sixties.

'Hi there, Tom. How are you – how's the kids?' The handshake was warm and genuine; the blue eyes sparkled.

'Gus, I'm fine thanks and Lucy's in good form; Andy will be home from law school for Easter.'

It would be good to have the family together again, even though the children's mother was no longer with them. Tom checked himself; in another minute he would be plunging into misery.

Gus was staring at him. 'I gather your Lucy saved a tricky situation last night.' He looked concerned, almost embarrassed.

'That's right, Lucy was brilliant – she saved Al's life.'

'Sure, I've heard and I won't forget it.'

'You know he claims someone attacked him.' Tom opened the front door and waved Gus inside. 'I spoke to him today and he's telling the truth. I found a man lurking in the kitchen as well.'

'I know, Tom. Gina's told me all about it,' Gus sighed. 'It's got me worried too. I didn't want to come home to this kinda thing.'

'Will you tighten security? I tell you something else, we had people tampering with the horses – Gina's Spider did a runner.'

'I know, I've heard nothing else since I got here. Come on; let's do a tour in the Jeep. You can tell me what happened as we go.'

Gus stopped the Jeep in the pasture on the summit of Crossfield Hanger. It was beginning to spit with rain and the sky to the west was black with advancing cloud.

'Charlie told me it was going to rain,' Tom grinned.

'Oh sure he did – all the way home in the car,' Gus laughed. 'We're filling the pool next week.' He looked mischievous.

Tom wriggled uncomfortably. He could never come to terms with Gus and Gina's peculiar open marriage. Particularly the way Gus seemed amused by his wife's conquests. Similarly, Gina appeared unfazed by her husband's collection of bimbos. Through it all the pair were clearly fond of each other. If Gina as a hostess was a real asset, then Gus must be a beacon of security for her.

The pool was set within the Manor gardens surrounded by a white Spanish style wall. It was oval shaped, bright blue, and although open to the elements it was heated. When not using the pool themselves the Fjortofts made it available to the estate's employees and their families. Apart from a few of the student casuals, only Tom, Tricia, and their children had taken up the offer. Everyone else had been frightened away by the Fjortoft Scandinavian ethos. Bathers were required, reasonably enough, to take a shower in the changing area. After that the rules were explicit. No costumes or clothing of any sort were allowed by the poolside.

It had been last July, the hottest day of the year. The final trailer load of the winter-sown barley was safe in the grain store. Dusty and soaked in sweat Tom had driven down to the Manor. He had earned a quick dip in the pool. He dived in and swam two lengths in a languid crawl. Preoccupied, he had failed to notice the svelte figure lying prone on the foam mattress. Nor did he hear a sound as he towelled himself on the edge. He had stopped in frozen animation, as light fingertips touched his shoulders and ran silkily down his back. He turned to face Gina, or rather he faced the golden tanned figure that had once graced the centrefold of *Penthouse Magazine*. Even though her beautifully sculptured breasts and bottom might be more a tribute to her cosmetic surgeon, Gina still looked magnificent. Tom had faced her mesmerised as she moved her fingers to his thighs and then ran them up his chest and around his neck. Tongue-tied, he could hear his ears singing and feel his face reddening. Gently she rubbed herself against him until his arousal was complete. Then she had taken his hand and led him to her poolside bed.

It was dark by the time Tom, with Gustav Fjortoft, had finished their farm tour. Tom was delighted at the way Gus responded to every detail; clearly the man loved his farm. Tom reasoned they were doubly lucky. Had the estate belonged to a London investment company their futures might well be in jeopardy.

Lucy was waiting for them at Boxtree. She gave both men a kiss and invited Gus to dinner. He shook his head. 'Sorry, and believe me I'd soonest be with you folks, but Gina's expecting me and it don't pay to upset that lady.'

Lucy was holding an envelope. 'I forgot to tell you,' she said. 'This letter came by recorded delivery – I signed for it.' She handed Tom an official looking buff envelope.

He tore it open and frowned. 'I'm subpoenaed to give evidence to the Mid South Coroner's Court on Monday.'

'There's been trouble?' asked Gus.

'I found the body of a girl by the waterline at Chichester. Police say it's suicide.'

Tom had been about to tell him of Magda and her link with the farm. He hesitated and changed his mind. Some intuition, some deeply buried instinct told him no.

CHAPTER 4.

'It says her name's Magdalena Sherakova. It's less than a week – they seem to be in an indecent hurry to tidy the whole thing up.' He passed the coroner's summons to Lucy. 'I'd better ring the police straight away and get it over.'

Gus had gone home. Lucy had walked out into the yard with him, leaving Tom brooding over the piece of paper in his hand.

'I think you're making too much of this,' said Lucy. 'You're the head of a big organisation here. Nobody would expect you to know every casual worker.'

'So you say, but the police have a suspicious mindset – they have to.'

Tom rang the Sussex Police. He was told that Sergeant Storey was not there, but he would be on duty again at eight o'clock. Would Mr O'Malley care to call then?

'I think I'll come down in person, if that's all right?' he asked. 'Good, eight-fifteen then.'

He put the phone down and looked at Lucy. 'You coming, you know – moral support?'

'Yes, if that's what you'd like. I still think you're making too big a deal of this. You've got your own witnesses when all's said.'

'No blame on you, Mr O'Malley. We've monitored the young lady's movements up to twenty minutes before you found her. You were definitely in the boatyard during that time – we've checked.'

'Hell!'

'Don't worry, it's all routine. Nothing personal – that's the way we work.'

'Who was she? I only know her name – can you tell us some more?'

'Magdalena Sherakova, age twenty-six, from Riga in Latvia.' Storey picked up a computer printout. 'I would be interested to know what she was doing digging spuds on your farm. We're not wasting police time on it, but I'd be grateful if you could make a few discreet enquiries. Just to tie up the loose ends.'

'I'll do what I can,' Tom was surprised. 'Why shouldn't she work on a farm? We've lots of migrant workers in summer.'

'Yes, but not her class.'

'What was she?'

'Top journalist in her own country – written two books as well.'

'That's interesting. I thought you said there were no papers on her.'

'Correct, but the following day a woman came in here and identified Magdalena.' Storey shuffled through his notes. 'Here we are, Hannah Berkovic, Israeli national – close friend of the deceased. She was a cracker.' Storey whistled softly. 'Dark hair, nice bit of crumpet.'

Lucy was stirring. 'Supposing, hypothetically of course, the woman had been fated with a squint and a hare lip?'

'Evidence is evidence,' Storey smiled.

'What'll happen to the body?' asked Tom.

'Nothing until after the inquest. Has to be because there's poison involved.'

'Then?'

'Ah now, there you have it. We rang the Latvian embassy. Told them what had happened and asked them to contact the girl's family. Since then we've heard nothing.'

'Has she got any family?'

'God knows. We were a bit put out by the embassy – they seemed almost indifferent.'

'What'll you do?'

'It's up to the coroner's office, but I gather she's to be buried here in the town cemetery and that the Berkovic woman's paying.'

'I want to go to the funeral.'

'Dad,' Lucy protested. 'Why?'

'Why not – she worked on the farm and I didn't even recognise her? Now she's dead and miles from home.' He was aware that his voice had risen and both the policeman and Lucy were looking at him strangely. He retreated into silence; at that moment he couldn't have described his motives anyway.

Tom dropped Lucy at the clinic. It was raining again as a new weather system worked its way across Southern England. Lucy was not pleased; she had passed a traumatic twenty-four hours and it was her turn to be on emergency call.

'Sod's law,' she said. 'Probably nothing will happen, but it's a lousy night to have to turn out for some kid with a stomach ache.'

'Think how much worse it would be if you were a vet out there on the hill with a sick cow.'

She screwed up her face in an expression that reminded Tom of her as a little girl. 'You know there's times when I almost envy them. Animals are so much nicer than the human race.'

Tom left the car in Taraton's central car park and walked the short distance to his father's photographic shop. Fred O'Malley was in his mid-seventies and had started the business to ease the boredom of retirement. This had meant in his words, "swallowing the anchor". After a lifetime at sea Fred had turned his photographic hobby into a business that supplemented his pensions enough to keep Tom's mother Lucille and himself in comfort.

The shop was closed so Tom walked down the side alley to the back door and let himself into the tiny kitchen. He called and heard his father answer. The old man was in the darkroom, so Tom put the kettle on and waited. Ten minutes later Fred appeared. He took off his white overall coat and hung it on a hook. As always it smelt of chemicals.

'Lucy's young man was in here today. Sold him a new digital Olympus.' Fred scrubbed his hands vigorously in the washbasin.

'I like Michael,' said Tom, 'I think she's struck lucky there.'

Lucy and Michael were both doctors in the same clinic. They had been together since medical school and seemed an ideal match.

'Maybe,' Fred grunted. 'But I don't hold with the situation.'

Tom knew what he meant. Lucy had set up home with her young doctor without benefit of a marriage service. Nothing so marked the difference between his parent's generation and his own, and Lucy's even more so. Forty years ago, in a rural area, the stigma would have made the whole family social outcasts.

'Lucy's an adult,' he replied, 'it's her life.'

'You heard from young Andrew?' Fred poured them both cups of tea.

'He phoned on Friday. He's coming home for Easter.' Lucy's younger brother was an impressively mature young man at nineteen. Tom had been mildly disappointed when Andy had rejected agri-culture for the law, but with the state of British farming who would blame him?

'You've come for those enlargements? You're not going morbid are you, boy?'

'No, I'm not, but I'm curious about her. You see she worked on the farm and I never knew it – she was just a number.'

'Still sounds morbid to me. You ought to get away for a bit – have a change of scene.'

'No chance, Dad, I've a job to do.'

'If Fjortoft really valued your work he'd make you take a break.'

'Well I wouldn't go, this isn't a good time and the Fjortofts have problems of their own.' He told his father about the incident at the Manor.

'All the more reason for you to get away. I never trusted those Fjortofts, not either of 'em. Maybe there's some chickens coming home to roost.'

'For God's sake, Dad. Why d'you always have to be the odd one out? Gus is a great guy – everyone says so.'

'Not everyone. Did I ever speak to you about Sammy Little?'

'The name rings a very faint bell – who was he?'

'Oppo of mine from the Benson Line – back in forty-eight. Later, Sam worked for Bensons in Seattle about the time Fjortoft became chairman of the board. Nineteen sixties that'd be.'

'So?'

'Sam would spit if you mentioned Fjortoft. It seems he had a score to settle.'

'What about?'

'Don't know – none of my business.' Fred pushed an envelope into his son's hand. 'Here's your bloody enlargements and you're welcome to 'em. I've got a hundred jobs to do. You'd best push off for an hour. Go down for a pint in the Dragon.'

It had stopped raining, but a bitter damp wind spiralled through the streets. The pubs were open and Tom walked into the saloon bar of the Swan. There, holding court was the local MP Roland Gannemeade. Tom instantly withdrew. He might have forgiven him for being a politician, but there was something about Gannemeade that Tom found hard to take. He couldn't quantify it; he simply didn't like the man.

He walked the hundred yards to the Green Dragon. The bar was half full. He nodded to a couple of people he knew and smiled as he saw two youths enter, recognise the magistrate, and scuttle back into the street. One of them was "Curly" Tong, Crossfield's principal ne'er-do-well. The atmosphere was warm and relaxing as Tom ordered a half pint of low alcohol lager. He didn't much like the stuff but in his position one must set an example. It wouldn't do for tittle-tattle to link him with drinking and driving.

He downed his beer, left the pub and strolled up the High Street into the Market Square with its greystone church and dignified Georgian buildings. A gaggle of youngsters was drifting towards the nightclub on the far corner. Those kids must be impervious to rain and cold, he thought. The boys in thin T-shirts looked almost protected compared with the girls in their flimsy shifts. Someone was staring at him. He turned away quickly; it wouldn't do for him to be seen ogling teenage girls. A second glance and he saw who'd caught his eye. A girl, or a woman rather, a few years older than the teenagers had detached from the crowd and was heading his way. Tom turned and walked quickly across the street and into the shopping arcade. A voice was calling. He looked back and saw it was the woman. She was looking straight at him as she called again, 'please…?' The rest of her words were lost in the passing traffic.

Now he knew her; she was the same woman he had seen in his headlights as she sat in her car that rain swept night. Tom realised he was being stupid and irrational as he ignored her and sped through the precinct to the car park. He looked back once; she was standing under the archway of the shopping mall in the full glare of the lights. Her face wore an expression of irritation and reproach.

Tom lay awake listening to the rain as the wind battered it against the windows. He looked at the red numbering of the digital clock; it said two thirty. This was always the witching hour when his inner demons came out and encircled the bed to taunt him. These black depressions had grown less frequent over the months, but the unsettling happenings of the last two days would guarantee a visitation.

He rolled over and ground his face into the pillows. He wanted a woman. God, he needed a woman. Why was Lucy so bloody protective? If she hadn't hung around last night he could have had Gina on a plate; ignoble thoughts but true, and Gina was good. Twice since Tricia's death she had made an excuse to call at Boxtree when Tom was alone. Lucy knew nothing of these trysts and Gina never boasted.

The nightmare was working its usual course. It was July, two days after his encounter by the pool. Tricia had confronted him and he had confessed; told her what had happened, factually and truthfully. For the first time as a grown man, he had broken down and wept. Tricia had listened in silence, turned her back and stormed out of the house. She had returned two hours later and sat quietly, saying nothing, staring at him until he'd broken down again and blubbered and blustered in total and complete humiliation. Tricia had put her arms around him and cuddled him as if he'd been an errant small boy, chastised and forgiven.

Amazingly she had burst out laughing. 'Gina lives on another planet. She went all weepy on me and then she said "we're friends, you've no right to keep that lovely man all to yourself. We're friends – we should share our good things."' Tricia had given Tom a less than playful slap. 'Well, no way! You're not getting inside her again while I'm around and you're not being shared.'

That night they had made love for the last time. Twelve hours later Tricia was dead.

He rolled over and looked at the clock; it said three fifteen. The demons were running true to form. He would have no respite from this torture, no sleep, until he'd been shown the complete reprise of that awful day. Tom swore, swung his legs out of bed, and stomped downstairs to make a cup of tea. On impulse he wandered into the study. He wanted to have another look at that inquest subpoena. The red light was flashing on the answer-phone and it hadn't been so when he and Lucy had left that evening. He walked over and pressed the playback button.

The male voice was heavily accented. 'Meester Omly, Magda's friends would be much honoured to be meeting you. Please, we would like you, after der inquest, to go to…' There was a pause with a second voice muttering in the background. 'Please, you go to der Crown and Anchor, by der yacht yard. After der inquest – you understand.' The message ended abruptly.

Now wide-awake, Tom punched the 1471 code. He glared as the prissy female voice replied: 'You were called yesterday at twenty twenty-seven. The caller withheld their number.'

He ripped the tape cassette from the recorder and snapped it into his pocket Walkman player. Ten times he listened. He assumed, from what he already knew that the man's accent was East European. The second voice was definitely a woman. He could make nothing of what she said, but he assumed she was telling her companion the name of the rendezvous. A non-stop, rumbling and roaring, in the background didn't help. He concluded the callers were using a phone on a main road. In the end he gave up, made his cup of tea, and went back to bed. He was relieved that his sleep was long and dreamless.

CHAPTER 5.

The inquest was at half past eleven on Monday and it was still raining. Tom had done half a morning's work around the farm and then showered and changed into the formal suit he wore for his own court. He wished he could define why he felt nervous. Certainly the last coroner's hearing when Tricia died had left a scar. Now it was another person's tragedy and this time he was no more than an observer. Once again he sat facing the enlarged photograph of Magda. He had always known there was more to her than an itinerant worker. A top journalist the policeman had said, and yet she had killed herself. She was a beautiful talented girl with her life before her; whatever the circumstances it was still a waste.

The courtroom was in a crumbling Victorian building with draughty echoing corridors. The coroner, a hearty military type, sat at a table with his clerk and a shorthand writer. Half a dozen spectators were scattered around the chairs that filled the remainder of the room. A lone press reporter sat at a table by the door. One among the spectators did stand out. He was a young man of a type who would draw attention anywhere: athletic in build, with dark good looks and black hair tied in a ponytail. In this drab room he looked out of place, with even a touch of menace.

Tom spotted Sergeant Storey in the witness seats and joined him.

'This one shouldn't take long,' Storey whispered. 'There's only you, the pathologist and me – should be over in an hour.'

The coroner banged a gavel and the clerk called Tom to take the stand. He retold how he'd found the body and waited for the arrival of the police.

The coroner peered through his bi-focal spectacles. 'Mr O'Malley, I understand you were acquainted with the deceased?'

'No, sir, the young lady had been a casual employee of the company I work for, but although she looked familiar I have no recollection of ever meeting her.'

'Of course,' the coroner beamed. 'I thought we should make the point a matter of record.'

'Thank you, sir,' Tom replied uncertainly.

He was told to stand down and his place was taken by Storey. The sergeant confirmed the identity of the deceased. He stated that Miss

Sherakova was a Latvian citizen of ethnic Russian extraction. She belonged to a minority community facing restriction and some persecution in her own country. She had made no application for asylum, but her entry visa to the United Kingdom was due to expire. It was not for him to speculate on the lady's motives, there may have been other pressures on her, but in his view all the facts indicated suicide. The coroner made no comment. Storey mopped his face with an enormous handkerchief and sat down beside Tom.

The last witness was the pathologist. He was a thin balding man who walked with a stoop. 'The cause of death was heart failure and general trauma, caused by entry into the bloodstream of some ten millilitres of the veterinary anaesthetic, Etorphine Hydrochloride, brand name Imobilon.' The man spoke with a slight Scottish accent and sounded bored. 'In my opinion death would have taken place within a few seconds – half a minute at most.'

'How was this anaesthetic administered?'

'By hypodermic, inter-muscular injection into the deceased's fore-arm.'

'Was there a syringe or any similar instrument present at the scene?'

'Yes, there was a twenty-millilitre syringe found within a few feet of the body. On analysis it was found to contain Imobilon.'

'Is this a common product?'

'No, in fact it has been withdrawn in the UK because of its danger.'

'Can you say how this young lady came by it?'

'Not legally, though it is still licensed for use in zoos.'

'The crux of the matter,' said the coroner, 'is who administered this drug?'

'Finger print analysis confirms that the deceased handled this syringe. Her thumbprint was distinct on the plunger.'

The coroner addressed the court. The evidence they had heard pointed beyond reasonable doubt to suicide while of unsound mind. They could only regret the loss of a young and talented life. The court adjourned and everyone shuffled out into the corridor.

Storey bid a hasty farewell and disappeared. Tom yawned and looked at his watch; it was a quarter to one. The man whom he had noticed sitting in the public seats of the court was staring at him. He was standing with another person whom Tom had also noticed in the courtroom, but this one was little more than a youth: tall and thin, with groomed black hair and large square rimmed spectacles. He reminded Tom of the singer Buddy Holly.

The boy walked over to Tom. 'Please, Meester Omly, I am Anton.' He held out a hand and Tom shook it politely. 'Meester Omly, I would be much honoured if you would come to meet my friends.' Here was the voice he had heard on the answer-phone.

'So, it was you who rang me?' Tom said by way of helping the conversation along.

'That is so. You have your car?' asked Anton.

'Yes, it's round the back.'

'That is good. We go to see Magda's friends – they are waiting.'

Tom knew the Crown and Anchor; it was a pub-restaurant a short walk from the boatyard. He suspected he was being conned into buying lunch for a gang of famished students. Magda's friends – yes, he wanted to know Magda: who was she, her homeland, her hopes, ambitions and loves? Above all he wanted to know why this girl's face, so peaceful and enigmatic in the moment of death, haunted his every waking moment.

Something else was making Tom uneasy: he spun round. The other man he had seen earlier in the courtroom was staring at him. Something about this individual was disturbing. His demeanour and flashy good looks were turning the heads of a group of passing office girls; to Tom he left only an impression of deep malevolence and it was all directed at him.

'Who is that man?' he asked Anton.

'He's Joel.'

'And what does he have to do with this?'

'Magdalena's boyfriend – bad guy.'

Tom watched the said Joel turn and walk away towards the town centre. Seconds later a car cruised slowly by. Without waiting for it to stop the man opened the rear door and slipped onto the seat. Tom tried to memorise the number: Ford Mondeo, 1998 registration, was all he managed.

'Was that man the reason she killed herself?'

'No.'

Tom left it there and led the way to the drab car park. He fumbled for his keys.

Anton examined the vehicle. 'Citroen Xanthia – good wheels. I like cars,' he added.

'My wife chose it. I'm only interested in getting from A to B.'

'Your wife, she drives many miles?'

'Not now – she's dead!'

Anton looked solemn. 'So, your wife is dead and you are sad.

Magdalena was my sister and now she is dead, so I also am sad.'

The boy looked so bereft and mournful that Tom regretted having snapped at him. Maybe Lucy was right when she said he was becoming self-centred.

The car park at the Crown and Anchor was full so Tom stopped the Citroen in the approach road to the boatyard. Another car a dark blue Volvo, pulled in behind him apparently with the same idea. He was surprised when Anton opened the passenger door and loped round to speak with its driver. He watched in the rear mirror as the doors opened and two others, a man and a girl, climbed out. The man was broadly built and in physique not unlike Gustav Fjortoft. The girl was tiny in comparison. Although fair skinned she had her dark hair set in neatly woven dreadlocks.

'Hi, I'm Pete and this is Chantelle.' The burly man was leaning through Tom's open side window. He had a cherubic red face, with closely cropped hair and a single earring.

'I'm Tom.' He studied the faces of these strangers. Magda's friends? They seemed harmless enough, though this man was older than he had expected, late thirties perhaps and definitely American. Both he and the girl wore identical clothing: jeans, denim jackets and walking boots. They might be from some new age commune, although had that been the case Tom would have expected them to be scruffier.

'You're the guy who found Magdalena?'

Tom nodded; he was watching this man carefully. He would give nothing away until these people revealed their motives. The man seemed to sense this as his face broke into a friendly and disarming smile.

'Say, maybe I'd better put my cards on the table. I'm Pete Little, from Seattle in the US, but I'm in England on a two-year lecture contract at University South.'

University South was a large academic campus a few miles to the east. It had an abrasive, politically radical reputation; a denim-clad don with an earring was probably par for the course.

'What do you teach?'

'Twentieth Century history and Mid European studies.'

Tom thought he understood. 'Was Magda one of your students?'

'Jeez no, she wrote books in her own right.'

Tom gave this professor a challenging stare. 'Why do you want me?'

'You found Magda,' said Chantelle.

'Correct.'

Chantelle returned the stare. 'We're her friends, she was Anton's sister, and the police won't tell us a goddam' thing.' The woman spoke with an accent that was vaguely American but with a strange underlying cadence.

'I sympathise, but what can I do?'

'Would you show us the exact spot – it can't be far?'

'All right, I can do that for you.'

'It was there,' Tom pointed. 'I pulled her body from the tide line and put it here.'

His companions stood silently staring at the waters of the creek. It was no longer raining, but the low cloud still scudded unbroken across the sky. The boy Anton began muttering in a strange language; his eyes were red and swollen with traces of tears.

'Did you tell the police you moved her?' asked Pete.

'Yes,' Tom suppressed his annoyance. 'I told them every last detail.'

Anton intervened with a long speech in his own language. Chantelle looked as puzzled as Tom felt, but Pete clearly understood.

'Anton says nothing was told in court about you moving her. I know his spoken English ain't that good, but he understands it OK.'

They had a point; all the questions in the court had assumed that the body had remained static. Tom had reported moving her at the time, but had said nothing about it in court because nobody had asked. He said as much to Pete. 'Does it matter?'

'Oh, man,' said Pete. 'It's crucial – it's the key to the whole darned tragedy and nobody's picked it up.'

'I don't see it – explain.'

'Magda died from an injection of poison that would have killed her instantly – right? You've just said that you found her by the water's edge with her head on a pillow but the syringe that killed her was found, nice and convenient, by the place you finally put her.'

'If you are saying I had something to do with her death, forget it. I was in the boatyard at the time and I've witnesses.'

Pete waved away Tom's protest. 'No, man. You happening by was coincidence. She was murdered and we know who did it and why.'

Tom was not impressed. 'If that's what you think, I suggest you tell the police.'

'Oh sure!' said Chantelle.

'Have you talked to them?'

'Yes,' said Pete.

'With what result?'

'Nothing, they were very polite, but they'd already made their minds up – suicide.'

That was true. Suddenly he remembered something Lucy had said. 'Your Magda had her hair styled recently. My daughter says it must have cost a hundred pounds and had probably been done not long before she died.'

'It didn't, it cost her one hundred and fifty at a top stylist in Brighton, and that's one helluva lot of bucks.' Chantelle was glaring at him. 'Say, mister, how come you know that?'

Tom reached into his inside pocket and took out the two photographs. He handed them to Pete. 'I took these in the original position. I thought they might be needed as evidence.'

'Oh, Jesus,' Pete muttered. He handed them to Chantelle. She grimaced and gave them back to Tom.

'You may not know that I'm a magistrate,' he looked at the three of them. These student radicals were unlikely to be impressed and he didn't want to sound pompous. 'I've no authority in this county but you are, I think, entitled to make a formal deposition to me.' Yes, they were listening and they were interested.

'Deposition on oath to a judge?' Asked Pete. 'Say we've got something like that in the States.'

'I think that would be the proper form in law,' he was definitely sounding pompous. 'Oh look, this is all bullshit, just tell me what you know.'

They looked at each other; Pete pulled a mobile phone from his pocket and primed a number. 'Hannah, we're with Tom O'Malley, the guy who found Magda.' His face puckered as he pressed the phone against his ear. Tom guessed the signal was breaking up. 'We're down by the water where it happened … yeah, we think you ought'a meet him … the guy says he's a magistrate. He wants to hear our side.' There was a pause as Pete listened and he glanced suspiciously at Tom. 'No, it's gotta' be a coincidence. OK, I'll show him the mug shot.' The conversation ended and Pete stuffed the phone back in his pocket.

'Look, Tom, do you have time to come with us and meet someone? We'll take you in our car and return you here.'

'That depends on who I'm meeting, why I'm meeting them, and I'd prefer to see them in my own time and in my own car.' Tom was interested but he was damned if he'd give in that easily. 'If it's that important they can come and see me.' The look he gave them was none too friendly.

Pete held up a hand. 'I'll level; we think Magdalena was murdered. The police won't listen, but you're a judge and I guess you've your own suspicions.' Tom tried to intervene but Pete waved away his protest. 'No, man, hear me out. Tom, you've a link to this business that you don't know about. It's old history, but it killed Magda and she's only the latest in a long line.'

'This is getting bloody obscure. I don't think I can help you.' Tom was less sure than ever about the people he was dealing with and it was beginning to rain again.

'D'you know this guy?' Pete handed him another photograph, carefully shielding it from the rain. It was a black and white shot of a man standing beside an elderly army truck. He was tall, fair-haired, aged about thirty-five and dressed in combat trousers and a short sleeved shirt. The ground on which he stood was featureless and dusty. Tom had the impression that the picture was taken overseas in somewhere tropical.

'Would you know him?' asked Pete. 'It was taken thirty years back but we've nothing more recent.'

Tom was certain he'd never seen this man, but on the other hand something about him was teasingly familiar. 'He vaguely reminds me of someone, but right now I can't say whom,' he replied.

'He's Gustav Fjortoft's brother,' said Pete.

Tom shook his head. 'Fjortoft's an only child, he hasn't got a brother.'

'You seem very certain about that,' said Pete. 'How much do you know about Fjortoft?'

Tom would have to admit he knew practically nothing about Gus's past, apart from his career in films. 'Why are you telling me this?' he asked.

'Your father's Captain O'Malley – used to work for the Benson Shipping Line?'

Tom was surprised. 'How do you know about him?'

'My pa and he were shipmates.'

Now he made the connection. 'Sammy Little – my Dad was talking about him only the other day.'

'Now, will you trust us. There's someone important wants to meet you, and she'll tell you the whole story.'

Anton sat beside Tom as he followed Pete and Chantelle in their Volvo. He still had no idea what lay at the end of this journey. If, as seemed increasingly likely the police had overlooked a murder, he had a duty to try and discover the facts and see justice done. He had taken the precaution of ringing the estate office to let them know that he would be absent for the rest of that day. If he wasn't actually being abducted he still had no idea where he was being taken.

Pete drove into the central car park in Taraton and Tom parked next to him. Tom was invited to leave his car and join the other two in the Volvo. Anton for some reason remained in Taraton. It was only when Tom had settled into the rear seats that he noticed the side and back windows had been covered with plastic screens. In no way was he nervous, only annoyed. He caught glimpses of the route Pete was taking. Much of it was through narrow lanes and minor roads. He tried to see direction signs, farms and other landmarks, but could make little of it. The journey ended abruptly as the car turned into a gravel drive and came to a halt. Chantelle, with a sweet smile, opened the door and invited him to step out.

He was standing in front of an expensive modern bungalow within a large neglected garden, surrounded by a gloomy hedge of Leylandii. Tom could see the roofs of neighbouring houses peeping above the greenery. At this point he smiled; he knew where he was. These people weren't as clever as they assumed they were; he had been driven on a route deliberately calculated to mislead. He was in Malvern Road in Rotherwood, less than four miles from Taraton. Through a gap in the hedge he could see the Crossfield Hanger, two miles away.

'Journey's end,' said Pete. 'There's a black hole in my belly that I wanna' fill. When did you last eat, Tom?'

'Breakfast, and you're right – I'm starving.'

'Well, this ain't a bad place to put that right. Great food here but strictly kosher – I doubt we'll get a ham sandwich.' Pete rubbed his hands together.

It was a large bungalow and its lack of furniture exaggerated the size of the entry hall. At least someone had taken the trouble to polish the parquet floor and the house had a pleasant smell of pinewood and cut flowers. A vase of daffodils on the long trestle table was the only object in sight.

'Hi, you guys,' Pete called. 'We're back.'

'Hoi, not so much of dat shouting, I gotta a headache.' A large man had appeared in a doorway behind them. He was grizzled and elderly, wearing a striped shirt and off-white cotton slacks. In another setting Tom would have taken him for a French café owner.

'You a bunch of hungry bunnies now?' the newcomer asked. He spoke in a foreign accent that Tom couldn't place although he certainly wasn't French.

'What've you been cooking for us, Mo?' asked Pete. 'We earned it, man.'

'Sure thing, I done rost-bif, all in honour of de English farmer here.' He grinned broadly at Tom who noticed this ebullient chef had three missing teeth.

'I ain't eating that crap,' sniffed Chantelle.

'She's a goddam veggie,' said Pete wearily.

'OK,' said Mo. 'I do you beans and pasta. Then you fart in your boyfriend's bed all night and he go sleep elsewhere.' Tom liked this character already.

'Tom,' said Pete, 'Mo's our friend, protector, guru, you name it, but mostly he's here to mind our Hannah. Where is she anyway? I've brought Tom to meet her.'

'Dat lady went to shower, 'bout ten minutes ago. Give her a break, Pete. Never was a woman keep a date on time – she ain't no exception.'

'Chauvinist,' muttered Chantelle.

'No way, she der boss. I give my life for her, but she's still a goddam woman come end of der day.' Mo changed to a foreign language; Tom guessed it was Hebrew. Pete answered in the same tongue although it sounded as if he was struggling. At this point Chantelle chipped in demanding to know what was being said. She spoke in French, an odd sounding French with curious grammar. If they thought this was over his head they were mistaken. Lucille, Tom's mother, was French and although his fluency had slipped over the years his understanding was still good.

'Mo says this man's Gina Fjortoft's lover,' said Pete. He spoke in the same odd dialect as Chantelle. 'I told him I know that already – Han told me.'

'So what,' she replied scornfully, 'that woman has a hundred lovers. He runs her farm and he is *jolie* – so tall, nice posterior, *très* sexy – I don't blame her.'

This was too much for Tom. His face reddened and he coughed.

'Say, man, you understood all that?' Pete grinned.

Chantelle at least had the grace to look embarrassed, before she retaliated. 'How is it that an English peasant understands *le Français*?' Now her eyes glinted.

'Probably because my mother is a Breton peasant,' he replied in the same language. 'Anyway, what part do you come from? I've never heard a Froggie talk like you do.'

He had hoped to provoke her and he succeeded. 'I am not of France. I am Quebecoise.' She was openly hostile.

'Canada?'

'Civilised Canada. We brought civilisation. The English bring only exploitation, rape, and pillage.'

'Bullshit,' Tom laughed, and for a moment he thought she would hit him.

'You can cut the xenophobic crap, Chantelle. Mr O'Malley is a guest in my house and I won't have you picking fights.' Tom looked for the source of this new voice. It had the scintilla of an accent, or otherwise he would have taken the cadence for Standard English Home Counties. It was a voice resonant of gymkhanas and village fetes, except that it was also soft and musical and it reminded him of Tricia.

The woman was standing in a doorway with the light behind her. Tom was not in the least surprised, it was almost as if he'd been expecting her. She was his dark woman, the one who had called out to him in Taraton Square, and on that stormy night in Crossfield, had sat in the car in the wind and driving rain.

CHAPTER 6

She held out her hand. 'Hi, I'm Hannah.'

'I'm Tom – Tom O'Malley.'

'I know that.'

He was struck by the maturity in her voice. He tried to estimate her age: probably in her early twenties, and yet these people seemed to regard her as their leader. Her eyes were scanning his face. They were huge eyes, dark pools of deep brown, framed by long black hair that brushed her slim shoulders. The face was narrow with high cheekbones, a small angular nose and a complexion already lightly tanned.

'Someone pointed you out to me in Taraton the other night,' she said. Tom felt uneasy; he remembered the incident all too well.

'I was there too,' Chantelle sneered. 'You ran away from her – you gay or something?'

That broke the spell. Chantelle was exactly the kind of chippy feminist who most got up his nose. There could hardly be a greater contrast between these two women.

Tom ignored Chantelle and faced Hannah. 'I saw you parked at night in that lay-by at Buttons End. You drove off in a hurry when I came out of the wood.'

Now she was surprised. 'That was you?' Her eyebrows raised. 'I'm glad you told me that. It was unexpected and I didn't want to be seen.'

It was time he took the initiative. 'I would like to know what you were doing within a mile of Crossfield Manor on the night when there was an attempted murder in that house.' That would shake her. Sod them all – he was weary of this play-acting.

Not a flicker of expression crossed her face. 'It seems to me, Tom, that you are lucky to be alive yourself.'

'What does that mean?'

'As I understand it, you were in the kitchen within two feet of a killer.'

For a moment he was almost speechless. 'What the hell d'you know about it?'

'We know, that's all.' The voice defied argument. 'We know a lot of things. We know about you, your background, your wife and family. We know about your relationship with your employer's wife.'

'Is this some blackmail scam?' Tom glared at the girl; attraction was merging into resentment and anger.

'No blackmail; but we're certainly interested in you. People here like you. You're a personality – down to earth is the expression we keep hearing.'

Tom was mollified, but still very wary.

'Yes, we were thinking of approaching you anyway, and then incredibly you found poor Magda.' Her eyes were scanning him again. 'Tom, I think that was fate, kismet, do you believe in such things?'

'Not really.'

'Isn't it fated that you and I co-operate?'

Tom didn't know what to make of that. He could take the remark in any way he chose.

Mo reappeared. 'Food ready, you guys,' he called.

'Come on then,' said Hannah.

Mo's cooking was everything that Pete had claimed. Even the vegetarian dish that he plumped down disdainfully in front of Chantelle looked tempting. The promised roast beef was a beautifully tender sirloin, marinated in juices that were outside Tom's experience. Hannah uncorked a mellow red wine. Tom had never seen the label before and asked her what it was.

'It's Israeli,' she replied. 'From my father's vineyard. It's only a small place, we don't make many bottles but we think it's good.'

Twice he tried to ask questions, but she waved him to silence. 'Wait until after the meal, then I'll put you in the picture – promise.' She smiled at him. 'And do try and relax – there's no hidden agenda and I don't bite.'

Tom was sitting in what Hannah had euphemistically called her study. It was a pleasant enough room with patio doors overlooking the garden and an unkempt lawn. The room was furnished with tables, a filing cabinet and two computers. Tom now had his emotions under firm control. He had questions that he intended to ask and he was not going to be walked over by this formidable young woman.

'Houses in this road value at around three hundred thousand pounds and upwards. Today, I've travelled in the same new Volvo that I saw you in that night – worth at least fifteen grand.'

Hannah made no reply but cocked her head on one side attentively. Tom was not deterred. 'Who's paying and what sort of organisation is behind you?'

'Who said anything about an organisation? I'm a journalist and I like to think I'm a free spirit.'

'No, I'm sorry, but that's not good enough. I wasn't born yesterday – shall I go on?'

'Of course, I'd like to hear your reasoning.'

'Right, if you were a millionaire's daughter who'd been given this place, it'd be fully furnished and not looking as if the bailiffs had just called. Second, if this was a student's squat there'd be wall posters everywhere, pop music blaring and piles of dirty washing. I know all this because my daughter's place was like that at medical school.'

'What was your place like when you were at Cirencester?' she smiled.

'Christ, you have done your homework, haven't you?' This was personal and he knew he sounded bitter.

'No problem, it's all in the records. You were at the Royal Agricultural College in the swinging seventies,' she raised an eye-brow. 'You met your wife there, Patricia Lansbury – a girl of somewhat higher class than yourself, I'm told. Please, Tom, don't be offended. We badly want to take you into our confidence, but we had to check you out first.'

'Tell me about Magda,' Tom was anxious to steer the conversation away from him.

'All right,' she paused as she stared at some papers on the table. 'You've been told that Magda was a writer. I'll be more specific – she was an investigative journalist.'

'Was that why she was murdered?'

'Ah, so you think she was murdered?'

'In view of what I've been told today – yes. Tell me something else. This morning Anton pointed out a man who he said was Magda's boyfriend. Frankly I didn't like the look of the fellow.'

'That was perceptive of you. Yes, the man is Joel, he's crazy but he didn't kill her. We warned Magda about him, but she always had a rotten taste in men.'

'You say she was a journalist – what did she write about?'

'Magda's speciality was the history of the Baltic states and more recently the crimes of the Germans in the Second World War and those of their local collaborators.'

Tom began to understand. 'That could still be dangerous?'

'Very dangerous.'

'So you say someone killed her. I'm inclined to agree with you about that, but I can't express an opinion about the motive.'

'There is only one motive that is obvious to us.'

'And who is us?'

'Not so fast, Tom. I told you I'm a journalist, I'm not showing you all my cards and I defend my sources.'

'All right, you may think I'm pretty thick.' Tom had switched to his aggressive tone and that alone would have cowed most youngsters. 'You tell me why a Latvian investigative journalist would be harvesting vegetables in Hampshire – for the good of her health?'

'Certainly not for her health, although they all had a lot of fun. There was a man called Steve some of the girls fancied.'

'These girls plural – were they all investigative journalists?'

'I doubt it, the guy who runs the employment agency is one of us, he arranged for Magda to join their group,'

'Us again,' he glared at her. 'What is so special about Crossfield Manor Farms, which I happen to manage? I have an absolute right to know why some subversive organisation is planting spies on my patch.'

'In a minute, Tom – you must be patient with me,' again that slow hypnotic smile. 'Your father's a photographer?'

'Yes what of it?'

'Nothing, but he used to be a sea captain. He and Peter Little's father were shipmates. Very old buddies, Pete says.'

'Yes he told me.'

'Kismet, you see, Tom – so many coincidences. What did your father have to say about Mr Little senior?'

'Only that he had some sort of grievance against Gustav Fjortoft.'

'Quite right, but you must ask him for the details. What you won't know is that Mr Fjortoft has a half-brother whom he finds embarrassing. Magda discovered the whereabouts of this brother and for that she was killed.'

Tom was outraged, this was a repetition of what Pete had told him and it had to be nonsense. 'I know for a fact that Fjortoft was an only child and his father died in the war. Apart from Gina and one illegitimate son he's alone in the world.'

'Did he tell you that?' She was unfazed by his outburst.

'Yes he did, and so did Gina.'

'Then he at least lied to you.'

Tom controlled his anger. 'I find that highly unlikely. You know what I think.'

'Tell me what you think.'

‘I think this is some stupid conspiracy by film people. Gus has enemies in Hollywood – I know that for fact.’

‘You’re way off track, Tom.’ She was gazing at him with that slow smile. She was devastatingly attractive, and now he knew for certain that she was an enemy.

‘I think,’ he said, ‘that the only true thing you’ve told me is that Magda was a journalist, and I believe that because the police told me so. You may call yourself a journalist, but I wouldn’t dignify you with that title. I would say you’re a tabloid scandal hack.’

‘Wrong again, Tom,’ she sounded sad as if she were disappointed in him. She picked up a small square of card and gave it to him.

TELAVIV INT NEWS AGENCY
Hannah Berkovic
Flat 6
107 Drake St
London W12

Now Tom understood. The Fjortoft charity ran international hospices for terminally ill children. There had been a mighty furore eighteen months ago when the Israelis had commandeered a Fjortoft home in the West Bank and evicted the staff and residents. The place was now a clinic for a new Jewish settlement. World opinion had been outraged and Gus had immediately flown to Saudi Arabia to secure funds for three further homes.

‘So you Israelis have got it in for Fjortoft because he cares for sick Arab kids.’

‘No!’ her eyes flashed with anger. ‘We are not like that.’

‘From all I’ve heard you are exactly like that. If not, why are you hanging around here watching his house and trying to link him with an unrelated crime, if it was a crime?’

‘Tom, you cannot escape the fact that Magda was murdered and that for now her killer is escaping justice.’

Tom stood up. ‘Miss Berkovic, I am leaving. Thank you for the excellent meal and for a most interesting afternoon.’ He turned and walked abruptly from the room.

The entrance hall was empty and the house silent, with neither sight nor sound of the others. For a few anxious seconds he had worried that these dangerous people might prevent him leaving. The front drive was also deserted; the Volvo had gone. He was beginning to resign himself to walking home when he heard the sounds of a vehicle turning into the driveway. He was astonished to see his Citroen with Anton at the wheel. He swung round to find Hannah standing in the front doorway, a mobile phone in her hand.

'Hey, I never said you could use my car. Anyway it's central locking and I've got the ignition key.'

'Anton's a wizard with anything mechanical – always in a good cause,' she said.

Tom confronted the wretched Anton as he climbed out of the car. 'Taking and driving away a motor vehicle's a serious offence. That'll be at least sixty hours community service if I report it.'

'But I don't think you will,' said Hannah.

'I should do. You're foreign nationals acting suspiciously on British soil. I ought to go to the police.'

'And tell them what? I'm an officially accredited journalist following a hot story.' She had walked across and was standing facing him. 'Tom, I fight for truth and justice – nothing more. I would like to think you were on my side.'

CHAPTER 7

Tom needed to be home; he had decisions to make. Magda was no longer a poor refugee girl who'd come to a cruel end; she was part of something more sinister. He wished to God that he had never gone for a walk that day and found her body. Kismet, Hannah had said. That woman fascinated him; everything about her was mysterious. It reminded him of the day, nearly thirty years ago, when he had first set eyes on Tricia. She had been standing in that little white mini dress, glass in hand, laughing with her snooty county parents. She too had seemed lovely and remote.

He drove into the yard to find Lucy's battered Ford Escort parked by the front door. Tom groaned, much as he loved and depended on his daughter, he wished that she had stayed away. He didn't want to answer questions. Couldn't Lucy leave him alone for once? Long enough for him to collect his chaotic thoughts and decide what in hell he was going to do.

'What were they like?' Lucy had her most enigmatic expression.

'What were who like?' he fenced back. Lucy was far too intelligent and they knew each other too well.

'Magda's chums. That's why you're late isn't it?' She was sitting in his office chair and in her hand was the tape he had taken from the answer-phone.

'So you've been listening to that call?'

'You bet,' she grinned. 'What were they like?'

'Weird; apparently Magda was an investigative reporter and her investigations landed her in more than she could handle.'

'What was the verdict at the inquest?'

'Suicide, it was all wrapped up neat and tidy. They got exactly the result they decided in advance.'

'You're not saying it was rigged?'

'Of course not. It was their attitude. Poor little foreign girl, facing extradition, maybe love life in a mess, can't hack it, tops herself – rubber stamp – case disposed of.'

'And her friends say different?'

'They produced enough new evidence to worry me.'

'Do they know who did it?'

'I've no idea.' He wondered if Lucy saw through the lie; she usually did.

'I've had a talk with the doctor who treated Al Otford,' she said. 'Off the record of course. It's patient confidentiality so I shouldn't be telling you really.'

'Where's Al now?'

'He's back with Gina, I suppose. The diabetes is stable – no reason why he shouldn't be at work.'

'What did your doctor say?'

'It was definitely assault. The lab findings have gone to the police.'

'So, it was more than a shot of insulin?'

'That's right. There were two injections. The one in his backside was some sort of fast-acting narcotic. The lab people are not sure precisely what yet; they're making further tests. The insulin was injected into the forearm – absolutely normal.'

'So, whoever did it was a medic?'

'Now, hold on, Dad, it doesn't follow.' Lucy was fervent as ever in defence of her profession.

'Come off it, love,' Tom laughed at the expression on her face. 'History is full of dodgy doctors.' He became serious again. 'If he wasn't a medic, he at least knew how to use a needle.'

'He could have learned that anywhere – Army possibly.'

Tom was drawn back to the events of the afternoon. Hannah again, she kept intruding into his thoughts. If the Israelis were gunning for the Fjortoft Foundation it might be his duty to warn Gus. In the meantime he would keep a wary eye open but say nothing.

Lucy was staring at him. 'Do you want me to cook you a meal?'

'No thanks, I had something earlier.'

'With Magda's lot, at the Crown and Anchor? How many of them?'

'Only three, her brother and a couple of lefty oddballs from University South.' He told her what had happened, omitting only the final trip to Rotherwood.

Lucy left for work at eight o'clock. Tom could neither sit still nor think coherently. He tramped upstairs and threw off the ridiculous dark suit and his best shoes, mud stained from his walk on the waterside path. He lay on the bed, but unable to rest he stood up and walked to the window. To his surprise a car was driving in from the road. It wasn't Lucy; this one's engine had a deeper and sportier beat. It was raining again; he could see the shards of water gleaming in the beam of the headlights. It was Gina's Porsche. Last night he might have welcomed her; now she was another intrusion. He knew that Gus was away in Edinburgh, which meant that Gina was at a loose end. He dragged on a pair of jeans, ran downstairs, drew a deep breath, and opened the front door.

'What d'you want?' he snapped.

'Tom, darling, don't be like that to me.' She was standing in the pouring rain, dressed in a full-length fur coat, looking at him with her best soulful expression. Beside her was a large container. Tom recognised it as one of those cool-boxes that plugged into a car's electrical system. 'I've brought you some supper. You've been to that horrid inquest. I'm not having you sitting here all on your own.'

Now she made him feel guilty. 'Come in then,' he sighed. He had a suspicion, that for all her wealth and security, it was Gina who was the lonely one tonight.

'Say, this is nice,' she said grinning mischievously.

'Just a minute – your car keys please?' She knew what he meant and handed them over. 'Put your coat on the peg, I'll be back in a minute.'

Tom slipped his waterproof over his head and ran out to the double doors of the barn. He opened them and drove the Porsche inside. If tonight was going to be a long session he would prefer that car to be out of sight. Indoors Gina was hustling around, laying the dining room table and disgorging the contents of her box. 'Darlin', I've smoked salmon and salad, and a bottle of Bolly. Chef's done the salad special.'

That was all he needed. It wouldn't have taken chef two guesses to know where Gina was headed; by midday tomorrow the whole village would be talking. She stood away from the table so that he could admire her under the light.

'What d'you think?' she said throwing back her blonde locks and performing a little twirl.

She wore a shimmering white backless dress, secured by tiny crossover straps. Her California tan glowed in the subdued yellow light while the dress revealed enough cleavage to be alluring, but still in good taste. Entering into the spirit of the occasion, he kissed her lightly on the forehead.

'What about your security – where's Al?'

Gina clung to him, pressing against his body and licking his face, before pushing her tongue into his mouth. Inwardly he smiled, wondering if she could taste Mo's garlic sauce. She withdrew and hung back in his arms gazing into his eyes. 'Al's resigned, just like that – pissed off. I can tell you Gus ain't pleased. He's off hiring a whole new posse of Mormons to guard the place.' She kissed him again and resumed busying around the table.

'Where are the candles'?' she called.

'I'll get them.' He felt uncomfortable. Last time there had been a candlelit dinner here it had been with Tricia on their anniversary.

Despite his earlier meal, Tom discovered he was still hungry. Gina laughed deliriously as he sent the champagne cork rocketing across the room. Tom rarely drank the stuff outside of weddings and other formal occasions, but he could taste that this vintage was special. The salmon salad was superb. The fish was the best he had ever tasted, and he wondered at the strange vegetables and the herbs that garnished it. Music filtered in from the CD player in the sitting room.

The meal over, Gina went into the kitchen to make coffee that she laced with brandy. Now they had both burned their boats, with no chance of Gina being in a fit state to drive back to the Manor, nor for him to take her. It was eleven o'clock. Gina was fumbling with a small paper bag that she had produced from her coat by the front door. Tom was intrigued as she produced three large perfume bottles. She held them to the light and danced a couple of steps in childlike pleasure.

'Got'em in LA,' she said. 'Sensual aromatic oils – all the rage.' She put the bottles down and put her arms around him. 'First darlin', we gotta' go upstairs and get in a good hot shower together – exfoliate the pores. Then we'll rub in the oil, it's great – there's nothin' like it.'

After three hours of strenuous lovemaking, both of them had spent their lust and lay naked in each other's arms. Tom rested with his mouth on Gina's left breast. She took her arm from around his shoulder and cradled his head between the palms of her hands.

'It's like I've gotten a little baby,' she whispered. He responded and gently suckled the nipple as it hardened once more.

'You've never had kids?' he murmured and knew he had said the wrong thing.

'I can't,' she whispered. 'Gus spent thousands of bucks on tests, but the gynos say I've something internal that's wrong.'

'Poor Gina, I'm sorry.' He tightened his arms around her body and gently cuddled her.

'My, you're strong,' she sighed.

'Gus has a son, hasn't he?'

'Sure – Craig. He's a US marine – real macho guy.'
'It makes me realise how lucky I am with my two.'
'Your Lucy doesn't like me.' She ran her tongue over his chest licking the sweat.
'Lucy is overprotective.'
'You mean she thinks I'm a whore.' She sank her teeth into his neck and bit him.
'She'll think you're Dracula if she sees that wound.'
'I'm no whore, Tom – not with you.' She ran her hands along his body as he rolled on his back. 'I love Gus, he's my rock, nothin'll change that. But I love you too, Tom, and I loved Tricia, she was like a sister to me and I never had a sister. I had a brother but he was killed in Nam.' Suddenly she was crying. She laid her head on his chest and he could feel the wet tingle of her tears soaking into his skin.
'Let it go,' he whispered. 'You'll feel better.'
'I love the farm here. I was born to it – did you know that?'
'No, but I'm not surprised.' It explained her affinity with everything that went on.
'I was raised in Massachusetts. My people had a little farm near Cape Cod. I can just remember seeing Jack Kennedy drive by.' She ran her fingertips along his thighs. 'We grew potatoes and squash – that's sort of pumpkins.'
'I know.'
'An' we lived in a little frame house. It was painted white and you could see it for miles against the trees.' She was sobbing again as he put his arms around her. 'We had pigs that I looked after and turkeys too for Thanksgiving.'
'What changed – how did you meet Gus?'
'I was a pretty girl then.'
'You still are,' he kissed her. 'Go on?'
'When I was finished with high school, I went for the Miss America competition and I got chosen to represent my state. I didn't win but it got me into modelling, then one day I met Gus.'
'And it was love at first sight?'
'Yes, and you shouldn't laugh all cynical – that's the English in you.'
'Not true, it was like that when I first met Tricia. It was all one way for a few days, but she came round. Not the parents-in-law though. They still think I'm an oik.'
'Gus didn't have a family and his relationship with Craig's mother

had turned sour. We married and we've never looked back.'

'Do you know where Gus comes from? What's his background?'

'He comes from Seattle and his pa made money in a shipping line, then he was killed in World War Two, that's all I know.' She kissed him again. 'Strange thing, he never talks about his family and I can't ask – it's sort of off limits.' She paused and suddenly she sat upright. Moonlight had broken through the clouds and her moist body gleamed in the light from the window.

'Tom, there's something in Gus's past that scares the wits out of him. I'm going to tell you what I've never told anyone else – not even my analyst.'

'OK, I'm listening.'

'It's confidential, you mustn't tell.'

'I promise.'

'I think that when Gus was little he once saw another kid murdered.'

'Did he tell you this?'

'It all happened one night not six weeks after we married. Gus was kinda restless; kept rolling over and over. About three in the morning he woke me up. He was lying there rigid, shaking all over, and then he started to scream.'

'Was he asleep, you know – a nightmare?'

'Yes, I'm sure of it. The strangest thing was that he was yelling in German. I know the language a bit. My family's German descent and my granma spoke it fluent.'

'I thought Gus's parents were Swedish?'

'They were Swedish Americans, all the newspapers say that.'

'Gina, darling, newspapers are not holy writ.' Tom began to massage her neck muscles. He was shocked by the tension. 'I guess you understood enough to know what he was saying?'

'Sure, he was screaming and he was scared, and I've never seen Gus scared of anything or anyone, and you'd better believe that.'

'I do believe it, but go on.'

'He was calling to his mother, like a little kid. He was shouting, "Mammy, Mammy, they killed little Josef. You promised they wouldn't – you promised!".'

'Could Josef have been a guinea pig or a pet rabbit – children can be sadistic little sods?'

'I don't think so. You see it's happened since. Only three months ago, he yelled in German again but the words were different.' Gina was staring into space.

'He was screaming, but he wasn't talking like Gus. I mean it was like a kid's voice.'

'What did he say?'

'He said, "they're killing all the children – they've killed little Josef. I tried to stop them – I tried to stop them". Oh, Tom, it was awful.'

'Did you ever ask Gus what it meant?'

'I thought about it but I let it be. You see I don't want to hurt him. But I tell you one thing. That wasn't some pet rabbit got killed. Gus saw kids murdered some place long ago. I bet my sweet life on it.'

CHAPTER 8

Tom had woken as usual at six o'clock. After ten minutes in the shower he had managed to remove most of the traces of Gina's aromatic oil. That lady was still asleep. For all that she had spent her childhood on a farm, early rising was not her forte. He stared down at the recumbent form watching the steady rhythm of her breathing and the childlike expression on her face. He picked up the duvet from the floor and spread it gently over her. Nakedness in the cold morning light was symbolic. Last night, for a few hours, the theatrical part that Gina lived had collapsed before his eyes. The phoney accent had vanished as she reverted to the little New England farm girl she had once been. Tom sighed; at least he could see Gina in a different light. He no longer felt humiliated by her. If the truth was told, he and she were two sad middle-aged people from different worlds who had turned to each other for mutual comfort.

Tom arrived at the estate office on the dot of seven o'clock. Parked outside was Muriel's Honda Civic. Miss Muriel Campbell was the estate secretary. Apart from both being female, Muriel was the mirror opposite of Gina. Muriel was fifty years old, Scottish Presbyterian and a spinster in more than title. It was a racing certainty that Muriel had never shared a bed with a man, or a woman for that matter, and had never had an ambition to do so. Tom looked gloomily at the office door. On this of all mornings dealing with Muriel would require a massive mental readjustment.

'Mr O'Malley, something will have to be done about the Rowridges. I dinna' think we can put the matter off any longer.' Muriel was eyeing him as a schoolteacher might regard a recalcitrant pupil.

Her dealings with him were always on this level of formality. He had been told that Muriel did not entirely approve of him. She had her prejudices and persisted in believing him to be Irish and a Catholic, when he was definitely neither.

'All right,' he replied. 'I'll go and see them.'

It was a duty he had been dreading. The Rowridge family owned Woolbarrow Farm. They had worked the place for one hundred and fifty years, generation after generation, through prosperity, war and recession, to war and new prosperity, then finally to a recession from which there could be no recovery. Woolbarrow Farm was facing bankruptcy and the Rowridges had appealed directly to Gustav Fjortoft to buy them out. Matthew Rowridge was a homespun countryman, a dying breed in today's climate. Gus liked Matthew; often he would walk up to Woolbarrow Farm to pass the time of day.

'Matthew's one honest guy,' Gus had said. 'The most trustworthy man ever I met – present company excepted,' he had laughed.

When Matthew's appeal for help had arrived, Gus had offloaded the whole problem onto Tom. It had become the most onerous and least appealing task of his year.

'Ring Matthew and ask if I can call this afternoon,' he said.

'Excellent, Mr O'Malley, I will do that.'

At least it had stopped raining, although it was bitterly cold and wall-to-wall rain cloud stretched as far as the eye could see.

'Matthew, we will purchase the house, the buildings and land of Woolbarrow Farm for four hundred and ten thousand pounds. That's our only offer and it's non-negotiable.' Tom knew now what it must have been like to pronounce a death sentence. 'However, in view of your family's connection with this place, I shall recommend to Mr Fjortoft that he offers you a nominal rental agreement for the house. In other words you can stay here as long as you like.'

Matthew's face was impassive but Tom could detect relief. The terms would clear the Rowridge debts with a lump sum to spare and the estate would gain three hundred acres of land.

'What's your time scale?' asked Matthew. He was a red-faced solid man in his early forties. Tom knew him to be going through the ritual of considering the offer. In practice of course he had no option.

'We want completion by the end of July. We will move our silage making equipment onto the land in May, but we will pay you the value of the standing grass.' Tom paused; this was a valuable concession that would help them both. 'You will dispose of all your livestock and equipment by the completion date. We will take first pick of any machinery and stock.'

Matthew felt the pain now. Tom could see the death sentence beginning to bite. 'Them'll have to go then?' Matthew pointed across the field to the forty pedigree Sussex cows with their newborn calves.

Tom swallowed, this was the moment he had been dreading. He had psyched himself all morning to play the hard-nosed businessman. He was nothing of the sort; he was a farmer. The dark red cows were staring mournfully at him over the fence. In the good times Matthew had sold bulls as far afield as Australia and Paraguay. That was before BSE, the so-called mad cow disease. The herd was almost valueless now. It was ironic, considering that Matthew's grass fed single-suckled cattle, were as likely to contract BSE as a nunnery to have an outbreak of AIDS.

'All right, don't sell the Sussex if you don't want to. I've got forty acres of grass at Boxtree. You can have it and I'll talk to Mr Fjortoft about the herd long term.'

Matthew's relief was palpable. A slow smile spread across his lined face. 'That'll be champion, Mr O'Malley. I accept your terms. Come indoors and we'll have a drink on it.'

'Are you going to take our ponies away?' Francesca, the Rowridge daughter, had advanced on Tom the moment he stepped inside the farmhouse. She was a formidable seventeen-year-old, and clearly out for a confrontation.

'Shuddup, Fran,' hissed her father. 'It's going to be all right.'

'Why should I take your horses away?' Tom grinned at the girl.

'Because Fjortoft is a fascist.'

'Put a sock in it, Fran.' Matthew looked embarrassed. 'Mr Fjortoft's being good to us, you don't know the half of it.' He turned back to Tom. 'It's that college – they gives 'em ideas.'

'Well, Francesca, I'm not doing anything about your ponies. You're going on living in this house and that includes the stable and the paddock,' he smiled at her. 'So, no problem.'

'What are those people doing in Becham's wood?' Francesca shot the question at him.

'She's right,' said Matthew. 'I reckon you could have some poachers up there.' Becham's Wood was four acres of straggling copse that belonged to the Crossfield Estate and adjoined Woolbarrow Farm.

'I wouldn't have thought it was poachers,' said Tom. 'We're not releasing any game birds up there – nobody has in years.'

'I think you ought to take a walk around,' said Matthew. 'My wife thinks it's spooky but that's all cobblers. Any road, there's no tale of it ever being haunted.'

'What on earth are you on about, Matthew?'

'No it's true. Just afore Christmas I saw a bloke I didn't know standing inside the wood. I got sharp eyes and I don't miss much.' Matthew took a long swig from his beer glass. 'When I walks over he's gone – no trace, no sound. I calls, and I stands there for a while, but no one comes in or out.'

'He must have had a guilty conscience,' Tom said. 'He probably hid behind a tree.'

'Could be, but I don't think so. The trees aren't that thick and there's no ground cover. I walked the place twice and I don't reckon as I'd've missed him if he were there.'

'The other time was at night,' said Francesca. 'I was scared then.'

'She was, I'll vouch for that. She ran in here screaming like a good'un. That time I grabs my gun and I takes my dog.'

'What happened, Francesca?' Tom was beginning to take this seriously.

'I never saw anything, but I heard them.' She looked pensive under his gaze. 'It was three weeks ago, come last Thursday. Dad asked me to go and shut the gate into five acre. It was a nice night, and I sat on the old oak stump, sort of thinking.'

'That's right on the edge of the wood,' said Matthew.

'I was thinking,' she continued. 'I wondered if I'd be up here next year and whether I'd ride here, or sit and watch the stars.'

'All right, Fran,' Matthew looked uneasy. 'Don't take no notice of her. It's that college made her all poetical.'

'I know,' said Tom, 'and Francesca, you'll be riding your horse and sitting on your tree stump for as long as you like.'

'Not at night I won't. You see I'd been there about twenty minutes and then I heard them. Someone walked up the track and when he called out it scared the shit out of me.'

'Fran watch your language,' said her father.

She ignored him. 'Then another bloke said, "keep your voice down, there was somebody shutting that gate over there". Then I froze, I was that scared.' Tom could believe it. With all the stories on television and in the press, it would have been a frightening experience for a young girl.

'I held my breath and hoped they'd go. Then the second guy spoke again and it was like he was as close to me as you are now.' Her voice faltered she was clearly recalling a bad memory.

'Did you catch his words?'

'Yeah, he said, "This place is fucking brilliant, made for the job"...'

Matthew was outraged. 'Fran, your mother'll wash your mouth out.'

'I'm only repeating what he said.'

Tom grinned. 'I'm sure you are. Go on, tell us the rest.'

'He said, "come on, I'll show you. We'll put all the dids down there. Seal 'em up tight – no one'll ever know where to find 'em". Then they both walked off into the wood and I didn't wait, I ran.' Francesca began to cry.

'She were in one hell of a state,' said Matthew. 'I tells 'er to lock the doors and wait. I grabbed my gun and the spotlight I uses on the hill, then me and the dog had a snoop around.'

'Find anything?'

'Not a thing, but she was telling the truth. You see, when them young girls lie you can tell. I expect you remembers when your girl was that age. Fran weren't lying – she heard something.'

'You tell PC Ross?'

'I told him we may have some poachers and he said he'd log it, but what more can he do?'

'Any ideas as to what it was about?' Tom addressed both of them.

'Dids be a name for gypsies,' said Matthew, 'but Fran reckons they wasn't gyppos.'

'Did you recognise either of the voices?' Tom asked her.

'The one in the wood sounded local, I reckon I've heard him before, but the other one was an American.'

'Are you sure?'

'Yeah, a proper Yankee Doodle, but not like Mr Fjortoft – different kind of accent.'

Tom was in cheerful mood when he returned to the office. His interview with Matthew had not left the bad taste it might have.

'Muriel, I've done the deal. We take over the place, end of July, and the Rowridges keep their house. I'll have to talk to Mr Fjortoft about the Sussex herd, we can't let that disperse…' His voice faltered. Muriel was eyeing him in a way he didn't care for.

'Mr O'Malley, that Mrs Fjortoft came in here asking where she could find you.'

Tom winced; the temperature had dropped to zero.

'I told the woman I didna' know.'

'Oh Jesus,' Tom muttered.

'I'd say ye were in enough trouble with the Almighty without blaspheming.'

'I'm sure you're right, Muriel. I shall have to do better.'

'Aye ye will,' she relaxed a little. 'If ye must know, I saw her talking to your Miss Lucy. It seemed the two of them were having a wee difference of opinion.'

‘Oh God!’

‘Mr O’Malley!’

‘Sorry, Muriel. Now, would you ring Taraton police and ask if PC Ross could give me a call?’

Tom drove home. He was pleased with his day, a contrast with yesterday and its bizarre encounters. Lucy’s car was parked in the yard. That suited him because he needed to know about this reported slanging match between her and Gina.

Lucy greeted him indoors; he was surprised to see that she was dressed in her knee-length doctor’s white coat. She looked at him balefully and held up an object in her hand. ‘What is this?’

‘Wine bottle.’

‘It’s an empty champagne bottle – a rather expensive empty bottle.’

‘So what?’

‘For God’s sake, I can see why you wanted to get rid of me last night.’

‘I didn’t …’

‘Oh really, I offered to cook you a meal, but oh no, you weren’t hungry. So what’s this?’ She launched a kick at an object on the floor; it was Gina’s cool box. ‘And what do I find in the kitchen? A load of dirty plates and the remains of smoked salmon – very nice.’

Tom was not prepared to take any more. Not from his own child. ‘Lucy, I’ve had enough of this. Yes, Gina did come here last night after you’d gone. I wasn’t expecting her and she didn’t come as a predator. I found her a desperately unhappy person in need of comfort.’

‘Oh sure, you comforted her all right.’ She picked up another object from the table, one of Gina’s sensual aroma bottles. ‘You do realise you still smell of this crap.’

‘Lucy,’ he glared at her. ‘I’m sure you mean well, but I’m not taking moral lectures from someone who is shacked up with a man to whom she is not married. I don’t care, but your gran and granddad do – they say so.’

‘That’s cheap,’ she replied angrily, ‘Mike and I are not shacked up. We’re only sorting out our relationship before we make things final. Neither of us wants to make a stupid mistake.’

‘Good, I accept that. Now you stop being overprotective and let me get on with my life. I’m old enough to make my own judgements, thank you.’

‘All right, Dad, if that’s how you want it.’ She scowled at him and then her face relaxed. 'Anyway, I gave Gina a piece of my mind this afternoon.'

'Yes, I've heard.'

She burst out laughing. 'I've had part of my own back. I've secured a trophy.' She unbuttoned her doctor's coat and let it fall to the floor. Tom gasped; Lucy was wearing Gina's white backless dress.

'Where did you get that?'

'The silly cow left it on the hook in the bathroom. Did she drive home starkers?'

'No, she had a stupid great fur coat and that's gone.'

'You realise this dress is a Versace. The label's genuine, it must have cost a fortune.'

'Well, love, it certainly does you justice.' Gina had looked stylish in this next-to-nothing creation, but Lucy looked absolutely stunning.

She grinned. 'She and I are much of a size. It'll need a few stitches and tucks and then it'll be fine.'

'You can't just walk off with it.'

'I'm borrowing it that's all, she can have it back week after next. We've got our reunion ball in London – all the students of our year. This'll really wow them.'

'I hope for your sake it's a warm evening.'

PC Ross arrived on his police motorcycle not long after Lucy left. He stood on the doorstep shaking the rain from his waterproofs. Tom invited him to dry off and have a cup of coffee.

'Any more news about the break in at the Manor?' asked Tom.

'Nothing,' Ross shook his head. 'CID are playing it very close to their chests. Having a high-profile character like Fjortoft around is always a worry.'

'I've searched my memory about the intruder in the kitchen, but I can't remember any more than I told you.'

'What's this about poachers?'

Tom repeated what he had learned from the Rowridges. 'If we catch these people, what are our rights?'

'You're a JP – you know the rules about citizen's arrest.'

'Of course.'

'However, at Crossfield you have my superiors worried.'

'Why?'

'Our superintendent has been informed that Gus Fjortoft is planning to bring in half the US cavalry.'

‘That’s an exaggeration surely. He’s stepping up our private security. That follows from the other day when it took you half an hour to get here.’

‘Point taken, but this is our official advice. If you encounter a gang of poachers and they have guns,’ Ross paused, ‘we will dispatch an armed response unit. It is vital that Gus Fjortoft’s boys do not start shooting – understood?’

‘Hey, wait a minute. They don’t carry handguns. Fjortoft respects our laws – this isn’t the States.’

‘No, but they might try to respond with licensed shotguns. You see if anyone, either cowboys or Indians, was to be injured there would be hell to pay. We would have to charge someone and the paperwork would be horrendous.’ Ross allowed himself a rare smile.

The phone rang. Tom excused himself and reached for it.

‘Hello, Tom,’ said a remembered voice. ‘This is Hannah, we met yesterday.’

‘I’m hardly likely to forget.’

‘Magda’s funeral’s on Friday. I understand you wanted to be there.’

‘Yes,’ he hesitated. ‘Yes, I think I should.’

‘That’s good. Two o’clock at the cemetery, there’s a little chapel just inside the entrance. We’re meeting there – see you.’ The line went dead.

‘You look as if you’ve seen a ghost,’ said Ross.

‘It’s nothing, I’ve got to go to a funeral.’

CHAPTER 9.

Tom parked his car and walked the remaining few yards to the cemetery gates. He could see the hearse and the small knot of mourners. Hannah, her hair covered and dressed in black, stood out from the group. She gave him a quick smile of greeting.

The undertaker's men carried the coffin slowly up the paved pathway towards the chapel. A Russian Orthodox priest led the procession. He was a young man with a black beard and a slight limp. Next came Anton. The boy was weeping openly, without restraint, as were two girls of whom one seemed familiar. Tom might have felt embarrassed had he not guessed that open displays of grief were *de rigueur*. The Anglo-American contingent walked diffidently behind, upper lips stiff, faces deadpan. These were Pete and Chantelle, Tom and, surprisingly, Sergeant Storey. A few yards behind came the Jewish group: Hannah, Mo, and a pace or so behind them, Joel, the young man with the ponytail – Magda's boyfriend.

At least the sun was shining and a gentle breeze blew across the ground, fluttering the daffodils and stirring the sodden branches of the ornamental trees. They stood quietly in the chapel while the priest performed the ceremony, then they were out again, walking across the soft wet turf to the newly dug grave. Hannah took her stand on the far side and delivered the address.

Magdalena, she said, had been born into a distinguished Russian academic family. She had never known her grandparents. Her mother's father had been murdered in Stalin's purges, her paternal grandparents in Nazi death camps. As young children, Magdalena's parents had somehow survived the Second World War, but an event in this period had left her mother traumatised. She had witnessed the murder of her younger brother, an atrocity that haunted her until death.

'This is not a call for vengeance, for Magda never sought that, only for justice. Her whole life was dedicated to that one aim.' Hannah's voice rang with a crystal-purity. Tom noticed that even the undertakers were spellbound. 'On the day her mother died Magda vowed she would hunt down and bring to justice the men who had murdered her uncle. That small child was but one of two hundred and sixty little ones who died on one day in that place.' Hannah swept her gaze around the gathering. So intense was the stillness that Tom could hear the town's traffic.

'My people talk of the Holocaust. The memory touches every moment of our lives. It is too easy for us to forget that we were not alone in our sufferings. Magdalena was a Christian gentile, yet she is the latest victim of these terrible events. Yes, the killing goes on. There are still those who will kill, no longer for their crazed ideology, but now for the strongest motive of all, self-preservation.' Hannah paused again. 'Shalom, Magda. Go now in peace with your own people. We, your friends honour your memory and pledge ourselves to seek the justice you were denied.'

The ceremony over, the participants began to drift away talking quietly. Tom looking back saw the tall man, Magda's boyfriend, standing alone beside the grave.

Tom caught up with Sergeant Storey. 'What did you think of that speech?' he asked.

'The lady spoke from the heart all right, but it doesn't mean her friend was murdered. What do you think?'

Tom weighed his reply carefully. 'I met these people the other day. I've had severe doubts about that suicide verdict, and from what they told me, I would say this matter isn't going to go away.'

'You know, Mr O'Malley, I'm rather afraid you're right.' Storey watched the others approach. 'Of course it's not my call, I'm not CID. Anyway, sir, keep in touch, eh?' He winked and made off towards the town.

'Your policeman has a guilty conscience?' Hannah was standing beside him.

'I really couldn't say.' Tom touched Hannah on the arm and pointed to the man still standing by the grave, head bowed.

'Yes, I know, that's Joel,' she said. 'I don't approve of the man, but he and Magda were very close. Let's leave him in peace.'

'What's wrong with him?'

'He probably calls himself a freedom fighter. I would call him something else. Look, Tom, we're off to a pub round the corner – you coming?'

'They won't be open.' Tom was wary.

'This one will be.' She turned and strode to catch up with the others.

The pub was a short walk to the edge of the town. Beyond it were green fields and the distant trees that Tom knew marked the edge of the harbour. Hannah led them round to the rear entrance. It was clear that this was the prearranged funeral party. Tom did not want to be here, he wanted to escape and he was still suspicious of the company he was in. Apart from that, it was their private moment and he was an outsider.

Someone pushed a half pint of beer into his hand and a small plate of the usual canapés. He selected a quiet corner and watched. The small group from the funeral ceremony had been joined by a dozen new arrivals, an odd mix of young and old. Nobody took much notice of him. He would give it another fifteen minutes and then make his exit. He would have fulfilled whatever obligation he owed the dead Magda. As he left the room to collect his coat, Hannah appeared. She had changed from her formal clothing into a pair of jeans. 'Tom, can you spare me an hour?'

'I don't know – what is it?'

'Show me where you found Magda?'

'Yes, I suppose so.' Tom had not expected this. He didn't want to go back to that place, but it seemed unreasonable to refuse.

'It was here,' he said. For the second time in days his best shoes were filthy from walking to this spot.

Hannah looked around. 'OK, now we'll walk back along the path, reverse direction to the one Magda took.' She set off at a brisk pace towards the town. 'Hello, what've we got here?' She was looking at the crumbling structure of the wartime pillbox. 'Let's have a look.'

'Somebody's cleared the bushes,' said Tom. 'This doorway was overgrown the last time I saw it.'

'When was that?'

'I don't know, last year sometime. It was blocked then, but the brambles have been cut back with a hook.'

Hannah walked through the narrow door and Tom followed. The interior was in semi-darkness apart from an eerie light filtering through the tiny slit windows. The box had been sited with an all round field of fire. Tom wondered what would have happened had a German army really come here in 1940. They would probably have waited five minutes to bring up a flame-thrower and the local Home Guard would have died horribly in this concrete trap.

'Tom, does anything strike you about this place?'

'It's sad and rather sinister.'

'Agreed, but I'll put it a different way. What is the odd one out among four things here?'

'Sorry, but I'm not in the mood for riddles and I can't see four of anything.'

'These rifle slits; there's four of them. Now what strikes you?'

'Two point over the water and two over the fields?'

'No, you're miles away – look.' She pointed to three of the slits. 'Those are full of cobwebs and greenery, but that one,' she pointed, 'has been swept clean.'

Tom walked across and looked out. The cleared window overlooked the footpath.

'You see what I mean,' she said. 'Anybody walking along that path will pass within three feet of you.'

'This has a bearing on Magda?'

'Yes, I think it does,' she spoke so quietly that Tom hardly heard her above the rustle of the wind through the bushes. 'Tom, could you go outside and walk past as if you were going to the boatyard?'

The glare on emerging from that gloomy hole made him blink. Tom walked a few yards towards the town, turned round as she had asked and headed back past the pillbox. A sharp pain on the side of his neck made him jump. He looked wildly around. 'Sorry,' she called. He could see her face through the slit a yard away. 'Wait there, I'm coming out.'

'What the hell was that?' he asked as he rubbed the spot.

She held up a tiny catapult of the type used by small boys to cause havoc. 'I brought this along to test a theory. Sorry if I overdid the act.'

'What was it you shot?'

'Only a tiny bit of gravel.'

'I wish you'd warned me – that hurt.'

'Somebody knew how to blow straight,' she said.

'What d'you mean?'

'Magda was set up. If you hadn't come along when you did, they'd have got away with it.' Her mobile face registered deep sadness and anger. 'She was supposed to meet someone here. She was excited, almost ecstatic and she wouldn't say why, or who she was meeting.'

'A set up, you say?'

'Yes, I'm certain they meant to kill her and pass it off as suicide. I couldn't work out how it was done.'

'But you know now?'

'I do and I'll show you how. Magda walked along this path. The man who killed her was waiting. I came looking for a bush or some other concealment – I had no idea this bunker was here.'

'Who killed her and how?'

'I think I know who ordered it, and how it was done. The killer put a blow dart into her from three feet. He couldn't miss and he's probably had enough practice.'

'It's possible,' Tom agreed. 'We once had a vet use a blowpipe when a steer went berserk.'

'My guess is that he knocked her cold with the dart and then injected the main poison into her.'

'Then he carried her to the waterline reckoning the tide would float her away?'

'That's logical, but remember, the hypodermic syringe was found by her body after you'd moved it,' she replied.

Tom felt a cold sensation. 'You're saying he watched me and placed the syringe when I ran back for my phone?'

'All speculation, but yes, I'd say he went to ground in this place when you first appeared and he was watching you all the time.'

There was something he needed to know. 'This boyfriend of Magda's...'

'Joel.'

'Yes, both Anton and you have implied he's the wrong side of the law.'

'He's done nothing to cross the police in this country, they've probably never heard of him. He's irrational, an idealist and he does my cause no good at all. I'm afraid Magda's murder could make him very dangerous.'

'If you think he's going to commit a crime you should report it.'

'Joel and I share the same enemies. His methods are not mine, but then dog doesn't bite dog.' Hannah stared moodily at the water.

Tom continued. 'There is one flaw in your theory. They would have had the body stripped in the mortuary for the pathologist to work on. In court he only mentioned the injection into the arm.'

'I know. As I said I'm speculating, but remember the dart wound could have been tiny and they were already assuming suicide.'

Tom had one last question. 'What did Magda know that would give someone a motive to kill her?'

'Magda came to this country to search for a man who officially is dead and buried. She found him – typical journalist – wouldn't tell us a thing and now she's dead we're no wiser.'

He did not know what to believe. The sky was darkening; shaping up for more rain. 'I don't want to hear anymore. Let's get out of this place.'

Tom's curiosity had been overtaken by dread. Somehow this business connected with Gustav Fjortoft. Tom had been prepared to defend his friend and mentor to hell and back if necessary. Now he felt this cloying feeling of doubt. They returned down the track in silence.

He made a decision. 'The other day in Rotherwood, you began dropping hints about Fjortoft. A few hours later I heard something in confidence that put a different perspective on the whole thing.'

'When was this?'

'I've told you it was in confidence. It didn't come from Fjortoft, it was told me by someone who probably regretted it later.'

'Very well, I respect that.'

'Was Magda looking for this alleged Fjortoft brother?'

'If you care to visit the Congo you can see his grave. The trouble is he no longer occupies it.'

'Having gone this far, you'd better explain.'

'Wilhelm Brown is the youngest surviving Nazi war criminal. He took an active part in killing children at the age of ten. Only two kids escaped to tell the tale and one of them was Magda's mother.'

Tom felt as if his stomach had filled with a lump of ice. He heard the echo of Gina's words. "Gus saw kids murdered some place long ago..."

Hannah stopped walking so abruptly that Tom almost collided with her. She swung round to face him. 'Tenacious is the quality that describes Magda. She traced this man's progress from Germany in nineteen forty-five, to the Congo in nineteen sixty-one. She was told he had died as a mercenary, they even showed her his grave. She told our people and they had a look. As I've said the corpse had miraculously risen. Rightly or wrongly, Magda believed that Wilhelm Brown was alive and well, not far from here and protected by his brother.'

'You claim this half-brother took part in killings at the age of ten. It's horrendous, but it's unlikely he could be prosecuted so long after the event.'

'Possibly but there's something else. Your Mr Fjortoft was present, and may even have taken part.'

'How do you know all this? Fjortoft couldn't have been more than eight years old.'

'Magda's mother saw him and so did the other survivor.'

'A living survivor?' This was crucial.

'Very much so. She's Greta Little – Peter Little's mother.'

It was growing dark when they reached the bungalow in Rotherwood. Hannah did not invite Tom into the house, which was a relief. The rest of her associates were already there and he had no wish to mingle with them, that day, or ever again. He drove the short distance home in a daze. While he had been with Hannah he had felt detached. It was only now that the implications were clear and to his mounting horror became personal. Hannah's story was all too well supported by Gina's testimony. He still liked Gustav Fjortoft, loved almost, in the broadest sense of the word, but it was true he hardly knew the man. Gus never mentioned his childhood, never mentioned a thing before his early days as a businessman in Seattle. Gus was a good man, he was sure of that. What should he, Tom, do? Confront Gus and betray Gina's confidence? Not yet – he would stay alert, listen, and do the only practical thing open to him. He would seek out his own father and demand the whole story of Sammy Little.

He called at the estate office. It was half past five and Muriel was leaving.

'Mr O'Malley; Mr Matthew Rowridge was in here this afternoon. He had a message.'

'Verbal message?'

'That is correct. He said he had been reading some papers of his father's and that he has found something of great significance concerning Becham's Wood. He would like to walk the ground with you. The man seemed somewhat excited I would say.'

'What on earth..?'

'You will have to ask the questions yourself. I am merely passing on the message.'

Lucy was waiting at Boxtree. 'How did the funeral go?'

'It was dignified.' It was the only description he could think of.

'Many people there?'

'The same lot as last time, and that copper, Storey.'

'Do you still think it was murder?'

'Yes.' He turned away. He didn't want to discuss the matter and this time Lucy took the hint.

'I've cooked you shepherd's pie,' she said. 'No smoked salmon tonight – your fancy woman's away in London.'

'Shepherd's pie will do nicely – lead me to it.'

'You can be a referee,' she said. Something odd in Lucy's voice made him forget how hungry he was. 'After what you said about Mike, we had a talk – that is I had a go at Mike,' she hesitated.

'Go on, tell Daddy all.'

Lucy took a deep breath. 'I've been on the phone,' she pointed at the study door. 'I hope you don't mind?'

'Paying the bill you mean?' He glared at her with mock severity.

'Well sort of…'

'Never mind, put me out of suspense, for God's sake.'

'All right, Grandmother Lansbury wants the wedding in Gloucester Cathedral. Granddad O'Malley wants it here, but Gran' wants it with her lot in St Brieuc. What do you think?'

The track along the ridge was rutted and slippery from the rain that had torrented down in the night. Tom drove the Land Rover towards the stunted trees of Becham's Wood. The little spinney lay in a dip in the ground on the reverse slope from the prevailing winds. The valleys, far below, were filled with fog vapour as the morning sun warmed the wet fields and trees. The weather forecast promised a change to hotter, drier days, a welcome interlude in this cold shivering English spring. The tractors were at work drilling forty acres of barley. These were contract machines. In times past everything on an estate this size would have been the work of proud local men. There would have been no need for Tom to scrutinise proceedings twice a day. Satisfied, he walked across to the wood.

The fences on the Rowridge side were in an acute state of disrepair. When times were this bad, farmers patched and mended, spending as little as possible. These fences were secure for the moment, but Fjortoft would have to invest several thousand pounds to put things right. Tom carefully straddled a low point of the barbed wire to cross into the wood. He swore as a strand nicked his jeans. That was careless; he must be stiffening with age.

The ground between the trees was covered in a mat of wild garlic and bare patches, dotted with a splash of yellow primroses. As the sun began to warm the earth this place smelt good. It had that magic feeling of spring – rebirth and renewal. He turned and stared across the two miles to Rotherwood. If only this trouble could all be bad dreams. It was real enough; he could see the belt of trees that surrounded the bungalow.

As for Becham's wood, the place began to lose its charm. It contained an ugly collection of old oil drums, plastic sacks and empty beer cans. Amongst this litter were older objects; lumps of brick and concrete, remnants of a wartime gun site on the ridge above. The coppice trees here were all dead or dying. The best thing to do would be to clear fell the lot. New trees would grow on the old stumps.

He noticed footprints in the mud. Instead of trailing through the reeking garlic somebody, actually more than one person, had been walking along a badger trail. The little path was only a foot wide, straight and undeviating. These were shoeprints, stupid town shoes, when anyone who knew a thing about the countryside would be wearing wellingtons or similar. Matthew was right; somebody had been here in the last two days and definitely not a poacher. Tom pulled the mobile phone from his pocket.

'Matthew, I'm in Becham's Wood. What's so special that you wanted me to look at?'

'I'm not sure myself yet, but there's summat strange about that place. I only found out yesterday.'

'What exactly am I looking for?'

'Mr O'Malley, there's something of my old dad's I've got to show you. Can't do it now – going to see the bank manager down Taraton.'

'I hope he's happy?'

'You keep your side of the bargain and we'll be fine. But as to Becham's Wood.' Matthew hesitated sounding if not worried, tense.

'Yes?'

'Could you come over this evening, after work – say five o'clock?'

'Yes, I suppose so.'

Tom returned the phone to his pocket and had one last look at the wood. It was a poor unsightly patch of vegetation of no use to anyone. His eyes strayed once more to the ridge above Rotherwood village and the bungalow behind the green leylandii. Even here, in a different world, the revelations of yesterday troubled him. He would make no move to contact Hannah again until he had spoken with his father.

At least they had Lucy's wedding to look forward to. How he wished they could all enjoy that event without this other trouble. And he longed for Tricia to be with them to share the moment. On reflection he hoped Lucy would accept the Lansbury offer to stage the wedding. It would complete the long overdue reconciliation and provide a wonderful day out for everyone. He suppressed the cynical thought that it would also save him a lot of money.

He saw Lucy again that afternoon. 'I had a call in the village,' she explained, 'Mike and the boss are doing the surgery. I'm off duty until tomorrow morning.'

Tom told her his views about the wedding. 'I think it would be a nice gesture. They really like you, and it's a once in a lifetime opportunity.'

She laughed. 'Yeah, all right – why not?'

Tom looked at his watch. 'It's half past four. I've got to go to Woolbarrow to see Matthew Rowridge. You want to come?'

'Why?'

'He wants to show me some paperwork – I've no idea what it's about. Afterwards we could eat out – you needn't cook me a meal.'

'Good idea,' she said. 'We'll take my car and then you can have a drink.' Suddenly she rocked with laughter.

'Now, what's so funny?'

'Sorry,' she said and laughed again. 'Remember what happened last time you took me on my own?'

Tom remembered only too well. Not long after Tricia's death, he and Lucy had spent a mournful afternoon with his Lansbury in-laws. On the return journey they had stopped for a meal. Tom, emotionally drained, hadn't wanted to eat. It had been Lucy who had insisted. She had caught his arm and steered him unresisting towards the restaurant door. Then she had thrown her arms around him accompanied by a kiss. Tom had noticed a clergyman in a dog collar staring at them.

'You should be ashamed,' said this unknown vicar in an irritating falsetto. 'That lady is young enough to be your daughter.'

'She is my daughter, you bloody fool!' Tom had roared, thereby stopping every activity in the street. They had made a hasty getaway to eat in the next town. There he found, to his surprise, that his appetite had recovered. Lucy still thought the incident funny, although it was a memory Tom would sooner forget.

The lights were shining from every window of Woolbarrow Farm. Lucy drove into the yard and parked by the open front door. Tom walked into the hallway and called. He peered around the door of the room he knew to be the farm office. He was surprised how untidy it was. Books had been swept off their shelves and the floor was strewn with paper. He could hear a whimpering and scratching behind an inner door. Tom opened it and was almost bowled over by a bedraggled collie dog that ignoring him ran out into the night. Through the open door Tom could see a washroom with clothes scattered around the floor. This was so out of character; Matthew must be really losing his grip. As well as all his financial problems, it was known that his wife had departed for her native Norfolk. Matthew still kept up the pretence that she was away on family business and would soon be home. Local opinion was sceptical.

Someone was screaming. It was an eerie high-pitch wail from outside the house. Without waiting for each other, Tom and Lucy ran into the yard. The screams were those of a terrified young girl; unending, awful full throated screams.

'Stay here,' he snapped at Lucy, then he sprinted, as he had not done in years, towards the gate of the cattle yard.

Francesca Rowridge was on her knees, as she screamed again and again, in agony and despair. Her whole body was convulsing as if by electric shock. She was staring at the overhead beams of the covered yard. Dangling from one of them was the body of her father.

CHAPTER 10

Lucy felt unable to move. It seemed as if the scene before her was frozen in monochrome. What seemed an eternity was probably only seconds, but nothing in her training had prepared her for such a horror.

Slowly her discipline returned; she was the professional so it was for her to do something decisive and fast. Was Matthew dead? She ran to the body; yes, it was warm but she couldn't feel a pulse. That was the only certainty she could work with.

Death from cervical spine fracture invariably proves fatal within sixty seconds... This odd snatch from some half-forgotten lecture came mistily back to her.

'Can we do anything?' Her father snapped the words, finally pulling her from her trance.

'It's no good, I'm sure he's dead,' she was blinking back tears. 'I want to check. Can you take the weight while I cut him down?'

He reacted at once, seizing the body by the legs and hoisting it up a few inches. Lucy had spotted a small hacksaw on a bench. She grabbed it and climbed on the stack of bales that Matthew must have used to launch himself.

'The police won't like this,' her father gasped. 'We're disturbing the evidence.'

'Sod the police,' she gasped though clenched teeth. 'It's hopeless but I've got to try.' As she spoke the last two strands parted and the corpse toppled to the ground, expelling a horrible gaseous emission from its anal orifice.

Lucy leapt to the ground. She deliberately blanked her mind of everything as she loosened the ligature around the bruised neck. She had never seen a body dead through strangulation, although she had looked at photographs. Matthew must have had the presence to ease his exit with a drop of a few feet because the neck was clearly dislocated. That would be enough to kill him outright, the body was cooling with no sign of a pulse. The man was dead; her duty must lie with the living.

Francesca was no longer screaming. She was on her knees swaying and making little bizarre hand twirls. Lucy put a supportive arm around the girl and led her back into the house. Next she sprinted to her car for her medical bag. She laid the unresisting Francesca upon a settee and administered a sedative. She had only one thought;

to curtail the misery and shock this poor child must be suffering. Lastly she rang the ambulance service and the police. On a whim she called her fiancé Michael, at the surgery. Even as the phone rang at the other end she thought better of it. No, she would handle this her way, alone.

She ran back to the barn. Her father had found a plastic trailer cover and between them they unrolled it over the body. Lucy wiped her face; the tears were beginning again. She must take a grip before the official police surgeon arrived. 'Why, Dad?' She looked at him pleading for the explanation she knew he couldn't give her.

'I don't know,' he replied. 'I thought we'd solved his problems, financially anyway.'

'Was it his marriage?'

'We don't know anything for certain, but I'd say it was something more complex.'

'How so?'

'The Rowridges have owned this land forever, or for over a century anyway. In farming you grow attached to land for its own sake. Imagine this place has been part of the family for all that time…' He stopped, turned and walked out into the fresh air of the night. Lucy was glad to follow him, but she still needed an answer.

'You mean although he'd solved his money problems it was at the cost of his heritage?'

'I mean that in a few weeks' time Matthew would have looked out of his window and everything that had been Rowridge land would have become Fjortoft's. Even the roof over his head would have been by grace and favour of us.'

Lucy remained silent. She knew her father's moods too well.

He kicked the ground angrily. 'If I'd had the tiniest scrap of imagination, I might have seen this coming and done something in time.'

This was too much for Lucy. 'Oh, come off it, Dad – you're not psychic.'

'I don't claim to be. If only I hadn't been distracted by that girl Magda and her bloody friends.'

They heard the police powering up the lane; two cars, all flashing blue lights and bustling urgency; too late for Matthew, thought Tom. The three officers stood in a sombre group while he and Lucy pulled away the plastic sheet covering the body.

‘Money trouble or woman trouble?’ The first police constable looked at the body. His tone and glance suggested that nothing in this world surprised him.

‘Probably a bit of both,’ said Tom.

‘Did you find him?’

‘No, it was his daughter, poor girl. She must have seen him seconds after we got here. We heard her screaming from the house.’

‘Whose bright idea was it to cut him down?’ The constable sounded annoyed.

‘It was mine,’ said Lucy. ‘I’m a doctor. If there was a chance to save him I had to take it.’

‘It’s against the rules, disturbing the scene. D’you realise the extra paperwork you’re causing us? You could be in trouble.’

‘Sod you, and your bloody paperwork.’ She glared at the man.

‘Any indications that he was about to top himself?’ the PC asked Tom.

‘No, on the contrary, he asked me to call here on a farm matter. I spoke to him on the telephone and he seemed normal. Not only normal, he seemed excited about something.’

‘Any last note?’

‘Not that we’ve seen.’

‘There’ll be one somewhere – there always is.’ He sighed. ‘How’s the little girl taking it?’

‘She’s in the house – looks completely spaced out.’ A fourth policeman had appeared out of the gloom.

‘That’s all right,’ said Lucy. ‘I’ve sedated her.’

‘You shouldn’t have done that. She’s a vital witness – we need to question her.’

Tom winced, like all the family Lucy had a fiery temper that was frightening when it was roused. She turned on the luckless copper, eyes blazing. ‘You insensitive bastard! Francesca’s a seventeen-year-old kid who had just seen her father die and all you can think of is your bloody procedures.’

The PC looked shaken as he took a pace backwards. ‘Please yourself, Doctor. You can deal with George when he gets here. I can tell you he won’t like you interfering with the stiff.’

Dr George Shaylor, the police forensic officer, drove in half an hour later. He was grumbling, not that that was unusual; George was a world-weary country doctor who had seen most things in a career spanning thirty years.

'Who cut the rope for Chrissake?' he groaned.

Lucy explained as she faced George with a truculent poise. Tom knew that inside she was worried. She had done her duty with a clear conscience, but if George and officialdom chose to make something of this...

'You'll learn,' George grunted. 'It means I'll have to phone the coroner at home before we shift this cadaver.'

'I'm sorry,' said Lucy contritely.

'Doesn't matter – we'll wake up the pompous old fool.' He glared at Tom. 'You're a bloody magistrate. Couldn't you have stopped her?'

'I've no more control over my adult daughter than you have over yours.'

'That's the trouble with women,' George sighed. 'They always act on impulse – don't think of the consequences.'

Lucy showed him the body and told him what she had done. Tom watching some yards away heard only parts of the conversation. At one point Lucy bent down and pointed at the corpse's left ear.

'Trouble with you, young Lucy, is that you've been watching too much television,' George growled.

Lucy stood up and she seemed agitated. 'But you will note it, won't you?'

'Of course I will; it's a serious observation by a professional colleague.'

George walked across to Tom, looking none too friendly. 'So, on with the march of progress and another loser bites the dust, eh?'

'What do you mean?' Tom was genuinely puzzled.

'I mean another poor bugger's lost everything to the onward march of agri-business.'

'He didn't have to kill himself, and we'd just rescued him from a real financial mess.'

'Rescued – bloody hell, man!' George's face had gone a deep shade of purple, visible even under the dim lights of the barn. 'Doesn't it mean a thing to you? I tell you for nothing, this is the fourth suicide by a farmer I've been called to this year.'

'I know, George,' Tom replied quietly. 'It's the way things are but it's not my fault.'

'You and your Yank. You ever talked to your father about Fjortoft?'

'I know he doesn't like him.' Tom was wary; George was blundering onto dangerously personal ground.

‘He’s not the only one around here.’ With that George stumped off to his car to phone the coroner. Tom felt uneasy; the man’s belligerence was wholly unexpected. He wondered how many people felt the same way.

Lucy came over and stood by him. ‘Am I in trouble?’

Tom put an arm around her. ‘You did what you thought was right. It’s not as if there’s been foul play.’

‘I wonder?’ Her face bore a puzzled introspective look. ‘I’m not sure.’

‘You’re not serious?’

Lucy made no reply.

By now a police photographer was busy, his flashgun making them blink in the subdued light.

‘What’s going to happen to Francesca?’ Tom asked.

‘I’ve rung her uncle.’ said Lucy. ‘He’s on his way now.’

‘They live in Taraton, don’t they?’

‘Yes, I’m going to call in during the night to keep her sedated. We’ll contact the girl’s mother and arrange counselling tomorrow.’

‘Poor child, it’ll probably traumatise her for life.’

‘Not necessarily. Francesca’s a lively independent sort of kid – a tough cookie. Give her time and I think she’ll bounce back.’

They waited until Francesca’s aunt and uncle arrived. Lucy offered to go with them. They declined the offer but arranged for her to call towards midnight. They departed with Francesca who sat in the car clinging to the very subdued collie dog. Lucy drove Tom home. Neither had an appetite for food and Tom was feeling shattered and depressed. Matthew Rowridge would be alive now if he, Tom, had used a scrap of common sense and humanity. Surely to God he could have foretold this catastrophe. He had been so arrogant, so patronisingly smug, thinking he was doing Matthew this great favour by rescuing him from financial ruin. He had been so pleased with himself for gaining the estate three hundred acres of land for a knockdown price. He hadn’t offered salvation. George Shaylor had been right. They had stripped a defenceless and unlucky man of everything that made his life worthwhile and then driven him to a lonely and awful death.

Gina’s Porsche was parked in the yard at Boxtree. They could see her sitting in the glare of the headlights. Lucy uttered a single expletive.

‘Wait here,’ said Tom. ‘I’ll get rid of her.’ He ran across to Gina’s car. She was already starting to climb out.

'No, Gina,' he forced himself to be firm. 'Not now, something's happened.' He told her about Matthew Rowridge.

'Oh gee – oh, Tom, that's awful – but why?'

'It's my fault, it was me that forced him out of his farm.'

'No you didn't,' she replied. 'He asked Gus to help him, I saw the letter.'

'Gus left me to drive a deal and I drove one,' Tom felt better now he had a sympathetic listener. 'I offered him a dirt low price, no negotiation, take it or leave it.'

'It'd be a darned sight less if the bank had foreclosed on him,' said Lucy. Tom had not noticed her standing beside him.

'That's what I say,' Gina agreed. 'I saw just this kinda thing happen in New England when I was a kid, and Tom, maybe you don't know it but it was me told Gus to let you have a free hand with Matthew.'

'I know,' he sighed, 'but I was using the estate's money. I couldn't have acted in any other way.'

'I'll go now,' said Gina. She stared severely at Lucy. 'I only came to talk. I've gotta get back. We've a guest in the house, that's why I wanted to get away.'

Tom was surprised and by the look on her face so was Lucy. Gina was the world's most attentive hostess. The idea that she would slip away to avoid a guest was totally out of character.

'I don't like it,' Gina turned to face him and grimaced. 'Gus has been acting strange. It's like I hardly know him. Now this guy's come here.'

'Your guest?' Tom asked.

'Not my guest. He's scary – like he comes from a horror movie.'

'Oh, one of Gus's film people?'

'No, Gus says the man's his brother.'

CHAPTER 11

'I never knew Gus had a brother,' said Lucy.

'I didn't until tonight and then this guy turns up outa the blue. Like I said, Tom – there's things in his past he don't talk about.'

Tom had never seen her so agitated. 'That recurring nightmare,' he spoke quietly, although Lucy was no longer in earshot. 'Has it happened again?'

'No, not exactly.'

'What do you mean by, not exactly?'

'Like I said, he's acting strange. It's like I don't know him anymore.'

'For how long?'

'For about a week. He was like it when he came back from Scotland. Then he'd gotten a letter he wouldn't show me.'

'Any idea who from?'

'No, but it was posted in Seattle.'

'Doesn't mean a thing, it's his home town.' Tom paused for a few seconds; he had a decision to make. 'Look, this brother; how much has Gus told you about his parents?'

'They were divorced and his father was killed in the war. Don't know nothing about his mother.'

That was all Tom had ever known; until now it hadn't mattered.

'Gina?' Lucy was calling. 'Will you tell Gus about Matthew Rowridge? I think he ought to know tonight.'

'He's all private in his office with that weird guy.' There was tension in her voice. 'I don't want to break in on them.'

'I'll call by and tell him, if you like,' said Tom.

'Say, will you?' Gina's relief was so heartfelt it startled him. Something to do with this alleged brother-in-law must have really upset her, and Gina although naïve was not easily frightened.

'Yes, I think I ought to anyway. Let's go now and get it over.'

Tom took his own car and followed Gina's Porsche down the road to the Manor House. This brief interlude was important; it gave him two or three minutes to think. He had not told Lucy, let alone Gina, about Hannah and her disclosures. He felt a mix of disquiet and anticipation. If Hannah was to be believed, he might be about to meet Magda's killer.

Outwardly the big house was in darkness. The battery of floodlights that bathed its front wall most nights was switched off. Tom drove up the familiar avenue through the acres of trim lawns and ornamental trees. The moon lit the scene for the first time in days from a clear sky. Was it only a week since they had searched the woods for Gina's horse? That was the night he had seen Hannah by the roadside. He remembered how evasive the woman had been when he had mentioned that. Somehow it seemed all this mystery stemmed from that night. He stopped the car on the familiar gravel sweep by the front door. Gina ran across to him; she still seemed nervous.

She squeezed his hand and then let go, pointing to a car on the far side of the gravel. 'That's the brother's.'

It was a Jaguar with a dark colour scheme. He walked across to have a closer look. It had a four-year-old registration plate and a full year's tax. It bore the sticker of a car hire firm in Edinburgh. He glanced inside but even in the poor light he could see the interior was bare. He found a pen in his pocket and scribbled the Jaguar's details on an old till ticket.

He followed the by now impatient Gina into the house. All the hall lights were blazing including an overhead one shining down on a large man sitting in a mock medieval chair. He was a young fellow, well-groomed wearing a sharp suit with a collar and tie. One glance was enough to confirm him as one of Gus's Mormons.

'What's doin', Zeb?' Gina addressed him.

'Mr Fjortoft's still in conference,' the man replied. 'Ain't nobody allowed to disturb him.'

'Is he still in the office?' she asked.

'Sure is, Ma'am.'

'Then we'll wait.' Gina indicated Tom. 'Zeb, this is Tom our estate manager. Tom, this is Zebedee Scanlon, though he's Zeb to everyone around here.'

Tom said he was pleased to be meeting him, which was true.

'Look,' he said, 'I can't stay all night. For a start I've had a really stressful evening and I haven't eaten a thing all day. Can't I have a quick word with Mr Fjortoft and then go home?'

'Sorry, sir – can't let you do that. I've specific orders. Mr Fjortoft ain't to be disturbed – no pretext whatever, sir.'

He wasn't buying that. Gus never treated him as a minion, in fact he encouraged Tom to consult him whenever and whatever. For two pins he would stride off down the corridor and barge straight into the office. Or he would but for the fact that Zeb would almost certainly stop him, and that Zeb was patently bigger than Tom.

Gina had read his intentions. She clutched at his arm. 'No, Tom, don't go near Gus. Say, I didn't know you hadn't ate.' Still holding his arm she tugged him briskly towards the passage to the kitchen.

'Down here,' she said. 'I'm gonna cook you something all on my own.'

Tom followed her down the well-remembered passage to the swing door. Tonight the atmosphere was good. The kitchen was a warm and friendly place bathed in light. The whole room suffused with the smell of spices, garlic and newly sliced vegetables; a mix of aromas that was overwhelming. In spite of the horrors he had witnessed Tom found he had recovered his appetite; his mouth was literally watering. One chilling thought still troubled him.

'Gina, I must wash my hands.' He stared at the palms; they looked clean enough, but an hour ago they had handled the body of a newly dead man.

'Of course you must,' she replied. 'Staff toilet's out in the passage, first door on right.' Clearly she did not realise the significance and Tom wasn't going to enlighten her.

In the little toilet room, he scrubbed his hands with hot water and soap and then again with a bottle of disinfectant. Shakespeare, wasn't it, who wrote: *All the perfumes of Arabia will not wash out...* something like that. He knew how the man must have felt. Lastly he took off his wax jacket, which had recently cuddled the legs of a swinging corpse. He hung it on a hook and returned to the kitchen. Perhaps now he could do justice to Gina's cooking.

'Where's Chef and the staff?' he asked.

'Gus told 'em to go early,' Gina sniffed angrily. 'I wanted to serve dinner for this so called brother, but Gus wouldn't have it.' This seemed to have affronted Gina's instinct as a hostess. 'You know,' she continued, 'it don't matter if the man came out of nowhere. Chef and me could've gotten a dinner ready.' She looked woefully around. 'Well, bad on 'em. I'm going to cook you a meal like you never had in your life.'

'I could take that more than one way.' Some of the tension was easing.

'Now don't you be gettin' all sarcastic, Tom O'Malley,' her awful Southern belle accent was back; a sure sign that Gina was beginning to relax. She began delving into cupboards and scouring shelves, all the while singing quietly to herself. She lit a gas flame under an enormous wok and began to hurl ingredients into it. Tom was feeling drowsy and the kitchen was so warm. He pulled a wooden chair close to the Aga range, sat in it and stretched out his legs. Somehow even the memory of that grotesque swinging corpse began to fade. It wasn't a dream, worse luck, but down here in this secure warm place it seemed detached: a piece of history.

'That guy, the brother,' said Gina. 'It was like I wasn't there. Gus said to him, "meet my wife", and he never so much as looked at me. Never said, "Hello", or nothing.'

Tom agreed. 'That was certainly rude. Did this man give a name? He's only a half-brother by the way…' Hell, eight words too many.

She swung round and stared at him open-mouthed. 'Say, Tom, what d'you know about it?'

'Sorry, Gina, I know no more than you do. The other day somebody mentioned that Gus had a half-brother. I'd never heard of this before and I wasn't sure I believed it.'

'That's why you asked me the other night about Gus, and where he came from?'

'I wasn't really prying but I was puzzled. Gus never talks about his background and that's unusual with film people. Actors can be bloody irritating. In this country they're always coming on telly or radio with posh accents, agonising about their working class backgrounds.'

'In the States we don't have class like you Brits. Mostly we're mighty proud of our ethnic origins. My people's German but we ain't ashamed. They were religious settlers, a hundred years before the Hitler thing.'

'Fjortoft's definitely a Scandinavian name,' Tom mused. 'He comes from Seattle and that place is full of Norwegians and Swedes – I know, I've been there.'

'Well I've never been in those parts. Don't you think that's strange?'

'Why?'

'Cos that's Gus's home town, it's where his folks come from, yet he never takes me there, you know, show me the places where he played as a kid – where he went to school.'

Tom agreed. 'By all accounts his father was a wealthy man. It's his fortune that started Gus in films. He financed *The Bear* out of his own pocket.'

'No, it's like he's scared of the place. Is that where he saw those kids murdered?'

'That I couldn't say.' Tom was troubled. Gina was an innocent in all this, but she could be in danger and she deserved a warning. 'The other day I met a journalist who wanted me to talk about Gus. I hope you believe me when I say I wanted nothing to do with it.'

She nodded. 'I believe that, Tom.'

'It was this journalist who told me about Gus's half-brother. She said same mother, different fathers.'

'Who told you this?'

'Never mind, she was only some newspaper woman who cornered me the other day.' He stood up and walked across to her. Gently he took hold of her hand and made her put down the whisk she was holding. He turned her to face him. 'What she had to say is this and it's a warning. She had a friend, another investigative journalist, who was also probing into Gus's past. Now she's dead.'

Tom watched the shot go home. Gina's face blanked for a second and then she shook her head. 'I think you're wrong there. Gus would never have someone killed. He's been pestered for years and he's never lost his cool; it's like water off a duck's back with him.'

Tom put both hands on her shoulders and forced her to meet his eyes. 'Gina, I never said Gus killed the reporter. I'm as certain as I stand here that he didn't. There are other people interested in his past who do not wish him well. I think you should be careful – that's all.'

'OK, Tom, I hear you.' She smiled a rather lopsided smile. 'Sure, I'll be careful if you say so, but we don't let this get to us.' She disengaged herself from Tom's grip and then steered him over to the scrubbed wooden table in the centre of the room. 'Stay there,' she ordered and flitted out of the kitchen. He heard her footsteps recede into the distance. Five minutes later she was back.

'Creepy pants is going,' she whispered.

'Who?'

'The brother, I just named him that – came into my mind kinda' spontaneous.'

'Shouldn't you be waving goodbye?' Tom grinned in spite of himself.

Gina glared. 'No way, Jose, I don't want that piece of horseshit in my house – not ever again.' She returned to the stove and examined her work. 'This is no darned good. I should've gotten you to stir.'

'It smells great from here.'

'OK, I'll make the sauce and then we'll tuck – is that what you say in England?'

'I think you mean tuck in – that's nice and old fashioned. It's what adults told us to do when we were kids.'

'Tuck means something else in our language – I don't get it.'
'It's only an expression you know, a colloquialism.'
They both started as they heard footsteps coming down the kitchen passage. The door swung open and there stood Gus Fjortoft. He looked tired, or weary, that was the word. A subtle change had come over the man in the few days since they had last met and happily discussed plans for the coming year.
'Hi, Tom.' Gus gave him a wintry smile. 'Zeb told me you were here. Sorry if I kept you waiting, I've been detained these last four hours.'
'Has he gone?' said Gina. There was venom in her tone.
'Sure, he's gone.' Gus flopped down in a chair next to Tom. 'Say, that smells good. You got some for me too?'
'I've got enough for the three of us, especially for my two favourite men.'
Tom winced, and glanced at Gus. Why was this man so unfazed about his wife's extra-marital love life? Tom would never understand it.
'Gus, you know Woolbarrow Farm? We've got a problem.' Tom told him about Matthew.
'Oh my God,' Gus was clearly upset. 'Poor man, I'd never have thought it.'
'You knew him well, didn't you, honey?' said Gina.
'Sure, I owed him.' Gus lapsed into silence.
'I did the deal to buy his farm,' Tom said. 'What should we do?'
'Hey, not now, man – let's enjoy this dinner. Seems you and I have had one helluva of a bad day.'

Gina stood with her husband on the front steps of the Manor House. They watched as Tom drove away, the taillights of his car glowing until he reached the end of the avenue and vanished. She put an arm around Gus; she could feel how tense he was. All she wanted to do was listen and understand.
'Great man Tom,' Gus murmured. 'Salt of the earth.'
'I know that,' she replied.
'Sweetheart,' he squeezed her arm. 'If something should happen to me, I would like to think you had Tom to run to. I would hate it if you were all alone.'
She felt an awful foreboding. 'Gus, darling, why should anything happen to you?'
'I'm a jinxter.'

'A what?'

'Jinxter – like Jonah in the Bible. I cast a gloom over this place and people die.'

'No they don't. Stop it, Gus, you're talking shite.' She was outraged. In all their years together she had never known him like this.

'I love this farm, I love this community and all its people, and every time I come back here someone dies.'

'Gus, honey, stop it – this is morbid. No one dies 'cos of you.'

'Tricia O'Malley, and that little girl who worked on the potato picking.'

'But she died miles from here,' Gina wailed.

'But it was Tom found her.'

'He had nothing to do with it. Don't you suggest such a thing – you jealous?'

'Oh, come on, you know I'm not. I want the best for you and I can't please you like I used to and as I said Tom's a great guy.'

'She reached up and put her arms around his neck, pressing against him with her full length. 'You're big and strong, they rightly call you the Bear.'

He leant down and kissed her softly on the lips. 'You remember in the movie? The Inuit, they corner and kill the bear.' He whispered the words in her ear. 'Why was that?'

'Cos they thought he was a harbinger. They thought he brought them bad luck.'

'You see, I've come home and poor Matthew's dead. Maybe I killed him.'

'Of course you never killed him,' she paused. 'What did you mean, you owed him?'

'Nothing you need worry about. He did me a favour a while back, and I can't help wondering if…' He shook his head. 'Aw, forget it.'

'It was suicide. Tom said Matthew's money troubles got to him.'

'Gina, do you remember a few years back, those two boys in Liverpool? How they took and killed a little kid – just for kicks?'

'Of course I do, it was horrible.'

'Listen – those boys, what do you believe? Were they born evil, will they always be evil?'

'I don't know,' she blinked unhappily; she could feel her tears brimming. 'Gus, it's cold out here. Come indoors; let's have a drink – talk about something else?'

He nodded, 'Sure, we can't talk out here. I think it's time I came clean. There's things you don't know and I think now is the time I should be telling you.'

CHAPTER 12

Lucy watched the two cars leave the yard and listened as they rolled down the lane and turned into the Crossfield road.

'Sod you, Gina!' she yelled into the night. 'I hate you!' Suddenly she was laughing hysterically. It was a good thing she was alone; her tantrum was hardly dignified.

What a bloody awful day it had been. Conducting a morning surgery full of whinging geriatrics and bellicose malingerers, then a fight with Mike over a triviality. She smiled, knowing Mike would be ever so contrite by the time she came home. With a bit of luck it would be her turn to have some good sex. Wasn't it strange that understanding the mechanics of the body did nothing to diminish the pleasures or the pain. Hell, she couldn't drive away the image of Matthew Rowridge. Twenty-four hours ago Matthew had been a living breathing man. Now all that remained was the shell of a body; its decomposition slowed in some mortuary fridge. Something about that body was wrong; not wrong perhaps, but unexplained. She forced herself to focus on the memory. It was something she had to do. She wanted to surmount this challenge and emerge as a better doctor. She was going to reach the top of her profession and not end up a boozy disgruntled cynic like George Shaylor.

So what was different; what had she seen that George had missed? The eyes of course: that was it, the eyes. It was so obvious. She suppressed an urge to run indoors and call George there and then.

Her thoughts were broken by the sound of footsteps. A dark figure was shambling through the gate into the yard. It was a male with an enormous backpack.

'Hi there, big sister,' he called.

'Andy,' she shouted, racing forward to greet her young brother.

'Where's Dad?' Andrew O'Malley set his pack down on the steps and looked around.

'You may well ask,' she replied tersely. 'He's down at the Manor with his fancy bit.'

'Eh?'

'Gina, of course.'

'Christ, is that still going on?'

'She spent the night here two days ago.'

'Gus Fjortoft doesn't mind?' Andy sniggered.

'On the contrary, it's almost as if he encourages it.'

'Well, what's your problem?'

Lucy was furious. 'How can you say that – when the woman is stealing our father.'

'No she isn't, she's sex mad, gagging for it – everybody knows that.' He sniggered again. 'Good for Dad, wish I had a red hot bimbo. None at the uni – they swot so hard they're too tired.'

'I won't waste my breath.' Lucy glowered. 'I've had a foul day. We've had something awful happen. You know Matthew Rowridge up at Woolbarrow?'

'Yes, of course.'

'He committed suicide this afternoon and I was the one that had to sort it.'

'Oh shit no! Oh, Lucy, I'm sorry.' Andy gave her a sympathetic look. 'Is that really why Dad's down at the Manor?'

'Yes it is. Sorry, Andy, I'm wild because my nerves are on edge, and when we got here Gina was waiting for him.'

'Poor old Matthew, why did he do it?'

'He was broke, the estate bought him out, but he was always a loner – never mixed much. Dad thinks it all got to him and he just snapped.' It sounded hollow; she wished she knew more about depression. Doctors talked about chemical imbalances and dished out antidepressants; like bribing kids with sweets to keep them quiet. Yet everyone knew it was more complex. She often wondered if she should have specialised in psychiatry. Perhaps it was a fear that depression lay not far behind the surface of her own mind. Physician, heal thyself – what balls!

She glared at her brother. 'Why are you here anyway?'

'Oh, that's a fine welcome. Term's over – it's Easter break.'

'Of course, sorry again, I'm not my usual self tonight. Say, what are you doing in your hols?'

'Two mates and me, we're going to France. Aunt Marie and Uncle Marc say we can camp on their place. We're taking mountain bikes and we're going to tour around Brittany.'

'Lucky you, it makes me nostalgic for student days.' Now she was an overworked GP whose own life was about to take a dramatic shift.

'Brother,' she said. 'Mike and I are getting married.'

'Brilliant, I've been keeping my fingers crossed for you and I like Mike.' He stood up and gave her another hug. 'When's it to be?'

'July sometime, in Gloucester – Grandmother Lansbury's organising the do for us.'

'Oh shit.'

Lucy grinned sadistically. Andy had something of a complex about the Lansbury connection. She eyed him closely as he stood in the glare of the yard lights. His ragged clothing and shaven head gave him the appearance of a Tibetan monk. 'Never mind,' she said. 'We'll fix you up with the right gear to wear.'

Tom returned at nine o'clock. He was surprised to see the house was ablaze with light and that Lucy's car was still parked where he had last seen it. As he walked indoors all was explained; Andrew was eating supper while his sister fussed around. Tom greeted his son happily and asked about the college and how long he would be staying.

'Yes,' said Lucy. 'He's pushing off to France on Wednesday. You'll have to wait until then before you sneak that woman in here.'

'Don't mind me,' said Andy. 'I won't hear a thing – when I sleep I'm dead to the world.'

Lucy was glaring at him. 'I was hoping for some support from my brother, not this laddish nonsense.'

'Leave it alone, love,' said Tom. 'I've other things on my mind.'

Lucy nodded. 'How was it down at the Manor?'

Tom flopped down in his chair. 'There's something odd going on. I've never seen Gus looking so vulnerable.'

'Gus, vulnerable?' Lucy's voice expressed surprise. 'Did you tell him about Matthew?'

'Yes, but I doubt he took it in. No, something's bothering him. Something really serious and it's getting to me as well.'

'Why?'

'Because I have a nasty feeling that all our cosy lives here are in for a shake up.' He looked at Lucy. 'Love, hand me the phone. I want to catch your grandfather before he goes to bed.'

Lucy passed him the portable handset. 'Why granddad at this time of night?'

'I want information – everything he can remember about a man called Sam Little.'

At seven o'clock the next morning Tom was ringing the front door bell of his parents' house in Taraton. The elder O'Malleys lived in a 1930s detached house in the leafy outskirts at Beech Hill. Fred still cycled every day to his shop in the town centre. Tom's mother, Lucille, pottered around the garden, did the weekly shopping in her

Renault 8, and taught French to adult evening classes. Lucille was a farmer's daughter from St Brieuc. At eighteen years old she had fallen in love with an Englishman; his name was Frederick O'Malley. The handsome young ship's officer had captivated Lucille. Fred had stories to tell of the sea and the awful war that had tarnished all their lives. As a young sea apprentice, aged only fifteen, he had taken part in the evacuation of Dunkirk. At seventeen he had been torpedoed and nearly drowned in Arctic waters. There were things he had seen that he would never speak of: things that moved this most phlegmatic Englishman to long silences and sometimes tears. It was then that the young Lucille would sit quietly with him, holding his hands in hers, saying nothing. She asked for no more than that her presence should comfort and heal.

Lucille's family were not happy. They could not understand why she wanted to marry this itinerant Englishman. They had hoped, indeed they had planned, that she should marry her cousin Antoine, thereby uniting two farms. For five long years the impasse lasted. The lovers would travel to meet whenever Fred finished a voyage; sometimes vast distances in far continents. The airfares alone took a sizeable chunk of Fred's meagre pay and Lucille's schoolteacher's salary. In 1950, Fred had been given his first command, a small coastal tanker from the Benson Pacific Line. For Lucille and Fred it had transformed their prospects. Lucille had travelled to Vancouver and spent an ecstatic happy month with her man. When she returned to St Brieuc she was pregnant. With this *fait accompli* her family's resistance crumbled. Fred and Lucille married and their son Tom was born six months later.

Tom had only the haziest memories of his childhood in Vancouver. When he was aged four his father, under pressure from Lucille, had returned home to a shore-based job with the shipping line in Bristol. Tom was never sure that his father was a particularly good business executive, but the job paid well. The family had a comfortable home in the Forest of Dean and Fred had kept his hand in at sea with a small sailing yacht. Tom loved the boat but he never had a feel for the wider world of seafaring. He supposed his call to the land must come from his mother and her family's thousand years of frugal peasant farming.

'More coffee?' Tom's mother leaned over and refilled his cup. Tom was sitting at his parents' breakfast table. No sparse French breakfast this; his mother had produced an array of his favourite childhood start-the-day dishes. On the table were eggs, tomatoes, mushrooms, and little pancakes with syrup. She pressed helping after helping on him until he was unable to handle any more.

'I think you are not feeding properly,' said Lucille. 'You will have to marry again. I do not think Lucy understands cuisine.'

'What she understands is all about cholesterol and blood pressure. I wouldn't dare eat a breakfast like this with her around.'

'Just so, I make my point.' Lucille laughed and went into the kitchen.

Tom's father stared at him. 'Right, what's behind this visit?'

'Dad, I need information urgently.'

'All right, tell all?' Fred drank his coffee and refilled the cup.

'You remember the night I came with that film of the dead girl?'

'Oh no, boy – not still on about her?'

'Not her, but you mentioned a man called Sam Little. You said you knew him in the old days with the Benson Line.'

'Yes, I know Sam. Haven't seen him for a while but we go back a long way.'

'The other day I met his son. He's teaching at University South. He mentioned that you and his father had been at sea.'

'Well, well,' Fred leaned back and looked at the ceiling. 'Was the boy called Peter?'

'Yes, Pete, they call him, and he's not a boy. He must be at least forty.'

'Come to think of it I suppose he must be. When I last saw him he was nothing but a nipper.'

'All right, tell me; what is Sam Little's connection with Fjortoft?'

Fred looked nonplussed. 'There isn't any connection. Sam didn't like Fjortoft – period, as the Yanks say.'

'That's what you told me before, explain why?'

'Why what?'

'Don't be obtuse, Dad. This could be important.'

'I don't know the whole story, but it was something to do with Sammy's missus.'

'Oh, I see.' Tom felt an overwhelming disappointment. 'So it was like that. Gus used to put it about a bit. I imagine he must have crossed a few angry husbands.'

'No, boy, it weren't sex,' Fred intervened. 'It was something a bit deeper than that.'

'Can you tell me?'

'Yes, I can tell you what I know, but Sam was quite close about the details. It cost him his job, so you can see why he had it in for Fjortoft.'

Tom stifled his exasperation. He knew the old man would not be hurried.

'Sammy's wife was called Greta. She was a pretty little thing – foreign though. Her people came from Estonia I think, Baltic anyway. Sam said all her family died in the war.' Fred took another drink from his coffee. 'It seems this Greta nearly died herself in some death camp. Somehow she survived. When the war ended she found her way to Sweden and then on to the States – all at the age of ten. Sammy said her story would make a book and a film any day.'

'Where does Fjortoft come in?'

'Gustav Fjortoft owns sixty percent of the shares in Benson Pacific. Sammy and Greta were at some big social bash. You know, one of those boring things you can't get out of going to. I wasn't there, it was after my time, but it seems there was the most God awful scene – spoilt the party.' Fred looked up at the sound of the post fluttering through the letter slit in the front door. He pushed back his chair and shuffled to pick up the pile. 'All junk,' he muttered.

'Dad,' Tom was impatient, 'what happened?'

'At the reception? It was like this; Fjortoft gets up to make his little speech. Remember this was nineteen-sixty, so the man was only a young pipsqueak in his twenties. He'd been asked to make the puff for the board because he had "a talent to amuse", as Noel Coward used to say. You see Gussy was a bit part actor at the time, being a business tycoon was his day job.'

'Yes, I've read all that. What happened?'

'All right, I'll tell you. Gussy gets up, all preening himself for his little speech and then Greta Little runs up on the platform jabbering in Estonian or whatever and tries to scratch his eyes out. Took four of them to pull her off him. Sammy drags her out of the place and then four days later the company fires him. Some trumped up charges about him not keeping a proper ship's log. Load of codswallop.'

Tom was beginning to see some light. 'Why did Greta react the way she did?'

'That I never did hear. Sammy made it clear her motives weren't up for discussion. He was mostly on about suing the Benson Line. From what I've heard that's what he did and lost most of what he had doing it.'

'Why?'

'Because this was America, boy. He wins who has the most

expensive lawyers.'

Tom returned to the farm at nine o'clock and plunged straight into work. He learned that Gus and Gina had gone away. Charlie Marrington had driven them to London, and they had left no instructions as to when they would return. Of course by now the whole village was buzzing with news of Matthew Rowridge's suicide. He could detect a faint air of hostility that was as depressing as it was unfair. Public opinion echoed George Shaylor's view that the tragedy was somehow Gus Fjortoft's fault.

Tom went moodily home to lunch. He had no appetite after his mother's enormous breakfast. He made a cup of tea and took it into his study. On impulse he picked up the telephone and called Frank Matheson. Matheson, a private investigator, had worked for Tom last year. A dealer had bought some redundant farm equipment from the estate and then vanished without paying. Matheson, a no nonsense ex-police superintendent had tracked down the miscreant and recovered the debt within a week. Tom had been impressed.

He was in luck; Frank was in his office. Tom gave him the details of the Jaguar car supposedly driven by Gus's brother. 'Could you find out who hired that car this current week?'

'Yes, I should think so.' Frank sounded cautious. 'May I know why?'

'That Jag's been hanging around Crossfield. Mrs Fjortoft met the driver and there was something about him that she didn't take to.'

'If it's a sex prowler you ought to report it to the proper authorities.'

'No, Frank, I'm sure it's nothing like that. There's not enough to interest the regular police. We're just being careful.'

'Understood, I'll see what I can do.'

'There's something else. Can you check the bone fides of an overseas journalist?'

'That depends – it'll cost you.'

'I'll trust you to put in a fair bill. She's a Miss Hannah Berkovic and she's been harassing us.' He gave Hannah's London agency address. 'Find out everything you can and come back to me.'

For his last call of the day Tom hitched a trailer on a tractor and loaded six full-size silage bales. He drove home with these, leaving his car at the estate office. It was six o'clock. At Boxtree he found Andy watching television and Lucy in the kitchen.

'How is Francesca?' he asked.

'She's spent the afternoon with a bereavement counsellor. Apparently she's bearing up rather well. Still in deep shock but not as distressed as I'd expected. I saw her an hour ago and she's refusing any further medication.'

'How's her aunt coping?'

'With great efficiency and her own daughter, Natalie, has taken Francesca under her wing. The dog was unhappy being stuck in a town. They've given him to Tessa Marrington, Charlie's grand-daughter to look after.

Tom had heard that Francesca Rowridge was an academically gifted child and that Matthew had valued her neither for that nor much else. Maybe this tragedy, however terrible, would be a blessing in disguise.

'You don't have to cook for us, love,' Tom told her. 'You've been burning the candle at both ends. We can manage.'

'No, I'm fine,' she said. 'Mike and John are covering tonight. I've got the whole evening to kill and I'd rather be with you.'

'Thanks, I appreciate that.' He paused. 'I've got to feed the cattle at Woolbarrow. If I don't leave it too late there should be some daylight.'

'What cattle are these?'

'The Rowridge pedigree herd. They're running short of feed so I've loaded some silage for them.'

'We'll both come with you,' said Andy. 'What about it, Luce?'

'That silage stinks.'

'There's some overalls of your mother's upstairs,' Tom replied.

'OK,' she said, 'might as well.'

'Good, one of you can drive the main tractor and I'll bring the loader.'

Lucy was at the wheel of the big John Deere tractor with Andy sitting nonchalantly on one of the plastic wrapped bales. Tom followed with Boxtree Farm's own tractor, a battered David Brown with a hydraulic loader. He had intended to press Andy into helping and had been surprised and moved when both kids had offered without prompting. It was dusk as he followed the trailer up the long winding lane to the top of the hill. The rear lights on his tractor were hardly adequate; he fervently hoped PC Ross was elsewhere. He had already told Lucy to take the public road to the top of the ridge. He wanted to avoid unnecessary damage to the grassland by driving across country. They would enter Woolbarrow Farm via the old flint track that coincidentally skirted Becham's Wood.

At first Lucy had been nervous of this huge beast of a tractor, but she soon relaxed and began to enjoy herself. The cattle had heard them coming and were clustered around the field gate, gently mooing. Andy jumped off the trailer and shooed them away, as Lucy and her father drove through. The job was a dirty and frustrating one. Tom picked up each bale in turn with the loader, while Andy and Lucy cut away the wrapping and the bindings. Lucy grumbled and swore as the tight strings bit into her fingers. The first two bales were the worst as the cows pushed and jostled her in their efforts to reach the rich feed. The subsequent bales were easier as the herd dispersed along the line.

'If this is farming,' she said breathing heavily, 'you can stuff it.'

'You should be grateful,' said Andy. 'First hand experience of how your patients get themselves bruised and battered.'

'Never mind,' said her father. 'This is a one-off. Tomorrow I'll get some help from the estate.'

Lucy was filthy. Her overalls were wet, she stank of raw silage, mud and cow dung, and she had loved it. What a wonderful release after the turmoil of yesterday. It was as if her childhood had returned in some time warp. "Helping Daddy with the cows." When she had been fifteen Mummy had allowed her to drive a tractor. It was only a little Ferguson, far smaller than this giant she was driving now. She had learnt to harrow grass and turn hay. Lucy was always thrilled by the power of the machine she sat on and by her perfect control over it.

In her early teens tractor driving came second only to horse riding, and definitely more important than boys. A psychiatrist, a Freudian anyway, would probably say both pastimes were psychosomatic sexual substitutes. A young girl aroused by sitting astride a powerful animal or machine. She had read some such nonsense in a psychiatric journal. She smiled; she was certainly getting a different sort of buzz from this tractor. Four times the size of her little Fergie and with power steering, four-wheel drive and a hundred and ten horses under the bonnet; this was a machine to kill for. She must ask Dad to let her have a go with it again.

She pursed her lips and dropped a gear as she began the descent of the long downhill stretch. She could feel the weight of the trailer pushing her and hear the roar of the diesel as the tractor took the strain. Ahead was a gentle right hand bend, with the mellow brickwork of the Woolbarrow farmhouse standing out in the beams of her headlights. She wanted to hurry past this awful place; she knew that long as she lived she would never feel comfortable here. So powerful were her lights that they shone inside the house. She could see pictures on the walls, a heavy old-fashioned wardrobe and then a man walking across the window of an upstairs room. As she watched he turned, white faced, to stare into the light.

Lucy felt the hairs on her neck prickle. She went cold as her body reacted in shock. The tractor and load had started to wobble; she had lost concentration and another sharper bend was coming up. Ahead of her was an open gate. Lucy flipped the indicator switch left, and drove straight into the ploughed field. She sat trembling, her heart pounding. She jumped, and stifled a cry, as a man climbed onto the outside step and thumped on the cab door. It was only Andy.

'OK, I saw it. Upstairs in the house…' Andy wrenched open the door. He too was breathing hard.

'You saw the man upstairs?' She felt an overwhelming relief as she jumped from the tractor and flung her arms around him. 'Sorry, Andy, I hate this place – it was only yesterday.'

'I know, I know,' he reassured her. 'But that was no ghost. He dropped to the floor seconds after the lights caught him.'

'Hey, you two – what's happening?' Their father had pulled the loader tractor off the road and was walking towards them.

'There's somebody mooching about inside the Rowridge house,' said Andy. 'We saw a man upstairs – caught him in the headlights.'

'Hell,' said Tom. 'I asked Ross to keep an eye on the place. I told him every light-fingered sod in the area would know it's empty.'

'What are we going to do?' asked Andy.

'I'll go and take a look. See if I can get a sight of him – chances are I'll know him from my court.'

'I'll come as well,' said Andy.

'All right, but do as I tell you. We're not into heroics. It's identification I want.' Tom began walking briskly up the road towards the house. Lucy followed the two men who for the moment seemed to have forgotten she existed.

'Andy,' Tom whispered. 'If you slip along inside the field you'll come out at the back. There's a rear door into the kitchen. Watch it and the windows. See if you can get a glimpse of the man if he comes out that way.'

'OK, Dad, game on.' Andy replied. Lucy could see her brother's face; incredibly he was enjoying this.

'Remember, no heroics, no macho stuff – it's evidence we're after. I'll go indoors and see if I can flush him out. I've left my mobile phone at home so I'll ring the law at the same time.'

Lucy felt cold again. 'Be careful.'

He swung round, apparently noticing her for the first time. 'What are you doing here? Go home!' He turned away.

She felt a flash of anger. She had ceased to be frightened and she was not going to be patronised by these stupid men. 'I won't go,' she whispered. 'If either of you idiots gets hurt you'll need me.'

'Stay here then and keep quiet.' Tom dismissed her curtly; Lucy seethed.

She watched her father walk openly across the yard and into the front porch. He groped in his pocket and produced a torch. Evidently the front door was locked. He emerged from the porch and walked round the side of the building. Lucy saw him stop, reach up and vault rather gracefully through an open window. That's not bad for a man pushing fifty, she thought. She walked across the yard and through a side gate into the garden. Her eyes had adjusted to the darkness and she could now see details clearly. She stood back in the shadow of an ancient apple tree. She could just see the outline of Andy standing against a small wooden shed.

A shrill yell sounded from within the house, followed by her father's voice in a triumphant roar, 'gotcha!' There was a pause and then Dad again, this time his voice less certain. 'What the bloody hell are you doing here?'

A slim figure had detached from the darkness at the rear of the house and began to slink away towards the fields. Lucy saw Andy race out of concealment. The intruder had no chance. Andy caught him with a flying rugby tackle and down they both went. A scuffle ensued with the pair of them rolling on the ground. Lucy could hear Andy grunting and swearing. Then the intruder was on his feet as he delivered a savage kick. Andy gave a strangled gasp and doubled up in silent agony. The lithe figure sped away into the shadows.

Lucy had stood transfixed. Now she ran to her brother and knelt beside him.

'Andy, what happened?' She knew she was panicking. She had visions of a knife wound; of blood flowing and vital organs damaged.

'Bitch, the bitch,' Andy groaned. He sat up both hands clasped in his groin. 'Oh God, what a girl.'

Lucy was annoyed. It seemed her brother was not mortally wounded, except in pride. 'Will you tell me what happened?'

'It was a girl – a little dolly bimbo. She slipped me, God knows how, and then she kicked me in the goolies…'

Despite the seriousness of it all Lucy laughed – worse, she giggled. All the horror and tension of the last twenty-four hours dissolved in a burst of hysterical schoolgirl giggling. She tried to control herself but it was no good. Lucy sat on the ground beside her aggrieved brother and laughed until she actually cried, and when she cried the tears rolled in huge sobs until she lay on the ground shaking. Andy put a supportive arm around her. He's a good brother, she thought. I think he's guessed something of what I've been through.

Andy climbed slowly to his feet. Lucy could see him staring at the house. Dad was outside now pushing a strange gangling boy in front of him. Lucy recognised the youth as the person she had first seen upstairs. The boy looked, if not frightened, very chastened. He was tall and thin with untidy black hair. He wore jeans and a dark T-shirt, and clasped a pair of spectacles in his right hand.

'Andy, what happened?' Tom asked.

Lucy giggled. 'It was a girl. She kicked him in the balls.'

'Andy,' said Tom. 'Hold this character. Don't let him get away. I've lots to say to him.'

He turned and walked to the edge of the garden, and seemingly addressed the night. 'Hannah, I know you're out there somewhere, and not too far away, I would guess. I give you two choices. You show yourself and explain, or I'll hand your sorry little sidekick straight to the police. It's up to you.'

CHAPTER 13

'Good evening, Tom.' Lucy's heart gave a lurch. She spun round to see a small figure that had seemingly emerged from nowhere. The voice sounded so measured and polite that Lucy nearly started to giggle again.

Her father shone his torch on this new arrival. She looked very young with wisps of jet black hair protruding under a dark beret. Rather than a fashion item it had a military look. For the rest of her clothing she wore dark jeans, a black sweater and her hands were encased in surgical rubber gloves.

She wondered how her father could know this woman. She didn't seem like a petty criminal who appeared before the magistrate's court; her posh speech and general demeanour were all wrong.

'So it is you,' Tom replied. 'What are you doing here?'

'Kismet, Tom, we meet again.'

'Who is this vicious bitch, Dad?' Andy faced the girl.

'This lady is Miss Hannah Berkovic. She's supposed to be some sort of journalist.' He indicated the boy held by Andy. 'This is Anton, who told me he's the brother of Magdalena Sherakova, the young lady I found dead by the harbour.'

'These are Magda's friends.' Lucy found her voice at last. 'The ones you told me about?'

'Yes.' Tom looked at Hannah. 'I don't understand any of this; I thought you had a legitimate cause. I can't see how you advance it by casual housebreaking.'

Hannah shook her head. 'We are here for that cause and for no other reason.'

Lucy was changing her view of Hannah. This woman, no older than herself, possessed such charisma that Lucy's own doubts began to fade. Whatever reason these people had for being at Woolbarrow Farm, she doubted a criminal intent. She glanced at her father and brother. Andy still visibly in a state of suppressed rage; Dad poker-faced giving nothing away.

'Lucy, take the tractor and trailer back to Boxtree,' he ordered. 'Hannah, where's your car?'

'Behind the hedge,' she pointed.

'Very well, we'll go back to my house. You will drive – I will sit in the passenger seat.' He looked at Andy. 'You, Andrew, will sit in the back with Anton here. I warn both of you that Andy is a member of his university rugby team and it will not pay to mess with him.'

'You're both covered in mud and you smell. I'm not letting you in my car without some paper on the seats.' Hannah's voice was a casual drawl. In spite of everything Lucy liked her.

'I'm sure the Israeli government is not so broke it can't afford to have your car cleaned,' Tom replied.

'Bloody Israel!' Andy snapped.

'Yes, Israel; I think we'd all better go down to Boxtree and Hannah can explain, if she can, what the hell is going on.'

They sat, all five of them, around the polished dining room table at Boxtree Farm. To Lucy the atmosphere had become surreal. She poured coffee into their cups and offered a plate of biscuits. Her father placed himself at the head of the table, his face immobile. Andy sat opposite, glowering, the only one to refuse the refreshments. Hannah seemed relaxed in an attitude of polite attentiveness; Anton looked scared.

'Hannah,' said Tom. 'I will give you a chance to justify what you've been up to this evening. It had better be good because my course of action will depend on what you say.'

'That's fair by me, Tom,' said Hannah.

'Not by me it's not,' Andy growled. 'For Christ's sake, these are burglars. We caught them breaking into the empty house of a bereaved family – you can't get much sicker than that…'

'All right, Andy,' Tom sighed. 'Let me explain. Hannah, as I understand is a journalist with an Israeli news agency. She's also a bit more than that I would guess, but I've never asked questions because I would only get lies. At the moment she's trying to set up some exposé of Gustav Fjortoft, on the grounds that he has a half-brother with a murky past. Am I right so far?' He stared at Hannah.

'Yes, as far as it goes,' she replied. 'But the plot is deeper and wider than Fjortoft's brother.'

'I don't doubt it. Hannah believes this unknown brother had a hand in murdering children in Eastern Europe during Hitler's time. Magdalena Sherakova, whose body I found, is alleged to have discovered something about this half-brother and in consequence she was murdered.'

'That was suicide,' said Andy. 'Lucy said so in her letter and I read about it in the paper.'

'That is the official position. However I have been shown enough evidence to convince a magistrate that this supposed brother, whose surname I understand is Brown, has a case to answer. In fact I can tell you now that Magdalena was never a suicide.'

'Well put,' said Hannah. 'What do you think, Lucy?'

'Doctor O'Malley to you,' said Andy.

'Shuddup, Andy!' Lucy silenced him. 'Hannah, will you tell me why this involves the Rowridge family and Woolbarrow Farm?'

'Mr Rowridge had the misfortune to hold a document that Brown wanted suppressed and he killed him for it.'

'Crap,' shouted Andy. 'I'm going to phone the police. I've had about enough of this shit.' He half rose in his chair; his shaven head and stubble chin seemed to exaggerate his hollow eyes.

'Sit down, and behave.' Lucy knew how to control her impulsive brother. 'I'm interested in Hannah's story and,' she stared around the room, 'I think I can contribute a medical opinion.' She raised an eyebrow and looked at her father.

'Carry on,' he said.

'Matthew Rowridge died from strangulation and the associated trauma. I examined his body about half an hour after death. I saw something that didn't add up and I told the police forensic officer about it. Frankly I don't think he took much notice.' Lucy suppressed a smirk of satisfaction. Stuff you, Andy; they were listening to her now, hanging, if that wasn't a bad-taste term, on every word she said.

Hannah and Anton had gone. Lucy and Tom watched as the Volvo drove away down the road towards Taraton. Andy had remained indoors actively sulking.

'I suppose I've done the right thing?' said Tom.

'Yes, Dad, absolutely, although I'm not sure I buy everything she said.'

'Me too,' Tom grunted. 'You seem fairly confident about your diagnosis.'

'I wouldn't stake my professional life on it, but I'd say Matthew was drugged up to his eyeballs before someone strung him up.'

'It's completely crazy, but it all fits a pattern. Magda of course, but why Al Otford? As for Matthew, what could he possibly have known that would make these people kill him?'

Lucy shivered despite the warmth of the evening. 'You might think about yourself; could you be in danger?'

'I've nothing they want. If Hannah is correct, Matthew did have something. It seems incredible but there's no other explanation.'

She linked her arm through his. ‘I’m still scared for you.’

‘I think they should take your diagnosis seriously. George Shaylor’s a drunken old fool – will you fight this one?’

‘Yes, if they find narcotic in the blood the police will have to act.’

Her father laughed. ‘George will probably say you’re after his job.’

‘No way – he’s welcome to it.’

They returned indoors. Andy still sat in a smouldering heap of melancholy. ‘You’re a gullible pair, letting that bird sweet talk you.'

‘Andy,’ Lucy’s voice was threatening.

‘All I’m saying,’ her brother continued, ‘is what possible connection could a dumb lot like the Rowridges have with Nazi Germany?’

‘Wait a minute,’ Tom said. ‘I’ve remembered – it’s only pub talk, but I do remember something.’

‘What?’ Andy sounded sceptical.

‘I can’t give you specifics, but I’ll ask Charlie Marrington tomorrow.’

‘It’s nearly tomorrow anyway,’ Lucy yawned. ‘I’m going home. Look, Dad, I think you should have a frank talk with Gus. All this trouble is linked to him.’

Lucy went out to her car followed by her brother. ‘I don’t like any of this…’ he began.

Lucy swung round and caught him by the arm. For a few seconds she stared into his face. ‘Andy,’ she said icily, ‘what are you on? Apart from fags and booze?’

‘Shut it, you daft bitch,’ he replied angrily but with that catch of uncertainty that Lucy knew of old.

‘Don’t piss me around. I know my job and I’ve seen the symptoms. What are you taking?’

‘I’m not your little brother any more – get off my back will you?’ He turned and stalked back to the house. Lucy sighed and climbed into her car. Troubles come in threes, she decided.

‘Muriel, do you know where Charlie is?’ Tom looked round the door of the main office.

Muriel looked up from her desk. ‘Mr Marrington is serving customers in the garden centre.’ Tom wished she wouldn’t look at him like that. If she thought him to be the village’s only adulterer she was suffering an illusion. Crossfield contained a population of sinners as active as any in the land.

He discovered Charlie sitting on a pile of peat sacks looking like a moody gargoyle. Tom could not conceive of anything more likely to frighten away the punters. He seized hold of the man, took him into the garden tearoom and bought them both a cup of coffee.

'When is Mr Fjortoft coming home?' he asked.

'He didn't say. Never tells I anything.'

Tom sized him up while trying to find the most tactful approach. 'Charlie, do you remember the war years?'

'Of course I does, though I were nobbut a nipper then.'

'Did you ever work on the Rowridge place?'

'Sometimes at harvest. Our school helped with the corn cart. Some of us older ones used to hoe beet up there.'

'What d'you remember of the farmer? Would he be Matthew's father?'

'No, his grandfather, old Joe Rowridge, and I tell you this – they was outcasts.'

'Why, Charlie?'

'Traitorous bastards – Joe was soft on Adolf.'

Tom had that gloomy feeling he always experienced when Charlie started a chain of muddled reminiscences. Tricia had called Charlie "the Ancient Mariner", *by thy long grey beard and glittering eye...* He resigned himself to a long session.

'Is that really true? I'd like the facts.' Tom emphasised the word facts, although he doubted if Charlie would have much notion of what he meant.

'It's true, guv'nor. Before the war, Joe Rowridge was a blackshirt, a Mosley man. They marched up and down the high street in Taraton handing out leaflets. People used to laugh at 'em.'

'I'll be blowed.' Tom laughed himself at the image.

'But it were worse than that. When the war come, Joe's son Reg wouldn't fight. He went for a conchie.'

'Conscientious objector?'

'Reserved occupation they called it.'

'But, Charlie, farming was a reserved occupation. It was a perfectly honourable thing to do if you were trained for it.'

'Joe Rowridge didn't need no extra on the farm. He were a fit man and there was plenty of help. Tell you some more; Reg had been a Territorial soldier. He were trained to fight, so he couldn't have been a conchie, could he? You answer me that, Guvnor.'

Tom wouldn't attempt to answer. Charlie must have something wrong. A Territorial soldier would have been called up for service anyway. Reg Rowridge must have had some injury problem and been redirected to farm work. Village prejudice would have made the Rowridges more isolated than ever.

'This Reg Rowridge, he would be Matthew's father?'

'That's right, he died ten years back. His brother, the other son, Roy, he showed 'em. He joined the Air Force, wireless operator and air gunner. He died on the bombers and his name's on the memorial in the church there.'

'You're talking about a second son?'

'Yeah, and now them Rowridges got no one to follow 'em – only that mad Francesca.'

'Poor girl, what makes you say she's mad?'

'Don't do nothing but read books.'

At five o'clock Tom went home and ran a bath. Tonight he was due at the annual dinner of Taraton Rugby Club. Tom, as club president, would have a busy evening ahead watching over a happy, if potentially rowdy festivity. It would be a welcome diversion from his present troubles. The one blot was the guest of honour. The committee had invited Roland Gannemeade, the local MP, and in Tom's opinion a prize bore.

He turned his car into the lane and headed for the centre of the village. He had agreed to collect Lonny, the estate's head tractor driver and the captain of Taraton's First Fifteen. Lonny was the archetypal gentle-giant: twenty-eight-years-old, black, sixteen stone, and a fitness fanatic.

'What made Matthew top himself?' Inevitably the first words that Lonny uttered. Tom tried to explain for the twentieth time, but he knew he sounded unconvincing.

'I'd say it was that Vanessa,' said Lonny.

'You reckon she's run off?'

'Yeah, the slag.' Lonny bluntly put the popular view of Matthew's missing wife.

'Lucy's been trying to trace her all day. Vanessa doesn't know it's happened, and she should be with Francesca.'

The Rugby Club had taken over the function rooms at the Wellbury Hotel on the outskirts of the town. Those gathered were a disparate collection of noisy males and some of their more tolerant female partners. The males naturally divided into two groups: "young bloods" and "old farts". Tom had no illusions as to which category he belonged. He left Lonny to join his team mates and wended slowly through the crowd to the bar. However convivial the evening he would have to watch his drinking; standing by the bar was Chief Inspector Oats, the supremo of Taraton Police.

'Mr O'Malley,' said Oats. 'I wanted a word with you.'

'That sounds ominous.'

'No seriously, I think you ought to know that they're releasing Alex Cornbinder on Monday. We've had a report that he's been boasting in the nick.'

Tom grimaced, he wondered if Oats ever relaxed, ever forgot work. Alex remained one of the district's least loveable villains. Tom had sent him for trial eighteen months ago. The man had launched an unprovoked assault on an Asian boy half his size. Allegedly it had been a dispute during a rush hour queue at the petrol station; but everyone knew the motive was racial. The victim had been taken to hospital with a broken arm and head injuries. Alex had been convicted of GBH and had spent the intervening months in Winchester Jail.

'He hasn't leant his lesson then,' said Tom as he collected his glass.

'No, and this is where you come in, I'm afraid. We've heard he's boasting he'll get you when he's out.'

'Why me?' Tom did not feel unduly alarmed.

'You sent him down and he says you're Irish. Alex doesn't like the Irish, just as he doesn't like blacks and gays.'

Tom laughed. 'I'm not a gay black Irishman, I'm an English farmer and I sent Alex down because he's a psycho.' He changed the subject. 'You've heard about the suicide at Crossfield?'

'Farmer Rowridge, would that be?'

'Yes, any developments?'

Oat's eyes narrowed. 'Your daughter's insisting on extra pathology tests.'

'Good, I know she's not happy about something.' Tom did not enlighten Oats further. If Lucy was correct about foul play there would be big trouble for the Inspector.

'Anyway,' Oats downed the last of his beer, 'the lab has taken a whole lot of blood samples. We won't hear the results for a day or so and then there'll be the inquest of course. That's booked beginning of next month.'

He refilled Oat's glass; apparently the man had a lift arranged and could drink himself legless if he felt inclined. A hand clapped Tom heartily on the shoulder.

'Mr O'Malley.' Roland Gannemeade had his most simpering smile. 'So pleased to see you.'

Gannemeade was certainly a master of his trade. He could give the illusion that you were the most important individual he had met that day and that he needed to wait on your every word. In appearance he had all the characteristics of the one-time tall athlete gone to seed: obese, balding and sweaty. In Tom's opinion the man was a charlatan.

'Mr O'Malley, I must introduce you to Tony Tallisment.' Gannemeade indicated another man standing a few paces to his right. Tom had already noticed this character. He had caught him staring intrusively during his conversation with Oats.

'Tony,' said Gannemeade. 'This is Mr O'Malley. He manages Crossfield Manor Estates.'

'How much land?' Tallisment was a broad-shouldered heavy-jowled man in his late sixties. He spoke with a touch of a foreign accent while eyeballing Tom in an over-direct manner.

'You mean, how much land do we farm?'

'I want viable sites. This area's hardly been touched. We pay the best rates – in these times you'll need the money.' Tallisment was certainly blunt and to the point: no mucking about with small talk.

'I take it you are a developer?' Tom replied with a touch of irony.

Gannemeade looked embarrassed. 'Tony is chairman of Vega Magna Holdings PLC. I'm joining their board next month.'

'I only manage the estate, but it's true we have some plots in the village centre that might be potential for infilling.'

'That's no good; we'll need four hectares minimum for one of our "over fifties" colonies. Very tasteful – minimum capital per unit half a million – no kids, no proles – should suit a place like Crossfield.'

'We have a village school to maintain,' Tom replied evenly, though inside he seethed at the crass insensitivity of this moron. 'The last thing Crossfield needs is a ghetto of snobbish, child-hating geriatrics.'

'Not your decision, Mister Manager. Who's your owner – it's Fjortoft, isn't it?'

'Mr Fjortoft owns the estate, yes.'

'I'm sure he'll talk turkey when he hears my offer.'

You should be so lucky, thought Tom. At that point he managed to escape. The rest of the evening was a blur. In spite of all his resolution he drank too much. He mixed pleasure with alarm when he had to fend off the lecherous attentions of a member of Taraton

Women's Fifteen: a strapping red-headed girl in a low cut dress. Since she couldn't have been a day over twenty-one Tom beat a reluctant retreat.

There had been one surprise. Gannemeade had made a genuinely witty speech. He had a fund of stories about his own sporting prowess as a boy in South Africa. Tom suspected most of the tale to be pure fantasy, but enjoyable for all that. He wondered how close Gannemeade was to the obnoxious Tallisment. He resolved to find out all he could about Vega Magna Holdings PLC.

Someone had laid an enormous hand on his shoulder. 'Reckon I'd better drive you home,' it was Lonny.

'Are you in any better state?' Tom focused bleary-eyed.

'Alcohol?' Lonny looked surprised. 'Never touches the stuff – not when I'm in training.'

'OK, Lonny, you be pilot for the return.' Tom glanced at his watch; it was ten minutes to midnight. 'Come on, let's go.'

It was a relief to find this sober young driver. It seemed that every taxi in Taraton had been booked for the other revellers. Tom had not wanted the humiliation of phoning Lucy. He could imagine the icy reception with which his daughter would have greeted his plea.

'What did you think of Roland Gannemeade?' asked Lonny.

'I thought his speech was rather good.' Tom opened his eyes and looked outside the car; still three miles to go.

'Maybe, but I don't vote for him.'

'I must say I wish I didn't have to.'

'I'm a black guy – I know the signs. Gannemeade's a stone bonkers racist – a natural.' He signalled and turned left; the headlights shone on the newly leafed hedgerows. 'Who was that po-faced looking sod with him?'

'He's called Tony Tallisment, he's a property developer, he's rude and if I wasn't a JP I'd be tempted to punch him.'

'Tell you why I asked. I've seen him around a couple of times this week driving a swanky Jag.'

CHAPTER 14

Lucy and Mike lived in a three-bedroom semi on the eastern fringe of Taraton. For her last call of the day Lucy left her car at home and walked the ten minutes that it took to reach Heather Road. She enjoyed the walk in the sunshine, with its first feel of summer and gardens bright with the colours of spring flowers. She would have enjoyed it more had she not dreaded this call of duty. She was on her way to see Francesca Rowridge. At her own request Francesca had refused any further sedation. Now fully conscious, she would be aware of her father's death and, worse, the memory of his body swinging from the roof of the barn.

Francesca was with her Aunt Marjorie, Matthew Rowridge's sister. Marjorie had married Alan Cunningham, a partner in an accountancy firm, and it was Alan who audited the books for Crossfield Estate. Lucy hardly knew the Cunninghams, but she had heard that Marjorie had left Woolbarrow Farm at the earliest opportunity. She was rumoured to be on poor terms with her brother. Now Matthew was no more and Lucy had been supremely grateful to Marjorie and Alan for the way they had rallied around that dreadful evening. With her brother dead and her niece distraught Marjorie could have been forgiven if she had too had broken down. In the event she had been magnificent.

Heather Road was a row of superior detached houses, dating from the turn of the twentieth century. The Cunningham house stood on a slope with a view of the golf course and the little lake that was the town's distinctive landmark. Lucy noted the blue Mercedes on the drive. At least Francesca would lack for nothing material should the Cunninghams adopt her.

Marjorie greeted Lucy with a welcoming smile and led the way into her living room. Francesca sat in an armchair with a teen magazine in her lap. She looked pale and tired but otherwise composed. Lucy knelt beside her, popped a thermometer into her mouth and took a pulse count. This gave her a breathing space, a vital minute before she had to talk. Lucy had never cultivated a doctor's bedside manner. She determined to always be herself with no theatre. She whipped out the thermometer, glanced at it, turned to Francesca and deliberately established eye contact. The girl stared back; her face had no trace of tears, only an expression of utter emptiness. Lucy did not ask how she felt; that she knew to be the most fatuous question of all.

'Francesca, I can't find anything physically wrong with you – OK?'

Francesca did not reply but she was listening. Lucy continued. 'If you want to go out, you can – in fact I think you should.'

The girl gave the faintest nod and then she spoke. 'Can I go home and fetch my things?'

Lucy was startled. The last place she would have wanted to go in Francesca's place would be that awful house.

'No, Francesca, I don't think you're ready. How say you make a list of all the stuff you want? I'll go there for you.'

Francesca shook her head. 'I want to see Ringer and Sophie, my ponies. I bet nobody's fed them or been near them.'

'I don't know,' Lucy was puzzled. The child seemed more worried about her horses than anything else. 'Tell you what, I'll go straight up there and see to them after I've said goodbye here – how about that?'

'Oh please.' Francesca shot a look of mute gratitude.

'My father's got the key to your house. If you want any of your things we'll get them at the same time.'

'Thanks,' she replied in little more than a whisper.

'Has the counsellor been back to see you?'

'You mean that shrink woman?'

Lucy glanced at Marjorie, who pulled a face and beckoned Lucy towards the door. 'Yes, the lady came again this morning.' She continued in a piercing whisper. 'I'll tell you what she said in a minute.'

'I wanna go back to college,' said Francesca.

Once again Lucy was surprised. 'Are you sure about that? I can sign you off for a while if you like.'

'No, I wanna go back tomorrow.'

Lucy exchanged glances with Marjorie. Marjorie nodded vigorously.

'OK, Francesca, if that's what you want,' Lucy smiled at her. Then she continued. 'I've something you can think about. No need to say yes or no yet, but this is it. I'm getting married in July. I've talked to my partner Mike and we'd both like you to be a bridesmaid.'

Now there came a reaction. Francesca's face lit for two seconds with a mixture of excitement and gratitude, then the expression twisted in pain as the tears flooded. Francesca sobbed as her whole body shook. Lucy was horrified; somehow she had made a ghastly miscalculation.

'I'm sorry, I can't,' Francesca gasped. 'I would spoil it for you.'

'What on earth do you mean?' Lucy was baffled.

'I'm ugly,' she wailed. 'I'll spoil your day.'

'I don't think you're ugly.' Lucy was horrified. 'Who says you are?'

'My Dad said so…' Francesca sniffed into her handkerchief.

Marjorie was tugging anew at Lucy's arm. 'A word in private, Doctor, if you please!' She led the way into the hallway.

'I'm sorry about that,' said Lucy. 'I should have realised that Francesca's a teenager. I guess being a bridesmaid in a frilly dress would be embarrassing – a bit un-cool.'

'No, that's not the problem – it's a great idea and thank you. I'm afraid that young lady has been brainwashed. She's been talking to our girl Natalie. I can tell you I am appalled!'

'What happened?'

'She was abused.'

'Oh no,' Lucy groaned.

'No, not that: I mean mental abuse. From the day she was born her father never lost a chance to denigrate her. Told her she was ugly, brainless – no good for anything.'

'But that's not true, she's got a good intellect, put her in some decent clothes, tidy her hair up and she'd be quite pretty.'

'I think the rot may have gone too far.' Marjorie was clearly angry, but her next statement had Lucy gaping.

'Matthew was my brother and I know he's not even buried yet, but I think this could be the best thing that's ever happened to Francesca.'

'But why should her father do that?'

'As I said, brainwashing. That Vanessa can't have more children, so I think Matthew planned to keep Francesca on the farm for ever and that was his method.' Marjorie slapped her hand against the wall. 'And now Francesca's free of them.' She had a glint of tears in her eyes. 'Last year I had a blazing row with the bastard and I've never spoken to him since. I'm sorry about the way he went, but I'm not sorry he's dead.'

'Marjorie was telling the truth,' said Lucy. 'Understated if anything.'

They were in Francesca's bedroom at Woolbarrow Farm. Lucy sat on the bed sorting through a pile of clothing, while Tom unwrapped a black bin liner.

'All these clothes look like sackcloth and ashes. Half the stuff comes from charity shops I'd guess.'

'I don't know about clothes, but I noticed the dressing table.' He laughed causing Lucy to stare sharply at him. 'Sorry, but I'm remembering your room when you were her age.'

'I know.' She laughed now. 'Lipstick messages on the mirror, all my gear strewn on the floor and Mum going ape.' She moved across the room and began to empty the last drawer.

Tom went to the window and looked across the fields. He and Lucy had made the decision to return to Woolbarrow and load all Francesca's essential possessions. Lucy had fed and exercised the ponies the previous evening. Although irritable, they seemed none the worse for their neglect. Tom had arranged to move them to an empty stable at Boxtree. The farm office was still in the same disarray that it had been on the night of Matthew's death. Hannah and Anton had been searching for something, but that had been the following night. Seemingly nothing upstairs had been disturbed.

'Hello, what's this?' Lucy waved a large buff coloured envelope. She handed it to him. 'This could be important.'

Tom tipped the contents onto the table. He wondered whether he should be doing this. A package buried deep in a teenager's bottom drawer would almost certainly be something emotional and personal, to be hidden from the adult world. This time he was wrong.

The first sheet of paper was a yellowing flimsy typewritten form with a purple stamped date.

On His Majesty's Service
June 21st 1940
Civilian auxiliary catering course. Devonshire Regiment.
Witcombe Camp. Ashburton. Devon.
Detail to report 12.00 hrs.
J.Z. Marrington.
T.W. St J. Reade-Coke.
R.L. Rowridge.
Enclosed; rail warrants and ration entitlement.

'This is a bit of a turn up,' he said as he passed it to Lucy.

'I can't make head nor tail of it,' she said handing it back. 'But this is definitely the envelope Francesca mentioned to the counsellor.

'What counsellor?'

'The bereavement counsellor told Marjorie. She said that a stranger called on the evening Matthew died and that the last time

Francesca saw him alive was when he rushed into her room and stuffed an envelope in with her clothes. He ordered her to stay there, but Francesca says she leant over the banisters and heard voices but couldn't make out a word.'

'This could be significant,' said Tom. 'Has Francesca told the police?'

'Marjorie says a WPC came to talk to Francesca but she's not certain what was said. She's calling the police anyway.'

'It adds weight to your murder theory. Whether it was suicide or not, this visitor will have to be traced. He's got some explaining to do.'

'Will Francesca have to testify at the inquest?'

'I'm afraid so – it looks as if she's going to be the key witness.'

'Witness to murder?' Lucy murmured the words. Her expression looked strained and troubled.

Tom had watched Lucy drive away, her car loaded with Francesca's possessions. Then he had driven home for a late breakfast. He spread out the contents of the envelope. Apart from the movement order, nothing was comprehensible – just two more sheets of yellowing paper covered with chains of numbers. Eventually he gave up, reached for the phone and called Inspector Oats at Taraton. Oats was not available, so Tom told an uninterested subordinate that he would drop in the papers that day. Next he went to his study and photocopied all the envelope's contents. The police might be indifferent, but he would not let this go. He picked up the phone and dialled another number.

'Rufus, this is Tom O'Malley from Crossfield, and I've got something that's right up your street.'

'I told you at the time. You watch too much television.' George Shaylor emptied his beer glass and glared.

Lucy had gone looking for George the moment she was free. It was lunchtime, which meant George in the bar of the Shepherd and Dog. That morning she had received a copy of the post-mortem report on Matthew Rowridge. She felt both triumph and fury. Matthew had died from strangulation; but force of gravity had not been the sole instrument of death. His blood stream contained enough narcotic to have rendered him unconscious and ultimately to have killed him.

'Look here, young lady. I've been thirty years in this business. I've seen the bloody lot.' George signalled to the barman for another pint. 'I've been there: murders, suicides, road deaths, derailments – had twenty cadavers out of an air crash once.' He took another huge gulp from his glass. 'So I don't take to wet-behind-the-ears little girls romancing about foul play, when the true verdict is bloody obvious – see!' George spoke quietly as Lucy bristled.

'Doctor,' she stared at him coldly. 'I came here for a serious consultation with a professional colleague. Not for a slanging match with a boorish inebriate in a pub.'

'Eh,' George's face had shaded from red to purple like a chameleon. 'No bloody woman talks to me like that.'

'Yes they do,' said Lucy wearily. 'I just have.'

'All right, come over here.' George staggered to his feet and led the way to a quiet corner of the restaurant. 'You had some lunch?'

'No.' Lucy had to admit she was hungry.

'Then you'll let the old drunk buy you some?' George grinned.

'I'll buy my own thank you, Doctor.'

'Oh come on, young Lucy, don't take it to heart. You're a pretty little thing when your dander's up. Just like my missus when she was your age.' He called across to the bar. 'Usual for me Barry and something vegetarian for the feminist here.'

'If he's paying I'll have steak and all the trimmings,' Lucy called.

'And a bottle of that Eytie red,' George added.

'You are paying?' asked Lucy with her most malicious grin.

'As a gentleman and your senior colleague, I suppose I shall bloody have to – Doctor.' He grinned. 'Is it true you and young Michael are getting spliced?'

'We're marrying in July, yes.'

'Doctor marrying Doctor, that'll never work.'

'That's our problem.'

'Sure, don't take notice of me – you go for it. Now about Matthew.' George's manner had changed. The boozy slurred speech vanished. 'I knew the bloke slightly. I wasn't his GP, so I didn't see him professionally and they tell me he was never ill.'

Lucy nodded. 'That's true, he was on our books but he never came in even for a routine check-up.'

'He was a loner, had trouble with that wife of his. Flighty bit, what's her name?'

'Vanessa.'

'That's it, Vanessa, "the Taraton bike" they call her down the social club. I'm told she pissed off with some fellow.'

'That's the rumour. She hasn't come back to take care of her daughter yet. Her sister-in-law is hopping mad.'

'Poor kid,' George sighed. 'You see the pattern developing?'

'Not really.'

'Life, Lucy – I have my theory of life. When the Almighty puts you on this earth he marks your card, winner or loser. It's with you from birth and there's not much you can do about it. I know which side I've been put,' George grunted moodily. 'Not you, young lady; I reckon you're a winner.' He paused as the food appeared and the waitress set down the dishes on the table. She was young and blonde with a very short skirt. George eyed her up and down speculatively.

'Ooo, Doctor,' she giggled, 'you should be struck off.'

'And not before time,' Lucy laughed.

'Don't forget our wine, darling,' said George before turning back to Lucy. 'Anyway, Matthew Rowridge was a natural born loser if ever there was one.'

'I'm into psychiatry a little and I don't buy this theory of yours.'

'Oh the self-confidence of youth. Look, Matthew was born at the wrong time. His farm's too small, he's committed to the wrong style of farming and he hangs on to it too long. He marries the wrong girl and their only kid's an oddball…'

'Not true, Francesca is a mature and clever child. She's also feminine and she'll be very attractive once her aunt has finished with her.'

'Is that so? First her father tries to shape her and then this aunt tries the reverse. The poor kid won't know if she's coming or going. She'll be another loser if you ask me.'

'I'm not sure, George, that anyone is asking you. Finish your theory about Matthew.'

'A few years ago he takes another wrong turn – borrows money like there's no tomorrow. That was in the eighties with bloody Thatcher. Bank persuades him to modernise, then when everything turns pear-shaped they demand it all back – bastards!' George shovelled a spoonful of curry into his mouth and chewed noisily.

Lucy knew that George's politics were what were generally known as "Old Labour". She braced herself for a lecture.

'In Crossfield Parish, where your daddy rules the roost, there used to be fourteen family farms. Matthew's was the last and now he's gone and a whole way of life with him.' George grimaced. 'Of course most were tenants, had to touch their caps to the squire, but at least he was a Reade-Coke – been part of the scene for centuries. Now it's that stupid Yank.'

'Gustav Fjortoft isn't a stupid Yank – he's very nice.'

'What about Mrs Fjortoft?'

'No comment.'

George laughed. 'I'll tell you. We've had plenty of farm recessions before. Everything went to pot, with bankruptcies all over the place, but it did give a chance for the young ones to break in – buy somewhere cheap and wait for better times. Not now, after this one there'll be no way back. All there'll be is a few agri-businesses and the likes of Fjortoft.'

Lucy could not dispute this. Her father had said the same several times.

'No, Lucy, Matthew was on a course to top himself from day one. My theory of life – take it or leave it.'

'You still haven't accounted for that drug in his system.'

'I reckon he hedged his bets. Thought hanging might be painful so he dulled it a bit. This is the fourth farmer suicide I've been called to this year. They're prone that way – it's their ethos. The sick animal – you shoot it to put it out of its misery. The unprofitable cow – you slaughter it, send it down the road, as they say. There's Matthew, broke, all self-esteem gone. His natural instinct is, "I'm useless, finished – let's make an end."'

Lucy was not impressed. 'There was another suicide. The woman my father found near Chichester…'

'Yes, saw the inquest report on telly – *South Today.*'

'That girl died from Imobilon as well. The coroner rubber-stamped the police view, but my father thinks there's a serious doubt about the whole thing.'

'Does your daddy make a habit of discovering bodies?'

'Oh, ha bloody ha – very droll. Seriously, the court never looked at other possibilities.'

'If you say so. The Chichester case was nothing to do with me. No, I tell you that nobody had a motive for killing Matthew. He was a man with no enemies and precious few friends.'

Lucy sighed. 'All right, but when the inquest comes, I'll have to point out the discrepancies and the medical facts you missed.'

'You want my job, don't you?' George glared.

'Oh God, my Dad said you'd accuse me of that. No I don't want your job.'

George gave her a quizzical look. 'You might do worse. I've only a year or so left then I'll stand down. Think about it. I reckon you've got what it takes. I don't agree with you about Rowridge, but I'm impressed with the way you reached your conclusions.'

Rufus Partridge lived in a leafy suburban street not far from Tom's parents. It was he who opened the door to Tom at eight o'clock that evening. Rufus dressed in his velvet jacket and bow tie; Tom could never remember him in any other uniform. He directed Tom to his chaotic study. Books were stacked ten high on the floor and newspapers and magazines overflowed the large central table almost burying a computer. Rufus's desk was awash with grubby sheets of A4 paper.

'Mock A levels,' he grunted. 'From last term and I'm up to my ears.'

Rufus was head of science at Taraton Sixth Form College. He was good at his job and it was he who had taught Lucy and set her on the path to her medical career. He waved Tom to a tattered armchair and offered him a drink. He accepted a tiny measure of scotch. While Rufus poured it, Tom cleared a space on the table for the photocopies of Matthew's documents.

His eyes were on the little glass-fronted bookcase. It contained his host's life's work, all the volumes of Rufus's magnum opus. *Medieval Taraton, the Merchants of Taraton, Royalist Taraton 1642–45,* and others including: *Queen Victoria visits Taraton* and *Taraton at War 1914–18,* and *1939–45.* On the wall above were the posters for Rufus's plays, those that he wrote annually for the town's theatre club.

'This is the material I told you about,' Tom pointed to the papers on the table.

Rufus picked up the first one. 'Where did you get all this stuff?'

'The originals belonged to Matthew Rowridge.'

'Of course you said – the farmer who killed himself.' Rufus paused. 'You know I only met him once and, although I'm not one to speak ill of the dead, I didn't take to the man.'

'Any special reason?'

'First time was at a PTA meeting. I wanted his daughter to aim high – Oxford even. Rowridge wouldn't hear of it – he was quite rude.'

'I can believe that,' said Tom.

'Second time he was a bloody nuisance. Francesca's mother, Vanessa Rowridge, acts with the town players. She's good too. We did *The Importance Of Being Earnest* last year and Vanessa was an excellent Gwendoline.'

Tom vaguely remembered reading a review in the local paper.

‘So we offered Francesca a small part in last Christmas’ panto. I wrote that myself,’ Rufus explained proudly. ‘She enjoyed it too, spoke the words well, no nerves. We reach the dress rehearsal, two nights before the real day, then in comes Rowridge and hauls his daughter off by the ear. Says no one asked his permission to let her act and he would have forbidden it anyway. So I can’t weep too many tears. I thought the man an oafish red-faced bully.’

‘What happened then?’

‘I had to recast the part within twenty-four hours and then rehearse the substitute girl. She looked all right, but she had a Brummie accent – awful – ghastly!’

Rufus turned his attention back to the papers and his expression changed. ‘I say! This is cipher – well I never.’ He flashed the paper in Tom’s direction. It was another thin sheet with lines and columns of numbers. ‘Well I never, genuine wartime cipher. James Bond, eat your heart out.’

‘How do you know?’

‘Seen examples before. No good trying to crack it. The thing’s probably a double encrypt. Not as complex as “Enigma”, but sophisticated stuff.’

Tom was suspicious. ‘British or German?’

‘Oh, British I would say for certain. Your man must have had access to a key code though.’

Tom thought for a moment. ‘I think you ought to know that the father of the man these documents originally belonged to was suspected of Nazi sympathies.’

‘You don’t say,’ Rufus picked out the next sheet. ‘If that’s so there’s something that doesn’t add up – read this.’ He passed it to Tom.

Ministry of War, 18th September 1945.
To R. L. Rowridge Esq.
Dear Mr Rowridge,
I have been instructed by the Minister to convey to you the thanks of His Majesty’s Government for your devoted service in the late war effort. The fact that the details of this service are to remain secret is unfortunate but must be born dutifully in the national interest by all personnel involved in your operation.

Yours sincerely

Walter Pumphrey, Private Secretary.

'I don't understand any of this,' Said Tom. 'For a start Reg Rowridge was a conscientious objector, and I told you his father was under suspicion as a fifth columnist.'

'Perfect cover, I should think, but for what?' Rufus shook his head and fumbled through the remaining papers. 'These are all pay and rations stuff – nothing secret there. Tell me, who are the people on this alleged catering course?'

'I only knew two of them. Old Zac Marrington; he died this year, in January. Used to be the estate gamekeeper – his son Charlie still works for us. As for the others, Reg was Matthew's father and although he died after I came to these parts I never met him. Freddy Reade-Coke was the squire when I first managed the estate and he certainly wasn't in the war. He had TB as a youngster and was medically unfit. He never married and the line died out.'

'Must have been a bit of a comedown for the squire to go on a cooking course. I don't believe a word of it. Cooking – and you say the man had TB – never!'

'I must say that had occurred to me.' Tom remembered. 'His sister, Clarissa, still lives in the village; she's an eccentric old dear but she may recall something. Rufus, I've got to hand the originals to the police. I know for a fact that someone tried to steal these papers. Could you do a bit of discreet delving for me – see what you can find?'

Tom reached home at nine o'clock. Lucy would be on duty tonight, which in some ways was a relief. He felt guilty at the thought, but he had to admit it was nice to have his own company and it gave him a chance to think. The answerphone signalled an unread message. Could he ring Frank Matheson at home any time up until ten thirty?

'You win some you lose some in this game,' said Frank. 'First your Miss Berkovic could be bad news. Tel Aviv International News Agency exists. It's a sort of Reuters outfit – got agents in most capitals. On the face of it they're legitimate but my contact says there's an underside to them.'

'What's an underside, Frank?'

'My source says they were mixed up in a botched kidnap attempt in New York last year. As for Berkovic herself, nothing specific but my contact says he wouldn't buy a used car from her.'

'That doesn't tell me much.'

'I know, but that's only a preliminary report. I may have some more for you later.'

'What about the Jaguar?'

'Bit of a disappointment there. It was hired out as one of a batch of four prestige cars. All were booked by a property company as part of their normal way of business.'

'Would that company be Vega Magna Holdings?'

'Quite right – that's them. A word of warning there, Mr O'Malley. Vega Magna are a right bunch of desperados. If they're interested in your village, then watch your backs.'

CHAPTER 15

Andy was at Boxtree Farm waiting for his sister. He stood dressed in walking clothes, boots and sitting on a heavy rucksack. Lucy had offered to drive him to Portsmouth to connect with the ferry for France.

'I'll be away ten days,' he said.

'At least Aunt Marie will feed you properly,' remarked Lucy. 'You need some weight gain; you look like an anorexic schoolgirl. How do you manage your rugby in that state?'

Andy looked evasive. 'Had to give it up,' he said shiftily.

'Why, you never told us – Dad will be disappointed.'

'Haven't been too well lately. Lots of aggro – stress.'

'Andy,' this was the moment Lucy had been waiting for. 'I think you ought to tell me what you've been taking. I could help you.'

'I told you before – none of your business.'

'You're my brother – I'm a doctor – I make it my business.'

'I'll think about it.'

Lucy pointed at the car. 'Get in and you can tell me as we go.'

Lucy drove while Andy sat beside her in aggrieved silence. They reached the intersection with the A3 and began to eat away the miles going south. Lucy knew better than to raise the subject again; instead she waited. She was certain Andy wanted to talk. His mind must be a confusion of pain, worry and false pride.

'Last September,' he began falteringly, 'I was feeling pretty down. Mum had died – it was terrible and I couldn't come to terms with it…'

'Andy, I know – none of us could.'

He sat silently while Lucy hoped and waited.

'I met this girl, Jessica. She was great, really cool, invited me to a party in her folks' place … big house near Godalming.'

Lucy spared a quick glance at Andy; his face was pale and she could see a single tear. She returned to concentrating on the road ahead.

'It was only when I got to the party that she told me who her father was. He's Roland Gannemeade.'

'The politician!' Lucy hadn't intended to intervene but she was surprised. She didn't like Gannemeade. The man made a lot of noise with ever-ready sound bites for the tabloid papers. Lucy personally found his opinions, especially on race and women, obnoxious.

'Yes, but I never met him, he was away overseas that weekend. Jessica had the place to herself with her mates.'

'All right, don't tell me,' Lucy sighed. 'You all got up to things that could be embarrassing for Mr "family values" Gannemeade. Good, the man's a bloody hypocrite in my opinion.'

'If we did, he's paid for it – his daughter died.'

'What, the one you mentioned, Jessica?'

'Yes.'

'How come we've never heard a thing about it?'

'Gannemeade covered it up. The press reported that Jessica died of a heart condition.'

Lucy dropped the car's speed to forty miles an hour. The driver of a transit van closed within two feet of the rear bumper, glaring at her through the mirror. She didn't care, she wanted to slow the journey and give Andy a chance to spill his whole confession.

'There was a man there that night, an American.' Andy was looking dreamily out of the window. 'Much older than us, strange bloke – sort of scary. Jessica said his surname was McCann, but I don't think that was his real name.' Andy's voice faltered.

Lucy could guess what was coming next.

'I didn't like him and I think the others were downright frightened. Anyway it was pretty clear what his game was…'

'Drugs.' At last we've come to the point, she thought.

'Yes, but McCann wasn't a back street dealer. He was big-time, and in a place like that he had it made … country house packed with spoilt rich kids.'

'Did you join in?' Lucy's tone was questioning, but not accusing.

'Yes,' he whispered the word so quietly Lucy barely heard him. 'They more or less forced the stuff down me, but I think I might have resisted if it hadn't been for Jessica telling him who I was.'

'Oh come on, what's so special about you – you're not a spoilt rich kid?'

'Jessica told him that Dad managed for Fjortoft and that had a funny effect on McCann. He seemed to make a special target of me. You see, I'd had a few drinks and Jessica had hinted that I could share a bed with her later. Then I took the snort of coke and the sex didn't matter, nothing did – you've no idea.'

'Yes I have, not personal experience, but I've listened to enough addicts. "A thousand times the greatest orgasm you've ever had – making love to the universe", sickening stuff.' Despite her resolution Lucy was becoming angry. 'You're abusing the body's natural defence mechanisms. Turning them around to destroy you. If you don't kick the habit, you'll die!'

'Sister,' Andy had turned to look solemnly at her. 'I did kick it. I'm not on the stuff. There's a clinic in Guildford where I've been going every day. It was bloody awful – no, worse – it was five months of the purest hell you'll never know.'

'So that's why you went away for Christmas vacation and wouldn't come near us. Dad was really upset about that. He thought you were blaming him for Mum's death.'

'No, Lucy, I had to clean myself. I had to do it before I could face him. But I'm free now and when I've finished this holiday I'm going looking for McCann.'

Lucy was worried. 'I wouldn't advise that. Have you gone to the police?'

'No.'

'You must!'

'What good will that do?'

'Leave off that student crap. The police will act, believe me – in this sort of case they're good.'

'If I thought they'd pull in McCann for Jessica…'

'Did he kill her?'

'Not directly, but we found her dead the next morning. She drowned in her own vomit.'

Tom had spent a routine day on the farm. That morning he had waved Andy off on his departure for his French trip. He hoped that would relieve whatever was worrying the boy. It had been unnatural the way his usually extrovert son had shrunk back inside himself. Clearly his mother's death had shaken the lad. College life could be stressful if approached in the wrong spirit. Andy's failure, with no explanation, to return home for family Christmas had hurt Tom. He suspected the boy was depressed and in the grip of some turmoil that went deeper than grief for his mother and unconnected with normal teenage angst. Anyway, a week with his St Brieuc cousins should cheer him up. Maybe the two of them could have a proper talk when he came home.

At five o'clock Tom drove the Land Rover to Woolbarrow Farm. He needed to move the Rowridge cattle to a fresh pasture. It was a simple enough job. No more than a brisk walk, opening a gate and calling the herd. They came slowly, sniffed the fresh pasture and spread out, munching their way slowly across the field. Tom checked the water trough and then, shutting the gate behind him, walked back to his vehicle. It was a lovely evening, and for a change, not a cloud in the sky. The setting sun lit up the countryside for miles. He could see the houses of nearby Rotherwood among the trees on the far ridge. Someone was having a good bonfire there. No, not a bonfire; a tongue of orange flame had leapt from the centre of the blaze and a pall of black smoke rose high into the still evening air. Tom knew he was looking at an intense oil fire and at the epicentre of it was a house. It was Hannah's bungalow in Malvern Road. He could pinpoint it by the tall pines on the edge of the garden.

Fire hoses ran the length of Malvern road and a bitter acrid smell penetrated even inside the car. Tom pulled over to let through a fire engine, with its blue lights flashing and its siren blaring. People stood in the street, interested and apprehensive: young children clinging to their elders, older children grinning with excitement. Through the thick oily smoke came a roaring noise, punctuated by tiny firecracker explosions. Twenty yards short of the bungalow, two fire appliances and two police cars blocked the road. A policeman in a peaked cap waved furiously at him with a white handkerchief, which he promptly replaced over his mouth. The man attempted to rub his eyes with the other hand that already held his radio.

'You can't go up this road – not for an hour at least.' The policeman was leaning through the open window a few inches from Tom.

'I know the people in that house. I came as soon as I saw the fire – are they all right?'

'Can't say,' the PC coughed smoke. 'I'm not in a position to tell you anything.'

'I know a girl who lives in that house, she's called Hannah. I don't know if she's safe.' Tom was desperate.

Another explosion rocked the surroundings as black fumes enveloped them. Both Tom and the policeman were choking.

'I'll let you park in that lay-by back there,' spluttered the PC. 'Talk to you later.' The man turned and ran across the road out of the worst of the smoke.

Tom backed the car slowly down to the parking space. Another vehicle, a casualty ambulance, came pounding up the street, siren screaming. His apprehension was turning to real fear and he wasn't sure why. It was natural to be concerned, but it was not as if Hannah was one of his own flesh and blood. He was out of the car and running wildly along the road towards the blazing house. He turned aside and sped up the drive of the adjacent property. A crowd of onlookers had gathered, peering through gaps in the hedge. They scarcely noticed Tom as he forced his way through the greenery, the fronds dragging at his jacket and scratching his face. He scrambled through a plain wire fence and stopped within feet of a team of fire fighters wrestling with a hose on full power.

The sight was horrible. The once elegant home crumbled before his eyes; a shell now, barely visible in the distorting heat. Another explosion rocked the site followed by a gust of hot wind and a choking foul-smelling odour. A small group of firemen wearing breathing apparatus hovered on the fringe of the inferno. Tom could wait no longer. He ran to the nearest fire fighter, a bulky figure, unrolling a further length of flat reeled hose. Tom banged him on the shoulder.

'Is there someone in there?' Tom yelled.

The fireman stared, eyes narrowed, from under his helmet. 'Where did you spring from?'

'Please, my friends live there. D'you know if they all got out?'

'Couldn't say, mate. We can't get in there at the moment.'

Tom felt a mad urge to rush towards the inferno. The fireman caught him by the shoulder, turned him around and pushed him back to the hedge.

'Better stay there, mate. Another twenty minutes and we may be able to tell you something.'

There was nothing more that Tom could do but return to the road and wait.

'His name's Anton and I think the surname is Sherakova, at least that was his sister's name. She's dead as well.' Tom hardly knew what he was saying.

He had turned away in disgust at the sight of the charred corpse, streaked with blackened dried blood. The features were recognisable; the face still had some white flesh and the metal rims of the spectacles had burned into the skin.

'Poor little sod,' said a voice in Tom's ear.

He turned round to face George Shaylor. The doctor had driven up unnoticed while Tom had identified the body.

'How do you come to know him?' asked George.

'Pure chance, I knew a woman who lived here.' Tom had no wish to expand on the circumstances to George.

'What woman?'

'Her name's Hannah. She's a journalist writing something about Gustav Fjortoft. I've only met her twice.'

George grunted something and turned away to talk with the chief fire fighter.

'Can I go now?' Tom asked the policeman. He was desperate to escape from this place.

He groped in his wallet and found the card Hannah had given him with her London address. The policeman radioed the details to his home base and returned the card. Yes, he was now free to go. Tom pushed his way through the ring of ghoulish spectators, recovered his car and drove home.

Tom's first instinct had been to tell somebody, anybody. He had rung Lucy at the surgery but she had been unavailable. He declined to leave a message; he needed the salvation of talk. Almost at once his mood changed, he knew he could never speak of what he had seen; particularly the charred wreck of the young man he had spoken to only a day or so before. The smell of burned flesh was nauseating, it seemed to cling in his nostrils and permeate his clothes even after he had showered and changed. Tom was unable to eat for the rest of the day. Lucy was not due at Boxtree and now he was glad. He had wanted to pour out the whole story to her – now the nightmare was closing around him; if he tried to talk about it he knew he would choke on the words.

At six-thirty the local TV news had shown pictures of the fire scene. The bungalow was blackened and roofless. The film showed investigators in white overalls probing among the wreckage. The television reporter said something about a fractured central-heating fuel tank. At nine o'clock Tom experienced another mood swing. He felt hungry, so hungry that he surprised himself. He scrambled some eggs, made four rounds of toast and poured himself a massive slug of scotch. As he sipped from the glass he heard a rapid tapping on the kitchen window. He could just make out the shape of someone on the other side of the steamed-up glass. Tom walked to the back door and opened it. A slim figure was lurking in the shadow.

'Tom,' whispered Hannah, 'turn the light out.'

He gasped in surprise. 'What happened? I saw your house today – are you all right?'

'Turn the light out.' The urgency in her voice stopped him arguing.

He ran across to the light switch and sent the room into darkness.

Hannah slipped into the room and shut the door. Seconds later she had reached along the wall and pulled down the Venetian blind over the window.

'OK, Tom, switch on again.'

'Why all this theatrical stuff?'

'When you're in trouble you don't stand in a lighted doorway and show the world where you're going to or coming from.'

'What happened at the bungalow? You know Anton's dead – the poor boy was burned to death. I had to identify the body – not that I really know who he is.'

'He wasn't burned to death. He was dead before the fire started.' Hannah was shaken and upset. Tom could see her usual mask of superior self-confidence had slipped. 'Poor Anton, I blame myself, I should have sent him home.'

'He wasn't part of your set-up?'

'Anton was a kindly simple-minded car mechanic. He was devoted to his sister, although he never really understood her work.' She had a catch in her voice. 'I let him stay with us because I thought I could keep him from doing something stupid.'

'How did it happen?'

'Our opponents have raised the stakes – it's open war now. I've got to disappear for a few days, right out of circulation. Would you put me up?'

'For God's sake, why me?' Tom was horrified.

'I need to stay around these parts. They think I've gone to London.'

'You're presuming one hell of a lot. This isn't my quarrel, why should I put my family and myself in danger for you?'

The gall of this woman, that she should expect him to help her, without notice, and without explanation.

She seemed shrewd enough to guess what he was thinking, because she made no further plea. Instead she moved over to the stove where he had been cooking eggs. 'You could give a hungry homeless lady a bite to eat?' She looked plaintive. 'Return of hospitality?'

'Help yourself. You'd better do your own cooking, you people have odd dietary rules and I wouldn't know where to begin.'

'The rules don't mean a lot to me – never have. It's true I don't touch your bacon, but that's loyalty to my heritage – sort of symbolic.'

'In that case, I'll do the honours. How about a big dish of scrambled eggs and a tin of beans? I'll make some more toast – this lot's stone cold. While I'm doing that you can tell me exactly what's going on.' He walked across to the stove. 'I accept this half-brother exists and I've reason to suppose he's not far away…'

'What reasons?' Hannah interrupted.

'I am asking the questions. What happened today?'

'Anton called me on his mobile just after four o'clock; he'd seen men in the garden. He was trying to tell me more and then he screamed, "They've put a dart in me" – he was speaking in Russian. I called into the phone but all I could hear were whispers and some bumping and scraping noises. Then somebody picked up the phone and laughed. After that, nothing.'

'Where were you while all this happened?'

'Halfway to London with Mo. I told him to keep driving while I phoned ahead for a contact to meet us at the next service area. Mo carried on to London with my colleague, while I drove back in a different car. When I reached Rotherwood it was all over. I was just in time to see you drive away. So that's why I'm here.'

'Why didn't you turn round straight away? If you suspected trouble Mo would be a good guy to have around.'

'No, it's very important that they think I'm in London. Mo will arrive there with my contact and she looks not unlike me.'

Tom let matters stand there. He didn't much like the idea of two Hannahs. He turned his attention to cooking. He served a portion of eggs on toast and put them in front of her. Hannah fell on the food as if she hadn't eaten for a week. He loaded his own plate and sat down opposite.

'Questions,' he said bluntly. 'I'm going to ask you some straight questions to which you will give straight answers. Any half-truths or evasions and you can forget about help from me.'

Lucy was due to take a surgery in Taraton at two o'clock that afternoon. First she drove to the town's police station. She asked for Inspector Oats and found she was in luck. Oats, a patient of the practice, made no trouble about seeing Lucy at short notice.

'George Shaylor's been complaining about you,' he said.

'I thought my ears were burning – I can guess what he said.'

'Damning with faint praise is the expression.' The inspector laughed. 'You're upsetting his quiet life.'

'We had a professional difference of opinion.'

'About the Rowridge post-mortem, I know.'

'I'm sticking to my guns on this one.'

'Quite right too. George has been challenged by our official pathologist – he's testifying the same conclusion as you.'

'That should settle it.'

'I'm afraid not. George is going to dispute your view at the inquest. Silly old bugger's set to make a public ass of himself and I'm not going to save him.'

'It was murder.'

'Hey now, wait a minute,' Inspector Oats looked mildly shocked. 'The circumstances are suspicious. We are conducting an investing-ation to ascertain if a crime has been committed.'

'Which in cop-speak means you suspect foul play?'

'I cannot make a personal comment.'

Lucy gave up; she had a more immediate problem. 'Inspector, have you ever come across a drug dealer called McCann?'

The inspector seemed surprised. 'I don't remember that name but we may have him on file somewhere. He is a him, I assume?'

'Of course – you'd hardly expect a woman…?'

'Dr O'Malley, your defence of your gender is praiseworthy, but in my world, which is the real world, there isn't a crime in the book that hasn't been perpetrated by a woman. Any crime, you name it, however despicable.'

'I find that hard to believe…'

'I don't care what you believe. Take it or leave it.' The inspector sat back and fixed her with a steady gaze. Then he relaxed. 'Tell me about McCann.'

After surgery, Lucy made one final call to the Cunningham's house. Francesca, home from the Sixth Form College was eating her tea. Lucy could see nothing outwardly wrong, although she wondered what might be fermenting in the girl's mind.

'I want to go to the farm,' said Francesca. 'I want to find some-thing.'

'My advice is not to go there,' Lucy replied.

'I'll be all right. Would you take me, Doctor?'

'I haven't got the key.' Lucy clutched a straw.

'Got my own.' Francesca held up a small bunch of keys on a ring.

'You see, Dad had something hidden away and it might be valuable. Could be what those burglars were after.'

'What burglars?'

'The ones the other night. Tessa Marrington told me that your Dad caught a burglar at our place the other night.'

Lucy was appalled. 'God, that bloody village. How the hell did she hear about that?'

'Curly Tong was hiding and he saw your Dad catch a burglar.' Francesca stuffed a huge forkful of chips into her mouth.

It was all so predictable. Curly Tong was the village's recognised poacher and general layabout. Once again she cursed the impossibility of keeping anything under wraps in Crossfield.

'Look, Curly's making a meal out of nothing. My father found some people trespassing in your garden. They had a reasonable explanation and that was the end of the matter.' Lucy felt relieved that Francesca accepted this. She supposed it was her authority as the doctor, coupled to the truth that she was a much better liar than her brother Andy.

'You'll take me?' Francesca persisted. 'It's important.'

Francesca unlocked the front door, stood hesitantly for a moment and then crossed the threshold. Lucy had watched her walk from the car along the narrow path to the porch. The girl was tense and white-faced. She never once glanced towards the barn where her father had died. Lucy followed her indoors. She saw a sad shabby place. Everything about it was dark: heavy stained furniture, drab old-fashioned wallpaper, faded prints of hunting scenes and framed family photographs. The faces in these photographs glared down severely. A bearded Victorian paterfamilias had eyes that seemed to follow Lucy around the room. One photograph was different.

'Who are these people?' she asked.

The picture was a monochrome enlarged snapshot of three young men, clearly of a later period than Victorian times. They wore sports jackets with heavy flannel trousers and flat caps. There was a comradely, conspiratorial air about all three.

'That's Granddad,' Francesca pointed out the young man on the left. 'I asked him about that picture once, but he wouldn't tell me a thing – just laughed and winked.' She grimaced. 'Then Dad clipped me round the ear and I was sent to bed.' She sniffed and turned away.

'That happened just because you asked about a picture?'

'It was so unfair – and what's special about the bloody thing anyway?' Francesca put her hand over her mouth and glanced around guiltily.

Lucy looked at the picture again. 'I've seen the man in the middle somewhere, although he looks younger there.'

'It's old Mr Marrington, Charlie's dad. He died in February.'

Lucy remembered. 'Yes, we all went to the funeral.'

'The one on the right's Mr Reade-Coke. He was the boss man of the whole estate in those days.'

'I know, he was bed-ridden, I only met him once.' Lucy made a quick calculation. 'That picture must be in wartime.'

'It says something underneath,' Francesca pointed to the white masking below the picture.

Lucy peered closer and read the caption. *The Three Musketeers. July 1940.*

'You could show this to Mr Partridge in Taraton. He may know what it's about.'

'Old Rufus? Sure, he can have it.' Francesca dismissed the matter and walked across to the fireplace.

Like the rest of the room it was old fashioned; a brick surround with niches for hanging fire irons. Francesca reached behind a settee and pulled out a piece of metal rod, a foot long, with a sort of hexagonal key welded on the end. She knelt down and inserted it into the back of one of the niches. The lock clicked. Francesca dropped the iron, thrust her arm into the cavity and rummaged around. She pulled out a jewel case, a small flat box, and a leather-bound book.

'That's the lot,' she sounded disappointed. 'Want to look?' She passed it to Lucy.

It was a much battered and stained farm diary, full of records of cattle sales and crop sowings. Lucy turned to see the date: nineteen forty-seven.

'Can't see this being valuable.' Lucy moved closer and examined the tiny metal door. If she had known she would have taken it for a flue access. It seemed none of the recent intruders had found it; assuming their target was these mundane articles. 'My great-granddad was a cattle dealer. He used to keep his cash takings in there – didn't trust banks. He was always banging on about Jews – so my granddad said.'

The great grandfather, it seemed was a suspected Nazi sympathiser whose son, the supposed conscientious objector, was involved in something covert. An intriguing mystery, Lucy mused, that should keep Rufus happy for weeks.

She looked at Francesca who seemed to be in a trance. 'Has anything been taken?'

'No it's all here. I've no idea what it is though. The other stuff that I hid in my room – that used to be in there as well.'

Lucy picked up the flat box. 'May I look?'

'Yeah, go ahead.'

It contained a single medal wrapped in a square of silk and a piece of folded vellum. Written on it was a citation. It recorded the award of The British Empire Medal *to Reginald Rowridge Esq, by His Majesty King George the Sixth. In recognition of services unspecified during the late conflict; 1939–1945.*

‘Would you lend this to Mr Partridge?’ Lucy asked.

Francesca didn’t answer. She was engrossed in the leather-bound diary. ‘My dad was reading this. He was excited about something in it. He wanted your dad to see it but then he…’ without warning the dam broke. All Francesca’s suppressed emotions engulfed and consumed her.

She collapsed on the settee and sobbed until finally she howled as she curled into a ball and buried her head in the cushions. Lucy sat with her arms around the girl. She worried that she had been mistaken in allowing the child to return to this depressing house. Maybe, on the contrary, it would be therapeutic. Lucy had been concerned all along by Francesca’s deadpan self-control. She waited until finally the shaking receded and the sobs quietened.

Francesca turned and opened one swollen red eye. ‘Sorry, Doctor.’

‘Don’t say that – I think this is the best thing for you. Don’t hold anything back – this is all a natural part of grieving.’

‘I know,’ there was a wan smile. ‘The shrink woman said that.’ She sat up. ‘Let’s open that other box.’

Lucy handed it to her. She fiddled with the catch and the lid opened stiffly. Francesca shrugged her shoulders and held up the sole object within. It was a key on the end of a piece of discoloured string.

Lucy returned Francesca to the Cunninghams. She stopped briefly at Rufus Partridge’s house. Rufus was out but she left the parcel with a quickly scrawled message. The evening surgery had been pleasantly quiet and she and her two colleagues had been able to shut up shop early at half past seven; still time for her to call at Boxtree and see her father.

The moment she walked into the house she heard Tom’s angry voice. The voice was not raised but it had the timbre that she long recalled from childhood. She followed the sound to the kitchen and stood silently in the doorway. A woman sat at the kitchen table: it was Hannah.

‘What’s going on?’ Lucy asked.

‘You may well ask,’ her father replied. ‘You’ve heard about the fire at Rotherfield?’

‘I’ve been with Francesca, but earlier I did hear a lot of fire sirens. What’s happened?’

Briefly her father explained. ‘I’ve given Ms Berkovic a meal and a fair hearing. In return I’ve had to listen to a lot of unsupported slander.’

Lucy looked at Hannah. ‘Don’t keep me in suspense. Who’s slandering who?’

‘Not me,’ said Hannah. ‘I’m a journalist following a hot story. I’ve told your father I’ve discovered the two youngest surviving war criminals of World War Two – Wilhelm Brown and Gustav Fjortoft.’

CHAPTER 16

Hannah left the house and quickly melted into the darkness. A few minutes later they heard a car stop in the lane and then speed off in the direction of the village.

'What have we done to be caught up in this?' asked Lucy.

'Nothing – we're in the wrong place at the wrong time. I've become entangled with the wrong people and frankly my main worry is for you and Andy.'

'I shall have to follow up the death of this man Anton,' she said. 'If he really had a hypodermic dart in him there'll still be traces.'

Tom was firm. 'No, keep out of it. Leave things to the official pathologists. If you start beating the drum they'll want to know how you knew of Anton and how you heard about the attack with the dart. You'll be in potential danger and you'll put us all in the spotlight.'

'Are you really suggesting that we do nothing?'

'No, as an officer of the law myself, I'll have a quiet word behind the scenes. It's time the police knew about Hannah Berkovic and her activities.'

'Her accusations about Gus – do you reckon there's any truth in them?'

Tom hesitated; he didn't want to think about this. 'Something must have happened. Gina says Gus has nightmares where he shouts in German about seeing children killed.'

'When did she tell you this?'

'That night you know about – the one you gave me a telling off for.'

'So it was pillow talk – yes?'

'It just poured out. She's worried; she says it's happened twice and the voice sounded as if he was a child himself.'

Lucy frowned. 'I don't know what to think. I'm interested in psychiatry and all this is flavour of the moment.'

'Explain?'

'Do you believe that a child that knowingly commits murder does so because it's incorrigibly evil, or can he or she be rehabilitated to lead a normal adult life?'

'I would say no. It's evil and should be put away, but I'm old fashioned.'

'It's being disputed among the professionals. There have been high-profile cases where they argue about how long a child should be detained. Some say it should be under supervision for life.'

'I look at it this way,' said Tom, 'there is no evidence that Gus has ever harmed another person in his life. He certainly witnessed something at a young age that traumatised him. Hannah's given me the name of the camp where Greta Little and Magdalena's mother were held.' He picked up a piece of paper from the table. 'It was called Gostanyn – apparently that's a place in Poland.'

'And Hannah says this Greta saw the killings?'

Tom sighed. 'I wish I knew what to say. Everything I believed in seems to have shattered since your mother died. Now I'm told Gus may have been a murderer, you may be in danger and none of us look like having a future.' He stood up. 'Let's catch the TV news and I want a stiff drink.'

'You've forgotten the one thing that's really bothering me,' she said.

'Sorry, I'm not with you.'

'What in hell is the connection between this business and the Rowridge family?'

'If there is one.'

'Hannah said there was and today I've found out some more.'

'All right, come in the sitting room and tell me.'

A week passed; one for Tom of comparative sanity. He had a talk with Inspector Oats. He had told his whole story to this sceptical police officer. Oats made little comment although he confided that the fire at Rotherfield was being examined for arson. The Fjortofts were still absent from Crossfield and had left no contact number or address. Rufus Partridge was becoming increasingly excited about the Rowridge papers. The man refused to elaborate, which had irritated Tom.

Brooding over everything was the prospect of the Rowridge inquest this coming Wednesday.

Francesca Rowridge, Lucy and Tom had all been formally subpoenaed to appear at the inquest and Tom was not looking forward to it. George Shaylor had turned awkward. He announced that he would dispute the evidence of foul play to be presented by the young police pathologist backed by Lucy. Tom suspected this was a conflict between disgruntled middle age and ambitious youth. He had tried to buttonhole Inspector Oats but the policeman was having none of it. Tom was a witness, and it would be most improper for him to discuss anything about the case with him. Tom suspected that Oats had a card up his sleeve.

The coroner's hearing was a very different affair from the Magdalena inquest. The courtroom was crowded and the authorities had empanelled a jury. The local press had clearly sensed something in the wind and were out in force. The remaining seats were filled with members of the farming community and others who had known Matthew in life.

Tom and Lucy stood outside the court with Francesca until the last moment. Francesca looked pale and beads of sweat were visible on her face. Tom hoped the coroner would have enough compassion to spare her an unnecessary ordeal. George Shaylor arrived and winked at Lucy. Seemingly he alone was out to enjoy the day. Everybody crowded into the stuffy courtroom. The coroner asked if they would like the windows opened and the proceedings began.

First on the stand was a police officer. He reported being called to Woolbarrow Farm at nine pm on the day in question. He confirmed that the dead man had been identified to him as Matthew James Rowridge. The coroner announced that he accepted this identification and would not be calling Mr Rowridge's daughter, whom he understood to have found the body. Francesca relaxed; Lucy squeezed her hand supportively.

Tom was next to be called. He described hearing Francesca crying and his and Lucy's discovery of the body.

'Was the man dead?' asked the coroner.

'Yes sir, my daughter is a doctor and she confirmed it, but there was no doubt in my mind anyway.'

'Why did you cut down the body?'

'My daughter needed to be certain he was dead.'

'You know I have received an official complaint from the police?'

'I think we can live with that.'

'Very well,' the coroner continued. 'Where was Miss Rowridge while all this was happening?'

'My daughter took her indoors after she'd confirmed Mr Rowridge dead.'

'Did you follow her into the house?'

'Only after I'd finished dealing with the body.'

'Did anything about the house strike you as unusual?'

Tom paused; he hadn't expected this kind of question. It struck him that the coroner was walking a rather fine line between his real province and the official police investigation.

'The only unusual thing was the state of the place. Whenever I've been there before it was spotless.'

'And it was not so this time?'

'It was a shambles: books and papers all over the place.'

Tom was told he could stand down. The coroner called Lucy.

'Doctor O'Malley, after the body was cut down you examined it?'

'I checked for a pulse but there was none. The body was also cooling. I estimated he had been dead for perhaps half an hour.'

'Wouldn't you have been better advised to wait for the police?'

'No, I wasn't concerned with the reason for his death, but I had a professional duty to check if there was a chance to save him.' Lucy's reply was sharp and a touch of colour had flushed her cheeks.

'Quite so, Doctor – nobody is suggesting you could have done more.' The coroner was soothing. 'Was there anything about the body that struck you as unusual?'

Lucy looked startled. 'There were two things that I noted. I thought the official medical witness might be able to enlighten me.'

'What was it that you thought might interest the police doctor?'

'There was a small incision or tear on the neck. It had bled, so I surmised he must have been alive when it was made. Secondly the pupils of both eyes were at maximum dilation.'

'What would that signify?'

'That he had a considerable amount of some drug or narcotic in his bloodstream.'

'In your opinion, Doctor,' the coroner spoke slowly and precisely, 'would such a drug have prevented him from hanging himself?'

The question produced a stir in the courtroom, a communal intake of breath and a subdued muttering.

Lucy looked around the room. 'I'm sorry but I really couldn't say.'

'Did the official surgeon confirm your view?'

Lucy appeared unsettled. 'He seemed … how can I say … he seemed to think I was over-imaginative.'

'Thank you, Doctor, you may stand down.'

George Shaylor took the stand. He wore a rumpled tweed suit with a beige waistcoat and a canary yellow bow tie. He confirmed that he had received a call by the police to attend Woolbarrow Farm. He had arrived there at five minutes past ten. He had pronounced the casualty dead and recorded demise by strangulation.

'Did Dr O'Malley dispute your findings?'

'No.'

‘But she says she drew your attention to some unusual details.’
‘Not unusual. Dr O’Malley asked my opinion on a technicality.’
‘Did you dismiss her views as over-imaginative?’
‘I made a joke about her watching too much television.’
‘Doctor, this was hardly an occasion for mirth.’ The coroner looked down his nose. Tom sensed the man had seen rather too much of George over the years and was enjoying cutting him down to size.
‘No indeed, I was making a serious point. I’ve seen many such sad sights; Dr O’Malley has not – no fault of hers. She is one of the most competent young medical practitioners it has been my pleasure to work with.’
‘Smarmy bullshitter,’ Lucy whispered in Tom’s ear.
‘I must make my point,’ George continued. ‘It is very easy to see the sinister dimension in everything when the obvious is simple and staring one in the face. Obscurity is the tool of the conspiracy theorist; would you not agree?’
‘Doctor, this hearing is not about conspiracy theories. We only want to walk out of here knowing how this poor man died.’
‘Then that is simple. Matthew Rowridge killed himself because he was depressed. The obvious, as I have said, is invariably the truth.’
George was told to stand down and the coroner recalled Lucy. Was she aware that Matthew Rowridge suffered from clinical depression? She replied that although Matthew was a patient of her practice there was no record of him complaining of depression or any related condition.
Now it was the turn of the official pathologist. He was a small earnest man of Asian appearance. He described the bruises and the abrasions on the neck and body. Death had been from strangulation. The condition of the heart and lungs supported this conclusion.
The coroner looked at him. ‘Doctor, you will have heard your colleague talk of an incision on the neck of the deceased. What conclusion did you reach in regard to this?’
‘It was a deep incision compatible with a badly handled hypodermic syringe.’
‘What makes you say badly handled?’
‘In my opinion a needle was driven in cleanly and with some force, then withdrawn rather clumsily.’
‘What further investigations did you try?’
‘I took blood and urine samples.’
‘You now have the results of your tests?’
‘Yes, the bloodstream contained the veterinary anaesthetic brand

name Imobilon.'

'Is this a dangerous substance?'

'Yes, in human terms a minute quantity could be fatal,'

'If the deceased injected himself, why did he stick the drug in his neck?'

'I cannot say, except that veterinary surgeons often inject cattle sheep and pigs in the neck region.'

The pathologist stood down and the coroner recalled the original police witness. 'Did you find a hypodermic syringe at the scene?'

'No, sir.'

The coroner glanced at Tom.

'No, sir,' he agreed. 'I saw nothing like that.'

The coroner had a glint in his eye. He reminded Tom of a children's conjuror about to pull his largest rabbit from the hat.

'Call Mr Elvis Darren Tong.'

Had he called the original Elvis, Tom could hardly have been more surprised. Darren, "Curly", Tong was the bottom of the social heap in Crossfield. The Tong family were not gypsies in the real sense of the word but they had been travelling folk who had settled permanently in Crossfield. "Diddikai" was the usual title given to these people. In most cases they were law-abiding citizens who paid their taxes and did no harm to anyone. The Tongs lived in a complex of mobile homes on the outskirts of the village. Here their children played unscathed among huge piles of lethal scrap metal. Curly at eighteen, the eldest of eight Tong sons, was the black sheep of the family. He had managed to stay one step ahead of the social-security inspectors in a subtle war that had lasted ever since he was excluded from school. He was an associate of the violent Alex Cornbinder; now released from jail and threatening retribution. Both men tended to be in the centre of pub fights and both were banned from Taraton's disco nightclub.

Curly shuffled to the front of the courtroom. He wore faded jeans and a leather jacket, both reasonably presentable. He had also taken the trouble to shave. There wasn't much he could do about the huge mop of black hair that had given him his nickname. To Tom he had that trapped look of a bull pushed into a market auction ring. Curly looked nervously back down the room. Two police officers standing in the gangway, arms folded, stared coldly back.

'Mr Tong,' said the coroner. 'Where were you on the night in question at eight o'clock?'

Curly shuffled his feet and looked around the room. 'At Woolbarrow, by the tractor shed.'

'Why were you there?'

'Just looking.'

'Are you admitting loitering with intent to commit a felony?' The coroner stared over his spectacles at the hapless Curly.

'No I weren't. I was waiting for some'un.'

'For whom were you waiting?'

'Her over there.' Curly pointed at Francesca.

'Could you please identify this person?'

'I said it were her – Fran Rowridge.'

Francesca had risen to her feet in an agitated state. 'I only asked him to come by and talk. I wouldn't do nothing – not with the likes of him.'

'Miss Rowridge, please sit down. You may have your say in a minute.'

The coroner returned to Curly who did not look pleased by Francesca's outburst.

'Mr Tong, let us accept that you were making a social call. Did you speak with the young lady?'

'Never got the chance. Her dad catch us.'

'This is Mr Rowridge the deceased you are referring to – what did he do?'

'He come at me waving his gun, shouting like a loony – I legged it.'

'And how far, as you say, did you leg it?'

'About a hundred yards down the road towards Boxtree. Then I turned and went back.'

'What happened then?'

'Fran's dad were yelling at her – mean old cunt…'

The coroner intervened. 'You must moderate your language, particularly as this man is now dead. Where did Mr Rowridge and Miss Rowridge go then?'

'Into the house.'

'But you stayed watching – why?'

'I thought Fran might have a chance to slip out when the old sod'd calmed down a bit. Then the other two come…'

'Please, Mr Tong, you are running a little ahead of me. You're telling me there were two more visitors?'

'That's right, they drove up in a posh car – a new Jag. Parked in the field gate right were I be standing. Never saw me though.'

'Could you describe these people?'

'Old geezer and another, bit younger – thin scrawny looking git. I never got too good a look; I kept me head down.'

'What so alarmed you?'

'Didn't like the look of 'em and the old'un had a gun.'

'Could you discern what calibre of weapon?'

'What you on about?'

'I mean what sort of firearm – hand gun, or rifle?'

'It were only a little 'un, know what I mean – airgun like.'

'Where did these men go?'

'The old 'un, he gave the gun to the other. Then he walks to the door and knocks. Matt Rowridge opens the door and in he goes.'

'Only the one man?'

'Yep.'

'And you stayed watching?'

'Yep.'

'For how long?'

'Not long, the door opens and old Matt throws the geezer through it. Shouting and yelling like a good 'un he were. Tells him to sling his hook double quick. Then he walks away into the barn.'

'Just a minute, Mr Tong, with respect I'm confused. Which person walked away and into which barn?'

'Old Matt Rowridge, he were showing them what shit he thought them – that's my guess.'

'Now, Mr Tong, as they say on the television – what happened next?'

'The thin bloke comes out the shadows and he gives the old'un the gun. He runs round the open side of the barn, aims the gun and fires one shot. Then they both runs inside and shuts the door behind 'em.'

'You never saw what happened inside the barn?'

'Sorry, and I didn't want to.' Curly paused and looked at the coroner. 'Sorry, mister, but I weren't going to die for old Matt – know what I mean.'

'How long did you stay watching?'

'Dunno – lost count – twenty minutes maybe. The old 'un comes out of the barn first and he goes in the house. The other bloke stays outside watching. When the other comes out and he talks to his mate.'

'Mr Tong, this is important. Did you hear the words spoken?'

'Yeah, he said, "can't find 'em, maybe they ain't here – we'll have to try again when the place is empty. Let's go before the little girl sees us".'

'Mr Tong, you do remember that you are under oath. There could be serious consequences were you to be found to have invented any of this.'

'I ain't made any of it up. It's as true as I stands here. Sod your oath – I'll swear on my grannie's grave…'

'Yes, all right, Mr Tong – I think we get the message.' The coroner beamed soothingly. 'What happened after these men had gone?'

'I was going to have a look around, but then another car come in the yard. It was gaffer O'Malley and that Lucy. He's a magistrate. I didn't want to be found, so I runs.'

Curly stood down while the courtroom hummed with suppressed excitement. The coroner had to call order.

'Miss Rowridge, in view of what we've just been told, I will have to ask you to take the stand.'

With the coroner's gentle prompting Francesca described how her father had asked her to hide some papers and how subsequently she had heard angry voices downstairs. She spoke quietly and confidently with only the occasional tremor. The court heard her in respectful silence.

The coroner made only the briefest comments before asking the jury to declare on the cause of death. Twenty minutes later they concluded. Murder by persons unknown.

'You've pulled a fast one. You've made me look a complete idiot.' George Shaylor glowered at Lucy.

They were out in the fresh air. Tom had managed to shepherd Lucy and Francesca away from the frantic press people, by dodging down a side passage into a service entrance. Unfortunately George had spotted them and he was justifiably angry.

'It's a bloody conspiracy. Nobody told me a thing about that weasel Tong. The little shit's out front now with the bloody reporters – basking in it.'

'George, will you calm down,' said Lucy. 'I didn't know a thing about Curly Tong watching us until I heard him say so just now. I backed my judgement on medical grounds and as it turns out I was right.'

'Of course you're right – your sort's always bloody right.' George rammed his bush hat on his head and stalked off in the direction of The White Hart.

Inspector Oats appeared and Tom looked at him with disfavour. 'I wish you'd told me about Darren Tong. I had no idea he was prowling about that night.'

'I know, I apologise, but we only found out ourselves two days ago. Tong was boasting in The Dragon and one of our off-duty officers heard him. We'd pulled him in on another matter and suggested it would pay him to co-operate.'

'That doesn't sound ethical,' said Lucy.'

'The means justifies the ends,' the inspector grinned.

'You're certain he's telling the truth?' asked Tom.

'Oh yes, Mr Tong was questioned for some hours and he stuck to his story throughout.' Oats looked at Tom. 'Mr O'Malley, we need to find this Miss Berkovic. She's a registered overseas journalist. Her agency is legitimate and they rented the bungalow at Rotherfield. So if she contacts you, please ask her to speak to us.'

'I'm not sure I want to see that lady ever again, but if I do I'll tell her.'

'One more thing,' said Oats. 'We pulled in Alex Cornbinder yesterday.'

'You said he'd been threatening to get me?'

'We've given him a warning, but all the same be careful.'

Oats left them. Lucy peered round the corner of the court building. The crowd was thinning, the reporters had vanished, although a local TV man was still addressing his camera. They made their way back to their cars.

'I'll run Francesca to Heather Road,' said Lucy.

'And I'll get back to work,' said Tom. 'I don't mind telling you this morning's revelations have shaken me.'

'Dad, I've got to ask; you think you know who this man Brown is?'

'Yes, I didn't want to talk to Oats in public but I'll ring him later. Gus's supposed brother called at the manor in a Jaguar. I've traced it to a car hire firm, but it's one of a dozen they own. Lonnie from the farm has seen a similar car around the village and now we learn that Matthew's killers arrived at Woolbarrow in a Jaguar. I know for certain who was driving the one Lonnie saw and I've already told Oats in the report I sent him.'

'Did you tell Hannah?'

'No, I'm not telling her anything. I don't want to see her again.'

CHAPTER 16

It was Saturday, and Lucy and Francesca were riding. Earlier that week Lucy had borrowed the Land Rover and horsebox and moved Francesca's two ponies to the stables at Boxtree.

Lucy had been quietly satisfied when the inquest had vindicated her diagnosis, but not for long. The implications of murder were too serious; it placed her in the spotlight and it was painful. George Shaylor had resigned his police post the next day. He was reported to be deeply depressed and drinking hard. Lucy felt awful; George could be infuriating but she was fond of the old fool. Now many fellow doctors, as well as staff at the local hospitals, were muttering about her. It was suggested by some that she set ambition above loyalty to a colleague. Her boyfriend Mike had an angry public confrontation with a doctor from another practice that had nearly ended in blows. Stupid men, they could have both been disciplined and it was all her fault. She had never set out to humiliate George; that stubborn man had destroyed himself. Did these people seriously expect her to stay silent and let a murderer go free?

The stable yard at Boxtree had not seen such activity for a year, not since that dreadful day when Lucy's mother had ridden out along the woodland tracks to fall and die from a crushed skull. Lucy was saddling Hero, her mother's old horse. Hero was an Arab, bred for the sport of endurance. Lucy had done her best for him during the ensuing months but she knew it had not been enough. Now the old horse was in the yard champing and stomping, anxious to be away to the hills where he belonged.

The two girls mounted and rode out onto the lane that led downhill to the Manor. To Lucy this day was an important step in Francesca's rehabilitation, a task that she had taken upon herself. She glanced sideways at her companion and felt a glow of satisfaction. Francesca's face was alight with contentment; for the first time since that awful night she seemed relaxed and perhaps a little at peace.

'Car coming,' Francesca called pointing at the bend ahead.

'Bugger,' Lucy grinned and Francesca giggled.

Most drivers slowed down to protect themselves as much as the oncoming horses. The majority were tolerant, a few irritated and some completely indifferent to the safety of others. The oncoming vehicle was a blue Ford Mondeo with a single occupant. The driver politely pulled over onto the green verge to let them pass. As they did so he wound the window down and called; 'Say ladies, where's Crossfield Manor, Mr Fjortoft's house?' He was an elegant grey-haired man of indeterminate age but certainly over sixty. The accent was American and he spoke the name literally as: Cross-Field.

'You've passed it,' she called. 'If you reverse into that gateway you can turn.' He nodded courteously and did as he was advised.

Lucy wondered who this man could be. If he was a business representative he would be out of luck. Gus was overseas and frankly she wished that he was here. She was frightened for her father and Francesca. Dad had not been frank with her; he shared secrets with Hannah. The man who had called himself Gus's brother had frightened Gina and she had told Dad he had altered his appearance. As an actress Gina recognised stage makeup, however skilful; now both she and Gus had vanished in a move that looked very like a cut-and-run.

With an effort Lucy expunged these thoughts. The sun was shining, the gardens were a mass of daffodils and wallflowers, insects were buzzing and the cattle from the dairy farm were happily munching the green grass. Lucy was not one for brooding; this day was too good.

'Come on,' she called. 'Let's try the gallops.'

Ahead of them lay the half-mile stretch of mown grass laid out at Gina's design. Lucy gave Hero his head and he responded joyfully. With the warm scented breeze in her face she felt she was flying. She stood in the stirrups like a jockey, forgetting everything in the joy of the moment. She looked back to see Francesca's little cob, already fifty metres behind, straining manfully to keep up. The belt of trees at the end of the grass was racing towards her. Lucy eased back to a sedate canter to allow Francesca to catch up. Hero seemed to have other ideas, he slowed reluctantly and swerved towards the gateway that led into the forest plantation. Lucy felt cold; how could she have forgotten, when Hero clearly remembered? This was the route her mother loved to ride, through the trees and onto the long bridle way to the summit of Crossfield Hanger. The way she had ridden to her death last summer. Lucy had determined never to see this track again. She pulled the horse to a halt facing the gate. Hero threw back his head in irritation and stamped the ground. Francesca rode up, face flushed and her eyes shining.

'Wow,' she shouted. 'That was wicked – doesn't your horse go!'

'I know, this is the first decent run he's had in weeks.'

'Can we go on up the hill?'

This was the question Lucy had been dreading. She nearly reacted stupidly by rounding angrily on her companion. Then she remembered; Francesca had overcome worse memory by returning to the scene of her father's death. How could she give professional guidance to the poor girl if she herself would not confront her own demons.

'Come on then,' she forced a smile. 'We'll ride round the circuit. It'll do both horses good.'

The forestry road was deeply rutted from the passage of the logging trailers all winter; Lucy slowed to a walk. The Reade-Coke family, a century before, had planted the original woods, now matured into oaks, magnificent beech trees and copses of ash, all heavily budded and ready to burst into leaf.

'Lucy, did Mr Partridge say anything about those papers of Dad's?'

'He says the papers are some kind of wartime code. Old history now, but interesting to him.'

Francesca looked at her suspiciously but said nothing. Lucy had seen a movement further up the track. A man emerged from the trees, stared at them and then slid back furtively into the shadows.

'That's Curly Tong,' said Francesca. 'Hi, Curly, come out of there – we've both seen you.' She pushed the little cob into a trot and rode forward to the spot. Lucy followed; there was no one visible.

'He's up to something.'

Lucy agreed. 'The shooting season's over, but there's still loads of pheasants about. Come on, let's go – it's not our responsibility.'

Ten minutes later they entered the bridleway that climbed the hanger. Lucy felt sick and her heart rate had risen alarmingly. She felt as though she was in that nightmare where the air was as ice, while feet and limbs became leaden. It was as if she was a spectator watching her participation in a pagan ritual. The path was a shelf cut in the side of the hill. It had been widened by the authorities and was normally safe, although its edge looked down a cliff-like slope dotted with small trees and bushes. Nobody would ever know what happened that day. Her mother had been seen to ride her horse like one possessed, but for her that was not dangerous. Somehow, experienced rider though she was and on a smooth unobstructed path, she had pitched from the saddle. It seemed incredible and even more so to learn that she had projected headfirst over the edge into the void. Fifty feet below her fall had ended; her skull crushed against the bole of a yew tree. Half an hour later a contrite Gina, riding out to seek reconciliation, discovered the body of her friend. Gina had been genuinely distraught and Lucy could concede her that. It was much harder to forgive Gina this silly affair with her father while her mother was no more than six months in the grave.

'This is where your mum died isn't it?' Francesca had slowed her horse and was staring over the edge.

'Yes, but they never told me which tree,' Lucy mumbled.

'It was that one,' Francesca pointed. Lucy tried to follow but her eyes wouldn't focus.

'Come on,' she said, 'race you to the top.'

Hero stretched his legs and pounded up the last stretch of hill. Lucy felt a wonderful sense of achievement; more like liberation. Not only had she confronted her personal nightmare, she had done so riding Hero. Perhaps both of them could now put the past in its place.

The path curved around the hill and emerged on the open downland. Lucy slowed Hero enough to let Francesca catch up. Ahead of them lay a broad expanse of thorn bushes and sheep pasture. Beyond that she could see the straggling trees of Becham's Wood. Beside the copse was the old farm track leading to the upper Crossfield lane. Lucy had no taste for a return by the route they'd ridden.

'Come on,' she said. 'let's go up the track and back by the road.'

'I don't want to go past our house.' Francesca looked worried.

'No need, we'll go the other way, and then down Button's Lane.' Lucy led off across the soft turf.

'I don't like this place,' said Francesca. 'There were men here – they scared me.'

'I know; my father said.'

Matthew had wanted to tell Dad something about Becham's Wood on the very night he died. Did Francesca know that?

There were two cars parked on the edge of the track. One was a battered Astra, the other was the same blue Mondeo that they had seen earlier that afternoon. They rode level with the vehicles and stopped. Somewhere nearby came the sound of voices.

'That Astra's Mr Partridge's car,' said Francesca.

Before Lucy could reply the man himself appeared from the trees. With him was the elderly American. Rufus looked mildly embarrassed as he saw the two riders; the American merely nodded.

'Good afternoon once more, ladies.' He sounded affable enough as he turned and sank rather painfully into the driver's seat of his car. He drove off up the track. They heard him turn left and head down the hill towards Woolbarrow and Boxtree.

Rufus always tended to look eccentric, but today his appearance was downright bizarre. He wore breeches tucked into long woven stockings and climbing boots. His head was covered in a balaclava and he carried a coil of rope.

'Hi, Rufus,' Lucy called. 'You look as if you're set to climb Everest.'

Rufus greeted each of them. 'Nothing so hard,' he grinned. 'I've rung your father, by the way, and my investigation has his blessing.'

'What investigation? This place is a rubbish tip.'

'On the contrary. You may see a rubbish tip, but I am walking with history.'

Rufus looked irritatingly smug. Lucy knew from long experience that the most mundane and boring local history would, in Rufus's eyes, be a Holy Grail.

'Who is that guy who's just left?' she asked.

Rufus dug into his back pocket. 'He gave me a card. Apparently he's an old friend of Mr Fjortoft's.' He looked warily towards Francesca who had walked her horse to the edge of the wood. 'May I have a word in your ear?'

'Go ahead.'

'It's awkward with young Francesca here after all that's happened.' He produced the card and passed it to Lucy. 'His name's Maxton Jiffers and he's very anxious to buy Woolbarrow Farm House.'

At seven o'clock Lucy drove Francesca home. The evenings were lighter now that summertime was on the clocks but it was dark enough to need headlights in the gloom of the sunken lanes. Lucy turned left to take the short cut through the village of Frapley. The lane here was especially narrow with banks of solid limestone and very few passing places. Traffic was normally sparse at this time of the evening but she noticed another set of lights behind her. The following vehicle was a Land Rover or similar and Lucy was annoyed when its driver turned the lights to full beam straight into her rear mirror. Now the bulky truck closed within inches of her rear bumper forcing her to increase speed; Lucy swore one short expletive. She steadied her pace: whatever happened she would not be intimidated by the tailgating of this mindless idiot.

Without warning the truck hit her. It was no accident. Amidst the confusion and shock Lucy knew the other driver had deliberately rammed her. A loud crunch and the car shot forwards slamming Lucy hard into her seat and banging her painfully against the headrest.

Beside her Francesca screamed. Lucy put her foot hard on the accelerator and momentarily her car surged away from the pursuer. It was beyond her comprehension, but she knew now that the other driver had been waiting for her, bent on intimidation if nothing worse.

'Francesca,' she shouted. 'Sit right back with your head against the rest.'

Her companion complied with a whimper. Lucy hadn't time to look at her; she could only concentrate on speeding away from danger regardless of what might be around the next corner. God knew what this was about and she hadn't time to speculate; the truck was coming at them again. She accelerated enough to lessen the impact as the attacker smashed into them before backing off and repeating the impact. Lucy let her body slump into the full protection of her seat. They were through the last of the bends and before them lay a ribbon of straight road with a grass verge to either side. The pursuer was coming again, but this time he was shaping to overtake along the grass to her right. Lucy pushed the throttle pedal to the floor. With all four wheels on the tarmac surface she could repel this attack that was clearly intended to force her off the road. If she could hold on a few minutes more they would reach the village and safety.

She saw lights ahead, another car on the road heading straight at her. Lucy instinctively braked. The black bulk of the truck was alongside slamming into her. There came a numbing jolt, a scrape of tearing metal, as the side of the car buckled. The window shattered showering her with fragments of glass as Lucy lost control. The car skidded onto the nearside verge, throwing her violently against the seat belt as they slid into a nettle-covered ditch. Distantly she heard the sound of a motor reversing at speed, its over-revving engine whining in protest. Lucy bent forward and turned off the ignition; beside her Francesca sobbed. She released both of their belts and tried to open the door; it was bent and jammed. She could smell petrol; for the first time she felt on the edge of panic.

'Lucy, it's me, Daddy – what's happened.' She looked through the broken window and felt a huge glow of relief. Her father heaved on the door and at the second tug it swung open with a bang. Lucy seized Francesca's arms and dragged the girl out onto the road.

'What happened?' Tom snapped the question; she could see the concern in his face.

'Did you get his number?' she asked.

'Sorry, no. I saw it was your car and that was all I could think of. Why on earth did he try to overtake you there and in the face of an oncoming vehicle – he's got to be drunk.'

'No, it was deliberate ramming. He came up behind me a mile back and he hit us three times. I'm certain it was a deliberate attempt to cause an accident.'

'We'll report this straight away,' Tom extracted a mobile phone and walked to the rear of the car. Lucy stayed with Francesca. The girl was crouching on the road hyperventilating.

Tom tapped her on the shoulder. 'I've called the police. I've told them there's a Land Rover with a drunk driver.'

'I think there's more to it than that. I'm sure I was attacked deliberately. It was so cold and calculated – but why me?'

'Come on, both of you, into my car. I'm not waiting for the police we're all going back to Boxtree.'

'My medical stuff's in the boot – drugs and all.'

'OK, I'll go and fetch them. I've rung Lonny, he's on his way with the tractor and loader. He says he'll wait here until the police have been and gone, then he'll bring the car home.'

Tom put the phone down. 'Lonny's on his way back,' he said. 'He reckons the car's an insurance write-off.

'Oh God, this is bloody crazy,' Lucy sat with her head in her hands. The delayed shock had hit her now with a vengeance. 'What's happening to us?' She tried to control her shaking but she failed and the tears flowed unchecked.

The police had departed; statements had been taken and signed. An hour after the event it had all seemed fantasy. The police had been sceptical and Lucy had to accept the humiliation of a breath test. The evidence at the scene though was compelling. The skid tracks on the road, and the shattered car were evidence that could not be ignored. A general call was put out to find a Land Rover and a driver suspected of being over the limit.

Lucy stood up. 'I'd better ring Mike. He won't believe my story. He'll be all chauvinist and go on about women drivers.'

'He'll change his tune when he sees the car.' Tom walked to the door. Outside in the yard was the drumming of a heavy tractor. 'Good, here's Lonny.'

The wrecked car looked even more grotesque sitting on the low-load trailer. Tom looked around for Lonny. The man was standing beside the tractor staring at the barn door. Tom turned and for the first time he saw it too. The headlights lit the scene as bright as day. He stopped transfixed. The door and walls of the barn were covered in ugly graffiti, the hurried work of someone with a paint spray can. There were a dozen four-letter obscenities and one tangible sentence.

Paddy coon lover
RON

'Who the hell is Ron?'

'It stands for "Reclaim Our Nation",' said Lonny. 'They're a racist political group and about as nasty as they come.'

CHAPTER 17

Inspector Oats's offer of police protection had shaken Tom. He had called at Taraton police station the morning following the assault on Lucy's car. He had prepared himself for a long argument with Oats and he had never expected to be taken so seriously.

'We pulled in Alex Cornbinder last night,' said Oats. 'Of course he claims an unshakeable alibi, but his old Land Rover has vanished off the face of the earth.'

'If it was Alex.' Tom was not convinced. 'His quarrel's with me, not Lucy. I know he's got a violent record, but it's always been drunken brawls.'

'I know,' said Oats wearily. 'It would be so much simpler if it was Alex and it does fit his profile, but his mates will perjure themselves to hell and back.'

'Tell me something about this Reclaim Our Nation group? My lad Lonny got really wound up when he saw that graffiti. He's a local man, but his grandfather was West Indian, so he's sensitive about racism.'

'The RON, you mean.' Oats's face was expressionless. 'I must say I was surprised to hear about the vandalism at your place. It's not their normal style. The RON try to be terribly middle class and reasonable.'

'There was nothing reasonable about the attack on Lucy, or the daubing on my barn.'

'I know, that's why we went for Alex – it's more his trademark. As for the RON, they're a far-right group that's making a bit of headway in the London suburbs and in the South Coast cities. As I said, they try to sound terribly reasonable. Always say they've nothing against the minorities except they'd like to ship the whole lot out. They've made a lot of converts among the gullible.' Oats paused; to Tom the man looked almost shifty. 'I've got to be careful what I say and for two reasons. Number one, they've built a bit of a following among the police, including some of my officers. Not the younger ones, but a couple of the long servers. I've had to issue a warning only last week.'

Tom could sympathise. Oats was a good copper, a traditional upholder of law and order. He enforced the law as he saw it regardless of class, colour, political affiliation, or anything else. To Oats, people were people: good, bad, and indifferent. In his eyes most belonged to the last two categories. But institutionalised racism in the police force would certainly be an anathema.

Tom changed the subject. 'Did you enquire about this man Tallisment? He was driving a Jaguar car. Fjortoft's supposed brother arrived in a Jag. Curly Tong swore on oath that Matthew Rowridge's killers arrived in a Jaguar. I say it's the same man. I think you should go for him.'

Oats reached into a filing tray and pulled out two sheets of A4 paper. 'I thought you'd ask me that so I've come prepared. We've traced Mr Tallisment's history as far as we can. He has no criminal form and there is nothing to connect him with Mr Fjortoft. Frankly, and I'm sorry to have to say this, but we think you've a bit of a misconception about Mr Tallisment.'

Tom was not impressed. 'Tell me what you did find?'

'He's recorded as Polish by birth. Grew up in England but went to South Africa as a teenager. It seems he made a pile of money in that country not all of which was entirely legitimate, but that's a matter for the South Africans. He returned to Britain in the nineteen-seventies and invested a small fortune in property. Now his company is so big, and he has so much pull in high places that our Chief Constable has ordered me to back off. Sorry, Tom, but that's that, and whoever he is he's not Gus Fjortoft's brother.'

'If you say so, I don't know what to think. Gina Fjortoft was specific that the man who arrived in the Jaguar was Gus's brother.'

'The firm that hired that car has a dozen similar – all the same colour and year of manufacture. It's true that four were leased to Vega Magna PLC, but not to any specific driver. Remember we're talking about a big concern here – nearly one thousand employees, not counting their spouses, children, friends and relations.'

'But doesn't he fit the description of the older man that Tong gave to the court?'

'We questioned Tong at length. We've constructed a photo fit of both suspects and neither looks anything like your Mr Tallisment.'

Tom knew he was beaten, with nothing to be gained by pushing the man further. He glanced at his watch. 'I'd better be going. I'm sitting in court at eleven. I can't do the first case because I know the defendant.'

'You mean Lady Clarry.' Oats grinned. 'I think her driving days are finished. We found her Morris in the ditch with her ladyship four times over the limit.'

Tom was not surprised. Lady Clarissa Hoskythe was the last of the Read-Coke dynasty still living in Crossfield. She was elderly, eccentric and much loved, apart from a weakness for the bottle.

'I was going to visit her to ask about her brother and Reg Rowridge. They were up to something secret in the war. Rufus Partridge is getting quite excited about it.'

Oats stood up and showed Tom to the door. 'There's one thing I think I can tell you – off the record, as the press boys say. It concerns the RON.'

'You told me you had a second reason for being wary?'

'Rumour has it that our Mr Gannemeade MP is retiring from parliament at the next election and that he's been invited to jump ship and take the leadership of RON.'

Tom remembered. 'You were there that night at the rugby club. It was Gannemeade who introduced me to Tallisment.'

'I know, but there's nothing suspicious about that. Gannemeade's a business associate and they're both South African. Another thing you'll be interested to know. Tallisment and Gannemeade share a motor yacht at Birdham.'

Tom looked him in the eye. 'Half a mile from where Magdalena was murdered.'

When Tom reached home, he found a police panda car parked in the yard. Beside it a constable was in conversation with one of Gus's Mormons. The Mormons had heard about the incidents at Boxtree and were insisting on taking their turn with security.

A surprise awaited him indoors. Sitting at the kitchen table, munching a plate of chips was Andrew.

'Ferry arrived in Pompey at seven this morning,' said Andy. 'Hadn't enough cash for the train, so I hitched.'

'Have a good holiday – how are your aunt and uncle?'

Andy launched into a detailed account of his time in Brittany. Tom listened with interest. It was good to see the boy had put on some weight and his face was no longer pallid.

Andy stopped in mid flow. 'Sorry, I forgot to tell you. In the study there's an email for you from America – you've been summoned.'

'It's from Gus.' said Tom reading the screen.

That's what I said,' replied Andy. 'He's summoned you – tremble and obey.'

From: Gustav Fjortoft
To:Tom@boxtree.supernet.co.uk
Sent: 05 May 2000
Subject: Request presence.
Tom, I need you here. Please can you fly here Wednesday? You can't be too busy with the farm right now? I've arranged tickets delivered to you today. Accommodation arranged in Seattle; all expenses on me.

Tom, I need your help. This is important. Whole future for us at stake. Can't emphasise how vital it is we meet soonest possible.
Please reply on receipt of this. Gina sends her love.
Gus.

It was three thirty in the afternoon. Francesca Rowridge stood in the road outside Taraton Sixth Form College. She looked quickly around before starting down the main road. She was anxious to avoid Daryl Barnes. She wondered what his game was. He couldn't fancy her; Francesca had no doubts on that. She had made her decision a week earlier. She would put everything she had into academic success. Old Rufus had told her she could achieve grades that would take her to university, even Oxford. Whatever she lacked in sexual attraction she would make up for in career achievement. That would be one in the eye for her miserable old dad. The horror of his death was no longer so painful despite the recurring nightmares. Sometimes she felt the old sod was watching her from beyond the grave. Her mother had either ignored or not received her pleas to come home. Marjorie had tried every way to contact her. In Marjorie's opinion, Vanessa had fled abroad with her fancy man.

Still no date was set for Dad's funeral. She was told that the police were still holding his body for tests. The impending funeral was hanging over her like a shadow and it wasn't fair. The college was awash with reports of the inquest. The teachers had all been supportive and kind, but some of her fellow students had been vicious. She had heard snide remarks about her mother who was being universally blamed for the murder. That at least had to be untrue. Francesca had her own theory and it scared her. She remembered with a chill the two voices she had heard in the wood that night. She had thought a lot about those voices. She had lain awake in her bed hearing the words over and over again. One had been an American;

he sounded like someone in that spooky X Files series. The other voice she'd heard before, but where – when?

Francesca reached the lake and stood for a while beside the children's swings. Marjorie would not be home yet and there was still half an hour to wait. She decided to continue her usual route around the water; it would give her space to think. The ground surrounding the lake was called The Heath, but today it was largely deserted. She stopped by the water and fed the remnants of her packed lunch to the ducks. Rufus had written a whole book about the lake and it was dull. Had he found something more interesting in Bechams Wood? She wished she could talk to Mr O'Malley, everyone looked up to him. The village rumourmongers said he was about to run away with Gina Fjortoft. Some in the village were saying that Gina had done away with Tricia O'Malley. But Gina was a lovely kind lady. She had even baked Francesca a birthday cake in the manor kitchen.

Francesca reached the golf course and set off on the path that would lead her to home. She could see a car under the trees where the path joined the road. She walked closer but could still see nobody. Then the man stepped out from behind a gorse bush. She knew him by sight of course, everyone did, and she knew the bloke by reputation and she didn't like what she'd heard. She had a clear conscience and she wouldn't be intimidated. She fixed her gaze on the path in front and aimed to ignore him as she walked past.

He grinned and stepped into the path blocking her way. 'Hello girl – Francesca isn't it? I've got some news for you.'

CHAPTER 18

Twelve hours cooped up in a 747 and an eight-hour time difference. Tom who had a strong aversion to sitting idle found his legs were beginning to twitch. He knew he should try and sleep but he couldn't and his reading matter had become a meaningless blur. He had not expected this summons; his position, farm manager, was that exactly. He could think of no reason for Gus to send him halfway round the world.

He had woken that morning determined to cancel this stupid trip. The sun shone, the trees were in leaf and the green fields, his world, had never looked so beautiful and inviting. He didn't want to go to America; he would tell Gus and the whole universe to go to hell. He had reckoned without Lucy and Charlie. Lucy had stayed overnight and cooked him breakfast. Then Charlie arrived with the Mercedes. Without a word spoken he picked up Tom's luggage and pointed him into the passenger seat while Lucy had given him a kiss and a cheery wave. Between the two of them they treated him like a fractious child.

In Seattle, having cleared customs and been reunited with his luggage, he passed into the outer concourse of the airport. He saw his contact man at once and hardly needed the neatly stencilled name placard. The clean-shaven, sharp-suited young man stood out from the crowd. Here was another of Gus's Mormons.

'Mr O'Malley, sir. I'm Lewis Gungenhorn – but everyone around here calls me Lew.' He held out a hand. 'Mr Fjortoft's out of town at the moment but he asked me to meet you and take you to the hotel.'

'That's fine by me, Lew. I could do with a decent bite to eat and some sleep.'

'There's no program laid on for you today. Just relax, sir, we'll do the honours.'

The hotel was called the Benson Criterion. It was a middle-sized high-rise block with a huge glass foyer filled with tropical plants. The brochure explained that the building belonged to the Benson United & Pacific Shipping Line and also contained the company's head office. Tom was led to the elevator and deposited in his suite on the fifth floor.

It was as if he had walked into some garish film set. The ground floor of Boxtree Farm could probably have fitted this apartment. The vestibule led into a cavernous reception area with Italian leather furnishings. The windows looked out across rooftops to the famous Space Needle. The curtains were gold cloth, the carpets deep pile and ornate chandeliers hung from the ceiling. A massive four-poster bed, with the same gold cloth curtains, dominated the bedroom. The bathroom contained a heart shaped Jacuzzi and showers, all with gold fittings. The whole place was a triumph of heavy over-lavish colour-clashing kitsch.

Lew and the hotel porter departed. Tom felt dizzy and his limbs were twitching worse than ever. He regarded the awful bed with distaste but after a few seconds fell on it. With total relief he sank into its soft inviting clasp and within thirty seconds he was asleep.

The house telephone was ringing. Tom sat up bleary eyed and looked at his watch; it was midnight. Then he remembered where he was and that his watch was still adjusted to Greenwich mean time. The phone rang again and he picked it up.

'Reception – I have a lady and gentleman to see you.'

'Really – who?'

'Ms Chantelle Trouvier and Mr Peter Little.'

Momentarily Tom could make nothing of the names. 'OK, ask them to come on up.'

He rubbed his eyes and swung his legs off the bed. It must be about four in the afternoon local time. Peter Little must be Pete, the college lecturer, still with that irritating Canadian girl. How the hell did that pair come to be here? He shuffled through to the main room and found a drinks cabinet stocked with enough beverages to host a conference. Tom set three glasses on a crystal-topped table and awaited his guests.

Neither had changed in appearance since Tom had last seen them. Pete was dressed in the same jeans and denim jacket, as was Chantelle; her black dreadlocks looking out of place against her chalky white complexion. Tom sat them down and poured the drinks.

'First question,' he stared at Pete. 'How did you track me here?'

'Hannah told us you were on your way. No secret, she asked your daughter where she could find you.'

Tom nodded; this made sense.

'Some joint this,' Pete remarked.

'Not my choice.'

'Sure,' Pete sipped his whiskey. 'Where's Fjortoft?'

'I'm told he's out of Seattle at present.'

'Any idea why he wants you?'

'No, and I wouldn't tell you if I knew.'

Pete nodded. 'Man, you must be at a loose end. How say you come out to Edmonds and meet my folks.'

'What, now?'

'Yeah.'

Pete's parents were Sam and Greta Little, his own father's friends. He had a letter from his father to Sam in his pocket and a promise to make contact. 'All right, Pete, I'd be delighted.'

'You gotta car?'

'I believe the hotel have one booked. You want a lift?'

'Could do, but that's not why we asked.'

Tom checked with reception and was informed that his hire car for the week was in the basement car park. Tom drove the car, a new Lexus, once around the block to accustom himself to the left hand drive; then with Pete navigating they set out for the sedate northern suburb of Edmonds. Now was the rush hour. Tom was staggered by the enormity of the sight. He was familiar with the traffic chaos around major British cities; what he saw exceeded anything he had experienced even in nightmares. End to end and wall-to-wall flowed thousands of vehicles combining like a lava stream. It was endless, frustrating and slow. Pete pointed him to the priority lane reserved for vehicles carrying more than one occupant. This helped for a while until that road too became strangled. It was nearly three quarters of an hour before Pete directed him off the freeway and into the little town that was their destination.

The older Littles lived in a spacious bungalow, or rambler as the Americans would say. It lay up a short driveway from a pleasant tree-lined street. Pete tapped Tom on the arm and indicated him to pull over near an obese individual wearing mechanic's overalls. The man leaned against the wooden fence surrounding the property. Another grey-haired man appeared from the shadows. He was tall and wiry and even from a distance of twenty yards he suggested menace.

'Nam vets,' said Chantelle. 'Pete's hired a posse of 'em – watch the place through twenty-four hours.'

'Why?'

'Why d'you think? If those Nazi goons find out Greta's the last survivor of Gostanyn, there's no knowing what they'll try.'

‘Tom,’ Peter spoke quietly. ‘Drive in the gate and stop. Then get out real slow and do what you’re told.’

Tom rolled the Lexus into the driveway. The tall guard was by his window. ‘Out of there, mister – shift your ass.’

Tom complied without argument; the man was holding a handgun. Both guards swung him round against the car and he was frisked from head to toe.

‘OK, fella, you’re clear. Go on up – you’re expected.’

The rambler seemed a modern house with steps leading up to a porch. Standing in the entrance was another guard. These sentinels had a cold detached fatalism that set them apart from the usual heavies. Vietnam veterans, doomed to fight a hellish war, that deep down they probably knew was wrong and unwinnable.

This time he was mistaken. The watcher by the door was an elderly black man, with grizzled greying hair, who radiated bonhomie.

‘Hi there, Henry,’ said Pete. ‘Tom, this is Mr Henry Henry, or HH as we call him. Those are his real names too.’

‘Pleased to meet you, Mr Henry,’ said Tom.

Henry grinned. ‘Glad to meet you, Mr O’Malley. I served at sea with Captain Little and I well remember your pa, and you too, man; though you was a babe in your ma’s arms.’

‘Henry was purser on Dad’s ship,’ said Pete. ‘He’s helping out until we’re clear of this trouble. Now come in and meet the folks.’

Tom recognised Sam at once. Though the man was well into his seventies he seemed unchanged from the photographs Tom’s father had produced. Short in stature, Sam made up for that with a deep voice and a glittering eye. A Cornishman by birth, Sam had spent a lifetime working on the Pacific seaboard. His speech had developed into a nice blend of Falmouth and American West Coast.

‘Well, no argument as to who your dad is.’ He stared Tom in the eye. ‘Chip of the old block, even if you are half a froggie.’ Sam had a cheerful abrasive manner and Tom liked him.

Greta Little had entered the room. She was a petite lady no taller than her husband. Even now she retained much of the East European beauty that had graced her as a girl. She gave Tom a friendly greeting and invited him into the living room for a drink. She seemed kindly, albeit her face was careworn and Tom suspected she had not slept well of late.

He reached in his pocket and produced his father’s letter. Sam opened it and sat reading without comment or expression. It was a long letter, four pages in Fred O’Malley’s tightly formed script.

Sam laid down the paper and regarded Tom. 'Your old man's written your life history. I'm sorry about your wife,' he looked embarrassed. 'I should've kept in touch with your father – we were great buddies.' He glanced over his shoulder towards the kitchen. Pete and his mother could be heard talking and clattering plates.

'Did your dad tell you about Greta's spat with Fjortoft?'

'He told me there was a row at a reception.'

'You know why?'

'Yes, it was about some wartime prison camp.'

'Gostanyn; Dr Brown's Kinder Clinic, they called it. Never Brown's Extermination Camp, although that's what it was.'

'Can you tell me about Gustav Fjortoft's part in this?' It was the question he had come thousands of miles to find an answer.

Sam shook his head. 'That's Greta's tale. So bide your time and wait 'til she's ready. I can tell you it's some yarn.'

Tom fought sleep. His watch said three o'clock in the morning although the company were sitting down to dinner on what for them was the previous evening. The food was good, though uncompromisingly American. Throughout the meal, Greta had been friendly but reserved, while Tom had felt himself to be under scrutiny. Sam had bombarded him with questions about his father, and added his own recollections. At no time was there a mention of Fjortoft. By the time they had regained the comfort of the armchairs in the living room, Tom needed all his willpower to stay awake.

Greta picked up a photograph in a silver frame and carried it across to him. It was a studio portrait of a young man in German military uniform. Tom had seen similar British pictures on mantelpieces and in family albums; the last proud memories of some son or father. This soldier was no different. He was nineteen or twenty, fresh faced with smooth dark hair and a slightly surprised expression.

'This is Gunther,' said Greta. 'He saved my life and my friend Sonja's.'

'Sonja was Magda's mother,' said Pete.

Sam looked up. 'Never condemn a whole race. Gunther was one good German.'

'Like Oscar Schindler,' said Pete.

'Sure, but Schindler was an influential guy who knew how to work the system. Gunther was just a simple boy with a good heart.'

'Tom looks lost,' Pete grinned. 'Would you tell him the whole story, Mother?'

Greta replaced the photograph and then tipped out the contents of an envelope. She selected another photograph, a modern colour print. She passed it to Tom. He could make little of it. The picture was a scene of weed-strewn concrete and some shattered brick walls.

'This,' she said, 'is all that remains of Gostanyn Kinder Clinic. I took this picture last year. It was the first time I have returned to that place.' Tom heard the catch in her voice.

'They brought kids there from all over Europe,' said Pete. 'Specially selected after medical tests. Only the fittest were taken. Gostanyn was like no other camp in the Nazi system.'

'That's true,' said Greta. 'There was good food, warm huts, swings to play on, and a grass square for ball games.'

'But no teachers or education,' Pete interrupted. 'No point where they were going.'

'To the treatment ward,' said Greta. 'Every week Doctor Brown would choose six kids, maybe more. They would go to the treatment ward in the great house and that would be the last we would see of them. A few days later in would come a truckload of more kids, and they would think they were in paradise until they guessed what was going on.'

'What was going on?' Tom had to ask.

Pete glanced at his mother. 'Spare part surgery: Brown was trying organ transplants, even arms and legs. All his victims died, or all but one; he couldn't crack cell rejection.'

'You say one survived?'

'Yeah, by some miracle he had one that worked.'

'Who was that?'

'Little boy, son of one of the SS guards. He was near to total kidney failure. Brown killed one of the Aryan kids and took his kidneys and somehow it worked. Modern science would tell you that's impossible but it worked – Mother saw it, she'll tell you.'

'How long did this boy live?'

'He may be alive now. We know he survived the war. That's the injustice of it; all the innocent kids died.'

'What happened to the bodies?'

'They shipped 'em down the road to a camp with a furnace. What did Brown care when he had an unlimited fresh supply.'

'Who were these kids?' Tom worried that he might sound insensitive, but he had to know.

'They came from every group. Jews of course and Slavs, but some blue-blooded krauts as well, but they were always autistic or Down's-

Syndrome.'

'Did all the children die this way?'

'About one hundred and fifty, but they always kept the numbers in the camp around three hundred. Then at the end of forty-four came the Russian advance. The Germans evacuated Brown and his team, but they never took the kids. They killed the lot and put them in a mass grave.'

'Except for Sonja and me,' said Greta. 'Gunther saved us.'

Tom forgot tiredness. He needed a tactful moment to quiz Greta about Fjortoft.

'Gunther worked in a field bakery. He was a fat boy, not too bright in the head. He drove the truck that brought bread into the camp. The SS didn't like it because the bread was fresh – Brown insisted his specimens were well fed.'

'Gunther was an ordinary soldier,' Sam explained. 'The guards on the camp were SS.'

'Sure,' said Greta. 'They reckoned a non-combatant cook like Gunther was the lowest of the low. They didn't care to associate with such, but they didn't mind him talking to us – that's me and Sonja.'

'He helped you escape?'

'God bless him, yes he did.' Greta dabbed at her eyes.

Tom felt increasingly trapped and uncomfortable. He was trying to imagine a world of horror that had previously touched him only through the pages of books and old scratchy news films.

'I'd better explain,' said Greta. 'Sonja and I were labelled Slavs. The bottom of the heap were Jews, and even in our camp they were housed away from everyone else. About half the camp were Slavs and we got to talk to the Germans sometimes. The SS were all evil bastards, no exceptions, but some of the ordinary conscript soldiers were OK. Like Gunther they missed their families.'

'Please, Mrs Little,' Tom intervened. He knew this was tactless, if not downright rude, but he had to know. 'Was there a boy called Josef or "little Josef"?'

To Tom's relief she was not offended; only surprised. 'It was a common name, particularly among the Jewish kids. Why do you ask, Tom?'

'My employer, Gustav Fjortoft…' he hung on the words for a full three seconds; Greta's face remained impassive. 'Gustav Fjortoft has nightmares about children being killed. His wife told me so and he calls out to save someone called little Josef.'

'So, he has an uneasy conscience,' Greta's voice was hard. 'Yes I remember Mr Fjortoft and I also have nightmares.'

'That's true,' said Sam. 'She has real bad dreams, but less so since she went back there.' He pointed at the photograph of the rubble. 'You know, that campsite is the most God-awful place. You can call me a superstitious Cornish bumpkin, if you like, but stand in that place and your blood chills. It's true that you never hear a bird sing there.'

'You can't say who this Josef was?'

'Sorry, Tom,' Greta shook her head.

'Please, I must know what Fjortoft did in that camp?'

Greta looked uncertain. She shot an appealing glance at her husband.

'Tell him,' said Sam. 'It's part of your story.'

'It was the day after we heard the Russians were near. Gunther warned us, then the SS sealed off the camp.' Greta stared blankly at the far wall; Sam closed a hand over hers and gave it a supportive squeeze.

'The guards came into the camp and called an *appel*, a roll call. All three hundred kids had to parade, even those that were sick. Doctor Brown came out of the main block and with him were his three boys, Albert, Wilhelm and Gustav. I can remember those three to this day standing in a little huddle. Wilhelm was laughing, I would call it gloating – until his father shouted at him.'

'What did Gustav do?' Tom had to ask.

'He just stood there; looked lost. But he was a good bit younger than the other two.' Greta was crying; her face buried in a handkerchief.

'Give her time,' Sam urged.

'The guards pulled twenty children from the first group,' said Greta. 'Then they told the rest of us to go back to the huts.'

'Lucky for her she didn't obey,' said Sam.

'That's right, Sonja and I slipped out of the back of our hut and went to find Gunther. He was in the kitchens. There was no sign of the guards. Gunther told us to get in his truck and hide under the breadboxes. Told us the SS were killing the kids in batches – lethal injections. He told us he'd seen it all through the windows of the operating theatre. Then he told us about the boys.'

'Fjortoft?' Tom asked.

'Doctor Brown's boys. Gunther said the SS were letting them take part. He told us Wilhelm had done it before; said sometimes he contaminated the drug doses with gasoline – make his victims die real painful and slow. Even some of the SS were disgusted, and that took some doing.'

There was a long embarrassing silence. Nobody wanted to look at Greta's tormented face. Tom didn't know what to think. He clutched at one last straw.

'Please, you never actually saw this?'

'No, but Gunther did, that's why he saved us. And he made a sworn statement years later when we met him again.'

'Is he still alive?'

'No,' she replied quietly. 'He died a year ago – killed himself. They found him lying in a stream. He used to go fishing there and his wife said he brooded a lot. It was the fifty fifth anniversary of that day.' Her voice cracked as more tears flowed.

Tom wondered: another convenient suicide?

'Gunther got the two girls out that night,' said Sam. 'He hid them in a cellar with some food and told them not to show until the Russians came. Then, would you believe it, the Russkies put both kids into a gulag.'

'Why?'

'The pair were Russian speakers. The girls thought that would get them favourable treatment – did it hell? The commissars said they must be traitors or they wouldn't be with the Germans. That was the official Stalin line.'

'We were in that camp for two years,' said Greta. 'It was terrible: bad food, always cold and all that stupid indoctrination. Worst thing was I got separated from Sonja. Eventually she made it back to Latvia where her people came from, but they were all dead by then.'

Magda and Anton, Sonja's own children, were dead too. Tom wondered if Greta knew that. It was not for him to add to her grief.

Suddenly Sam grinned and the tension eased. 'My girl here was too smart for the commies. Soon as she got out of the gulag she was sent on a labour detail in some place not far from Riga. She lit out and made it onto a ship for Sweden. I keep saying it would make a class movie.'

'There's one thing I don't understand,' said Tom. 'You talk about three boys. Does Fjortoft have a second half-brother?'

'There were three brothers,' said Greta. 'Wilhelm and Albert were twins, and Gustav was their half-brother.'

'Where is Albert?'

'We've checked and double checked,' said Pete. 'All the indications say Albert was killed in an air raid in nineteen forty-five – that may be true. But we know Wilhelm is still alive. We have reason to think that your man Fjortoft is protecting him and not far from where you live in England.'

It was a mile down the freeway on the journey home that Tom first noticed the motorbike. A huge brute of a machine, with a single blazing headlight, it closed up behind him and held station for the rest of the way to his exit for the city centre. Tom assumed the rider would use his extra power to overtake. He felt puzzled, more than alarmed, when the motorbike followed him into the city still keeping station. At the second set of traffic lights he lost it. Tom felt relieved although he didn't know why. He concentrated on the street grid, trying to remember how many blocks to count before his turn to the hotel. Ten minutes later he was lost in a business district with featureless modern buildings. He knew that he had passed none of them on the outward journey. He was tired and disorientated in a strange American city, that might or might not, be dangerous at night. A single headlight in his rear mirror, the motorbike again. Of course he couldn't say for certain it was the same bike, but his instinct said so.

Tom turned right at the next intersection. The bike was still behind. These were meaner and shabbier streets and he guessed they were heading for the port area. He glanced at his fuel gauge and saw with alarm that he had less than a quarter of a tank. He would not be intimidated, nor would he indulge in unnecessary bravado. He took one hand off the wheel and took his wallet from his pocket. He emptied it of all but sixty dollars in cash and then hid the rest of his money and credit cards under the seat. Five minutes later he found himself driving downhill towards the waters of Puget Sound. He guessed he was not far from the infamous Skid Row. Then, with relief he saw a filling station; no different in design and layout to those outside Taraton. Tom pulled in beside the first set of pumps. He looked over his shoulder; the motorbike had also entered the precinct and stopped. The machine was a large Yamaha, the rider dressed in all black leathers with full helmet and visor.

The well-built black lady at the pay window took Tom's money and told him to have a nice day, an odd suggestion in the pitch dark. Tom's watch now read six am GMT. He had passed through a whole home-time night without sleep and amazingly he was awake again. The motorbike was still there, its rider watching as Tom walked back to his car. He felt a mood change, almost one of exhilaration. The comforting normality of the filling station drove away irrational fears.

Now he was angry. He took off and sprinted towards the bike determined to have an explanation. The motorcyclist saw him coming, gunned his engine and rode straight at Tom who dodged behind the last line of pumps. The man's visor was raised. He caught the briefest glimpse of two dark eyes set in a surround of white skin. They were deeply expressive eyes and he had seen them before – but where he couldn't remember.

Tom turned the car around and retraced the way he had come. Ten minutes later he caught a distant glimpse of the Space Needle. He pulled over and took a mental compass bearing. On regaining the city centre he stopped to ask directions from two friendly cops who pulled up behind him in a patrol car. This bewildered dumb Limey had apparently made their day. They pointed him to the Benson Criterion Hotel. They explained amidst stifled guffaws that he was now parked outside the rear entrance.

He left the Lexus in the hotel's underground garage and went up to the reception area. As he threaded his way through the tropical plants in the foyer he heard voices; the soft deferential tones of the girl receptionist, then the noisier bluster of an awkward male complainer. Tom detested bullies, particularly those who took their sadism out on inoffensive employees. He felt even more irritated, and surprised, because he recognised the owner of the voice.

'The name's Gannemeade for God's sake – Roland Gannemeade MP.' The disembodied roar echoed through the building.

Tom reached the reception desk to see the confrontation for real. The girl behind the desk seemed completely unfazed by the man who glowered down at her.

'I'm real sorry, Mr Empey,' she said sweetly. 'I'm sure your reservation's in the system somewhere.'

'Not Empey – MP,' roared the outraged guest.

Tom beamed his friendliest smile at the beleaguered receptionist. 'MP are the initials after the name, it means Member of Parliament. In this country he'd be Congressman.'

'Say, d'you have a Congress in England? I thought you was ruled by Queen Liz and that guy with the toothy grin. I think he's kinda' cute.'

'He's the Prime Minister and he leads our Parliament of which this gentleman is a member – hence MP.'

Tom looked at the man with disdain. He didn't like politicians and this one was more odious than most. Lucy had confided that it was in Gannemeade's house that Andy had been introduced to drugs.

'Good evening, O'Malley. They told me you were visiting Seattle with your employer – it's a small world.' Gannemeade had reverted to his simpering vote-catching mode. The man really ought to be an actor.

The girl behind the desk was trying to retrieve some information from her computer. She was pretty with eastern features, Korean, or perhaps Filipino.

'To think we've let this nation of half-breeds rule the world,' Gannemeade snorted.

Tom was appalled and embarrassed by the bellicose rudeness of this buffoon.

'Say,' the girl shot a dazzling smile. 'I love your English accents.'

Tom left Gannemeade MP to stew and took the elevator to his floor. It was dark outside but he no longer felt the least bit tired. He was surprised to find the lights on in his suite. The ridiculous chandeliers were gleaming, throwing light into every corner, though only one light was in use when Pete and Chantelle had called. He could have sworn he had turned everything off before he went out. He ran across to the bedroom, by contrast in semidarkness, broken only by a single bedside light. Above the bedclothes protruded a bare shoulder and a mop of blonde hair. It was Gina.

CHAPTER 19

'Gina, no!' Tom, weary, confused and worried, had no appetite for whatever Gina had intended by invading his bed.

'Darling, what's wrong?' Gina was sitting up staring at him doe-eyed.

'For a start, I've travelled halfway round the world at your command and I've been given no good reason.'

'Gus wants you – he's in trouble.'

'Well, I've heard some things about him tonight that I don't like. Apart from that, I've just escaped being mown down by a raving lunatic on a motorbike. Then I find that prize shit Gannemeade shouting the odds.' Tom took off his jacket and flung it across a cane chair. 'Finally just as I need some peace and quiet to think – I find you here.'

'Why shouldn't I be here?' Her lower lip drooped. 'I booked this specially. It's the bridal suite.'

'I'm not a newly-wed and nor are you.'

He was fed up with this moronic spoilt woman taking him for granted. The full horror of Greta Little's tale was slowly taking hold of him. Tom had run out of excuses for Gustav Fjortoft. Nothing could absolve this man who had taken part in a mass murder of small children.

'I've nothing against you,' he said quietly. 'You're a victim too and I'm sorry about that.'

She stared at him with an expression so woeful that he almost relented. 'I am resigning as your husband's employee. I no longer wish to work for him, to meet him, or to be associated with him in any way whatever.'

Gina wailed; she laid full length on the bed, fists clenched, head buried in the pillows. Tom felt remorse now. This was not a contrived tantrum; clumsily he had penetrated the inner soul of this poor woman and unleashed the terrors and insecurities that she dreaded. He sat beside her on the bed while she clung to him until her tears subsided and her shaking stopped.

'Tom,' she whispered. 'Who told you about Gus?'

He told her everything he had learned, without mentioning Greta by name. 'How much of this have you heard?' he asked.

'Gus told me most of it that night his brother called on us at

Crossfield. After you left us he kinda broke down.' She hesitated. 'Tom, I think you should hear Gus's story from himself and not go jumping to conclusions.'

'What other conclusion can I come to? Witnesses saw him, and the German soldier saw the killings. I'm sorry but I heard the evidence and it convinced me.'

'Tom please?' She clung to him her face still wet with tears. A new edge and timbre rang in her voice. Tom who knew most of her moods was surprised.

'Tom, you owe it to us to hear Gus out. Will you come with me tomorrow – for old time's sake?'

'Go where?'

'Place in the country – way out of town.'

'All right, I will listen, but I warn you I don't think it'll make much difference.'

'Where are we?' Tom rubbed his eyes. The rhythmic drone of the car engine had sent him to sleep.

'We're headed for Oregon,' Gina replied without taking her eye off the long stretch of freeway.

'Sorry, couldn't keep awake.' He glanced at his watch, now finally adjusted to local time.

It was eleven thirty in the morning. They'd been on the road for two hours.

'You still haven't told me where we're going' he said.

'It's a kinda college campus out in the woods. No town near, only an old reservation.'

'Red Indians?'

'Sure, but I've never seen 'em – Mulgrum don't like 'em.'

'Who is Mulgrum?'

'He runs the joint; says he's a Christian pastor, but he ain't no Christian in my book.'

'So he's a friend of Wilhelm Brown?'

'I guess you'd better wait and see the form for yourself.'

Tom was aware that something was bothering Gina. Three times in the last minute she had glanced in her rear mirror. Tom twisted in his seat and with some difficulty looked round. He said nothing to Gina, but now he too had seen the powerful motorbike and its black-leathered rider. It seemed that few vehicles were on this stretch of road and the way ahead was clear. Nothing need deter the bike from overtaking and the man could do so easily without exceeding the speed restrictions.

Gina seemed to read Tom's thoughts as she slowed to forty miles an hour. The motorbike still held station.

'What's wrong with this guy?' said Gina.

'I'm sure it's the same bike I saw last night.' Tom was wide-awake now. If this biker was tracking them he certainly didn't care who knew it.

'Say, can you reach my shoulder bag?'

He turned and with a struggle caught the strap and pulled the exquisite artefact over the top and into his lap.

'My gun's down the bottom,' said Gina. 'Point thirty two, full magazine – you reckon you can use it?'

'No I can't! What in hell are you doing with a thing like that?' Tom was horrified.

'OK, keep it cool. It's mine – I gotta permit. If you can't shoot it we'd best change places.'

'We don't want to shoot anyone. Gina, I am not going to spend the rest of my life in Alcatraz.'

'There ain't no Alcatraz – these days it's a museum. I'll take you there when all this is over.'

'You can't go shooting at people. If you do we'll be in real trouble.'

'Not if that guy tries a hi-jack. This is the States, Tom. It'd be self-defence – all within our rules.'

Tom gave up; here was a culture he didn't comprehend. He fished in the bag and found the gun. It was smaller than he expected and fitted easily in the hand. He examined the cocking mechanism and checked that the safety catch was on. It might be male ego but he preferred the gun to be in his hands.

They crossed the state line into Oregon and refuelled at a station on the outskirts of Portland. The motorbike did not on this occasion follow them onto the precinct. Instead it passed them, motoring slowly down the road. The respite was to be short. Within minutes of the restart it was tucked in behind them again. Gina drove on past Portland for another half-an-hour, before she took a branch road away from the freeway, heading east into the Cascade Mountains. They were in wooded country now, amongst great stands of mature timber stretching as far as the eye could see. In other circumstances Tom would have stopped to explore, but he felt unnerved by the following bike, while Gina seemed focussed on the road ahead. Apart from a crude notice pointing to logging camp there was no sign of the human race; yet the teeming city was less than an hour behind them. Gina had turned the car onto another side road and this time the hard surface petered out after a mile into little more than a dirt track. They bumped and jolted for a further half hour before turning into a side lane marked by a large signboard.

Academy of the Aryan Nation
Principal. The Revd Randell Mulgrum
Strictly no admittance.

'Charming,' Tom muttered. 'Where's our shadow?'

'He's pulled back. I guess he's still there though.'

'Gina – slow down!'

'Why?' she complied, slowing walking pace.

'I'm going to have a word with that bloke.' He released his seat belt, opened the door and dropped onto the roadside.

He stumbled, fell, and rolled over in the dust. The car had stopped ten yards further up the track. He gesticulated urgently to Gina to keep moving. He caught a glimpse of her face, apprehensive and alarmed. But she did as she was ordered and the car drove away round the corner. He heard the gear change as it climbed further up the hill.

Tom clambered to his feet and stood by the roadside listening. For three minutes he stood still, watching – waiting. Keeping to the edge of the trees he began to move back down the road to the place where Gina had last seen their shadow. The bike was parked under a bush a little way past the first bend. A casual passer-by would never have noticed it. Tom moved quickly off the road and into the trees. He began to work through the forest parallel to the road. These hemlocks grew tall, shutting out the light and their dense foliage made movement slow and frustrating. The whole place had a moist, pine-scented smell and the ground was covered in a soft carpet of needles and fallen cones. Tom had a vivid flashback to childhood games in the Forest of Dean. He stopped and froze, just as he used to then. He wondered what creatures roamed these woods; everything seemed as still and peaceful as in those days long ago. He heard the beat of a diesel engine. He managed to catch a glimpse of the vehicle through a gap in the foliage. He saw a pickup truck, a red Toyota Hilux with rough terrain tyres. Two men reclined lazily in the back. They wore combat fatigues and balanced across their knees were automatic weapons. Here was another development that Tom could do without.

What had he let himself in for? A week ago he was an ordinary English farmer; now what? A pathetic amateur sleuth blundering around an American forest, whose only inhabitants were members of some lunatic fascist cult.

It was not easy to move through these trees. The green fronds brushed against his clothing with a rasping noise that must be heard even over the wind in the treetops. Tom stopped, he could see nothing but he knew he should be within yards of the spot where the bike was hidden. He moved slowly step by step until he found a gap in the greenery. So dark had it been under these trees that instinctively he closed his eyes against the glare of the road. Twenty feet away was the biker. At last he was able to take a long look at the man. He was a small, lithe effeminate figure, but something about him spelt perfect physical fitness. Tom had visions of a karate fighter, a latter day Bruce Lee. For the first time Gina's gun in his jacket pocket became a source of comfort. Slowly the biker turned back to his machine and carefully slid the helmet off his head. Tom held his breath; he was about to have a close up of his persecutor's face. With nerves already taut, Tom received as big a shock as he could remember in forty years. The biker was not a martial arts hit man. It was not even a male.

'Hannah!' he gasped.

CHAPTER 20

Hannah dropped her helmet as she turned to face him; it was satisfying that she too had received a shock.

'Hello, Tom.' Her self-control was maddening; she sounded almost bored. 'Where's Mrs Fjortoft?'

'Gone on in the car. Why are you following me – you could've been shot.' He showed her the gun.

'That's a chance I take every day of the year.' She looked back up the road. 'We'd better get under these trees. There's another of their trucks around.'

Tom followed her into the dense shade of the firs. 'You haven't told me why you're following us.'

'For your own good. I've shadowed you ever since you left England. I was on the same flight.'

'I never noticed.'

'You were in top class, courtesy of Fjortoft.'

'If you think I'm protecting Fjortoft, forget it.'

'So you were impressed by Greta.'

'None of your business.'

'I think you see Mr Fjortoft in his true colours.'

'Tell me about this place,' he demanded.

'This is Fjortoft land. The part of his estate he hasn't told you about.'

'So what, he's got property all over the globe.'

'His father built a hunting lodge out here.' She stopped and pulled him further under the trees.

Tom could hear it too. A vehicle was descending the hill. He recognised a Jeep, not unlike the one Gustav Fjortoft used at Crossfield, but this one was camouflaged. Standing in the back was a man. He wore combat overalls and a bush hat; he leant against the swivel mount of a heavy machine gun. The Jeep passed them and disappeared. They waited listening, as its engine faded away.

'Do the authorities know these people are here?' Tom whispered.

'Of course,' she replied in a normal voice. 'But they won't do anything. None of the federal agencies are looking for trouble – not post Waco.'

Tom remembered the Waco siege. Apparently the FBI had grossly over-reacted, alienating moderate public opinion that might have been expected to support them.

'These mountains are full of gun toting nutters,' Hannah continued. 'Over in Montana it's even worse. You'll find eco-warriors and militia-men who think the outgoing President is a space-alien. We're concerned with this lot; Mulgrum's Aryan nation.'

'Nazis?'

'You said it, not me.'

'You know Gus Fjortoft's in there?'

'I guessed he might be; was Mrs Fjortoft taking you to see him?'

'I agreed to listen to his version of the death camp story – that's all.'

'Perhaps you should be getting on up there. The lovely Gina will be worrying about you and I don't want her shouting about a girl on a motorbike.'

'We both thought you were a man. Why did you try and mow me down last night?'

'I could see you were nervous. I thought I'd intensify it.'

'Trying to make a fool of me?' Tom was not pleased.

'I was hoping to wake you to danger. I'm not sure I was the only watcher.'

'I still want to talk to Fjortoft.'

'Go ahead, if Gina has reported to Mulgrum, he'll be expecting you. If you don't turn up he'll come looking for you and I'd much rather he didn't.'

'All right, I'll go and find Gina.' He met her eyes. 'What about you?'

'I'll be around.'

Tom started walking. He was apprehensive certainly, but not frightened. The whole scenario was unreal, dreamlike. The track was steep as it circled around a pine-covered hillside. As he walked, he had glimpses of the chimneys of a house. He was dusty and sweating as he reached the end of the trail. Across the road was a barrier pole and beside it a wooden hut. Beyond was a gate and to either side stretched an eight-foot high fence topped with razor wire. Two guards stood beside the hut under a large signboard.

ACADEMY OF THE ARYAN NATION
Past this point: NO Jews, Afros, Ameroindians, Arabs, Asiatics, Irish, Slavs. NO Sexual Deviants, or Persons With Hereditary Deformity.

‘This is private property, Buster. You got an appointment?’ The nearest guard was a seedy little man with a stubbly chin and dark glasses. He wore jeans and a brown shirt. On his arm was a broad cloth band, red with a white circle and a double flash of lightning. A flag hoisted on a nearby pole bore the same logo. The second guard was equally unprepossessing, though fatter, with a cigar drooping from yellowing teeth. Both carried automatic weapons.

‘I’m with Mrs Fjortoft. I think she came in here a short while back.’

‘Sure, we know the dame – got a nice butt. How come you’re not in the car?’

‘I told her I’d walk the last stretch. Fascinating flora and fauna hereabouts, don’t you know.’ Tom replied. Possibly by playing the stage Limey he could deflect further questions.

‘Aw, nuts,’ said the guard. He began talking into his pocket radio.

‘You gotten an ID, Buster?’

Tom held out his passport.

The guard compared the photograph with the subject in front of him.

He scowled. ‘Can’t you read.’ he pointed at the signboard. ‘It says – no Irish.’

‘I’m English.’

‘O’Malley’s an Irish name.’

‘I was born in Canada but I’m English through and through.’

Tom stated no more than the truth. He was not going to descend to the level of this unwashed oaf. ‘What’s wrong with the Irish?’

‘Mister Mulgrum says they ain’t proper Aryans. Not as bad as Hymies or Nigras, but still not pure.’

Tom sighed. ‘Hadn’t you better check that I’m expected?’

‘Done that already. Mister Mulgrum’s on his way down.’

Tom could already hear a vehicle beyond the line of the wire. It was the same Jeep. It drove through the gate and stopped by the guard hut. The gunner jumped down and walked towards them. He was fat and sweaty and carried a handgun. The driver was a contrast to everyone that Tom had seen so far. He was a slim man, around forty years old, in a nicely tailored blue suit. He had close-cropped greying hair and glasses. He also had a presence unlike the others around him.

‘Good day to you, Sir.’ The accent was American Deep South, refined with the rough edges smoothed. ‘Mrs Fjortoft is worried about you.’

‘There’s no need,’ Tom tried to reply as if he met paramilitaries every day. 'I wanted to look at the woodlands.'

'You'd be safer inside our campus, sir. We've bears around here – I wouldn't want you hurt.'

'Thanks for the warning, but I never went far from the road.'

The man seemed to accept this. 'I'm Randell Mulgrum, principal of our college. Honoured to meet you, Sir.' The handshake was firm as Mulgrum stared into Tom's face. 'Your eyes are blue. That's good – that's real good, but we'll have to find you a better name.'

'I'm very happy with the one I've got.'

Mulgrum ignored him. 'I think Manley would be better. Tom Manley, welcome to our family.'

Tom did not demur. If he had to enter this madhouse it would be prudent to humour the inmates. It was ironic that Mulgrum should choose a Jamaican surname to replace an Irish. He wouldn't let the issue go entirely unchallenged.

'Why don't you like the Irish?'

'Never said I didn't. Mister, I'm a Christian minister. I love all species. Just like I love my dogs and I leave those bears out there alone. I can live with sub-humans too. I just don't like 'em breeding so fast and I don't want 'em in government, raising taxes and interfering in my culture and my Christian way of life.'

Mulgrum's voice had risen. He sounded almost camp and his vowels were rounder. He was also unstable and dangerous. Tom wondered what Christian denomination could conceivably have ordained this mad bigot.

Mulgrum invited Tom into the Jeep. The fat machine-gunner resumed his post and began to track imaginary aircraft. Mulgrum put the vehicle in gear and they moved off through the gate. Tom tried not to panic at the thought of being taken hostage. The mere fact that Fjortoft was willingly in this place condemned him in Tom's eyes. As far as he was concerned his promise to listen to Gus was void.

They drove through more pine forest and then past a greensward laid out for baseball. Finally they reached the house. It was a large flat-roofed building with rounded corners and large multi-pane windows. Art Deco, nineteen thirties, Tom thought. It reminded him of one of those old seaside lidos. The place was surrounded by mown lawns but without flowers or colour of any kind. In front was a gravel square with a white flag pole, flying the same double lightning banner. Like everything else the main entrance was square, with heavy wooden double doors, fronted by wide stone steps. Standing there with Gina by his side was Gustav Fjortoft.

Tom felt confused; emotionally torn in two. Gustav Fjortoft had been much more than an employer. He was a true friend and benefactor; Tom had liked him from the first. Tricia had adored him and she was an infallible judge of character. How could he confront Gus and say that he believed him to be a criminal and a murderer?

'Tom, thank you for coming out here so prompt – I appreciate that. How's things at Crossfield?'

All Tom's resolve had vanished. He found himself grinning and talking banal farming matters as if nothing had changed. How could a child willingly murder one of his fellows? Why didn't this man look like a murderer? Tom had preconceived notions of serial killers. One saw their pictures in the newspapers; there was no doubting their evil. The same primitive logic told him that Gus too should show these facial characteristics. Yet Tom had liked and trusted this man; loved him, in the best sense of the word, would not be too strong.

'We'll talk later,' said Gus. 'I'll fix it so we're alone,' he dropped his voice. 'Some place these punks can't listen.'

Tom could see the Reverend Mulgrum walking toward them clearly intent on breaking up the conversation.

'So, Tom, you've found your friends.' Mulgrum's smile was not mirrored in his eyes.

He looked suspiciously at both Tom and the Fjortofts. 'We've quarters prepared for you.' He tapped Tom on the shoulder and beckoned him to follow.

The entrance hall felt cool and well proportioned with light streaming through the windows. The wooden parquet floor was polished to the point where one could nearly skate on it. On each of four walls was a portrait. The largest was undoubtedly the host. The Reverend Mulgrum dressed in academic robes stared back from the canvas. Knowingly or not, the painter had brilliantly conveyed the paranoia of the sitter. Tom's eyes switched to the next frame. The subject was Adolf Hitler; somehow the room seemed colder.

'Tom, I'd like you to meet Mr John Van Zyl. John this is Tom Manley from England.'

For the first time Tom noticed a young man who had somehow appeared from the shadows. He shook his hand politely. Van Zyl looked like a stereotype American college boy. He was tall, athletic, with tidily groomed fair hair and dressed in casual slacks, sports jacket, and open neck shirt. He could have wandered down some time warp from the nineteen fifties.

'Honoured to meet you, Mr Manley.' The voice was educated Ivy

League.

'John's from an old New York Dutch family – pure descent – no taint,' said Mulgrum. 'He'll show you your quarters.'

'If you would follow me, Sir,' Van Zyl beckoned.

Van Zyl led the way up a wide wooden staircase to a first floor landing that encircled the building like a gallery and opened a door. Inside was a minimalist bedroom, the sort of place one would find in a student's hall of residence. Everything was wooden and polished until it shone.

'Mr Manley, have you luggage?'

'My overnight bag's in Mrs Fjortoft's car – and my name's O'Malley.'

There was no reaction from Van Zyl. 'I'll leave you now, Sir. I'll see your things are sent up.'

Van Zyl vanished closing the door silently. Tom was thankful to be rid of him. Van Zyl had about him an air of obsequious menace. The dandified college boy act concealed something else. Tom could well remember such people from schooldays; those who graduated from pulling the wings off flies, to setting fire to the cat. If the man had any redeeming features they were not apparent. Mulgrum's comic book militia soldiers were one thing. Van Zyl and his sort were infinitely more dangerous.

Tom walked to the window and looked down on the gravel square. The Jeep had parked in the centre facing the entrance. Distantly he could hear singing; for a moment Tom thought it to be a Gregorian chant. Then he recognised the tune; it was the call and response marching song of the American Army. He tried to understand the words but the caller's guttural accent was incomprehensible.

A double line of men was marching onto the square. Tom counted fifteen in each file: an infantry platoon. Their jungle fatigues looked tatty and the march was an unpractised amble. They shouldered their assorted weapons at a dozen different angles. On command the files formed a single line behind the Jeep. Tom noticed that the flagpole had been joined by two more. From one flew the Stars and Stripes and the other the British Union flag.

Tom could see traffic on the road, another open-topped truck followed by an ordinary road car. Somebody rattled a snare drum and the platoon produced a shambling present arms accompanied by a tolerable bugle call. The car halted and a man climbed out. The Reverend Mulgrum strode forward to greet this new arrival. Tom recognised the unmistakable shape of Roland Gannemeade.

The MP stood briefly and doffed his cap to the flags. Tom had never liked this man; now he felt real loathing. He could think of no respectable reason for a British parliamentarian to be in a place like this. He was distracted by a sharp knock on the door of his room.

The new arrival was a young man, around twenty years old and a distinct improvement on the militia thugs. 'Mrs Fjortoft asked me to bring you this.'

This lad was tall, with an aura of physical fitness that marked him out from the others. There was something teasing about him. Tom felt he had seen this man before, but where he couldn't think.

'I'm Craig – Craig East at your service, Sir.'

Now Tom understood. 'You're Gus Fjortoft's son. I've seen your picture in his house.'

'Say, man, keep you voice down. Nobody here knows that.' Craig looked warily up and down the corridor. He moved quickly inside the room. 'I'm real honoured to meet you, Mr O'Malley. My Dad talks about you all the time.' He held out his hand with a firm confident handshake. 'D'you know who this Brit guy is? Why should Mulgrum lay out the red carpet for him?'

'He's Roland Gannemeade. He preaches male supremacy and family values, while kids die at drug parties in his house.'

'Another piece of horse shit to add to the pile.'

'All right, Mr East. Where do you fit into the scheme of things?'

'I'm not part of this outfit from choice. I've infiltrated them and I want to go on living, so keep that to yourself, Mr O'Malley.'

'I thought you were a marine?'

'I'll be a United States marine until the day I die. But I'd like that day to be fighting in battle – not messing with these goons.'

They were both staring out of the window. The militiamen were dispersing, slouching away, many dragging on cigarettes.

'Oh, Jesus,' Craig muttered.

'So I take it you don't approve of these people?'

'I said, they're horse shit.'

'I'm told your father owns this place. Why doesn't he put a stop to it.'

'Of course he'd like to, but it's not that easy. You'll have to ask him yourself.'

'When can I see him?'

'Look, Mr O'Malley. Gina bringing you here wasn't part of the script. It's thrown Mulgrum somewhat and it could put you in danger.'

'Is Fjortoft's half-brother here – the man called Brown?'

'He's not here now, but I guess he's not far away. Father's looking for a showdown with the guy. I think he's come here hoping for just that.'

Tom was trying to digest this and he was aware of sounds in the building.

'Please, could you tell your father that I must see him. He asked me to come to America and I still don't know why.'

'Sure, I'll try and fix it for you to see him while Mulgrum's out of the way.' Craig stiffened, half saluted, and slipped from the room.

Tom found a shower and toilet at the end of the passage. Refreshed and in a change of clothes he began to plan. He wondered what he should do with Gina's gun. He had no intention of using the thing, so he put it on top of a corner cupboard pushing it until it touched the wall. Shortly afterwards he heard a tap on the door; it was Van Zyl.

'Mr Manley, the Reverend Mulgrum would like to speak with you. Would you come this way please, Sir.'

Van Zyl led down the stairs and along a corridor that branched off the entry hall. At the far end was a militiaman guarding a door. Van Zyl knocked and entered. Mulgrum sat facing them behind a heavy wooden desk.

'Take a seat, Mr Manley.' Mulgrum waved him to a leather-backed chair.

It reminded Tom of being summoned by his college principal. That time, thirty years ago, when he had been found in his future wife's room after permitted hours.

'Mr Manley, who are you and why are you here?' Mulgrum's eye contact was unfriendly.

'You ask me that?' Tom stared back. 'I don't know myself why. My employer, Gustav Fjortoft, summoned me to America and his wife drove me here.'

'Are you a religious man?'

Tom was taken aback. 'I believe there's a power behind things that we don't understand. Most farmers would tell you that.'

'I would commend you to study the Bible, Sir.' Mulgrum's manner was intense. 'We may not be far from the great day. God Almighty will take those that are true to his Book and are of pure race.'

'All in one day?'

'Indeed he will, all in the same minute of the same day. The great rapture will be the day of our Lord's second coming. The consequences will be terrible for those that are not chosen.'

'Does that include me?'

'Mr Manley, you may be among those rejected and that saddens me. I would recommend you study the Revelations of John.'

'What happens to those left behind?'

'They will suffer the consequences. Think, who are the people of intelligence? Who controls our industries, our power supplies our airlines and railroads?' Mulgrum stared at Tom, inviting a reply.

'See here,' he continued. 'When the hour comes, good Aryan folk will be taken. Think of that, captains of airliners, drivers of freight trains, truckers and ordinary car drivers. Their craft will be abandoned, thousands will crash and burn. Nuclear plants will go critical, cities will blaze while calls to fire-fighters go unanswered. So great will be the vengeance of God and the days of tribulation to follow.'

Tom could think of no rational reply.

'Think of it.' Mulgrum's voice had a husky quality; he seemed to have forgotten Tom was there. 'The surgeon poised to operate, the moment comes and he is taken, maybe the others with him. If the patient is not of the chosen, he will die.'

'The last surgeon to operate on me was Jewish,' Tom finally intervened. He knew he was provoking Mulgrum but he'd had enough of this insanity.

'Jews will die, they are disfigured mutant souls who have invaded human bodies. Their doom was sealed when they killed the Lord Jesus.'

'Wasn't he a Jew?'

Mulgrum drew in his breath; he was clearly very angry. Tom wished he had kept his mouth shut. He suspected his own fate could be on a knife-edge.

Mulgrum stood up. 'Come with me.'

Tom followed him. The guard on the door made a clumsy attempt at a salute; Mulgrum ignored him. At the end of the passage was a feature completely out of character; a studded wooden door set in a Gothic arch. The room was a chapel, although unlike any that Tom had seen. The whine of electric motors and a smell of polish that was almost overwhelming greeted him. It seemed that among other things Mulgrum, like Hitler, had a fetish for polished wood. Two persons were operating the polishers. Both were women; the first, apart from Gina, that Tom had seen in this place. They wore ankle length woollen skirts and blue cotton tops with mutton leg sleeves. Both had hair perms in nineteen sixties style. They switched off their machines and stood watching the men with a deferential poise, like children in a school activities day.

'Keep right on with your work, ladies. Don't mind us,' Mulgrum called.

Tom took in the surroundings. The chapel was a long bare room filled with wooden pews. At the far end was a raised dais and lectern. Behind was the forked lightning flag and beside it, draped in black mourning ribbon, was a portrait of Adolf Hitler.

'Mr Manley, see here.' Mulgrum touched him on the arm and pointed at another painting hanging near the door. It was a strange highly coloured manic affair, its style a mix of William Blake and Hieronymous Bosch. In the centre a tall Christ-like figure stood proud from a background of fires, lightning bolts and black clouds. From behind broken walls and stunted bushes there peered distorted figures of goblin-like humanoids. Those nearest the Christ figure were flinching and covering their eyes.

Mulgrum stood in front of the painting. 'Here are illustrated many truths. Jesus was a Galilean, a good Aryan people whom fate had compelled to live among Jews. Galileans were the true people of God, descendants of those believers led out of Egypt by Moses.' Mulgrum's voice had a smouldering intensity. Tom was no Middle East scholar, but he knew enough to know that Mulgrum was turning facts into fantasy, with the zeal of one who believed the world to be flat; which very likely he did.

Someone coughed behind them. It was Van Zyl trying to attract Mulgrum's attention.

'Excuse me, Mr Manley,' said Mulgrum, 'I must go now. Please feel free to take a walk, but keep away from the firing ranges.'

Mulgrum and Van Zyl left the chapel. Tom, to his overwhelming relief, was alone.

CHAPTER 21

Tom closed the door of his room, sat on the bed, once more holding Gina's gun. He felt a comfort with it in his hand although he still wondered if he could really use it. He could hear footsteps in the passage, so he stuffed the gun back in his bag and waited. The steps ceased outside, followed by a tap on the door; it was Van Zyl. Something about this man unsettled Tom. Mulgrum was mad, Tom had no doubt of that, but Van Zyl had an aura of calculated cruelty. He suspected the man would kill without conscience and without a second thought.

'Mr Manley,' Van Zyl was coldly obsequious. 'Mr Mulgrum would be honoured if you would join him and the company at dinner.'

'Whatever you say.'

'Please be ready at eight o'clock. I'll tell Militiaman East to call on you.' Van Zyl withdrew or rather he flitted silently from the room.

Tom knew he would have to be wary. He might have deceived Mulgrum, but he had not fooled Van Zyl. That man would be watching and waiting; somehow this night he knew he must escape.

Craig appeared on time dressed in a magnificent tuxedo. Tom wore the dark suit in which he had travelled to America.

Craig looked him over. 'Yeah, you'll pass.' Craig opened the door and glanced at the landing.

'Mr O'Malley, I'll try and get you to see Dad later.'

'When's later?'

'After dinner when the boys have swallowed enough liquor. Wait for us to show.'

Craig pushed Tom into the dining hall towards a knot of people all with glasses in hand. One of the women he had seen in the chapel offered him a drink from a tray. Tom took a cautious sip; an insipid fruit concoction and definitely non-alcoholic. He stood on the edge of the group carefully avoiding eye contact. Tom's spirits sank as Gannemeade spotted him.

'Mr O'Malley, it's nice to run into one's constituents in a far-off land.' Gannemeade had the doorstep politician's smirk.

'My employer owns the freehold of this place and he wanted to see me.' Tom was cool but polite.

He needed to probe; he wanted questions answered. Did Gannemeade know about the drug culture in his own house?

'Ah, Gustav Fjortoft, the director who made *The Bear*.'

'Yes.'

'A most interesting man, I've no doubt. I must pay a call on him sometime. He lives in, let me think, Crossfield, is it?'

This was crazy, Gannemeade knew damn well where Fjortoft lived. Tom wondered where this was leading.

Gannemeade sniffed. 'My daughter was friendly with a student from Crossfield.'

'Really?' Tom knew where Gannemeade was coming from now.

'A nasty little Irish-French half-breed.' He sniffed again.

This was provocation, a declaration of war. Tom hid his fury but he resolved that one day Gannemeade would pay for that remark.

'Your daughter's a student?'

'Was – she's dead.' It was a bald statement almost neutral.

'I'm sorry.' Tom meant it. He knew nothing of Jessica's mother and from all Andy had said the girl was not like her father.

'Yes,' Gannemeade took a gulp of his fruit juice and grimaced. 'She went to the bad – leftist views, mixed with blacks and the little half-breed. It was probably him that gave her drugs.'

Tom wasn't standing for that. 'Can you substantiate where she got drugs?'

'I wasn't there, I was overseas. My daughter used the opportunity to let all those scum into my house. She paid for it – subject closed!' He turned his back on Tom and began a conversation with Van Zyl.

Somewhere near at hand came the boom of a dinner gong. Mulgrum led the way to a dais with a high table, rather like a college refectory. He invited Tom to sit on his left. The militiamen were entering in orderly files all wearing tuxedos, mostly ill fitting. They could have passed for a convention of nightclub bouncers. Through an archway in the far wall Tom could see another table occupied solely by women, eight of them, presumably the wives of militia leaders. Their attempts at formal glamour failed miserably, apart from one. Tom saw Gina in an elegant strapless gown. Of Gus he could see no sign.

Through the doorway came a procession led by six women of the same soberly dressed type. Following them came a procession of younger serving girls; all were drab and zombie-like.

Mulgrum noticed his interest. 'We don't permit women in our militias, but we allow them to do their duty as comfort girls. All of pure race of course – good breeders.'

Tom examined the plate he had been given. It was a mixture of rice, beans and sauce; a vegetarian dish and wholly unexpected. He remarked as much to Mulgrum. It might seem rude but Tom was past caring.

'Many great men were vegetarians,' said Mulgrum, 'including Adolf Hitler and he was a great man. You British should never have fought him. – you were suckered by that Jew Churchill.'

Tom could think of several robust replies to that but he let it go. Frankly he wondered how much more he could take. The Mad Hatter's tea party had nothing compared to this gathering. He looked around the hall. The nearest militiamen were eating a meat dish and most were broaching beer cans.

'Sure, we have to give the foot soldiers meat,' said Mulgrum. 'They wouldn't fight well without it – same thing with liquor. But officers don't touch it – got to keep clear heads. In this we follow the teachings of the Lord Jesus.'

The oldest trick in the book, thought Tom. Keep the men fuzzled with booze and they won't question the leadership.

'I've another guest due here tonight,' said Mulgrum. 'Dr Hellmunt, a distinguished man of science. My friend Fjortoft tells me your daughter is a doctor.'

'Where is Fjortoft? I'm here to talk to him – he sent for me.'

'Mr Fjortoft asked to be excused. It seems he's got gut trouble.'

'Really.' Gus didn't seem to be in bad health earlier. Craig had hinted that his father was under restraint.

The militiamen began to thump the tables in unison. An odd chant rolled around the hall. It was one word: "Chief", shouted repeatedly. Tom glanced at Mulgrum. The chief was positively preening. The absurd puffed up fuehrer with his little private army. Mulgrum stood and raised a hand; instantly the hall subsided into hushed attention. Every eye in the place was fixed on this man. Mulgrum opened his mouth then hesitated. He was staring towards the back of the hall. A militiaman, this one dressed in uniform, had run into the room. He was red faced and clearly out of breath.

'Mister Mulgrum, sir, there's intruders in the woods. Same lot of hymies as last time.'

The dining hall emptied in a shambling chaotic rush as the militiamen streamed from the building, shouting incoherently. Tom looked for Craig but couldn't see him.

The whole mob, now armed with an assortment of guns, streamed towards the entry gate. Two pickup trucks loaded with militia roared past. A more un-military shambles would be hard to imagine. Tom followed, keeping in the shadow of trees and bushes. The raging mob was too preoccupied to notice him.

The pole at the entrance was raised. A short distance down the road stood a parked car; beside it on the ground a uniformed militiaman nursed a cut head. Another body lay doubled up and twitching. The leading truck pushed its way to the front, its headlights making a lurid tableau of the scene. Tom could see Van Zyl in the passenger seat.

The incoming car had not stopped from choice; all four tyres were flat. Behind it lay a spiked chain, in police jargon a "stinger". Beside the car stood an elderly man; expensively suited, he looked somewhat out of place. He blinked uneasily in the oncoming lights. Mulgrum had descended from the second truck and was addressing this new-comer.

'Doctor Hellmunt, I can't believe this – I can't.' Mulgrum was deferential, even nervous.

'Never mind, Reverend. I'm a great survivor and I'm glad to be here.' Hellmunt's accent sounded English with a touch of Mid-European.

'Men,' shouted Mulgrum. 'Search the timber, every inch of it – shoot on sight.'

The troops needed no second invitation. They dispersed into the trees in a babble of shouting. Whoever was there would have no difficulty escaping; the incompetence of Mulgrum's men was breath-taking.

Tom watched Van Zyl as the man walked towards the disabled car. Two more militiamen were treating their colleague with the cut head. Van Zyl ignored them. He walked to the wounded man on the ground. Tom had seen the prone figure trying to crawl away. It was agonising and made him feel uneasy and slightly sick. Van Zyl walked casually to stand over the twitching figure. He pointed a handgun against the neck and fired a single shot. The body convulsed and then lay still.

Tom stood mesmerised. He was witness to a cold-blooded murder and he was sickened. He stiffened with shock as a hand touched him on the arm. It was Craig.

'Sorry, Tom, but it's time for you to run.' Craig's formal tone had gone. He spoke quietly while appearing to look elsewhere. 'Walk back to the lodge and go to your room. I'll be with you soonest I can.'

Tom sat on the edge of the bed. He had made a quick change into jeans and sweater and he wore his waxed jacket with its poacher's pocket. In this recess he had concealed Gina's gun. Outside the window came the sounds of moving vehicles, accompanied by shouts and the occasional gunshot. It seemed an age before Craig reappeared with Gina.

'Big trouble,' said Craig. 'There's a group in the timber. I've seen them before – got to talk to their leader once, British guy by the way he talked. Never thought they'd try something like this.'

'What's it about?'

'They were out to get this Hellmunt. Tried to abduct him but they blew it.'

'You saw Van Zyl murder that man?'

'Sure, he's a killer, done it before; means nothing to him.'

'These people in the woods. Was there a girl called Hannah?'

'Hey, man, what d'you know about it?'

'Hannah's an Israeli woman journalist. I saw her in Seattle.'

'I don't know about Israelis. It's a New York Jewish group, but their leader's an English guy.'

'What did he look like?'

'Kinda tall, dark hair tied back. Pretty boy – looked like he oughta be in the movies.'

'I think I've met him – there can't be two to fit that description. In England he's called Joel. What do you know about these people?'

'They're as crazy as Mulgrum, and they're mighty keen on this Hellmunt guy.'

'Could he be the half-brother?'

Craig smiled. 'I leave you to make your own speculations.'

Tom looked at Gina. 'Are you staying here?'

'I'll come with you, Tom. I can't stand this crazy place.'

Tom looked to Craig. 'We can't take off cross country with her dressed like that.'

'Can't you fix her up?'

'Tom, you got a spare pair of slacks?' asked Gina.

'They won't fit.'

She snorted and began to wriggle out of the dress and its underpinning; Craig turned away, embarrassed. Tom groped in his bag while Gina stood naked apart from tiny thong briefs. Tom threw her his spare jeans and a T-shirt.

'Craig, we've got to get out but where do we make for?'

'Listen, there's a Toyota Land Cruiser, full gas tank, and they've left the keys in. It's parked round the side by the kitchens. Take this,' he handed Tom a plastic orienteering compass. 'Head east for the mountains. There's a trail that starts far side of the sports field.' He looked at Gina. 'You ready step-ma?'

Gina was still struggling to belt the trousers, the bottoms of which were rolled to her ankles. Craig produced a knife and cut the cord from the window blind. Gina threaded it through the waistband and pulled it tight; it was clear this proud fashionable woman was deeply humiliated.

'Craig,' said Tom. 'I'm grateful for what you're doing but will you be OK?'

'I'm all right, Mulgrum thinks I'm a dishonoured marine and he's mighty proud to recruit me. Not Van Zyl – I know he's watching me, but if he tries anything, he's taking on the wrong guy.'

'What'll you do if he catches you?'

'I said, I'm a marine. They teach us to kill people.' Craig opened the door and looked out. 'Come on, you guys – let's go.'

'Wait,' said Tom. 'What about your father?'

'He'll be safer with you and Gina out the way – now go!'

He led them along the passage to a fire door. Craig pushed it open and they found themselves on a balcony leading to the metal steps of a fire escape.

'Can't stay longer,' Craig whispered. 'East of here's an Indian reservation. Head for it, you'll be safe as long as they don't think you're Mulgrum's goons.'

'Understood.'

'Right, down the steps, then round to your left. You'll see the truck by the kitchen bay. God bless you both.' Before they could reply he had turned and was gone.

The building's lights were ablaze but the place seemed deserted. In the far distance there was shouting and the odd gunshot. Ahead of them exactly as Craig had said was the outline of a four-wheel-drive vehicle. They reached it in seconds. Beside them was a flight of steps leading to the basement. Tom could see the brightly lit window of a kitchen; this too was deserted. He reached for the car's door handle.

'Hold it there, Mister.' The voice came from behind. Tom turned slowly; standing in the shadow was Van Zyl. Tom felt cold with shock. Van Zyl seemed almost to have an ability to dematerialise and reappear at will. He was holding an enormous handgun and Tom knew him to be a killer.

'Where were you hiding?' Tom snapped. 'Since when has it been good manners to spy on guests?'

'Not if the guest is a goddam spy. Come on – who sent you here?' Van Zyl waved the gun menacingly.

Tom stood still not daring to move a finger or even flick an eyelid. Slowly Van Zyl lowered the heavy gun until it was pointing at the ground. At that moment Gina sprang at him.

It was as sudden as it was unexpected. Gina moved silently and Van Zyl, unaware of her, paid the price. She leapt on the man's back with the athleticism of desperation and clenched her hands around his neck. Van Zyl swung round and the gun fired into the dirt. Now he screamed, a cry combining pain and fear. Gina had her long manicured fingernails embedded in Van Zyl's eyes. She had wrapped her legs around his waist locking her feet together. Van Zyl cried out again, staggered and toppled to the ground. He rolled over, blood streaming down his face. Tom gasped in disgust. One of Van Zyl's eyeballs had been half forced from its socket. The assault had blinded him in that eye at least. Gina was on her feet staring at the body. She was shaking, all her manic energy gone. Tom lifted her bodily and dropped her in the passenger seat. He could hear shouting from the nearby trees and see running figures speeding towards the lodge. Tom picked up the gun, climbed into the driver's seat and turned the ignition key. The engine started first time.

CHAPTER 22

The Land Cruiser drummed along the trail, eating away the miles. Tom could count on years of rough terrain driving, but he needed to concentrate, as the track was potholed and eroded by rain. He was concerned only to cover as much distance as possible before Mulgrum could organise a pursuit. That would depend on Van Zyl. The man had been semi-conscious and in a poor state. Tom felt no twinge of guilt about that. Van Zyl was the most evil individual he had ever encountered; he was indifferent whether the man lived or not. Gina slumped in the passenger seat had yet to utter a word.

'You all right?' he asked.

'I'm OK.'

'Thanks for what you did. You shook me, let alone Van Zyl. He's lost an eye, I think.'

'Don't ask me to feel sorry.' Her words were barely audible above the drone of the engine.

'I don't like running out on Gus and Craig,'

'They'll be OK. Mulgrum won't touch Gus, and Craig can look after himself.'

'Gina, we're heading east because that's the only way we can go. Do you know of any villages out this way – any population whatever?'

'Nobody lives out here but a few hicks.' Gina used the term with all the contempt of a New England sophisticate.

The gloomy pines shut in the way on either side. In a couple of places, brushwood and broken branches littered the surface. He could only hope that no fallen trunks blocked the road because the trees were too dense to allow the car to leave the trail. The track ahead was rising steeply. Tom knew from memory that in front of them lay mountainous country, the foothills of the ranges that the early pioneers had crossed with such hardship. Whether they would find sanctuary was in the lap of the gods.

They had been running for an hour and the trees were fewer. They were moving into a country of heath land, not unlike parts of Surrey. Tom's lights caught a reflection: glass and the outline of a building. A hundred yards further and he could see an area of cleared ground, a range of derelict buildings and a broken conveyor on stilts. He stopped and climbed out. Gina moved to follow but he told her bluntly to stay in the car.

It took Tom all of five minutes to ascertain that the place was abandoned. The only building with a semblance of a roof had its door secured with a rusting padlock. He wasn't sure what the complex had been, probably a sawmill. Reluctantly he returned to the car and resumed driving.

The gradient was steep and the track now entirely obscured. The ground was still passable but covered in loose sand and stones. Trees were sparse and Tom could see a light frost gleaming on the vegetation. They must now have reached a thousand foot altitude; probably more. He stopped and climbed out. The moon was bright enough for him to use the little compass. He stood for a while wondering what to do. Ahead loomed a massive hill with a skyline that seemed miles above him. He knew this was an illusion distorted by darkness.

'Tom, there's lights – they're after us.'

Below in the forest were headlights and judging by their speed they were four-wheel drive trucks on a mission. Inwardly Tom cursed himself for the time wasted.

'We'd better move.'

The terrain was awful. The topsoil was loose and covered with boulders. Tom spun the wheel to avoid a jagged piece of stone. Gina squealed with fright as the vehicle slewed across the slope at an angle, so steep that Tom too felt a qualm.

'Look back,' he ordered. 'Where are they?'

'Coming out the trees past the sawmill.' Gina sounded scared.

He concentrated solely on driving, the car twisting and lurching as the wheels spun on the uneven surface. With difficulty he fought his way to the summit of the first slope. In front of him he could see a short plateau and then an even steeper hill. He glanced back to see the headlights of two pursuers; Mulgrums's trucks presumably. He knew that these vehicles, with their lower centre of gravity and off-road tyres, would be more than a match for the Land Cruiser. He put the car in gear and began to pick his way across the flat ground. He reached the next hillside just as the beams of the pursuing headlights lit the sky.

This new slope was daunting. Tom would never normally have attempted such a climb. The vegetation was sparse but the rocks fewer. It took fifteen minutes to climb the mountainside. It was probably around five hundred feet of what sometimes seemed like sheer cliff. Tom had to keep moving. If he stalled the engine or lost momentum in any other way they would be done for. At times the front wheels lifted from the ground. Tom felt cold fright as he imagined the Land Cruiser toppling over backwards. He could see nothing in his rear mirror only the awesome drop behind. Slowly the top crept nearer. They were yards from the summit. He could see it in the headlights; half a minute more and they would make it.

Something slammed into the rear of the car; metal on metal like the blows of a sledgehammer. Tom saw a line of dust streaking away to his right. Without warning, the car slewed sideways. Tom fought to stay straight and level but the momentum had died. The front wheels spun wildly as the vehicle climbed slowly over the edge of the summit. Tom pushed down the accelerator but the car failed to respond as it settled into a hollow. He could smell burning rubber; then the engine stalled.

'Gina out! Come on, make it quick – they've shot out our tyres.' They both stumbled and fell on the ground. 'Come on, follow me.'

A pile of stones lay to the left not far from the edge of the slope; Tom sprinted to it. Gina followed and flung herself down beside him. He realised with a shock that she was barefoot.

Far below, he could hear a truck grinding up the mountainside. Its lights below them were probing the sky. A red light winked at him as a hail of bullets swept the hilltop to their right.

Gina tugged at his arm. 'You got my gun?'

Much good that would be. Mulgrums's men had a machine gun. Then he remembered; Van Zyl's heavy calibre weapon was still in the Land Cruiser. Gina squealed in alarm as he stood up and raced back to the car. He knew he was in a state of near madness. He reached the car and dropping on hands and knees he groped for the gun. With a grunt of satisfaction he found it. The gun was a 44 Magnum, a huge cannon of a weapon. Stooping low, he ran back to the rocks. He knew no fear; indeed he had no feelings of reality. He seemed to be detached watching himself in some dream world. He saw a brief vision of Boxtree Farm and the quiet Hampshire countryside; that too faded.

Below he could hear the scream of overheating engines and spinning tyres. Tom examined the pistol. It weighed heavily in his hand with its exaggerated long barrel and revolving six-shot chamber. Tom sneaked a quick look over the edge, as once more not far away, bullets raked the crest. A beam of white light swept the hillside. It was a handheld halogen searchlight. He steadied the gun aimed at the light and pulled the trigger. The kickback was vicious and unexpected, as was the report that left his ears singing. Where the bullet went he had no idea. Tom surprised himself with his inner calm. He remembered one had to grip the gun with both hands and aim low. Secondly he would have to hold his nerve and wait until Mulgrums's men were close enough to present a real target. He risked another look over the rocks. He worried that the men might abandon the vehicle and try and rush the crest on foot. He was banking on the militiamen being too slobbish and unfit. He risked another look. The truck was below him traversing a shelf in the hillside. Tom could see it in the glare of the moonlight and its own lights. He stood, gripped the gun and extended his arms. He aimed at a point between the ground and the side of the truck. He fired and the gun slammed upwards. He felt a savage joy as he heard the shot smack home, metal tearing metal. The truck reached the end of the traverse and turned upwards pointing straight at him. The hunting light was sweeping the length of the crest. In seconds it would find him. Again he gripped the gun, exhaled, and aimed straight into the approaching lights. Three times he pulled the trigger until finally the gun clicked empty. All five of his shots had gone. Tom hurled the pistol down the slope and fell flat. He heard a new sound, the engine racing accompanied by a hissing sound. There came shouts, followed by a slithering bumping noise. Below him he could see the truck's lights cartwheeling down the mountain. Bouncing ahead of it went the halogen light. The truck reached the flat ground, with a single metallic crunch, then an eerie silence.

'What's happened?' asked Gina.

'I think I may have killed someone.' The realisation hit him like cold water. 'I hit the truck and then the driver lost it.'

Gina put an arm around him. 'Tom, honey, you were great – like James Bond.'

'I don't feel it.' His mouth was dry as he began to shiver convulsively. 'Have I really killed a man?'

'More than one, I hope. Don't worry about those punks – they're better dead.'

'It makes me a murderer.'

'No it doesn't. They fired first – it was self-defence.' She started to giggle a trifle hysterically. 'You've me for a witness. Oh boy, when we report this to the Feds they'll have to do something about Mulgrum.'

'Why haven't they years ago? For Christ's sake, Gina – what sort of country is this?'

'It's a great country, that's what! Don't you play the patronising

Limey with me, Tom O'Malley – I don't buy it.'

Tom gently pushed her away. 'We're not out of trouble – listen.'

From below came shouts accompanied by the engine of the second truck. If a new assault came they would have to run and find somewhere to hide. For five minutes he watched and listened. Then he heard the sounds he hoped for; the second truck driving away down to the forest trail.

'I think we've won,' he said. 'All thanks to you.'

'Why me? It was you shot them.'

'I'm thinking of Van Zyl. If he'd been there he'd never have let them turn tail and run.' He stood up and pulled her to her feet.

'Tell me what we do now.'

'We don't stay here, that's for sure. We go some place else.'

Tom had been too preoccupied to notice the cold; now he was shivering. They were stranded miles from any known habitation without food or shelter and very little clothing. They might well have seen off their pursuers but at the price of exposure and starvation. He kept these thoughts to himself.

'Come on, let's go back to the truck.'

The Land Cruiser was useless; one glance was enough to see that. The rear tyres were ripped to shreds and the fuel tank had ruptured leaking diesel onto the ground. A petrol-driven vehicle could well have exploded in ball of fire. Gina had climbed inside for shelter. She was shaken and visibly trembling with cold and shock. He must find her some warm clothing. He searched the back seat and sighed with relief as he found a camouflage combat jacket. It was too big for him but it would serve. He pulled off his waxed waterproof and handed it to Gina. He gave the combat top a grimace of distaste and put it on. He looked behind the seat and found a grey army-style blanket and a shoulder bag, containing a dozen cans of Budweiser. In a last resort they would have some liquid.

'You're right,' he said. 'We can't stay here – Mulgrum will be back.'

'Yeah, I guess so.' Gina sounded distant and remote.

'We're going to have to walk. Where are your shoes?'

'At Mulgrum's. Couldn't walk in them anyway – they're my Guccis – I threw 'em away.'

'I wish you hadn't,' he tried not to sound severe. 'I'd better rip up this blanket. You can tie strips around your feet.'

'No way, we'll need that to wind around ourselves if we stop. I'll be OK – just so long as we keep moving.'

'Are you sure?' This was difficult ground and he didn't fancy carrying her.

'I was born to it. Never wore shoes when I was a kid except when the snows came.' She was emphatic.

Tom left it at that; time would tell.

The terrain was all uphill and made of loose sand and small rocks. Gina strode along with seemingly no problems. It must have been bitterly cold for her but she made no complaint. Tom offered her the blanket to wrap around her shoulders, but she refused it. She would be all right, she said, as long as she kept moving. Tom looked at his watch and was surprised to see that it was only ten minutes past midnight. So much had happened in so short a time.

'What has Gus told you about the camp in Poland?' It wasn't the most tactful question he knew, but he wanted answers.

'He says his stepfather ran it. Gus didn't like the guy – I believe him.' She sounded vehement and on the edge of tears.

'All right, love, I don't suppose he did. What about Wilhelm?'

'He was the man's real son, the blue-eyed boy. Both the other two had to follow him.'

'What other two?'

'Gus and the other half-brother, Albert.'

'Follow him in what?'

'Wilhelm killed his friend, his special playmate. That was the Josef that he shouts about in those dreams.'

'Do you know what part Gus played?'

'What could he do? Oh leave it, Tom. I've been through enough today – just leave it.' She was crying for real now.

Tom didn't want to increase her distress. He doubted she knew the answer that really mattered. Had Gus handled the needle himself?

Suddenly she spoke again. 'The other brother, Albert, Gus liked him – they were close.'

'I heard he was dead.'

'How did you hear?' She sounded suspicious; accusing.

'That journalist, the one probing into Gus's past. She said there were two half-brothers and one had been killed in an air raid.' Tom hoped this excuse would suffice; he would not mention Greta Little.

She seemed to accept this. 'I've got a feeling Gus didn't tell me all the truth about Albert. I think the guy may still be alive and Gus knows it.' She walked on now clearly in discomfort. 'I tell you something. All these people are mighty keen to make Gus leave England; that's the real reason they're intimidating us. My guess is that brother Wilhelm lives in England and not too far away from Crossfield.'

Tom gave up; it was all very puzzling. 'How are your feet?'

'Kinda sore, if you must know. I'm not as hard as once I was.'

The moonlight lit her face; she grinned ruefully at him. His admiration for this woman was growing by the minute. He had long dismissed her as a witless bimbo and he felt ashamed. He didn't want to alarm her, but he knew they had reached a critical point in their march. If they stopped moving, hypothermia would take them before morning. They needed somewhere out of this biting wind. He was feeling thirsty and he guessed Gina was too. The beer cans in his shoulder bag seemed tantalising but he had a feeling the contents would do them more harm than good. He said nothing as they walked on into a new flat wilderness.

He could see vegetation here; a sort of short pampas grass. He had no idea of their altitude but breathing seemed harder. To add to these other woes the terrain had become damp. They were walking into some kind of wetland, by no means impassable but the water was leaching into his shoes. It was his turn to suffer as Gina forged ahead.

'Say,' she said. 'There's gotta' be a stream around here. I could use a drink.'

'Don't talk about it.'

Tom didn't want to raise their hopes but he had heard something. Away to their left was a rocky outcrop almost a mini-hill standing isolated on the plain. He could definitely hear something, a musical, rippling sound. A sound he had heard a hundred times before: the water feature in the Crossfield Manor Garden Centre.

'It's a spring – follow me.'

He ran, splashing over the moist surface following his ears towards the sound. He felt a pang of apprehension that this might be an hallucination. Not so. In a hollow under the jutting base of the rock bubbled a little spring of clear water.

He knelt and scooped the delicious icy cold liquid into his mouth. Gina had flopped down beside him and was burying her face in the waters. She rolled over on her back and grinned at him.

'Say, Tom, I thought these parts were all desert?'

'If I remember my geography it's this side of the ranges that catches the rain off the Pacific. Once you cross the high mountains it's desert.'

'Say, my feet feel real sore. Can't we find somewhere to rest?'

'I agree, we can't go on – let's look around.'

Tom began to examine the rock. It was smaller than he'd first thought but had deep fissures worn by time and weather right into its base.

'Hi,' called Gina. 'Someone's had a camp fire.'

She was right; deep in one of the fissures was a neat little grate of rough stones with a metal grill and the remains of a wood fire.

'We're not the first here anyway which is something to cheer about.' He yawned, he felt very tired now the adrenaline rush had gone. He distantly remembered an essay that Lucy had written about hypothermia. He recognised the symptoms in himself all too well. Gina must be even colder.

'Let's get into this place as far as we can – at least we'll be out of the wind.'

The fissure ran for some thirty feet, narrowing to a cleft at least forty feet high, and no more than two feet across. At last they were protected from the wind.

'Tom!' Gina grabbed his arm. 'Look, there's a light – no, it's gone again.'

'Where?'

Surely to God Mulgrums's men couldn't have reached here already? Then he too saw it. A point of warm yellow light glowed across the landscape. Tom fumbled for the pocket compass. 'North plus ten degrees.'

'What is it?'

'Not sure but it's stationary.'

Slowly the light faded and now Tom knew what he was seeing. The light had a distinct rectangular shape: a door being opened and shut. Somewhere out here in this wilderness was a house.

'What do we do?' asked Gina.

'We stay until daybreak. We're in no state to walk any further. That light could be miles away.'

Tom set down the shoulder bag and pulled out the tightly folded blanket.

'We'll roll up together – share our warmth until daylight.'

'Say, that sounds good.' Gina flung her arms around him. 'You'd better take those wet shoes off.' She was serious now.

'That's true – my socks are soaking. I nearly offered them for you to walk in earlier.'

She laughed. 'That's like the Bible. "Greater love hath no man;

that he gives up his socks to his wife".'

'And you're not my wife young lady – behave.' They clung together laughing. Both were becoming light-headed.

Under the blanket it was utterly miserable and bitterly cold. Tom could find no comfortable position on the rocky ground.

'Tom, are you awake? Gina whispered in his ear.

'Yes, try and sleep.'

'I can't. Say, Tom, sweetheart – make love to me.'

'You've got to be joking.' The woman really was incorrigible.

'No, it's something medical I once heard. I think it could help us.'

Already she was loosening his clothing and reaching into his groin. Her hand was warm and in spite of everything he felt himself arouse to her. She wriggled out of her oversize jeans. Tom found himself gently rolled onto his back. The blanket above formed a tent as Gina kneeling astride thrust him deep inside her. It was incredible but true, that when she had finished they somehow lay together and slept sound and warm for the rest of the night.

The sun was shining. Tom opened his eyes and closed them against the glare. His head ached, as did every bone in his body. He reached out and pulled the blanket tighter around him. Gina gave a soft moan and huddled closer. The whole of yesterday's horror returned to Tom in a total recall. At least they had survived the night and now the sun was definitely warming the rocky cleft. It was time they searched for the house they had seen.

He thought he heard something. He lay still listening. Yes, there it was again: a scraping sound like small footsteps. Tom froze in alarm. Could it be the bears that Mulgrum had warned him about? So concerned with human enemies he hadn't thought of wild animals. He reached for Gina's gun lying on the ground beside him.

The thing was moving closer; the light pattering sound was too small for a bear. Could it be a lynx? He sat up and stared at the entrance of the cleft. A figure stood there. Tom relaxed with an audible sigh of relief. It was a small boy, probably aged no more than seven or eight. He was the first person that Tom had seen since coming to America who wore a cowboy hat. The rest of him was clad in a little logging jacket, jeans and tiny rubber boots. With a round face and shock of curly brown hair he put Tom in mind of a hobbit. Only the point two-two rifle, that the child carried casually in the crook of his arm, spoilt the illusion.

Tom grinned cheerfully. 'Hello, who are you?'

The boy tilted his head. 'Hi, I'm Mitch.' His face creased into a huge smirk. 'I guess I know what you folks are doing.'

CHAPTER 23

Lucy had promised her father to call daily at Boxtree and collect his mail. Three days had passed since his departure and she had heard nothing. She felt both worried and annoyed. He could at least have reported a safe arrival. The police guard at the farm had been reduced, but the Mormons were still watching.

Ed, the afternoon guard appeared. 'In the office, Miss Lucy, there's an email for you.'

'To me – who from?'

'Your pa.'

'What's he say?'

'Didn't look too close – none of my business. The site's some place in Oregon.' Ed began to put on his jacket. 'Miss Lucy, d'you know we've TV people picketing the Manor?'

'What's happened?'

'Zeb says there's two TV vans parked there. The guys are setting up satellite dishes; seems they're in for a long stay.'

'But why?'

'There's some fool rumour that Mr Fjortoft's gone missing. There's no moving 'em. We've got CNN there as well as your Brit TV.'

Lucy could make nothing of this. She went into the office and read her father's message.

Lucy,
I'm staying with friends out in the country. I need some information urgently. In the top right-hand little drawer of my desk you will find Hannah Berkovic's business card. Please could you email back all the information on it to this site. I'm well and you'll be pleased to hear I've just done a massive cross country hike and burned off lots of cholesterol and all in the line of duty.
Take care and all my love
Dad.

Lucy sat staring at the screen. She knew her father better than anyone in the world now Mum was gone. He was hiding something from her. He'd made no mention of Gus in this cryptic message. Something had happened; she was being protected from bad news. She felt that childish mix of resentment and foreboding.

She pulled herself together and searched for Hannah's card. At least it was where it was supposed to be. Since Mum's death her father's office had become increasingly chaotic. Several times she had calmed his rages as he pulled the place apart, looking for some supposed lost document. Lucy had always found the missing papers, but inevitably the system had become more disorganised than ever. She sent the email and went to the kitchen for a cup of tea.

Here she found the day's second surprise. Zebedee the Mormon was taking over the new guard shift. With him was Al Otford.

'Hello, Al, I thought you'd left us?'

'Only temporary, Doctor. Now I'm back and raring to go.'

'It's good to see you fit and well.'

She meant that. Never would she forget that dark rain-swept night.

Al was clearly remembering too. 'You saved my life. If ever you're in trouble I'm here – all for one and one for all.'

Lucy was puzzled. Al was supposed to have left the Fjortoft organisation. She wanted to ask questions but this wasn't the moment. A car was drawing into the yard.

The driver was heading towards the front door. It was the elderly American, Jiffers; a fellow medic if she remembered rightly. She ran to open the door.

'Doctor Jiffers, I'm afraid my father's away – can I help?' She beckoned him in.

'Well maybe. I've been talking to Mr and Mrs Cunningham about Woolbarrow Farm. It seems their attorney has advised them to break negotiations with Mr Fjortoft. I've been around the house with Mr Cunningham and to be straight with you the place suits me fine.'

'Come on in and have a cup of coffee,' she offered.

'Thank you – doctor, isn't it?'

'That's right but only a humble GP. What's your speciality?'

'General surgery, but I'm the one who should be humble. You people do the real work. I part millionaires from their appendices and rich women from their varicose veins.' He grinned. 'It pays the cheques and then some.'

Lucy could imagine that. 'I'd still rather do what I do. Money's not everything.'

'Ah, idealism – I was like you once.'

'I can't help you about Woolbarrow,' she said. 'But you won't fall out with Mr Fjortoft or my father. We only want the best for the family. I take it you know why the property is on the market?'

'The farmer died.'

'No, the inquest brought in a murder verdict.'

'I didn't like to ask too many questions but…'

The Doctor's words were drowned as an aircraft passed over the house almost scraping the chimney pots. Lucy ran outside followed by Jiffers and the Mormons.

A large helicopter was quartering the ground to the south of the house. They felt the draught of the rotors as it drove at them, only to turn away moving slowly across the field. Lucy's anger burned; she could hear the whinnying of frightened horses in the stables. It was only by chance that she had been too busy to turn them out into this same field. She ran back to the yard and began to soothe Francesca's ponies. Her Hero looked more irritated than frightened. Jiffers and the Mormons were watching the sky as the helicopter soared over the house to land gently in the paddock behind the barn.

Lucy strode through the gate in fury. As the amused Mormons told her later, she personified the English country lady in high dudgeon. A man was standing on the ground by the chopper with another still inside, presumably the pilot. The stranger ambled towards Lucy. He was an elderly thickset man with greying hair, dressed in a well-cut business suit. She noticed he was breathing heavily and looked sallow faced and sweaty. He might have had an air of menace, but Lucy was past caring. She knew her eyes blazed and her pulse rate had risen alarmingly.

'Who the hell are you? You're frightening our horses and invading our privacy. I'm taking the number of that bloody machine and I'm reporting you to the police.'

'You can tell them I'm Anthony Tallisment. They know the name and they won't be interested in your complaints. I'm paying a business call on the owner of this house. Is that you?'

'No.'

'Then stop wasting my time.' The man strode on, ignoring her.

Lucy resisted an overwhelming urge to hit him.

He called over his shoulder. 'This place is Fjortoft's, I suppose.'

'It's Boxtree Farm and it belongs to my father. If you want Mr Fjortoft you'll have to wait; he's in America.'

'I know that. He's not coming back.'

Lucy steadied her temper. She must stay calm; in no way would she be the hysterical female.

'Of course he's coming back.'

'Your father must be O'Malley.'

'He is Mr Tom O'Malley and he manages Mr Fjortoft's interests.'

'Not any more. I'm buying this village and you'd better believe it. O'Malley's not coming back either.'

'Of course he's coming back. I've just had a message from him.'

Tallisment swung round glaring straight into her face. Lucy forced herself to make eye contact. She would not be found wanting in any trial of strength.

'What message?'

'A private message from my father.'

'That's impossible – you're lying.'

'Mister, she ain't lying.' Zeb was standing beside her. In her anger she had not noticed. 'Her father sent her a message this morning – saw it with my own eyes.'

'Where from?'

'That, Mister, is no concern of yours. Miss Lucy, d'you want this guy outa' here?'

'I've nothing useful to say to him. I'd prefer he left.'

'There you are, Mister. You heard the lady – shift your ass.'

Lucy began to relax; surely this awful man would take the hint. She was not prepared for what happened next.

'Well I never.' Dr Jiffers had moved to stand in front of her. 'My-oh-my, if it isn't Rudi. You know, Lucy – may I call you Lucy?' He turned and smiled shyly. 'This guy here is Rudi.'

He addressed Tallisment. 'Am I right?'

A change had come over that man. Lucy could see his neck tendons tensing; beads of sweat were rolling down them into his shirt collar and his face had turned an odd yellowish tinge. You're heading for a coronary, she thought.

'Rudi and I go back a long way,' said Jiffers. 'So long ago that I wouldn't have recognised him, had not my old friend Gustav told me he was in these parts. Your manners don't seem improved either, do they, Rudi. Tell me was Gus avoiding you – is that why he's in the States?'

Lucy was wholly confused as, by their faces, were the two Mormons.

'Come on, Mister, on your way.' Al Otford spoke as both men closed in on either side of Tallisment.

Together the three of them walked to the helicopter. Tallisment almost seemed to shuffle. All the bluster and arrogance had vanished.

'Lucy,' said Jiffers. 'You've heard the expression, "dead man walking"?'

She nodded, wondering what was coming.

'Well, now you've seen it for real.'

Lucy was driving homeward in her new car, but she was too troubled to enjoy the moment. Dad's odd message, then the arrival of the odious Tallisment. What did he mean? "O'Malley's not coming back".

Somewhere in America her father was in danger. Dr Jiffers had refused to answer her few guarded questions. This mystery man knew something, and the sight of him had deflated Tallisment like a pricked balloon. Something she could do was drive to Taraton and call on the Cunninghams.

Marjorie ushered her indoors. 'Lucy, I was going to phone you – we've a problem.'

'If it's Woolbarrow, don't worry. Mr Fjortoft won't stand in the way if you can get a better deal.'

'Yes, I know, but it's not that – it's Francesca. We don't seem to be getting anywhere.'

'What's happened?'

'Last Saturday she went out with our daughter Natalie and some of their friends. By all accounts they had a wonderful time. We really thought it was a turning point.'

Marjorie lapsed into silence; Lucy waited.

'She went to college on Monday morning in high spirits. That afternoon she came home and ran upstairs and locked her door. She came out for a meal but wouldn't say a word. She's been to college yesterday and today but that's it. She's in a dream world. It's as if we've lost her.'

Lucy was not really surprised. In Francesca's mental state she would expect mood swings. She suspected something had triggered this episode. Professionally she would like to know what. From upstairs came the distant bump – bump of a pop drumbeat.

'That's Natalie's room. If you'd like to talk to Fran she's up there.'

Lucy's ears led her to the bedroom. The music was deafening and she wondered what manner of consultation she could hope for. Francesca and Natalie were sprawled on the floor amidst the chaos of cast-off clothing, shoes, books and papers. Ten years ago her room would have looked much the same; she could almost hear her mother's reproving tone.

Natalie Cunningham was also a patient of Lucy. A precocious seventeen-year-old blonde nymphet, already sexually experienced, Natalie was not Lucy's ideal choice to show Francesca the real world.

Natalie grinned at Lucy and turned down the CD player. Francesca stared apathetically.

Lucy smiled at her. 'How's things?'

'All right.' The voice was deadpan.

'I'm free Saturday afternoon – want to come riding?'

'All right,' Francesca hardly bothered to look up.

'You don't have to.'

'All right.'

It was as if Lucy's questions were bouncing off a brick wall. Natalie caught hold of her elbow and nodded towards the door. Lucy followed the girl outside.

'I think I know what happened,' said Natalie in an excited whisper.

'Go on.'

'Monday, after college, on the Heath – I think she saw the phantom flasher.' A mischievous gleam lit the girl's blue eyes.

'The what?'

'Flasher; there's a creep who hangs around the Heath – shows his dick.'

'Have you told the police?'

'No, haven't seen him myself, but some of the girls have.'

'Oh God!' This really was too much.

'I was first home. Fran won't walk with the crowd – she's a loner.' Natalie paused. 'She ran indoors bawling her eyes out and she won't say a word – it's got to be him.'

Lucy found Marjorie and told her. 'We'd better alert the police at once.' She was so angry her own troubles were almost forgotten.

'I'll do that of course, but frankly this sounds like Natalie stirring things. That rumour about the man's been going for years. We used to whisper about it when I was at school. The police do patrol the Heath anyway. They were there that afternoon.'

'Are you sure?'

'Yes, I was on my way home and I saw that PC Witherrick – you know the officious one. He came out by the golf hut.'

'I take your point. Witherrick would love to catch a pervert. Someone to beat up in the cells, given half a chance.'

'It still doesn't help us with Francesca.'

'I know,' Lucy sighed. 'I'll ring the coroner's office and see if we can speed up Matthew's funeral.'

CHAPTER 24

'Caught'yer at it – didn't I? The boy grinned. 'Yeah – you're making a baby.'

'What?' Tom could hardly believe what he was hearing.

'Sure,' the lad was unfazed. 'This is the birth-rock. I got made here – right where you are now.'

'Hi, Mitch – did you say that's your name?' Gina was sitting up and smiling.

Mitch stood watching them, his legs apart, head tilted to one side. His cocky self-confidence belied his age.

'Look,' said Gina. 'We're here because our truck broke down. We wandered around half the night. Could you take us to your house?'

'Sure – soon as you finish making your baby.'

'All we want is somewhere warm and some dry clothes,' said Tom.

'What makes you think we were doing whatever?' Gina asked.

'Cos' this is the birth rock – the Klamath use it all the time. Mr Johnson'll tell you.'

'And who is Mr Johnson?'

'He's out hunting with my dad. They'll be back come evening.'

'What about your mother?' Gina asked.

'Sure, she's indoors.'

'Where's indoors?' asked Tom. 'We saw a light over there.'

'Yeah, that'll be our cabin.'

'So, will you take us there?'

'Sure, come with me.'

Mitch ran to the entrance of the cleft and stood waiting.

Gina sniffed. 'What bunch of hicks have we landed with?'

Tom helped her to her feet. 'This is no time to be snobbish – be thankful for small mercies.'

Gina limped out of the cleft. Clearly last night's walk had taken its toll. She went to the pool and plunged her feet into it.

'Hey,' said Mitch. 'Did you folks drink any of that water?'

'What's wrong with it?' Tom glared at the boy.

Mitch spluttered with laughter.

They followed their guide round the rock. Nearby a little pony was grazing the rough grass.

Mitch looked at Gina. 'Lady, how say you sit on Lucky? Let him take the weight off your feet.'

Gina stared dubiously at the pony.

'You never rid' before?'

'She rides every day,' said Tom. 'She's good too. Come on, love, up you get.'

Gina smiled and swung into the saddle.

'Mister, you talk funny. You sound like Michael Caine.'

'He's a Brit as well,' Gina laughed.

'Limey? My granpa's Irish – he don't like Limeys.'

'Tom here's Irish too.'

'No I'm not.'

'From now on you are if it'll smooth our path.'

Tom was struck by the magnificence of the scenery. All he had seen last night were slopes, plains and high ridges in silhouette. Now he stood in awe. Beyond the undulating landscape the ground rose steeply culminating in a vast snow-capped peak. Further away other mountains were visible. Mitch led his pony on a well-trodden path skirting the marsh. Now Tom could see the cabin and beside it, glinting in the sun an antique wind pump. The cabin was a single storey built of timber with a stone chimney on one end. It was a much-enlarged version of the log cabins one saw in books about the old West. A wisp of smoke from the chimney gave the place a welcoming touch. Tom was already revising Gina's perception of "hicks". The house had a trim lawn and a colourful garden in bloom. A smart pickup truck was parked to one side and a satellite dish adorned the roof. A woman stood on the lawn hanging her washing on a rotating frame.

Mitch sprinted ahead. 'Ma,' he yelled, 'we've got people.'

'Hicks,' muttered Gina. 'Haven't they got a washing dryer?'

The woman walked to the garden gate. A pretty girl, maybe in her early thirties, she wore jeans and the same style logger shirt as Mitch.

'Hi there,' she smiled a greeting. 'I saw you coming from afar. You look like you've hit hard times.'

'You could say that,' Tom replied. 'Our truck broke down and we've been trying to find help all night.'

'Know where I found'em?' said Mitch. He pulled on his mother's arm and whispered in her ear. 'They drank the water too,' he added loudly.

'Now, none of that, Mitch,' the woman was blushing. 'I don't know what youngsters are coming to these days.' She smiled at them. 'Hi, I'm Lisa and you're very welcome.' She was staring at Gina.

'Say, haven't I seen you before – like on television?'

'Could have,' Gina was wary. 'I once played a waitress in Miami – Vice.'

'You're in movies?'

'My husband works in them.'

'Well, what d'you know.' Lisa was grinning in delight. 'Is this your husband?'

'I'm a sort of bodyguard,' said Tom. He wondered what Lisa was thinking.

Gina pushed Tom forward. 'This is Tom O'Malley from England and I'm Gina. Lisa, we'd sure appreciate a hot shower.'

Tom appreciated the shower although he would rather have wallowed in a hot bath. At last he felt wholly warm again accompanied by a pleasing languor that almost, but not quite dispelled his worries. He was touched by the generosity of these people. Would two bedraggled strangers have had such a welcome in England? Lisa had asked no questions. Certainly she was broad-minded enough to ignore Mitch's comments, even though the boy had clearly caught them in a compromising position. Lisa had raided her wardrobe and her husband's and found them each a set of warm well fitting-clothes. Then she had cooked them an enormous breakfast. Gina and Tom fell on the food with such gusto that they uttered hardly a word for twenty minutes. Mitch sat in a chair, watching fascinated. Later Lisa came and shared a large pot of coffee. It was time, Tom decided, to give her a full explanation.

'On the way here we ran into some bad trouble,' he began. 'That's one of the reasons we're in this mess.'

'I guessed something happened,' said Lisa, 'I didn't want to pry.'

'Have you ever come across the people who call themselves The Aryan Nation?'

'Oh sure, we've heard about them, but they never come near us – they wouldn't dare.'

'Why not?'

'This is Klamath country; we're on the edge of the reservation. If those guys came toting guns, the Indians would think Christmas had come early – it'd be a reprise of General Custer.'

'Thank God for that,' Gina sighed. 'You know they chased us and shot us up. Tom saved my life – he's a hero.'

'I think it's time the Feds got off their asses and did something,' said Lisa. 'It's not good when you've young kids out here with all those nuts roaming around.'

'Well, why don't they do something?' said Tom, more sharply than he intended.

Lisa grimaced. 'I guess that Mr Mulgrum pays his taxes and that's all they care about in Washington.'

'Leave it, Lisa,' Gina grinned. 'Or else we'll have Tom on with a lot of bullshit about how much better the Brits run their goddam country.'

'Do you live here all the time?' Tom asked.

'No way. I'd love it, but this is our vacation cabin. My husband Don's a lawyer – got a practice down in Oakland but he enjoys hunting and he writes about wildlife – had pieces in *The National Geographic.*'

Gina intervened. 'What was it Mitch was on about? A "birth rock", he said.'

'Oh dear me,' Lisa laughed. 'I'm not saying anything, but Mitch is right – it worked for us.'

'What did?'

'You'd better ask Mr Johnson. It's his heritage.'

'Who is he?' asked Tom. 'Mitch mentioned him several times.'

'Luke Johnson, that's not his real name; he's a Klamath. Don and he were at law school. Luke practices law, but a lot of his work is with civil rights.'

'He found us this cabin,' said Mitch.

'That's true; Indians don't much like outsiders moving in on their territory. You'll meet Luke tonight. You'll like him but you must always call him Mr Johnson – he's one proud fella.'

'You know,' said Tom. 'I hate to admit it, but I rather like Americans.'

'That's mighty generous of you,' said Gina. 'I kinda like Brits, though half the time I don't know where you're coming from.'

'What do we do now? We can't impose on Lisa forever.'

'I'm worried about Gus,' she replied. 'I feel all guilty. I sort of forgot him while we were in trouble.'

'Put your trust in Craig.'

'What do we do?'

'We wait; Lisa's husband and this Johnson are both high-power lawyers. We do nothing without their advice.'

Lisa had departed in her truck. She was going, she told them, to collect her mail from a box on the nearest highway. Mitch was around somewhere; otherwise they were alone. Tom thought long and hard. He doubted Mulgrum would harm anyone as prestigious as Gus. A lot would depend on the state of Van Zyl. If that man was sufficiently recovered his urge for revenge might be unconfined. He said nothing to Gina because he knew she was more worried than she pretended.

'I think I know what's going on,' she said. 'Gussy's got something that creepy brother wants real bad.'

'Any idea what?'

'I don't know, but whatever it is, it's in England, not here.'

Lisa returned at midday. She greeted them cheerfully and called Mitch to help her in the kitchen. Something was troubling her. When Gina left them to find the toilet, Lisa beckoned Tom into the living room.

'I know why I've seen Gina before. It's been worrying me all day. Now, mister, look at this.'

Her tone hardened, not hostile, but she wanted answers. She handed him a newspaper: that morning's edition of the daily paper in Portland. Tom saw the item immediately. Staring him in the face was that two-year-old shot of Gus and Gina at the Oscars. Gus was wearing a magnificent tuxedo, while Gina stared demurely at the camera, in a dress containing hardly any material above the waist. *Top Movie Director Missing,* said the headline.

It reported the disappearance of Gustav Fjortoft who apparently had last been seen driving south from Seattle to keep a private appointment. The police did not rule out abduction but suspected that Mr Fjortoft had been under stress, *"and may be seeking privacy and solitude at an undisclosed location. Mr Fjortoft's wife, the model and actress, Gina Heidfelt, is also missing. She was last seen leaving Seattle with Tom O'Malley, an employee of the Fjortoft organisation".*

'OK, Tom, I guess you haven't kidnapped the lady; so what's going on?'

This was the moment for absolute honesty. 'Gustav Fjortoft is being held captive by Mulgrum. Gina and I managed to escape, but it was a close call. We couldn't take Mr Fjortoft; he's being held somewhere we couldn't reach.'

Lisa seemed satisfied. 'You want to call the County Sheriff?'

'I'm not sure that's such a good idea at the moment. I'd rather tell the whole story to your husband and ask his advice.'

'Is this Fjortoft in danger?'

'We think not at the moment.'

'No ransom demand?'

'No that's not the problem – it's something different.'

'All right, Tom, I'll not pry further. Tell your story to the two boys tonight and we'll see what we can do.'

Tom had the glimmer of an idea. 'Lisa, are you on the Internet?'

'Sure we are – you want to send a message?'

'I want to contact my daughter in England. It's partly to tell her I'm all right and it's just occurred to me; I've one card left and I'd like to play it.'

Dusk was growing outside the cabin when they heard the sounds of the returning hunters. Lisa ran up the roadway to intercept them. She waved the truck to a stop and held an animated conversation with the driver. As she talked she gave occasional glances towards the house. Then she left and ran back to them.

'It's OK, Don's heard all about Mr Fjortoft on the radio. He says you're welcome.'

Neither of the two men seemed the least put out by such unexpected arrivals. Don was a slim man in his early thirties. He greeted them cordially and introduced them to his companion. Tom had never knowingly met a Native American and tried to restrain his curiosity. Mr Johnson was the same age as his friend, but was a stockier figure with short dark hair and a swarthy complexion. If he had not known better Tom would have placed him as a Spaniard.

Johnson bowed gallantly to Gina. 'My people think highly of your husband. *The Bear* portrayed our Inuit cousins as real people and you can't ask for more than that.'

Lisa appeared at the kitchen door. 'Come on, you guys. First we eat – explanations later.'

Mitch was tugging at Johnson's arm while pointing at Gina.

'They were doing it by the rock – I caught 'em.'

Lisa rounded on the boy. 'One more bleat out of you, young man, and it's bed.'

The boy was safely in bed, when later in the living room Don poured drinks and stoked the open fire with logs; the flames reflecting on the varnished wooden walls and ceiling. Outside, the same chill wind as last night wafted around the building. Tom could hear it, but the sounds only increased his feelings of ease and security. Like all countrymen he could appreciate a warm fire and a snug house. Gina was surprised that the cabin had mains electricity in the midst of this wilderness, but Don explained that the grid from Portland passed within a hundred yards of the cabin.

Tom cradled his glass of Scotch. In this pleasing languor he was finding it difficult to keep his eyes open. He had given his account; now Gina had taken the floor and was giving an exaggerated tale of their escape. She was blatantly casting Tom as some sort of film hero.

Don intervened. 'You sure the gun was a Magnum? Funny sort of handgun for anyone to carry.'

'It was,' said Tom. 'I've seen one before. I'm a magistrate in England and we had a man up before the bench for keeping one without a licence.'

'I'm not surprised you busted Mulgrum's truck,' said Johnson. 'They made those guns in Prohibition times. It's said a bullet from one will darn near knock an automobile engine off its blocks.'

'Anyway,' said Gina. 'We lit off cross-country until we found shelter by that big stone, and,' she glared at Johnson, 'what's special about it?'

Johnson smiled. 'It's an old site and sacred to my people. I'm no shaman and I wouldn't want to get into a discussion on the nature of belief, but sometimes things happen at places like that.'

'Such as?'

'Things that defy logical explanation.'

Tom looked at both men. 'Please, we're in your hands; what do we do?'

'We report to the police,' said Don. 'That means Sheriff Morsen. What's going on in his county is a disgrace. It's time he got off his butt.'

'That would be the local police?' Tom asked. His knowledge of American law enforcement was confined to television drama.

'That's right,' Don rose and walked to a large map pinned on the wall. 'This is a Geological Survey sheet – what you'd call an Ordnance map. We're here, just inside the reservation, so this is Klamath tribe territory – a different administration. Along the top of that bluff you climbed is the county line. West of there's Grattan County, Sheriff Morsen's domain.' He pointed again. 'That there is the old Uplands Hunting Lodge, which is where your Mulgrum is. Contrary to what you're told in England, the rule of law does apply in these parts. You tell me you witnessed this Van Zyl shoot a wounded man in cold blood. That's a State and Federal offence: Murder One.'

Don turned away from his map. ‘So, Tom, you trust us to put the wheels in motion while you have a good night’s sleep.’

CHAPTER 24

The next morning Lucy took surgery as usual and tried not to let her despondency show to her patients. Yesterday had unsettled her. She had made a dangerous enemy in Tallisment and all her hard work for Francesca seemed to have come to nothing. These were minor matters compared with her concern for Dad. She had sent an email with the information he wanted but as yet had no reply.

It was a relief to be asked to make a house call on an elderly lady. Lucy had driven to the village, not three miles from Crossfield. She noticed the blossom on the trees, the early flowers and the road verges shooting with greenery. Here was real spring at last and it lightened her mood. She completed the visit and said goodbye to her patient. She had a clear three hours before her next surgery. The road took her along the high ridge with its view of three counties. Ahead of her was the turning that led to the old flint road and the former gun site by Bechams wood. On a chance whim she turned and drove down the track.

She had come here as a child to picnic with her mother and baby Andy. The old wartime huts, still standing then, had long since vanished. All that remained were piles of rubble and an old water tank. It was a peaceful spot where she could be alone for an hour with her thoughts and worries. She grimaced as she saw another car parked on the grass: Rufus Partridge's Astra. She wondered why Rufus should be so obsessive about this derelict place.

She parked next to the Astra and strolled down the hill. She felt a lump in her throat as she remembered the picnics with Mummy. Andy snug in his carrycot, Mummy teaching her the names of the wild flowers: the sandwiches and the fizzy drinks, hot sun and nettle stings. Her reverie was broken as Rufus walked out of the wood carrying a rucksack.

'Hello, Lucy – nobody ill today?'

'You have got to be joking,' she laughed.

Lucy was fond of Rufus and grateful. Rufus had taught science at Taraton College as long as anyone could remember. It was he who had urged her to raise her sights and try for medical school. The man never seemed to age. His narrow face was perhaps a little more lined and the untidy hair had more grey flecks. Today he looked red-faced and happy and his boots were caked in mud.

‘What are you up to, Rufus?’

‘Ah, please don’t take it amiss if I leave you in the dark. My thesis is almost ready for publication and when it is I’ll take you round the site on a privileged tour. Can’t say fairer than that, can I?’

‘I shall look forward to it,’ Lucy smiled politely.

She could raise no enthusiasm for Rufus’ historical projects. Taraton and district seemed to have been ignored by the world. Rufus had scraped the barrel with his half-dozen self-published books. They seemed only to confirm that nothing had ever happened around Taraton and was never likely to. Sir Isaac Reade-Coke might have ridden forth for the Parliamentary cause in 1643, and much good it had done him. A blow on the head at the Battle of Cheriton had dampened his enthusiasm for soldiering. Since then nothing much had happened in Crossfield until the arrival of one Gustav Fjortoft.

Lucy parked in the yard at Boxtree and ran into the house. Ed the Mormon was in the kitchen. He confirmed that there were no more messages and no callers at the farm. Lucy went out saddled Hero and rode into the lane.

She turned and headed up the hill towards Woolbarrow. She was going to make the effort to beat her phobia for that place. She gave her horse his head and let him amble while she tried to think. She became distantly aware that a car was coming down the hill too fast. Suddenly the vehicle was upon them, a dark green transit van that filled the width of the road. It made no attempt to slow, on the contrary the driver put his foot down and seemingly drove straight at her. She tugged on the rein and kicked her mount into a hard turn to the right. Thank God that Hero was so disciplined and well trained. He took two nimble steps to the wide grass verge. Lucy felt a gust of air as the van swept past within a foot of her. She caught a glimpse of the driver’s face; she would know him again. She tried to read the registration plate and the lettering on the van’s rear door. Something “Motors” with a Taraton phone number. Witnesses or not, the police would hear from her.

For five minutes she rode on blind with fury, a prisoner of the metaphorical red-mist. It was unlikely the man had meant to harm her, maybe he never even saw her, but he could have killed poor Hero. It had been the horse’s calm response that had saved them both. She rode as far as Woolbarrow listening nervously for more traffic. She had lost her appetite for riding that day. She turned round and made the return journey across the fields.

It was only when she was in the car and heading for home that Lucy missed her pocket recorder. It was one of those talking notebooks that fitted in the palm of her hand and it contained today's patient's notes. She stopped the car and searched her pockets and then the whole vehicle. She was certain she hadn't taken it riding. It was just possible she had dropped it on the ground at Bechams Wood. A hundred yards short of the turning she saw Rufus's Astra appear and head home towards Taraton. Lucy turned into the track and drove down to where she had parked earlier. An inspection of the ground revealed nothing. She climbed back into her car and set off in pursuit of Rufus, on chance that he might have picked up the recorder.

The way to Taraton ran down Milbury Hill, or "Little Switzerland" as the guidebooks called it. The road, a shelf excavated in the side of Taraton Down, formed a series of tight turns and blind bends. Above the road was a hillside of beech trees beginning to spread into leaf. Below was a cliff-like drop of four hundred feet to the floor of the valley. It was a stunningly visual route with sightseeing parking spaces at intervals. Lucy had driven the road a hundred times and today was oblivious to its charms. Halfway down the hill she was forced to slow by stopped cars blocking both narrow carriageways. Lucy sighed; this was turning into one of those days. She caught sight of a policeman standing by his motorbike. It was PC Ross, their local bobby. He was gesticulating at the traffic trying to ease the blockage. He ran up the line until he was almost level with her. She wound down her window and called.

Ross was red faced and breathing hard. 'Doctor, I need your help. A car's gone to the bottom. Over the edge past the next bend. Hasn't happened long – hell of a mess. I've radioed for backup.'

'You want me to go down there?' Lucy heard her voice; inwardly she filled with dread.

'Please – park in the layby on the next bend. It's already reserved for the ambulance. There's a guy volunteered to keep it open.' Ross raced back down the line.

She reached the layby. A burly lorry driver with a shaven head waved her away.

'I'm the doctor,' she called.

Lucy stood on the edge of the drop and felt giddy. Far below she could see the wreckage. In all her time in medicine she had never confronted a situation like this. She deliberately blanked her mind and started to scramble down the slope. The hillside was covered in saplings and small bushes. The falling vehicle had left a trail of destruction behind it. Lucy tried to forget her vertigo as she slithered down the slope; the going was made harder by the plastic bag she clutched. It contained a few hastily assembled bandages and phials of morphine. Ross had had to stay up top but she had the muscular lorry man for support.

'They'll need a mountain stretcher,' was all he said.

Lucy guessed he was an ex-soldier.

Five minutes later, breathless and scratched by brambles, they reached the wrecked car. It lay half on its roof with framework bent and windows smashed. The radiator steamed and she could smell petrol.

'Watch for fire, lass!'

Lucy felt the same; she was frightened. Was this what it meant to be a hero? She knelt down and forced herself to look into the driver's side. She saw a mayhem of bent bloodstained metal and in the midst the body of a slender man. She finally registered what she had subconsciously known. This was no longer impersonal. She remembered all those medical student stories of doctors called to accidents, only to find the bodies of their, mothers, wives or children.

'Rufus, it's me Lucy.'

She wanted to cry. She mustn't do that – she must be professional, especially with this dour ex-soldier watching.

'Car's on't balance. Reckon I can turn her right ways up,' he said.

'If he's alive the shock could make it worse – I know him,' she added.

'They'll never get him out like this.' The man took the decision himself. He walked to the car, grasped it around the bent window frames and heaved. Slowly it tipped and rolled onto its four wheels. Lucy pulled at the driver's door. It flopped open throwing crystal shards of glass. Rufus was bent forward. She couldn't move him without a neck brace and some skilled help. She reached in and took a pulse reading; he was alive.

'Rufus, can you hear me?'

'Hello, Lucy, can you get me out of here?'

'Of course we will.' She felt a wave of exhilaration and hope.

'Stupid thing,' Rufus muttered. 'Steering went – only had her tested a week ago.'

The lorry man was kneeling down peering underneath the front of the car.

'Well, I'll be buggered,' he said.

CHAPTER 25

The pole barrier was lowered. It looked as if the Aryan Nation expected trouble. Six men guarded the gate, all armed to the teeth.

The forces of law and order had driven out in two patrol cars. Don and Tom had been allowed to follow, but Gina had been left behind.

Sheriff Morsen strode to the gate flanked by his two officers, one white one black.

'Hey there,' shouted a militiamen. 'If it ain't the sheriff with one of his niggers. You ain't coming in here, black boy.'

Morsen stood, hands on hips. 'I'm here to interview Mr Mulgrum. I don't care where we talk, but you get him down here quick.'

'Maybe he don't want to talk to you, Sheriff. What d'you do then?'

The FBI man intervened. 'We understand Mr Mulgrum is holding Mr Gustav Fjortoft against his will. If so, that's a federal offence.'

'And I have a warrant to question a suspect to murder,' said Morsen.

'I say again, what'you going to do about it?' the guard chortled.

'You've a choice,' said Morsen. 'Mr Mulgrum co-operates or we bring in as many armed officers as it takes. You tell him that.'

The guard muttered into his radio.

'He's on his way,' he said.

A light aircraft had begun to circle, shortly to be joined by a helicopter. More cars were bumping up the track the first was driven by Lew Gungenhorn, the Fjortoft aide; the others contained TV crews and newsmen.

'Mr O'Malley, I'm sure glad you're safe,' Lew clasped his hand.

'What's all this activity?' asked Tom.

'Media people; can't say how they found out Mr Fjortoft's here.'

Mulgrum walked to the barrier and stood face to face with Sheriff Morsen.

'What can I do for you, Sheriff?'

Morsen repeated his charges against Van Zyl and demanded access to Fjortoft.

Mulgrum was staring at Tom. 'So, you've brought your goddam spy. That guy seriously injured Mr Van Zyl; jumped him from behind – no warning. My doctor says he may lose an eye.'

Tom could have laughed. Van Zyl blamed him because he could never admit it was a woman who had outsmarted him.

Morsen was uncompromising. 'We need to talk to both Mr Van Zyl and Mr Fjortoft. Now, Reverend, do we do this peaceful or not?'

'Very well, you gentlemen may come to the lodge and see if you can find them. The Irishman and the nigger stay here.'

Mulgrum returned to the Jeep. The guards raised the pole and the two patrol cars followed him into the grounds. Tom was deeply thankful not to be included in the party. He never wished to see Mulgrum's house again.

Another carload of reporters had arrived and was setting up a satellite dish. A man in a leather jacket carrying a radio-mike tugged at Tom's sleeve.

'Who are you, fella?'

Tom was about to give a sharp riposte. Lew Gungenhorn intervened.

'The gentleman is a member of Mr Fjortoft's personal staff. He is not entitled to answer questions, Sir.'

Don's mobile phone was shrilling a jingle to the tune of Offenbach's barcarolle. 'O'Brien here ... who are you – how come you know this number?'

'For you,' he handed the set to Tom.

'Hi, Tom, you wanted to talk to me?' It was Hannah.

Tom felt guilty. He had contacted Hannah's agency via Don's computer. Somehow she must have tracked the number of this mobile. Don did not look pleased.

'We must talk – there're things I need to know. Can you wait for me at Grattan County police station? Gina Fjortoft's a guest of the Sheriff's wife.'

He rang off; Hannah would know there were people listening.

An hour passed before the Sheriff returned, clearly empty-handed. He looked dour and displeased. He walked straight to Tom.

'Mister, I must ask you to come to my office. We've gotta talk.'

'You haven't found Mr Fjortoft?'

'No we have not. The Reverend Mulgrum, says you entered his campus under false pretences. You injured his personal assistant and you stole an automobile.'

Don spoke. 'Sheriff, I'm Mr O'Malley's attorney. I suggest you be careful.'

'Sure I will,' Morsen switched his displeasure to Don. 'Reverend

Mulgrum don't cause trouble to nobody. We leave him alone and he leaves us alone. We don't necessarily agree with everything he preaches, but he's a respected citizen of our county and he pays his taxes.'

The Sheriff's words echoed exactly Lisa's opinion yesterday.

Tom was defiant. 'I saw Mr Fjortoft, forty-eight hours ago in that place. I have three witnesses, including Mrs Fjortoft, and a British Member of Parliament Mr Gannemeade. I will swear on oath that I saw Van Zyl shoot a wounded man exactly on the spot where you are now standing. Look man, there's still a blood trace.'

The Sheriff took a rapid step backwards and stared at the ground.

'Jeez, what've I done to deserve this?' He looked at Tom. 'Sir, I think we should talk back in my office.'

Tom nodded agreement. The pressmen with their microphones had been shuffling ever closer.

Don looked worried. 'Sheriff, we're losing time here.'

'Mister, I'll be the judge of that.' Morsen turned back to Tom. 'Sir, you'll ride with us. Mister Attorney, you can follow.'

Tom made his statement in the Sheriff's office. He told the basic facts omitting only Craig's role. Halfway through the proceedings he heard a hubbub in the reception area and in marched Craig, resplendent in the uniform of the United States Marine Corps.

Tom gaped and then made the introductions.

'I never mentioned Mr East,' he explained. 'I gather he's an undercover agent and at risk, but he's the man who helped us escape. Craig, what's happened?'

'That guy Hellmunt's taken Dad with him. Van Zyl went in the same car. Hellmunt's taking him to some clinic – that's all I know.'

'Hellmunt is Brown – he's got to be?'

Craig shook his head. 'Maybe – he's from Dad's past, that's certain.'

Morsen interrupted. 'Lieutenant, I'd like your statement next.'

'Where's Gina?'

'Mrs Fjortoft is at the local Inn. I'm due to interview her when I've done with you folks.'

A tight-lipped guard of Fjortoft Mormons patrolled inside and outside the hotel. The event could hardly be classed an interrogation. It was as if Gina was holding an audience. Tom supposed a Hollywood celebrity to be the American equivalent of minor royalty. He would not have been surprised had the Sheriff concluded by bowing and walking from the room backwards. She confirmed everything that Tom and Craig had reported, and repeated her over-dramatised account of their flight.

'Mulgrum says you drove off down the regular road.'

'He's lying.'

'I've had a call from Luke Johnson,' said Don. 'He's up there with some of his people. They've found that Toyota shot full of holes.'

The police and FBI conferred, then Tom and Craig were told they could leave.

'I want to go home,' said Tom.

'We can't stop you,' said the FBI agent. 'We'll ask you to give a formal undertaking to return should you be required as witness in court.'

'Gladly – no problem.' He remembered. 'My hire car's in Mulgrum's compound. I need it back.'

'I ain't stopping you fetching it,' said Morsen. 'The Reverend'll be real pleased to see you.'

The media were waiting and Gina's reappearance signalled mayhem. She had dressed for the moment in a light blue trouser suit. Her blonde hair shone in the sunlight; she looked stunning. Gina had been in his thoughts a lot these last days. He realised how facile were first impressions. She had transformed before his eyes. She had responded to danger with courage. She had disabled the murderous Van Zyl, kept her head in the subsequent chase, and finally walked barefoot across miles of rough terrain in near freezing conditions. He seriously questioned whether he could have survived without her presence.

Gina smiled radiantly for the cameras. Yes, she was well. Her husband was well. He was taking a short rest before reappearing in public. His visit to the Aryan Nation had been a research project. The clamour from the press had by now increased four-fold as the Mormons closed in and ushered her to the waiting car. As they drove her away Tom experienced new feelings of emptiness and loss.

With Gina's departure the entire pack turned on him. Tom was saved by Don O'Brien. Mr O'Malley, he said, was a Fjortoft company employee and was not permitted to answer questions. Lew Gungenhorn appeared with a second car into which both Tom and Craig were able to escape. Tom saw Hannah on the fringe of the crowd. He badly needed to speak with her but this was probably not the time or place. Tom just had time to thank Don for all he and Lisa had done for them. Don grinned and exchanged a high-five hand slap.

'Tom, keep in touch. If I can do anything – say the word.'

'What's going to be done about Mulgrum?'

'I shall deal with Reverend Mulgrum within the law. Luke warned me the Indians are talking of paying that gentleman a visit. Luke won't have it. That kinda gunplay finished a hundred years ago.'

'You could've fooled me, Don.'

At last he was going home. Tom made his way to his allotted seat in the 747 and settled himself by the window. He glanced at his watch: half an hour before the scheduled takeoff. He leaned back and shut his eyes.

A hand touched him lightly on the arm as someone slipped into the seat beside him, a slight person with a whiff of perfume. 'Hi there, Tom. We've a long trip ahead – plenty of time to compare notes.'

'Hannah, how in hell did you know I was on this flight?'

CHAPTER 26

'We're treating the incident as potential manslaughter – even attempted murder,' said Inspector Oats.

'Why – why Rufus?'

'We don't know yet but we intend to find out. Tell me about the man – everything you can think of.'

Oats looked tired. Lucy speculated that he hadn't slept much of late.

'Where can I start? He's the most harmless person I know in the whole world. No one has a grudge – everyone likes him.'

'No, Doctor,' Oats slapped the table. 'Someone didn't. Tell me about his private life.'

'I don't think he has one. He's always working flat out at college or on his hobbies.'

'I understand he's divorced.'

'I think his ex-wife's in Australia and he's got a married daughter in Scotland.'

'We'll check it; any other relationships?'

'I don't think so; all his energy goes into his interests.'

'Obsessions from what I've heard. Amateur dramatics – that can inspire murder.'

'And history,' Lucy was quick to defend her mentor. 'He'd been working on some archaeology at Crossfield only half an hour before the crash.'

'I know, at Bechams Wood. Did you see anyone near the place or on the hill?'

'Sorry, no.'

'Anyone within a mile that you didn't recognise?'

'Some mindless oaf nearly killed my horse. Drove a bloody great transit van straight at me.' Lucy had intended to report the incident but it had been submerged in the greater tragedy.

'Description – vehicle number?'

'It was so quick, but it had a Taraton phone number and I think it was a motor firm – garage maybe?'

'This isn't getting us anywhere. PC Ross has walked the ground at Bechams Wood – there's nothing there.'

The aftershock of yesterday's drama had finally hit Lucy. Following evening surgery she had driven to the general hospital through the rush hour traffic only to find the staff car park was full. Forewarned, a junior house doctor was waiting in the intensive care wing. He was a callow bespectacled young man, apparently suffering from terminal acne. The ward sister gave Lucy a quick smile and waved her to a chair by the bed. Rufus lay motionless connected to drips, his bruised face covered by a mask and his legs in traction. The heart monitor bleeped in counterpoint to the chatter and bustle of the corridor outside.

'How is he?'

'Multiple fractures, including pelvis, four broken ribs, abrasions to the head and upper body. But no spinal damage, and we think nothing bad internally. If he pulls through he'll walk.' The doctor showed her the x-rays.

'He's been in and out of consciousness,' said the sister. 'He squeezed my hand on command just now.'

'Thank God for that.' Lucy could have stood and danced. 'He was still conscious at the scene of the crash – has he said anything?'

'For a few seconds about an hour ago,' the sister smiled. 'I think he was recalling his breakfast.'

'What were the words?'

'Something that sounded like – "real cook's bangers".'

'You've had the police here?'

'They called at the front desk. They want to talk to Mr Partridge when he's conscious.' She looked concerned. 'Was the accident his fault?'

'On the contrary – the car was tampered with.'

'You don't say – what happened?'

'Someone took a hacksaw to the track rod on the steering. They cut within a few millimetres, so that it broke in two at the first serious bend. Then to make sure they puncture his brake pipes and let the fluid out.'

The young doctor's eyes narrowed and Lucy could predict his thoughts. She mentally dared the little wimp to question her female grasp of mechanics.

She returned to her car, paid the extortionate fee to raise the exit barrier and set herself on the road for home. Her mobile phone was calling; she pulled over and answered.

'Lucy, it's me – I'm home.'

'Dad, where are you?' Lucy was overjoyed; a huge weight had lifted from her.

'I'm fine – never better. I'm at Heathrow – can you see if Charlie could collect me?'

'Never mind Charlie; stay where you are. I'm on my way.'

Francesca Rowridge waited for Natalie before setting out for home. She missed her solitary walks across the Heath but she would not risk another confrontation with that man. Natalie had an unhealthy prurient interest in this supposed person. She assumed that Francesca had seen the pervert, the flasher. In the end it was easier for Francesca to tell the truth.

'It was PC Witherrick.'

Natalie released a delighted squeal. 'Witherrick's a flasher?'

'No, of course not.'

'Well, what did he do then?'

'He told me I'm in trouble with the law.'

'Never!'

Francesca wanted to talk, wanted to tell someone, anyone but her garrulous friend.

'Go on, what are you supposed to have done?'

'He said…' Francesca hesitated. 'He said my Dad had stolen something valuable from Mr Fjortoft and unless I found it and brought it back the police would charge me and I'd go to jail.'

'Stole what?'

'He said it was a leather case and it was full with something valuable.'

'You ever seen it?'

'Of course I haven't.'

Francesca stumbled; her eyes so filled with tears that she could hardly see.

'You'd better get yourself a lawyer.'

'No, I mustn't do that. Witherrick said if I give him the case back no one will ever know. But if I talk to a solicitor, or anyone else, they're going to charge me. He said Mr Oats was being kind about it; just as long as I don't tell anybody.'

'Fran, this is all shit! I don't believe it. The police wouldn't do that.'

Francesca turned in fury. 'It is true – you calling me a liar?'

'Of course not. I don't like Witherrick, nobody does – he's creepy. He's winding you up,' she giggled. 'I bet he's a perv on the quiet.'

'What am I going to do?' Francesca sobbed.

'Yeah, all right – I believe you.' Natalie put a supportive arm around her. 'I think you should go to the Bill – confront them.'

'I can't,' she sniffed. 'Witherrick said it'd be in the local rag and everybody at college would know. I'm not to go to the police station. I've got to deal only through him'

'You must get help. Tell Dad, better still, talk to Doctor Lucy.'

'Yes, I think I will.'

The college had been awash with the news of Rufus's crash. Lucy had refused to discuss the incident and was circumspect about Rufus's work in Bechams wood. Francesca remembered, with a chill, the two voices she had overheard in the copse that night. When she had heard that voice again it had seemed like a stab from a knife. She knew she must tell the whole story to Lucy: no half-truths, no evasions.

'We keep ringing your mum's mobile,' said Natalie. 'She either doesn't answer or she's not there. She wouldn't just abandon you – I don't believe it.'

Francesca did not believe it either. She had never been close to her mother, who had been too busy with her own wild life to bother much about her daughter. What a terrible mismatch her parents had been. But she knew one thing for certain. Her mother would never willingly desert her only child at a time like this.

Tom felt desperately tired but he had to talk. He poured out his story to Lucy as she drove. He told her everything: from Greta Little's tale to the nightmare of Mulgrum's campus and his meeting Hannah. He played down Gina's part in all this; he knew Lucy's opinion of her too well.

'Where is Gina now?' was all she said.

'She's still with the Fjortoft men in Seattle.'

Lucy drove on without comment.

'I had a gut feeling you were in trouble,' she said. 'I'm only glad I never knew how big the trouble.'

'I think fortune rode with us that day. Finding Don and Lisa was a miracle.'

'What's Gus's family background? Why has he never said a thing about these two half-brothers?'

'I was wondering that as well. Gina knows nothing about his past. I asked Hannah before I flew home.'

'Does she know?'

'This is her version. Gus's mother is British by birth, Welsh to be precise. She married an Anglo-German doctor called Ernst Brown. At that time he was working in the States. She had two children born in the middle to late nineteen thirties, Wilhelm and Albert. Then it seems she divorced her husband and briefly married the elder Fjortoft, but not for long. Gus's father was a rich sadistic bully. At one stage he locked his wife and all three boys in a cellar with rats.'

'Typical of that type of male,' Lucy grunted.

'Anyway, it seems the lady fled back to her first husband along with her three children. Ernst Brown had meanwhile settled in Hitler's Germany with a research position that turned into the horrors we know.'

'Then what happened – I mean when the war was over?'

'Brown was tried and hanged. Gus's mother came back to Britain with her son Wilhelm – the other boy Albert vanished. He was supposed to have died in an air raid but Hannah's thinks he's still alive and her people are looking for him.'

'What about Gus?'

'His father died in the war, but he still had an uncle and family. They went to law and won custody.'

'So, where is this Wilhelm?'

'Hannah would dearly like to find him – I'd rather not know.'

Lucy told him about Rufus Partridge. For some reason Tom did not feel surprise or shock.

'Bechams wood again. There's got to be something about that copse. Francesca heard strangers there and her father wanted to talk about the place only hours before he was murdered. Then there's all that wartime stuff that Rufus was researching.'

'Are you going to tell inspector Oats?'

'No, I'm going to have a restful night's sleep – but tomorrow...'

'What about tomorrow?'

'Let's just say, tomorrow is another day.'

CHAPTER 27

Gina was livid having woken to find herself a virtual prisoner in the Benson Criterion Hotel. Never had she been treated this way since childhood. Ten minutes ago she had decided to go for a walk. She crossed the hotel foyer only to find the way to the outer world blocked by two security men. They treated her with a patronising respect that drove her to fury.

'I'm going outside,' she snapped.

'No, ma'am, I don't think so.'

'Don't you tell me what I can or can't do.'

'You don't want to go out of here – not today, Ma'am.'

'I am Mrs Fjortoft. My husband owns this lousy joint. If I want to go outside, I'll go.'

'No, ma'am, I've specific orders from Mr Gungenhorn. He says you don't want to go outside.'

Gina withdrew with an icy dignity acquired from long practice. How dare they treat her like this? She strode through the foyer and stormed into Lew Gungenhorn's office. Chief of Company Security was the label the man gave himself. Lew was in conference with four seedy-looking men; law enforcement officers, city police and Feds, she guessed. By this time she was beyond caring.

'Lew, why are your goons keeping me from going outside?'

She watched while everyone in the room gaped at her; exactly what she wanted. Gina was never a shrinking violet in company and she demanded answers.

'Gentlemen,' said Lew grinning broadly. 'This is Mrs Fjortoft and we, ma'am, are planning your personal safety.'

'Where is my husband?'

'Lady, I just wish I knew.'

'OK, why plan my safety?'

'You tell her Lieutenant.' He indicated a podgy little man with a sallow complexion. The guy put Gina in mind of Nixon and she'd never liked that man, even before he was proved a liar.

'Mrs Fjortoft,' he began. 'We have identified three groups hanging out around this place. All three are taking an unhealthy interest in who comes and who goes.'

'What people?' Gina's temper was cooling.

'Tell her, Lieutenant.'

‘Group one,’ said the officer, ‘we’ve identified as a New York Jewish organisation, although their leader’s British. They’re a suspected terrorist cell and potentially dangerous, which is why we’ve been alerted. We believe they are the ones who lost a man dead at the Aryan Nation. Group two: we’ve identified three of the Reverend Mulgrum’s finest. Group three: we can’t make nothing of them – look like a bunch of hippies, but it don’t follow they’re not dangerous.’

‘What makes you so sure they’re all after me?’

‘Mrs Fjortoft, please, who else in here would they be after?’

‘We know you’ve had a real bad time,’ Lew pleaded. ‘Why don’t you go and rest. I can send the doctor with something to help you sleep.’

‘Jeez, I don’t need sleeping pills. I want my husband back.’ Gina turned and left the room.

She took the elevator to her suite. As she stepped onto the landing she came face to face with a man. It was that fat Brit; some kind of politician Tom had said. He had been with Mulgrum and that was enough to condemn him.

‘Mrs Fjortoft, I believe. May I introduce myself – I’m Roland Gannemeade.’

‘Pleased to meet you, Mr Gannemeade,’ she lied coldly.

The man was obese and almost bald; a one-time athlete reduced to blubber. He looked of an age with her Gus, but Gus was still muscular and fit.

‘I understand your husband is out of town. I was looking forward to meeting him.’

‘Can’t help you there, Mr Gannemeade. If you’ll excuse me I need the bathroom.’

Gina turned her back and unlocked her door. She knew she was being rude and didn’t care. She walked to the window and stared at the city skyline. She wanted Tom here to comfort her in this lonely place where she knew no one. *Sleepless in Seattle*, a movie title she remembered, but so appropriate. It was raining outside, like in England. She stared down into the street at the slowly moving traffic and scurrying pedestrians. She could see no sinister watchers but it didn’t mean none were there.

Gina moved from the window and fell on her bed. She clenched her fists as she lay flat on her face. Never had she been so utterly miserable nor felt so alone. She wanted to be with Gus, he was her rock; the strong man who had rescued her from a career of modelling and bit-part acting. She wondered what he had seen in her. Gus’s relationship with Craig's mother had failed, but she knew Gus still hankered after the woman. She had no right to feel jealous, not with Gus being so generous about her adventures. Gina was a passionate woman. She needed a man for physical pleasure and love. She had been hurt by her husband's failing sex drive and wondered if it was her fault. It was different now she knew the truth of his awful childhood. She guessed the roots of his problem lay there. Gina had compensated with a whole series of different men. She knew she was still an attractive woman with lovemaking skills to please any man. Did that make her a whore? That's what some people called her; like Lucy O'Malley. It was all right for Lucy, with her career and her handsome boyfriend. Lucy had it made, so what right did it give her to sneer? Lucy would marry her man and have children, something fate had denied Gina. What did riches and fame mean compared to that? Her memories drifted back to her childhood in New England. She had travelled a long way from that little farm girl gathering fire-wood and feeding the pigs. She longed to return to Crossfield and her own farm. She longed to be with Tom, whose wife Tricia had been her dearest friend, and whom she had betrayed. She loved Tom like no man she had ever known, remembering the nights when he had shared her bed; the scent of him, his firm muscular body and his strong arms around her. Gina lost all restraint as she lay, face down, and bawled her eyes out, her tears wetting the soft pillows. Her whole body shook as if suffused with desolation and failure. After a while she drifted into sleep.

Gina awoke at six o'clock in the evening. She stared in the mirror and was horrified. Her hair looked awry and her complexion blotchy. Two swollen red eyes stared mournfully back at her. She grabbed her makeup bag and began to do running repairs. It more an exercise in damage limitation but she would not appear in public as she was.

At seven o'clock she made her way to the smallest and most secluded dining room, the area normally used for those with confid-ential business to discuss. The headwaiter recognised her and fussed around with a smarmy deference that she could do without. She had no appetite but her self-discipline told her she needed to eat. The sight of that haggard face in the mirror had alarmed her. Soup, bread and a bottle of wine appeared. The soup looked good and smelt good; already she was feeling better.

'Mrs Fjortoft, may I join you?'

It was Gannemeade. Gina wanted to tell that son-of-a-bitch to go to hell, but already he was sitting down not two feet from her.

'Please yourself, Mister. Maybe you know where my husband is.'

'I'm afraid I don't.'

Gina delivered her coldest stare. 'I saw you at Mulgrum's joint.'

He laughed. 'An interesting man, don't you think?'

'No, he's a goddam Nazi.'

'Ah, but he only endorses the positive aspects of that creed.'

'Like killing poor Jewish kids?'

'An event much exaggerated in the reporting – there was some unfortunate starvation of course.' He paused and lowered his voice. 'Mrs Fjortoft, I am writing a book and for that role I have to research. I am hoping very much that your husband can help me.'

'With what?'

'I would like to talk with him about his stepfather, Dr Brown. He was a pioneer with no recognition, but he was a great man.'

Gina nearly choked on her soup. Brown had killed over one hundred small children with his botched transplant experiments. Not content with that he had colluded at the mass extermination of his surviving specimens. She struggled to form the words needed; the kind of devastating put down that Gus would have delivered. She became aware of Gannemeade staring at her, his face, eyes and mouth twisted in lechery. He was coming onto her, slavering over her, when she had made it plain that she found him repulsive. Then she felt him touch her, his horrible sweaty palm feeling her thigh.

'Get your hands off me, you shite!' she whispered the words.

Gina had often had to repel drunken advances, but no man had ever groped her so coldly and arrogantly as this.

'Oh come on, Gina,' he leered. 'Everybody knows what you're like. You want a bit of fun, don't you?'

'Mister, if you don't hit-ass outa' here this minute I'll scream the house down and you'll be thrown out – got me?'

Gannemeade's face had reddened. 'You'll be sorry you said that – very sorry. I am a powerful man in England and a dangerous person to offend. You might be wise not to return there.'

'Get out of my sight!'

Gannemeade rose and walked from the room. In spite of everything Gina began to giggle. The man waddled like a disgruntled brown bear.

'Trouble, madam?' asked the waiter.

'Yeah, but it's finished,' she smiled at him. 'How about a rare steak and side salad.'

Gina did not linger in the public sections of the hotel, unwilling to risk another encounter with the loathsome Gannemeade. In her bedroom she began to pack her overnight bag. The moment Gus reappeared she was out of here. She found her gun, that she had recovered from Tom and checked it, taking a few practice aims. Hands together, breath in, aim low, squeeze the trigger. Satisfied, she dropped the weapon into the bag and zipped it shut. She kicked off her shoes and fell backwards onto the bed. She still felt the effects of that long hike in the mountains. Her feet were in good shape, but her ankles hurt and her back was stiff. The experience had given Gina a confidence boost. She felt not one iota of guilt about wounding Van Zyl. He had threatened Tom, so she had done what she needed to do and would do it again tomorrow; the man was horseshit. It mattered to her that the deed had impressed Tom. He had been magnificent that night, as if he was in a movie. She stood up and walked to the window. The streets shone in the rain. Cars were moving on the road, but few people on the sidewalks, and no obvious watchers.

A double knock sounded on the apartment door. 'Security,' called a disembodied voice.

She strolled lazily to the door. 'What d'you want?'

'Mister Gungenhorn asked me to check for electronic devices.' The voice was a deep mid-west drawl.

'OK, wait.' She yawned as she opened the door.

A figure, like a charging bull hurtled into the room shoving her to the floor; Gannemeade. Gina's fury and disgust was initially with herself. How could she have been so naïve. One glance through the spyhole would have prevented this intrusion. It took two seconds for her to scramble to her feet. She turned to face him.

'Get outa' here. Get out – you evil bastard!'

Gannemeade leered at her, red-faced and triumphant. Naked, apart from a towel around his waist, he looked more repulsive than ever. His blubbery folds of fatty skin were chalk white and she caught the odour of sweat and stale body spray. The guy wasn't playing games. Gannemeade was a heavyweight, bent on having his way and vengeful with it. Gina measured the distance to her gun and likewise to the house telephone. The phone was nearer and she inched towards it; Gannemeade anticipated her. He leapt, pulled the set from its socket, and hurled it across the room.

'Come on, little girlie, don't play hard to get. We all know what you're like – let me help you get naked.'

His tone, sneering and self-confident, brought Gina to the edge of panic. Gannemeade was a man who got what he wanted, and right now what he wanted was her. She edged nearer to the bag with the gun, just managing to release the zip. Gannemeade lunged and Gina lashed out at him. Her manicured fingernails had been damaged beyond repair by her recent adventures, but as weapons they were surprisingly effective. Gina's right hand connected with Gannemeade's chest and drew blood. He stopped in mid attack and winced, staring in disbelief at the scratch marks. Gina reached for her bag as Gannemeade, with a roar of animal fury pushed her sprawling onto the bed. She screamed and again kicked, this time connecting with empty air. She could smell his foul breath as grunting like a pig, he fumbled with the waistband of her jeans. The towel around him slid down to reveal a horrid little purple erection. He never saw Gina reach out, grab the gun from her half-open bag, thumb the safety-catch and teeth clenched, pull the trigger.

The explosion was deafening. Her ears sang and her nostrils filled with the expended cordite. Gannemeade, screaming with pain and rage, fell backwards clutching his shattered right arm. He gaped in utter disbelief as Gina stood up and raising the gun butt, brought it down on his head with all the force left to her. Gannemeade slid into a pool of blood groaning and twitching.

Instinctively she pulled up her jeans and fixed them. Then she staggered to the bathroom, seized the rim of the washbasin, and vomited her recently consumed dinner.

CHAPTER 28

'Charlie, may I ask a personal question?'

'For why?'

Charlie Marrington looked at Tom suspiciously. Tom sighed; this was going to be hard work.

'What did your father do in the war?'

Charlie's face creased into a smug grin. 'That'd be telling.'

'Go on, don't keep me in suspense.'

Charlie picked up a box of bedding plants and carried it to the display table. 'My old dad, he were Secret Service.'

'With Mr Reade-Coke?'

'That's right – if you knows already, why ask?'

'Honestly, that's all I do know. Could you tell me more?'

Charlie shook his head. 'The old man wouldn't talk about that, not to his dying day. Said as it'd break his oath to the King.'

'But you were around at the time?'

'I was only a nipper; he wouldn't tell I nothing,' he paused. 'I do remember Freddie Reade-Coke sitting with Dad in our kitchen. They used to talk in some foreign lingo – Spanish I think.'

The idea of an old countryman like Zac Marrington being a linguist seemed surreal. He said so tactfully to Charlie.

'Not so, my old dad were in the navy when he was a lad – merchant service; told me half his shipmates was South Americans. He could talk their lingo good.'

'Charlie, I really do need to know what Mr Reade-Coke was doing in the war. It's got a bearing on Rufus Partridge's work.'

'My granddaughter told me about that. Real cut up she is – they young'uns liked him it seems.'

'Anything you can remember will help.'

'Guv'nor, why don't you ask Lady Clarry, she were Freddie's sister. If anyone knows she will.'

'Charlie, that's brilliant. Why didn't I think of it. Although God knows if she'll be very co-operative – my court have just done her for drink driving.'

Tom pushed open the gate of Lilac Cottage carefully fending off the Jack Russell terriers that snapped at his trousers. He noticed the battered Morris Minor parked against the hedge. He hoped Lady

Clarry would be persuaded to sell it. With a three-year ban her driving days were clearly over.

Clarissa Hosskythe, sister of the late Freddie, was the only surviving member of the Reade-Coke family still living in Crossfield. Clarry was in the garden on her knees weeding. As usual the little plot looked immaculate. She rose to her feet and stared at him myopically. At seventy-six she still retained some of the aura that had once made her a society beauty. Her husband had died years ago, leaving Clarry a posh title and very little else. She had returned to live out her days in the village of her birth.

'It's young Tom?' she stared again.

'Clarry, can you spare me five minutes?'

'I can spare you more if you'd care for a cup of tea,' she smiled. 'Since your infamous colleagues stopped me driving I find I have unlimited time.'

Tom followed her through the French windows. The house had a pleasing aroma of wood smoke and scented flowers.

'I hear young Gina is still away. I hope she'll be home in time for the next fete committee.' Clarry waved him to a floral pattern armchair. 'Some of my ladies are rather caustic about Gina, but I like her. She has spirit – feisty is the word my grandson uses.'

Tom felt a sense of triumph. On the wall in front of him was the same photograph, *The Three Musketeers* that Lucy had described at Woolbarrow Farm. Clarry returned pushing an antique trolley. The tea was China, not Tom's normal choice of brew, accompanied by scones and homemade cake.

'I've got a new pot of honey somewhere.' She squinted vaguely.

Tom pointed at the picture. 'I gather there is a copy of that one in the Rowridge house. Can you tell me anything about it?'

'That's my brother's wartime unit. They had a secret mission.'

'I've heard rumours but nothing definite.'

Tom knew that Clarry had been close to her brother; he needed to be tactful.

'They wouldn't let Freddie join the army because of his health,' said Clarry. 'Very stupid of them; he was an experienced soldier. He'd already killed enemy in combat.'

'When was this?'

'In Spain – don't you know his story?'

Clarry shuffled across to the photograph; Tom waited.

'My brother had TB, so the specialists sent him to a mountain resort in Spain. It was 1936 and he'd only been there a few months when Franco's men massacred the people in a nearby village. Slaughtered everyone: old men, women, children, babies – even farm livestock. That was enough for Freddie. He tagged on to a refugee column until he reached Spanish Government territory. He joined their army and fought in the civil war until he was wounded.'

Clarry began pouring tea. 'Freddie was a Reade-Coke; we've always bred crack shots and top game stalkers. Freddie was one of our best ever. So they gave him a sniper's rifle, a special one made in America, and set him loose.' Clarry rubbed her hands together. 'He killed one of Franco's generals. The man was stark naked copulating with a whore. Freddie killed them both – same bullet right through the pair of them.' Clarry blinked around the room. 'I'm sure I've got a fresh honey pot.'

'It's over there.' Tom stood up and fetched the jar from the side-board.

'Well done. Now, as for Freddie, he killed over thirty fascists before he took a bullet himself. The British diplomatic mission intervened and he was shipped home.'

'Clarry, this is an epic. What about his TB?'

'Poor boy, he never full recovered.'

Clarry turned away from the picture and the sadness on her lined face vanished. 'Tom, you want to know about the Three Musketeers?'

'It would be interesting. We've found some papers relating to this that someone tried to steal.'

Clarry sniffed. 'It's still supposed to be secret but that's nonsense. Those men were brave and they should be given credit.' She sat down and sipped her cup. 'They were a special unit trained to deal with a German occupation. They were to compile a list of collaborators and fifth columnists. When the word came they were to assassinate them.' Clarry's eyes gleamed. 'Yes, take them out, slit their throats – make an example of the bastards.'

Tom felt shocked. The sight of this gentle old lady, teacup in hand, positively applauding terrorism was wholly unexpected. But he hadn't lived through the dark months of 1940. It wasn't for him to pass judgement.

'What about the other two in the group?' he asked. 'Reg Rowridge was a conscientious objector and Zac Marrington had only one leg.'

'That was the clever part. Rowridge was never a conchie, he was a fully trained territorial soldier. It's time people knew that. Marrington was our gamekeeper; he knew every inch of the ground for miles. Do you follow? The Germans have no imagination and less sense of humour. They would have been fooled for a while but not for long. The death of our men was inevitable and not a pleasant death either if they were captured. It's time their story was told.'

Tom spent the remainder of the day touring his domain, but his thoughts were far away. Clarry's story fascinated him. Freddie Reade-Coke had died ten months after he employed Tom to manage Crossfield Estate. Tom remembered him as a kindly but frail elderly figure, confined to a wheelchair. He couldn't relate the man he remembered to the furtive sniper, dealing destruction behind enemy lines. Zac Marrington was an elder version of son Charlie. Reg Rowridge, Tom had never met. Yet this unlikely trio had trained together for a specific purpose: rooting out collaborators. Maybe the Woolbarrow mystery had nothing to do with Wilhelm Brown and Gostanyn. Could its roots be not in 1944 Poland, but England in 1940? Was that coded sheet of paper the list of local Nazi sympathisers? Would someone, even so long after the event, kill to suppress it?

Tom completed his tour at the garden centre. It was five-thirty and the shop was closing. Tom was suffering from reverse jet lag. It might be evening but his body clock was telling him it was barely midday. He strolled through the electronic doors to be greeted by Muriel. She had her most judgmental expression; Tom wondered what he had done now.

'Mr O'Malley, I have an email message for ye. Mrs Fjortoft will be arriving at Heathrow Airport at seven-thirty. She asks to have transport arranged.'

Muriel turned and walked away. Even her back expressed disapproval.

'Don't look at me, Guv'nor,' said Charlie. 'I ain't turning out that time of night. You fetch her – she's your woman.'

CHAPTER 29

Gina clung to the washbasin as she fought a spasm of giddiness. Again she vomited until it hurt. Feeling better, she staggered to the shower and put her head under the stream of cold water. She had to escape. She no longer trusted these Benson Company men. For two days she had detected a growing hostility and now she had just escaped been raped by this foul-smelling ape.

Gannemeade was sitting holding his head and moaning; his shattered arm caked in congealing blood. Gina grabbed her overnight bag and fled the room. She locked the door on the outside but left the key in place. She stood listening, but all seemed quiet. She knew her chances of leaving by the main entrance were nil. Once, long ago in LA, she had worked in an hotel with basement storage areas and a loading bay. Gina heard the elevator stop and the doors open. She tiptoed into an alcove off the main passage and froze. Three people emerge from the elevator: Lew Gungenhorn and two other men. It only needed one of them to glance sideways and she would be discovered. She assumed they were heading for her room. Instead they passed it, unlocked another door and shut it behind them.

Gina ran for the elevator and pressed the button for the basement. The doors opened into a corridor of painted brickwork, so brightly lit that it almost dazzled her. In front stood a forklift truck and wooden pallets stacked with cardboard boxes. The arched roof of this subterranean passage stretched for some twenty yards ending in a pair of steel doors. The unloading area: so far so good. She steadied herself and drew a deep breath. To the right were wooden doors with circular glass panels: the kitchen. She could hear the murmur of voices and the rattle of utensils. Ahead lay the outer world and escape.

A wicket gate opened in the steel doors and a man stepped through. She knew him, his name was Kelly and he'd done duty at Crossfield. She wanted someone to talk to, almost as much as she wanted to escape from this trap.

'Kelly,' she called.

He stopped and swung around.

'Mrs Fjortoft,' he smiled, 'how come you're down here?'

'Kelly, I've gotta get out of this place. I must contact the police.'

'Police!'

'A man's just tried to rape me.'

'Jesus – you told Gungenhorn?'

'I can't – the man's a friend of his. I doubt he'll even report the offence. Man, will you help me, or do it for Mr Fjortoft? I guess it's my husband who pays you.'

He looked unsure. 'I don't know where Mr Fjortoft is. I'm told to watch this gate – nobody to go in or out.'

Gina felt near to despair. Kelly was blocking the way and he looked less and less friendly. She dodged him and sprinted for the far door. Kelly let out a yell and began to follow her. She felt a wave of pure terror mixed with mad exhilaration as she scrambled through the gate and ran up the ramp to the street above. Kelly had stopped and was imploring her to come back.

A black figure rose from behind a garbage bin. A man who seemed a giant, silhouetted against the street lighting, arms outstretched. Gina tried to dodge him but he caught her arm. She screamed as Kelly ran at him.

'Joel, you son-of-a-bitch,' Kelly yelled. 'She done nothing to you – back off!'

Her captor released her as Kelly lunged at him. The two men grappled swaying and stumbling on the rough sidewalk. The tall man swung an arm, there was an object in his hand that he brought down on Kelly's head; the Mormon collapsed to the ground. Gina thought about her gun, but it was securely zipped in her bag. That bag was a hindrance, but she would not let it go. She ran as best she could, but her ankles and feet hurt. Please, God, let a cop patrol come by. Instead the street was deserted, not a single walker in sight; nothing, apart from one car, an ancient Ford parked on the far side.

The big man was shouting in an English accent. 'It's the Fjortoft woman – she's broke out.'

'You don't say Jewboy, Joel?' sneered a nearer voice.

Gina saw the man and she knew him; the podgy platoon commander of Mulgrum's militia. She sobbed as she drove herself for one last desperate burst of running. She had fifty yards more to reach the intersection. If she could make it there she would find people who could point her to the police precinct station. She risked a glance over her shoulder. A handgun cracked; the sound made her duck in fright. The Mulgrum man was crouched behind another garbage bin; the tall one was nowhere to be seen.

She could hear a car; it was the old Ford. It performed a U-turn and was racing down the road; seconds more and it would catch her. She ran on gasping and wailing. It seemed this whole damn town was nothing but enemies. Another gunshot and she heard the bullet hit metal. The car swerved and accelerated; now it was level with her and slowing. Gina was finished; she had done her best and it was not enough.

'Mrs Fjortoft – it is Mrs Fjortoft?' The man's voice was pleasant, with a touch of Canadian burr. 'Please, answer me – are you in trouble?'

The car had stopped beside her. Very slowly, still trembling, she turned towards it. The passenger window was down and a man was looking at her. She couldn't see the driver but in the back sat a waif of a girl. Suddenly she felt easier, these people were mysterious, but not overtly threatening.

'Mrs Fjortoft, I think it'd be safer you come with us.'

As he spoke the girl opened the rear door and beckoned her in.

'Who are you, and why are you here?' Gina forced the words.

'My name's Pete and we're friends of Tom O'Malley. We've been watching those other guys. Get in, Lady, no more talking.' He turned to the driver. 'Go, Henry, take it away – let's outa' here!'

Gina heard a babble of shouting from further up the street and another gunshot. She hurled her bag inside, nearly flattening the girl, and dived after it as the car accelerated away in a screech of hot tyres.

'Mrs Fjortoft, I guess we were in the nick of time. You're one very lucky lady.'

Lucy returned to an empty house. Her partner Mike was out on call but he had left a meal in the oven and an untidy scrawled note. She ate the food, cod and chips from the takeaway down the road. In her troubled world it tasted of dust and ashes. She gave up and turned on the television, but the sounds and pictures only irritated. On a whim she grabbed a coat and went out to her car. It was not too late to pay a call at the Cunninghams.

Marjorie hustled Lucy into the kitchen and poured her a cup of coffee.

'Mathew's funeral's on Wednesday,' she said. 'Crossfield United Reformed chapel, eleven thirty.'

'Thank goodness for that.'

'Agreed, it'll be a closure of sorts,' said Marjorie. 'Would you let your father know?'

'Of course – how is Francesca?'

'Still very withdrawn. Natalie knows what it's about but she's being stubborn. They're closing ranks against the adult world.'

'I'll talk to her if you like, but let's get the funeral over.'

Lucy drove home, still feeling restless. Nobody was being entirely truthful. She suspected Dad of being evasive about his experiences in Oregon. Then there was Gina – something had happened between Dad and that awful woman. The relationship had gone beyond the carnal into something deeper. She had no proof, but intuition told her so.

Lucy put the dirty plates into the kitchen sink. The clock said bedtime, though she knew too well that this would be a non-sleeping night. Her brain was too active and her troubles too deep. She made a spontaneous decision; late as it was she would drive down to the hospital and see Rufus.

Lucy smiled as she took the parking space reserved for one notoriously self-important consultant. The clock on the dashboard said ten minutes to midnight. Lucy avoided the main entrance and walked in through A and E; the people there knew her and she would invite no comment. She had been told that Rufus was semi-conscious and out of intensive care. He had been moved to a single room on the third floor for observation.

Ward F1 combined a series of single rooms adjoining a long corridor. Halfway down was Rufus's room adjacent to the reception desk. Lucy knew the hushed air was deceptive. Night staff would be around to answer calls however frivolous. Lucy reached the reception and groped in her pocket for her doctor's ID. She wondered what explanation she could give for being here at this hour. Only two people were at reception. One was a restless patient with a heavily bandaged head. He wore a towelling dressing gown over outdoor trousers and shoes, which seemed odd. The charge nurse sat at his station but slumped forward asleep. A half-filled paper cup had toppled over dampening some paper charts. The ward sister would not be amused. Sleeping on the job was dereliction of duty and spoiling paperwork high misdemeanour. Lucy felt sympathetic; how many times had she been there in her hospital days. She turned away and walked to the three observation rooms.

The middle one had the door slightly ajar. The card read: *Mr R. Partridge,* the name of the consultant, and: *GP. Dr. L. O'Malley.* She pushed the door gently open and slipped inside. The semidarkness was relieved by the red glow of the bed-head light. She was not alone; another male nurse was bending over the form in the bed. Lucy started to mutter an apology but left the words unfinished. This nurse was distinctly overdressed. Apart from the standard jacket he wore a surgeon's theatre cap and mask. The man had taken one of the patient's forearms and was examining it with a pencil torch. In his other hand he held a large hypodermic syringe filled with oily liquid. Slowly he began to probe for a vein.

Something was wrong. Lucy had that strange out-of-body sensation; a spectator, observing herself, watching some dimly lit scene.

She screamed. 'Stop that – no!'

Too late, the man emptied the contents of the syringe into the arm. Lucy driven by a madness that blotted out everything including fear, hurled herself at the hooded figure, clasping her hands around his throat, kicking and screaming as she did so. For a second he froze; then he turned on her. She could not believe any human being could have such animal strength. He picked her up as if she was a rag doll and threw her against the wall. She staggered and nearly fell headlong. Her only thought was escape; through the door into the world she knew. She saw a man framed against the brightly lit corridor. He was the restless patient with the bandaged head. Could he save her? She sobbed as she ran into this stranger's arms. He caught her and savagely closed his right hand over her face, clamping her jaws together. His hand had a sickly taste of body perfume as he turned her towards the door. The bogus nurse was coming for her; she saw the glint in his eyes highlighted in the space between cap and mask. These were expressive eyes, both intelligent and powerful, but without humanity. Behind those eyes was an empty void – a lost soul. She watched apathetically as he examined his syringe, holding it vertically to the light, blowing out the air with the plunger. She could see a tiny residual dose, maybe a single millilitre. She tried to fight but her captor held her expertly and the pain was excruciating. The macabre figure reached out and took her right arm. It was silly but all she could think of was how professionally trained he must be.

Tom had driven Gina home accompanied by two Fjortoft security men. Their presence had inhibited him from asking questions, while Gina had slept the whole journey. Something had happened in Seattle. Earlier that evening Tom had received a cryptic email message from Sam and Greta Little. It seemed that while Pete and Chantelle had been shadowing Mulgrum's men, they had discovered Gina wandering the streets alone and in danger. He delivered her to the Manor and went home.

He half expected Lucy to be at Boxtree with a meal for him. In this he was disappointed; maybe she had an evening call-out. An hour later the phone rang. Mrs Fjortoft needed to talk with him – urgently.

Gina was lying on her bed still dressed in her travelling clothes. It was Tom's first view of the master bedroom. He thought the place over lavish, although not as awful as the bridal suite in Seattle. One wall was dominated by a huge full figure oil painting of Gina totally nude.

'I like your picture.'

She sat up. 'Gus commissioned it. I guess it's worth a lot of bucks. It took a whole month, every day, holding that pose for hours.'

She reached across to the bedside table and passed him a newspaper, The Seattle Times.

'Page two – down the bottom.'

It was a short report of a gun wounding forty-eight hours ago. The victim was stated to be a British visitor, Mr Roland Gannemeade.

'Don't ask me to sympathise,' Tom replied.

She told him everything: her time in the Benson Hotel culminating in the attempted rape and her escape.

'What are the police doing?' he asked. 'There's nothing said about a rape charge.'

'Gannemeade's cooked up some story about saving a girl from rape, quite a hero, and Gungenhorn's backing him.'

'God, the bastard – bastard! You're not going to let him get away with that?' Tom felt stunned – words were inadequate.

'No, Tom, I don't care – I shot him, I won. I'm a tough cookie, he's the third man I've punished for coming on too strong – first time with a gun though.'

'Did you report to the police?'

'Not worth the hassle – I know how things work over there. I took the first plane out. I never want to see that city again.'

In spite of his fury, Tom could understand her logic. He could see no way of bringing the odious Gannemeade to justice without damaging Gina.

'It's a bit of luck you finding my friends.'

'Not really, they've been watching the hotel to see if Brown was there. There were two other lots as well: some Jewish group and Mulgrums's boys.' She laughed. 'While they had a shootout, Pete and Chantelle snatched me.'

'Where were the police?'

'Search me.'

'You Americans – for God's sake!'

'I know, just leave it, shall we.' She sank back on the bed. 'Tom, I'm worried about Gus. I think that brother's got him.'

'Gina, love, I want you to think back. When the brother came here, did Gus name him?'

'Sure, he said, "Meet my brother, Will".'

'You've never met the other brother?'

'No, Gus told me about him, but he's a good guy, another victim. He's made himself a new identity and Gus doesn't want things spoilt for him.'

'You say the man you met was disguised, but would you know him if you saw him for real?'

'I can't say.' She frowned, her face tense. 'Oh my God! Could it be the same…?'

'What is it?'

'It's nothing, or maybe I'm going crazy.' Her whole demeanour had changed. 'Tom, please leave me, I want to lie down for a while.'

He smiled at her and walked to the door. She looked back with wistful, doe like eyes. Slowly she rested her head on the pillows. Seconds later she was sleeping like a child.

Tom returned to Boxtree. Gannemeade haunted his thoughts like a stench. That vile slug; had forced himself on a seemingly defenceless woman. At least he'd had his deserts and that made Tom feel good. He thought of Gina; he was becoming dangerously fond of her. Shared experience had bonded them, but she was Gus's wife, and so long as he retained a shred of loyalty for him, that would remain a point of honour. He yawned and looked at the clock; it was three in the morning. Then the phone rang.

CHAPTER 30

Lucy sat in a chair, ashen faced; on her lap lay a plastic bowl and a box of tissues.

'Hello, Dad.' She forced a smile.

Tom tried to reply but the words wouldn't come. His own eyes were misty and he had a lump in his throat.

Lucy's partner, Michael, took her other hand and kissed her. 'How are you?'

'I feel lousy. I've been vomiting all night and I'm too giddy to stand.'

'They've sent your blood samples to the lab,' said Mike. 'We'll know what the poison was tomorrow.'

'Apparently you were found in a broom cupboard,' said Tom.

'I'm remembering things. There was another man,' she dabbed her eyes. 'The one with the needle, he was strong, but I took him to be old. The one who grabbed me was young and there was something about him…' She closed her eyes and bowed her head.

'Don't talk if you don't want to,' said Tom.

'I do want to. You see, the man with the needle – I looked into his eyes; something about him seemed terribly sad. Do you know what I mean?'

Tom didn't, but he said nothing.

Lucy wiped her eyes with a tissue. Mike knelt beside her and put his arm around her shoulders.

'It was the other one holding me. I got the most terrible vibes from him. I think he's the nearest thing to absolute evil. I can't describe it any other way.' She sat staring glassily. 'Rufus is dead, isn't he?'

'Rufus died last night,' said Mike.

'It's all coming back. They killed him – it was murder.' She sat upright, wild-eyed. 'Dad, you could be next, nobody's safe. What are you doing?'

Tom squeezed her hand. 'Don't worry about me. I've got four of Gus's Mormons, one of them's sitting in my car right now. The police have finally woken up and there's an armed response unit on call if we meet real trouble, and…' he smiled, 'Hannah's turned up at Boxtree with two Israeli cut throats. I tell you they frighten me, let alone anyone else.'

'Hannah – what's she got to do with it?'

‘I have no idea, but I imagine she’s on the track of this man Brown. She’s asked to stay at Boxtree for a couple of days. This time I agreed – safety in numbers.’

‘What about the practice, Mike? The boss and you will never manage alone. I’ve got to get out of here.’

Mike gently kissed her. ‘Darling, cool it. We’ve a new locum and the other clinics are helping out; even George Shaylor’s taking a turn.’

Lucy smiled weakly. ‘Dad, take Mike away. I don’t want to be seen by him – he’s a rotten doctor.’

The two CID officers, an inspector and a woman PC, were waiting in the nurse’s office, as a well as the ward sister and a hospital administrator.

Tom spoke to the police. ‘I think it’s OK to question her if the medical staff agree, of course.’

‘Trust us, sir,’ said the inspector. ‘Has she said anything to you?’

‘Only that she remembers two men. I think she feels guilty about Rufus Partridge – she was trying to save him.’

The Inspector shook his head. ‘No chance; you know they doped two of the night staff?’

‘No, I didn’t.’

‘They’re both in recovery. The charge nurse had his coffee cup laced with something, we think it was probably rophypnol, the so called date-rape drug. His female colleague was in here. They held a pad over her mouth until she passed out – bastards.’

‘It’s an all-round disaster,’ said the administrator. ‘There’s got to be an internal enquiry and almost certainly an independent investigation. It could damage our funding.’

‘I doubt that’ll be much comfort for Mr Partridge’s family and friends,’ said the inspector.

Tom kissed Lucy goodbye; he felt it tactful to leave her alone with Michael. Ed, the Mormon guard was standing beside the parked car. It was raining again; typical of early May when winter returns for a last throw.

‘You shouldn’t stand out in this,’ said Tom.

‘Mr O’Malley, we’ve a problem. I’ve had a message,’ Ed held up his mobile phone. ‘Those Israelis at your place. They’ve grabbed a guy who called on you and roughed him up.’

‘Who was this?’

‘Don’t know his name, but he’s been around for a week or so. We think you should get home quick before they do something stupid.'

Hannah and the two Israelis had turned up late last night. Tom had just had the news from the police of the attack on Lucy. He had wanted to rush straight to the hospital but had been told firmly to stay at home and await a call. In his irrational state Tom had accepted Hannah's offer of support. Now he was beginning to wonder if he had imported more trouble. The Israeli minders exuded an air of menace that bordered on the downright nasty. There had been an immediate stand off between these two and the Mormons. As Hannah put it, the Mormons were Fjortoft men. In her view, as Fjortoft was a war criminal, the Mormons must quit. Tom had ripped into her. She was a guest in his house. The Mormons were staying and if Hannah didn't like it she could leave and take her thugs with her. The infuriating woman had listened to his tirade with a sweet smile and gracefully accepted the position. Now, with this latest news, Tom had taken enough.

He strode through his own front door and shouted for Hannah. She was in the kitchen with one of the minders. Outside in the yard he could see the other Israeli with Mo, the toothless chef from the Rotherwood bungalow. The pair was sheltering from the rain under an overhanging roof.

'What the hell are you playing at?' Tom roared at her.

'We've secured a prisoner.'

'No you haven't. You've physically attacked a visitor to this house. You've abused my hospitality and in our law committed a criminal offence.'

'No, Tom, we apprehended a man who may have come to kill you. Guess his name?'

'I'm not even bothering to try.'

'He's hiding behind a false identity but we know him. He's Albert Brown, brother of Wilhelm and Gustav.'

Francesca sat on the edge of her bed. She knew Natalie was staring at her but avoided eye contact. Near the end of her tether with worry she found Natalie's attitude irritating. That horrible Alex Cornbinder had approached her. Worse, it had been outside the college in full view of everyone. Of course Natalie had seen him and had insisted she tell all.

'Look, Fran, you're so naïve.' Natalie had been impatient. 'Everyone knows your mother was screwing with Alex, so what's the big deal?'

Francesca sat and stared in horror. It was all right for Natalie; she was attractive to boys. She knew about sex, that dark other world that half-fascinated half-frightened Francesca. She knew for a fact, that Natalie had done it with two of the lads from college and worse with one of the adult DJs from the club. It had been an experience, Natalie explained, out of this world – quite unlike fumbling with fellow teen-agers.

Francesca had no idea what Natalie was talking about. She had a ferment of mixed feelings, but mainly jealousy. Natalie was destined to experience sex, marriage and children: all things beyond the hopes of Francesca.

She rounded in fury. 'You know nothing about my mother – only disgusting rumours.'

'Oh yeah,' Natalie yawned. 'Go on, what did Alex say? You can tell me.'

Francesca wanted to tell her, wanted to pour out the whole sordid tale. She knew her mother was promiscuous. She well remembered her father's manic fury the day he assaulted Mum with a riding whip. She had fled the house and Francesca had not seen her since.

'He said Mum was involved in a bank robbery. Alex says she knows where the money's stashed. He says if I don't help him find it he'll tell the police and I'll be charged as an accessory.'

'This is weird,' Natalie gaped at her. 'First PC Witherrick says your dad nicked something from Fjortoft and now this – it's crazy. Have you seen Witherrick again?'

'No, and I can't help him; I've never seen any leather case.'

'Alex won't drop himself in it just to spite you. The only bank robbery was the one at Winchester, back in March, when Alex was still in the nick.'

'I know, but Alex says he planned it and he never got his share of the money. He says Mum knows where it is and he can't find her.'

'Well, nor can we.'

'Trouble is, Nats, it may be true. Mum had some crazy scheme to save the farm. I overheard her talking on the phone.'

'Not planning a robbery?'

'I heard her say, "I've found the keys, I'm sure they're the right ones. Bring the stuff tonight, outside the kitchens. They know me – I'll say I've come to offer help tomorrow. You'll have to keep the lady out of the way – shouldn't be too difficult". That was all, except Dad overheard and he went for her with a riding crop. That was the last we saw her.'

Francesca sat back and sighed. For the first time in these nightmare days she felt relieved. That phone call had been in the back of her mind; with the voices in Bechams Wood, it haunted her dreams. Now she knew for certain who owned one of those voices and that had been a double shock.

Natalie sat cross-legged saying nothing.

Francesca pulled down a suitcase from the top of the wardrobe. It was her case stuffed with her drab clothes. From it she pulled out a piece of discoloured string with an odd shaped key on the end.

'This was in my granddad's old hidey-hole at the farm. It doesn't fit anything that I know and I'd never seen it before.'

Natalie inspected it. 'Any idea what kitchen your mum was talking about? You say she said keys, plural?'

'It can only be the kitchens where she helped part time. And this key is odd, I've never seen one that shape and it's nothing to do with our house.'

'I didn't know she did kitchen work – where would that be?'

'Crossfield Manor of course.'

'Wow, Fran, what date was that Winchester robbery?'

'I can't remember.'

'The newspaper office is still open. Jonathan there fancies me – we'll make him check it out.'

'If this man's locked in my coal shed; you release him now.' Tom blazed the command with such force that Hannah visibly wilted.

She spoke rapidly to her man in, presumably, Hebrew. How much English he understood was anyone's guess, but he threw Tom a look of amused respect. Tom suspected this macho man did not care to be ordered around by women. It was a dishevelled individual who emerged from the coal shed. He had an air of dignity in spite of the rough handling he had suffered. His well-cut jacket was soiled, his tie askew, and he had a bruise over his right eye. Tom thought he could discern a faint resemblance to Gus, then maybe not. He beckoned him into the kitchen.

'I'm Tom O'Malley. If you are my employer's brother, then you deserve a better welcome than this.'

The man said nothing.

'Miss Berkovic says you came here to kill me – well?'

'No sir, I came here to warn you.' The accent was American but different to Gus's West Coast speech.

'Warn me of what?'

'My other brother, Wilhelm is a mad dog. He will kill, and go on killing, anyone who obstructs him. That includes you but also me – especially me.'

'Last night, a man who could be this brother, killed a patient in hospital. The victim was a harmless schoolteacher. Why should that be?'

'I don't know but I fully believe you – I'm sorry.'

'Having killed his victim with a lethal injection the murderer used his needle on the patient's own doctor when she tried to intervene. She is my daughter. What have you to say, Mr Brown?'

'That I'm horrified. I met your daughter the other day: an impressive young lady. May I ask how she is?'

'She's alive and recovering.'

The relief on the man's face could only be genuine. Tom's suspicion was turning into curiosity. Gina had mentioned Albert Brown whom Gus had claimed to be a decent man with a new identity.

The visitor brushed his coat with his hands. 'I can't come into your house with this dirt on me, and my name is not Brown. I adopted my wife's name by legal deed. Today I'm Doctor Maxton Jiffers, of Freetown, Connecticut. If I can do anything to bring Wilhelm Brown to justice, I will do so, Sir, with no equivocation whatsoever.'

CHAPTER 31

Tom took his place at the head of the dining room table, opposite him sat Doctor Jiffers. Hannah and Alan Otford were in chairs against the wall. Tom had banned the Israeli guards and Hannah had ordered them to wait outside the house.

Tom opened the proceedings. 'This is a quasi-judicial hearing. You will be making a deposition before a justice of the peace. Do you agree to a record of these proceedings?'

'No problem,' said Jiffers.

Tom pressed the start button of the office voice recorder, knowing the tape would run for thirty minutes. He placed the family bible on the table and administered the oath.

'Thank you,' said Tom. 'I need a record of this hearing because I have no independent unbiased witness.'

He spoke slowly and deliberately while staring at Hannah. She had already decided that Jiffers was guilty.

'Doctor, would you care to explain who you are and why you've adopted your current name?'

'I was born Albert Brown son of Ernst Brown. In March nineteen forty-five when I was eleven, I was in Bremen with my mother and two brothers. We were sheltering in the basement of a hospital when an allied bomb penetrated it. I received multiple injuries. I remember very little from this time only the cold, pain, fear and bewilderment. I was treated in what was left of the hospital, but it was crowded and there were few medical staff. I was alone because my mother and brothers had left the city. I knew another patient, a boy I met in Poland, but he was no friend – I hated him.' He paused.

'You know it's such a relief to tell this tale. I've hidden these things away so long.'

Tom nodded. 'Please remember your testimony is confidential at this stage.' He smiled. 'Go on, doctor – you're doing fine.'

'After a few weeks I had the greatest luck. The Americans arrived and took over. I was assigned as patient to a US Army doctor. I guess he was intrigued to find a German kid who spoke perfect English. He discovered that my father was under arrest for his part in Gostanyn and that my mother had deserted me. I told him my mother was English and my stepbrother an American. He asked about Gostanyn and that was hard for me. I'd tried to bury the memories of that place.'

Tom intervened. 'I shall have to ask you about Gostanyn, but I take it you somehow reached America.'

'That was my doctor's doing; he accepted my story, and you see the medics had kinda taken a liking to me. I spoke English, I was alone and in deep trouble for something that was not my doing. To cut the story short they put me in an orderly's uniform and I went to the States with them.' For a second he smiled.

'That must have been irregular?'

'You bet, I was breaking immigration laws, but this was in nineteen forty-six and a million men returning home, so no way the authorities could check. Somehow they smuggled me in and I wasn't the only one.'

'So you became an American?'

'And very proud of it, sir.'

'Doctor Jiffers, in America I met one of only two surviving children of Gostanyn.'

Jiffers looked agitated. 'They all died, there couldn't have been any survivors.'

'Two East European girls escaped with the help of one of the Germans.'

'I'm sorry, but that couldn't have happened. The guards were SS; there was no scrap of humanity in them. They were conditioned to cruelty – it was hard-wired in their minds.'

'An ordinary soldier, an ancillary who worked in the kitchens, saved the girls. He was called Gunther, I don't know his other name.'

Jiffers gaped at them in genuine surprise. 'Gunther Brandt, fat boy cook? But he was dumb, kinda simple-minded.'

'So I'm told, but he formed a friendship with these girls and he put his life at risk for them.'

'Oh my God, to think of Gunther a hero, when the rest of us did nothing,' Jiffers muttered.

'It's what you did, Doctor Jiffers, or didn't do that interests me. I must warn you that my witness described the whole of that last morning in Gostanyn camp to me. She claims that you and your brothers took part in the extermination of the children.'

'Then she's lying!' Jiffers hammered a fist on the table. 'I saw it, I was forced to watch, but I never laid a finger on one of those kids.' He stared wildly round the room.

'Mr O'Malley, there isn't a day in my life I don't have total recall of those killings. There's not a night when I don't go to bed and wonder if I'll dream a return of that day. Please God, Sir, I was only a kid myself, and brother Gustav was just seven years old, and Wilhelm forced him…'

Jiffers face was ashen, he pulled a white handkerchief from his pocket and began to dab his eyes.

Tom looked at him. 'Do you want to break for a minute – have a glass of water?'

Hannah spoke. 'They always play it this way when they're cornered.'

Tom rounded on her. 'Miss Berkovic, one more interruption from you and I'll call my security men and have you removed.'

'I'd like to finish,' said Jiffers. 'We were all prisoners in that place. My father was a prisoner of his work. I don't believe he started out evil, but his obsession gripped him until he couldn't tell right from wrong. My mother stayed loyal but hated all of it. Little Gustav clung to her, but he was her kid, not Father's. Poor little guy, I never once saw him laugh or smile all that time. As for Will…'

'Take your time. If you want to stop say so.'

Tom shot Hannah a cold look. He sensed they were now close to the truth.

'I'll be OK,' Jiffers murmured. 'I don't know if you've been told, but Wilhelm and I are twins. Twins are supposed to be inseparable, but I hated Wilhelm from the earliest I can remember.'

Tom pushed the recorder closer. 'Doctor, I must ask you to speak up.'

Jiffers nodded. 'Will was blood brother to those SS men. He loved to see the killings. You see, when the transplants failed, the kids were put to sleep. Father said it was the humane thing and I suppose in a mad way he was right, but it doesn't condone his work. Will loved that. He would pester the lab men to let him do killing injections. Tell you something; Will hated Gustav, I guess he still does. He despised him because Gus made friends with some Jewish kids and of course he wasn't our father's son.'

'Can you tell us what happened the day the camp was evacuated?'

'The SS had the whole operation planned. Bring the kids to the lab in batches, give 'em the needle then wheel the bodies to the trucks. Father left it to them, but Will forced Gus and me to watch.'

'How could he force you?'

'He had a tame guard, a young teenage guy, not much older, but a whole lot bigger. Between them they dragged us in there. I just froze but Gus went crazy.'

Tom interrupted. 'Did they kill a child called, Josef?'

'Sure, little Jewish kid, friend of Gus – how d'you know that?'

'It so happens your brother also has nightmares. Tell us what you saw.'

'When Josef died, Gus went crazy. He broke free and ran out to find Mother. Will's SS friend went after him and he brings Gus back. That's when Will got hold of him and …'

Tom waited, watching the torment in the man's face.

'They laid a little girl on the table; she was called Gudrun. She was a pure bred Kraut, but she had Down's Syndrome. She never understood much but she was a cute little thing,'

'Did Wilhelm kill her?'

'He dragged Gus to the table, then the SS creep held him there while Wilhelm put the syringe in his hand and forced the needle into the kid's vein.'

'Which of them applied the pressure?'

'Will made Gus work the plunger. He held the wrist with the syringe. Then the SS guy began to break the fingers on his other hand, one by one, until Gus gave in and pushed the plunger home.' Jiffers sighed and looked up at Tom. 'That's it.' He reached out and touched the bible. 'This is the truth, as I swear by God.'

'I think we'll leave it there for the moment,' said Tom as he stopped the recorder.

He looked at Hannah. 'Are you satisfied?'

'I admit I'm disappointed, but despite a lack of corroboration, I suppose I will have to accept what I've heard.'

'Why are you disappointed? Is it such a bad thing to hear a man declare his innocence, or that of his young brother?'

'You wouldn't understand, Tom.'

'I think I do. You lot believe in atonement. The difference is that I believe atonement must come from those proved guilty beyond doubt.'

He addressed Jiffers. 'Tell me, did you visit Gustav Fjortoft here on the twenty-first of April last?'

'No, I was in the States. I only arrived in England a week back.'

'I didn't know that you and Wilhelm Brown were twins. Are you identical?'

'No we're not identical; same height, maybe same nose but that's all. But I haven't seen Wilhelm for thirty-five years. That was in Africa; since then he's vanished off the face of the earth.'

'Would you know him again? In the light of the murders here the police will want to speak to him.'

'If I came face to face today, I guess I would – worse luck.'

Jiffers had gone, and shortly afterwards Hannah and her party had vanished. Tom was not sorry to see the back of them. He walked indoors and sank into his armchair. He was still not fully recovered from his American ordeal. Everything had turned sour since Tricia's death. His beautiful, ordered life was crumbling around him. How close had he come to losing Lucy as well? The thought of her dying crossed his mind like an icy shadow. He too would be dead on the inside.

The telephone in the study was ringing. He stood up in alarm; what now – could this be the hospital? Had Lucy had a relapse? He ran through the house and seized the handset.

'Mr O'Malley, it's Frank Matheson.'

The private investigator; Tom relaxed. So much had happened in the last few weeks that he had forgotten him.

'I've info for you; lots more about Anthony Moncrief Tallisment.'

'Fire ahead, I'm all ears.'

'Our man is never a Scot, he's a South African, and his real name is Rudi Kolkinnen, probably Finnish parentage. Kolkinnen made a fortune in the Cape developing land. Later he was involved in racketeering in the Congo during the early Sixties.'

'Wilhelm Brown was supposed to have died in the Congo.'

'Kolkinnen was never Brown, but we gather he's a sick man. Whether he picked up some nasty virus in Africa I couldn't say. Now here's the spicy bit. When Tallisment, alias Kolkinnen, was in South Africa he met a smartarse accountant called – wait for it – Roland Gannemeade.'

'Gannemeade's still connected to Tallisment. He told me that himself.'

'He's on the board of Vega Magna Holdings, Tallisment's company. It's difficult to know what they were up to in Africa, because both men used half a dozen aliases.'

'Well done, Frank, brilliant. May I ask how you found all this?'

'My Edinburgh associate discovered a former employee with a grievance. I'll mail you my full report tomorrow.'

Tom felt a satisfying inner glow. With luck he would gather enough material to destroy Gannemeade as a public figure. He rang the hospital and was put through to Lucy.

'I'm fine now,' she replied. 'I'm being discharged tomorrow.

They won't let me work for a week but I can go home.'

'Good, I'll collect you. You'll be coming here to Boxtree. I want you safe and sound where I can see you.'

Tom's last call of the day was to Gina at the Manor. The flood-lighting had been switched on and in the growing darkness the house shone like a beacon. He slowed, surprised at the throng of people milling around the entrance gate. He stopped the car as the headlights lit the scene. In front of him stood two Mormon guards supporting a large man who swayed unsteadily between them. It was Gustav Fjortoft.

'Gus, what's happened – where've you been?' Tom stared at the face in front of him.

'He's real spaced out,' said one of the Mormons. 'Drugged to the eyeballs.'

'Where did he spring from?'

'He was rolled out of a car, about ten minutes back. The car never stopped; drove off like the devil was after them.'

Gus's expression was deadpan and uncomprehending.

'Put him in my car. I'll run him to the house.'

Gina arrived sprinting down the road, her blonde locks flying. With a wild cry she flung herself at Gus with such force that she nearly brought all three men to the ground. She buried her face in his chest before releasing him and rushing with equal force at Tom. She began to bombard everyone with questions. Now came a further distraction. From the direction of the house came more shouting, followed by a female voice wailing and sobbing.

The Mormons lifted Gus into the back seat of Tom's car, followed by Gina. Twenty seconds later Tom was parking by the front door of the Manor. Someone was being half-carried, half-dragged by two guards. Incredulous, he recognised Francesca Rowridge.

'What's happened?' he called.

Francesca broke into a fresh fit of wailing.

'Caught this one, trying to break into the house. She got right through our security – don't know how…'

The man was interrupted by a further uproar from around the corner of the house, by another girlish voice, angry, high-pitched and laced with obscenity. Al Otford appeared, dragging a diminutive figure that he brought to a halt under the lights. She was a slight, blonde-haired teenager who looked vaguely familiar.

'Who are you?' asked Tom.

'I'm Natalie.'

'Natalie who; and don't play games with me – you're in trouble, both of you.'

'We haven't done anything,' Francesca whimpered.

'You've been caught in a high-security area after dark.'

'We've solved one of the secrets,' said Natalie. 'It's in the coal cellar.'

Tom scowled at her and was not amused when this tiresome little girl refused to wilt. He had no idea what game these kids were playing and he had more urgent matters to deal with.

'We think it's hidden in the cellar – the robbery money.' Natalie struggled in Otford's grip. 'If you don't let go of me you great ape, I'll sue you for sexual harassment.'

Tom took control. 'Take these two indoors. Send them down to the kitchens and keep them there until I come. Feed them anything that'll keep them quiet and don't let them out of your sight.'

Tom ran into the building along the ground floor corridor to the housekeeper's office. He didn't bother with a treble nine call; he rang Inspector Oats at home. Oats was disgruntled but he listened. Tom told him about Gus's reappearance. The Inspector asked for a description of the car. Why hadn't Tom consulted the witnesses before phoning? Tom told the man forcibly that Gus had almost certainly been abducted. He was linked, however indirectly, to three murders. He was a high profile figure in his own right. However inconvenient for them, the police should get to Crossfield Manor right now!

Tom put the phone down and ran upstairs to find Gina. She was sitting by the bed. Gus lay on it breathing heavily and twitching.

'How is he?'

'Out cold,' she replied. 'I think he's not so bad, but I didn't want him home this way.'

'You've phoned the doctor?'

'Yes, they're sending Lucy's boy, Michael. He's on his way now.'

'I've reported this to the police. Gus has been abducted, no doubt of it; they'll need to talk to him.'

'I guess so,' she looked up. 'Where's little Francesca? I've told the boys they're not to frighten her or her friend. I've said it's OK for them to be here.'

'I've sent them to the kitchen. I've told the guards to feed them and keep them quiet until I come. If it's all right here I think I'll go and see what they've been up to.'

The girls were sitting facing each other across the central table. A security man stood by the door arms folded. Tom thanked him and told him he could go back to his duties. The appearance of these kids was a secondary matter, but one he had better deal with. He fixed the pair of them with an icy stare. The little blonde girl remained unabashed.

'How did you two get here?'

'My boyfriend drove us,' said Natalie.

'Where is he?'

'Waiting outside the garden centre.'

'All right, tell me what this is about?'

Natalie groped in her pocket and produced a crumpled sheet of paper.

'Read this,' she said.

It was a photocopy of a news report from the *Taraton Herald.*

Mystery of Crossfield's Last Squire. The dateline was six months after the death of Freddie Reade-Coke. *Hampshire's chosen resistance leader,* as the writer termed him.

The story was roughly the same as that told him by Clarry Hosskythe: so much for the Rowridge family's oath of secrecy.

'Read the end bit,' said Natalie.

'You be patient, young lady.' He glared at her. 'Where did you come by this?'

'My friend at the newspaper found it for us.'

Tom resumed reading.

It is known that the resistance cell had a secret armoury already prepared, believed on good authority to be concealed in the cellars of Crossfield Manor. There was a good deal more, the product of the reporter's imagination, rather than historical research. Tom returned the paper.

'Now, I've had a very stressful day, so I want straight answers. Do Mr and Mrs Cunningham know you're here?'

'No,' said Natalie, 'they think we've gone to friends.'

'Instead of which you go snooping round a house that's awash with security and expecting violent intruders.' Tom glared and then softened his expression. 'I think you'd better tell me all about it.'

Francesca did so, very hesitantly, recounting everything she had told Natalie.

'You're telling me that Alex Cornbinder planned the Winchester bank robbery from his jail cell?'

'Yes, that's what he said.'

'Why should your mother, of all people, be involved?'

'I'll tell him,' said Natalie. 'Alex is one of her fancy men.'

Francesca joined in. 'Mum was planning something. Some crazy idea to save the farm.'

'Mr O'Malley,' said Natalie. 'The Winchester robbery was on the 28th March and that was the night when Mrs Fjortoft lost her horse and got locked in the stables.'

'I am aware of that – I was there. What would you know about it?'

'I think my mum was here, that night, meeting someone,' said Francesca.

For the first time Tom wondered if this was more than a childish fantasy. He was not likely to forget the incidents that night and there had never been an explanation for them.

'If it's true, will you have to tell the police?' asked Francesca.

'That depends on what we find.'

'So you are going to let us look?' asked Natalie.

'If only to put a stop to this nonsense – yes. Where are the cellars in this place?'

'There's a hatch outside – that's where your thugs caught us,'

Tom was beginning to find Natalie irritating; the police could be here any minute and these stupid children were a distraction he could do without.

'Come on,' he sighed. 'There'll be a way in from the house – let's find it.'

Tom discovered the entrance near the main storeroom. A flight of worn stone steps led down into a black hole. Tom found a light switch, and the cellar stood revealed, brightly lit and swept clean. One wall held a wine rack, fully charged with bottles. Tom circled the space and in a couple of places kicked the brickwork; the walls were clearly solid. He moved to the wine rack, lifted out a bottle and read the label. *Chateaux Laffite 1978.* He looked at a few more; Gus certainly knew his wine. The rack was a beautifully crafted artefact of wrought iron. He looked closer, admiring the craftsmanship, and now he saw the hinges linking the two halves of the rack. Gently he pulled on the right hand section; it held fast to the wall. Tom studied the left hand. Whatever happened he mustn't pull the whole lot over and smash thousands of pounds of vintage wine. Tentatively he gave the left section a pull. He jumped as it yielded. The thing was a gate; leading to what? He slowly eased the rack open; someone had recently oiled the hinges. Revealed was a five-foot high metal door. Tom examined it and found it locked.

'Try this,' said Francesca. She held an odd key on a piece of string.

'Where did you get this?' he asked.

'I found it hidden at home. Mum said keys, plural. She must have the other.'

'Give it to me and we'll see if it fits.'

It was strange object, obviously designed for a sophisticated multi-lever lock. He heard voices in the kitchen above and somebody calling his name.

'Down here,' he replied.

Ed appeared with a young man in a leather jacket.

'You, Mr O'Malley? I'm Detective Sergeant Chilvers. You called us about a suspected abduction.'

'That's right.'

'We're taking statements from everyone,' said Chilvers. 'I've a woman officer talking to Mr and Mrs Fjortoft.'

'You're here in force then?'

'Too right, we've picked up a young lad loitering around your retail premises. Says he's waiting for his girlfriend.'

'He's Shane,' said Natalie. 'He's nothing to do with it – leave him alone.'

'He can make a statement first.' The policeman looked at Tom. 'What's going on here?'

'Do you mean the entire Fjortoft affair, or just this cellar?'

'We shall require a statement from you – everything you know.'

'Then I hope your attention span is good, because that will just about fill a book.'

The detective laughed. 'All right, Sir, this cellar – is it relevant?'

'Give me a chance and I'll answer that.'

Tom inserted the key and the lock turned sweetly. He tugged on the handle and the door swung open. He noticed that it was set in a frame with a rubber seal. He staggered back choking from a vile cloying stench as bad as anything he had ever smelt. Detective Sergeant Chilvers pulled a handkerchief from his pocket and held it over his mouth and nose.

He turned round and caught Ed's arm. 'Get those kids out of here. Guard the upper door and don't let anyone down.'

Ed nodded; then pushing two subdued girls ahead of him he departed upstairs. Chilvers produced a small torch, and with the handkerchief to his face, walked into the cavity.

'Jesus Christ, what a mess,' he muttered. 'Woman for certain – any idea who she is?'

'I hope I'm wrong but I can make a guess. I'd say she's Vanessa Rowridge. She's the mother of one of those kids, and thank God you came before they saw it.'

CHAPTER 32

Marjorie and Alan arrived and Tom took them to the drawing room for a quick word before uniting them with the girls.

'Don't be too hard on them,' he said. 'It's one of those silly pranks that turned sour.'

'Are the police certain it's Vanessa?' asked Alan.

'They're not saying anything but I think it's her. The body's very decomposed but the face is recognisable.'

'We'll be firm with the girls but no recriminations,' said Marjorie. 'You're certain they saw nothing?'

'Quite certain, we pushed them out of the place before they could.'

'It had better be me that makes the official identification,' said Marjorie. 'I don't know what this'll do to Francesca. She was never close to her mother…' She sighed. 'We'll do the one thing we can do; give her all the love and support in the world.'

Michael had arrived to see Gus, but his visit had been overwhelmed by events. Francesca and Natalie had been put in Gina's care and sent to a bedroom. Gina had brought them each a cup of tea. Natalie sipped hers; Francesca lay flat on the bed. Gina sat holding her hand.

Francesca looked blearily at Tom. 'It's Mum, isn't it – she's dead.'

'Yes, I'm very sorry.' It sounded so trite, but what could he say.

'Was she murdered?'

'I don't know; we shall have to leave that to the police.'

Francesca closed her eyes and rolled over shaking. Gina lay beside her an arm around the girl's shoulders.

'We should never have come here,' said Natalie miserably

'It makes no difference, darling,' Marjorie whispered. 'What's done is done.'

'Mr O'Malley,' said Natalie. 'Can you find what the police have done to Shane? I only asked him to drive us. They're not to beat him up and hurt him.'

'All right,' he was glad for an excuse to escape. 'Whatever you've been told, they won't do that.'

The Incident Room had been set up in the housekeeper's office. Tom put his head round the door and enquired after Shane. He was informed that the boy had been sent home and told to report to Taraton police in the morning. In the passage Tom encountered

Sergeant Chilvers.

'We've something we think you should see, sir.'

Tom followed him back to the cellar. The body had been removed, thank goodness and someone had opened the trap hatch to the outside air. The smell was present but much reduced. Figures in white overalls were busy in the secret room; a photoflash made Tom blink. A man with a clipboard was examining a stack of plastic wrapped parcels.

'Money,' said Chilvers. 'We've been searching for weeks. Half a million – part of it anyway – proceeds of the Winchester raid.'

Tom awoke next morning to the sounds of wind and rain. He showered, dressed and rang the hospital. He spoke to Lucy who sounded her cheerful normal self. He had slept as soundly as ever he could remember; he wondered if he was becoming too hardened. If only this mystery made sense. His gut instinct told him all these events were connected. Making the police agree was a different matter. He snatched a quick breakfast and drove to work.

A solitary gravedigger was excavating in the grounds of the United Reformed Chapel. This dour brick building stood on a mound near the junction with the Taraton road. The coroner had released Matthew Rowridge's body and the final rites would take place tomorrow afternoon. Marjorie Cunningham had formally identified Vanessa's body, so the whole doleful ritual would be repeated in a week or so. Vanessa had died from two savage blows to the back of her head. The pathologist put the likely death to some time in late March or early April. Tom had no doubt as to when that had been. It was the storm-lashed night, when Gina's horse had bolted and later he had stood within inches of someone in the darkened kitchen.

Tom threw himself into work. As a means of escape this was less than successful, but somehow he came through the day. To everyone's relief the incident room at the Manor had been dismantled. Both Rowridge murder investigations were to be merged and co-ordinated in Taraton. Gus was fully conscious but had only a hazy memory of his life after he had been forced into a car and driven away from Mulgrum's campus. Michael had been in attendance and had told Tom that Lucy would be discharged that afternoon. He would collect her and drive straight to Boxtree.

'Where's Gina?' Lucy asked.

'She's at the Manor tucked up with a dozen security guards'

Tom laughed at the expression on her face.

Michael had delivered Lucy to the farm in the early evening. Tom had made a bed for her in her old room, a place filled with childhood memories.

'Don't be hard on Gina,' he said. 'She's worried sick about Gus and she was a revelation when we were adrift in the middle of Oregon. She's a most resourceful lady; very different from what we thought.'

Lucy grunted and Tom left it at that.

On Wednesday, the day of the funeral, it was still raining. A dozen cars had parked along the sodden verge outside the chapel. Tom had never visited this building before and it depressed him. He waited outside the door; his waterproof zipped tightly over his dark suit. People began walking up the sloping path from the road talking in subdued voices. Tom recognised local farmers, cattle dealers and some tradespeople from the town. Then came Gina with Clarry Hosskythe clinging to her arm. Charlie Marrington followed making a determined effort to shelter both ladies with an umbrella.

Gina greeted Tom with a sweet smile. 'Gussy's not well. He's running a temperature so I told him to stay home.'

'How is poor Francesca?' asked Clarry.

'I think she'll be all right; her aunt and uncle are with her.'

Tom watched as a melancholy procession made its way up the path. First came the coffin with its bearers careful not to slip on the gravel, then the minister in a black gown and behind him the family. Francesca, white faced, walked with Marjorie and Lucy on either side. Alan and a very subdued Natalie brought up the rear. Tom remembered the last funeral he had attended: Magdalena's. Two human beings from different worlds, victims of the same conspiracy; how many more, he wondered?

Tom slipped into the back of the chapel to be greeted by Muriel. He knew this was her home territory and he suspected that some of the visiting minister's stipend came from her own modest salary. Tom remembered Tricia saying that people received the funerals they had earned in life. This quiet little gathering of country people was intensely moving. His own eyes were moist as the congregation sang the hymn; *Come ye faithful people come; sing the song of harvest home*.

He was less impressed by the minister's address. The man, recounting Matthew's last days, told the gathering it was a blessing that the death was not, as first reported, a suicide. Suicides, he intoned, were damned before God and would suffer eternal torment, as would adulterous women and other such sinners for whom there could be no forgiveness. He spoke this part with a distinct relish.

Now they were outside again in the rain, squelching across the wet grass to the open grave. Marjorie and Lucy held tightly to Francesca walking zombie-like between them. At last it was over; the company stood for a few moments before dispersing.

Tom walked across to Marjorie and Alan. 'Come back to Boxtree; we've everything ready.'

Lucy had spent the morning preparing a post-funeral wake with help from the Manor staff.

Marjorie glared. 'You heard what that black crow said about adulterous women?'

'Yes.'

'Bloody cheek – no mention of adulterous men of course. I hope we don't get him when we bury poor Vanessa.'

Surprisingly, the wake was a great success. The adults had reminisced quietly while Francesca her ordeal over had visibly brightened. She and Natalie had drifted away and Lucy had found them playing video games on the office computer. Tom stood with Lucy at the front door saying goodbye to the guests, then he returned to the sitting room to survey the debris of discarded plates and left-over food. Only the Cunninghams and the two girls remained. Francesca and Natalie took over the sofa. Both seemed fully restored to their normal selves, Natalie the more so. She made Tom uneasy; the wretched girl kept staring at him with those startling blue eyes. In an adult woman he would have read a "come on" signal. He made a mental reservation never to be alone with this precocious sex kitten for a single moment.

'Mr O'Malley,' said Francesca. 'Did my Dad ever say anything about Bechams's Wood?'

This was unexpected. 'Yes, he did; that's why I came to see him that…' He faltered.

'You see, I think it's all to do with Bechams Wood.'

'In what way?'

'I think I know something. I've talked to Natalie and she says tell you.'

'D'you want to talk in private?'

'No, that's all right. You see it was that night I told you about. The night I heard those men in the copse – remember?'

Tom nodded.

'One was a Yankee – sounded a bit like Mr Fjortoft but it wasn't him of course. But I've heard the other one since and I know him.'

Francesca's quiet determination impressed Tom.

'I know him now,' she said. 'It's PC Witherrick from the town.'

Oh dear, thought Tom. To the youngsters of Taraton, Witherrick was a bogeyman. An ageing bad tempered policeman, passed over for promotion; he worked off his surly ire on everyone who crossed his path; especially children and harassed housewives. He was certainly a bully and Oats had named him to Tom as a covert supporter of the racist RON organisation. The community looked forward, as one, to the man's retirement at the end of the year.

'Francesca, I know you don't like him, but can you be really sure it was his voice?

'Yes, it was him. He cornered me the other day and threatened me.'

'OK, take your time. Tell me what happened.'

Francesca repeated exactly the account she'd given Natalie. She was telling the truth – no fantasy now. Tom was shocked at the blatant deceit of the man and his stupidity. Giving her a chance to return a stolen item, but only to Witherrick in person; what utter rubbish. So their own bent copper was up to his eyeballs in something sinister concerning Matthew and Vanessa. Oats would not like this, and with no reliable corroboration he would be bound to resist taking action.

'OK, Francesca, I hear what you say. Keep quiet and leave things to me.'

Alan Cunningham touched him on the arm.

'Tom, a word if I may?' He glanced meaningfully at the two girls.

'Come in the study,' said Tom.

Tom closed the door and waved Alan to a chair.

Alan looked unsure. 'This may not be the time or the place but I've got a query about the Rowridge accounts. I've been winding up Matthew's finances and I've hit something odd. Gustav Fjortoft was paying Matthew a thousand pounds a month by standing order from his personal account. He's been doing it for a year – any idea why?'

Gus was sitting on a cane chair in the Manor garden while Gina lay on cushions. Yesterday's rain had gone and a warm sun beat down as clouds of vapour rose from the sodden fields. Gus waved Tom to a second chair and poured him a glass of iced orange juice.

'How are you?' Tom asked.

'Very confused,' a smile flickered on Gus's face.

'Can I ask what happened?'

'Hellmunt drugged me and took me out of Oregon with one of Mulgrum's guards. After that I lost all sense of time. They wanted information from me. They suspected I held some evidence and they wanted to know if I knew where brother Wilhelm was. Every time I woke to the world they'd start the third degree. I can just remember an air flight – didn't know where I was bound. I think they passed me off as a an air phobic on heavy tranquillisers.'

'But they let you go.'

'I was becoming too hot a property. It's crazy to think that me being missing was headline news. Anyway, next I know I'm in bed here with young Michael glaring at me and a rather lovely lady cop asking questions I couldn't answer, because I don't remember a darned thing.'

'Gus, you sent for me from Seattle and I still don't know why.'

'Tom, I'm sorry. I should never have involved you. I didn't know where to turn and who to trust.'

'I know about your past and about Gostanyn camp.'

Gus stared at Tom. 'How could you know?' he muttered, clearly shaken.

'Magdalena, the girl who was murdered, was on your trail. Through her associates I met the last surviving child of Gostanyn. That lady believes you were complicit in the killings. However I have now met the man who calls himself Jiffers, and I'm happy to say he convinced me otherwise.'

'Brother Max,' Gus murmured. 'I call him that, not Albert. He's my guest in the house now. I reckoned he'll be safer here until this is settled.'

'He impressed me, but what's more important he convinced the journalist who's been investigating you.'

'Tom, it's good of you to take my part, but you're wrong. I did kill one little girl and I've had to live with that all my life.'

'Yes, my darling,' said Gina, 'but never willingly.'

'I do not accept my innocence. I know that I should have let those men break every bone in my body before I hurt that little girl. I killed her and there's no going back from that.'

'Can you tell us anything about your other brother – the one that came here on the night Matthew died?'

'I don't know where Will is or who he is. I was supposed to meet him at Mulgrum's and I'm still waiting for a showdown. As for

Matthew, I as good as killed him.'

'Gus what are you talking about?' Gina was indignant.

'Matthew died because I used him.'

Tom intervened. 'Gus, I was told in confidence that you were paying Matthew some sort of retainer.'

'Who told you?'

'Alan Cunningham is sorting out the Rowridge estate. He was puzzled and he asked me about it.'

'Then I'd better talk to your accountant man today. If we don't move quick little Francesca will inherit the danger.'

'I think she may have already.'

Tom told them about PC Witherrick's threats.

'Oh, my God, a little embossed leather case – yes that's it. I'd better get it back right now.' Gus stood swayed unsteadily and sat down again.

'Where is this case, and secondly who wants it that badly?'

'It's in safe deposit box in Taraton under the name of Matthew Rowridge.'

'What's so special about it?'

'It's like this. In nineteen seventy-four I hired a man to research Gostanyn and everything about it. He was the doctor who rescued brother Max in Bremen. It was he that first put me in touch with Max again, which was a shock because I knew him as Albert and I'd been told he was dead. By the way, Maxton is his second given name; Jiffers is his wife's surname – all logical.'

'You never told me any of this?' Gina looked aggrieved.

'I never told you anything of my bad side. I didn't want to hurt you. I guess I failed in that too.'

'Tell us now – don't hold secrets back.'

'My researcher was obsessed with Gostanyn. He wanted to trace those surviving SS men and bring their deeds home to them. I provided the bucks and off he went to Europe. He found the camp but there was nothing left. He met the war crimes investigators, but they'd drawn a blank. After six weeks he had a break, a phone call from an old SS man who wanted to unburden his soul, so he said. Truth was he needed money bad and he had red-hot property to sell: a great fat dossier. It had the names of all the Gostanyn kids and when and how they died, plus fifty photographs.

'My man wired me that night and asked permission to trade. He said they didn't have enough to prosecute the SS guy, but he believed the file to be genuine. I agreed because I remembered that little SS tick. He was the one with the *Leica* – real happy snapper – always getting the kids to pose in groups. I never knew that he went in the operating theatre making a record of the transplant foul-ups. Anyway, there's five pictures of Will holding his needle over dead kids and grinning all over his fat face.' Gus sat back. 'This is why we're all in such trouble.'

'What made you pick on Matthew?'

'I liked the guy; he taught me a lot about England. Clarry Hosskythe told me about his father and the wartime resistance. I asked Matthew about it but he clamped up. Said he was bound by his Dad's oath; he wouldn't discuss it with any damned Yank. Put me in my place properly.'

Tom smiled; that sounded authentic Matthew.

'Why did you involve him?'

'I wanted the dossier safe in the hands of someone who didn't know what it was and would never talk. He put it in his bank and I paid him.'

'But people still knew, and not only the Nazis. We caught an Israeli agent searching Woolbarrow when the house was empty.'

'I know,' Gus sighed. 'I don't understand it. Matthew would never have talked and let's face it the man was darned near a recluse.'

'But his wife wasn't. I would say Vanessa was your weak link.'

'And now she's dead – and in my own house.'

Tom drove home feeling more depressed than he could remember. They were all floundering in this morass and he could see no way out. A figure was running down the lane towards him; arms waving like a windmill – it was Charlie. The old man seemed at the end of his tether, his face red as he struggled for air. Tom pushed his brake pedal to the floor and skidded the last few feet.

'Hey, Charlie, slow down or you'll bust a gut.'

'Guvnor,' he gasped, 'there's a car – over there – on fire – looks like an accident – nasty!'

CHAPTER 33

Hannah turned off the main road three miles short of Taraton and drove into the narrow lanes leading to the hills. After three months these roads were as familiar to her as if she had lived here all her life. This was the England she remembered from childhood; a magical green countryside compared with her own hot and dusty homeland. She remembered that day in March a few weeks ago, when Anton and she had dropped Magda on the fringe of the village. Magda had a secret she wouldn't disclose: now she was dead and poor Anton with her.

Hannah was close to the place where Tom had driven out of the woods that gale-ridden night. She had been parked waiting for Magda to rendezvous. Magda never kept the meeting. She was already a corpse by the sea thirty miles away.

She dropped her speed as she crested the brow of the hill. The other car came fast out of the dead ground and slammed into her head on. She had a brief glimpse of a square fronted vehicle with, bull bars. The Volvo crumpled with a hideous tearing crunch as Hannah slumped forward against the exploding air bag.

'It's that fuckin' yid-girl – the one I told you about.'

Hannah heard the voice somewhere in her painful dream world.

'Has she croaked it?'

'Who cares?'

She felt cold, her head ached and she was frightened; a sensation she never liked to admit. Of the two voices: one was a local Hampshire accent, the other London probably, but more cultured.

'Are you going to finish her – make it look accidental like?' said the local voice.

'Not bloody likely, Alex. I don't want another one like last July.'

'What other one?

'The farmer's wife, Patricia O'Malley.'

'It was her old man sent me down for slapping that coon. Heard about his missus when I was in stir. It was an accident, wasn't it?'

'Shut up and give me a hand to get this one out.'

Strong hands gripped Hannah, and she was pulled onto the grass, her feet trailing in the mud.

'Skinny bird,' said the one called Alex. 'I likes 'em with a bit of fat – something you can catch hold of.'

Hannah could restrain her gut no longer. She vomited her breakfast on the ground.

'Dirty bitch,' Alex grunted. 'Stay with her, Ricky, while I put a tow chain on her motor.'

'Why?'

'Get it out the way before anyone sees it.'

Hannah opened her eyes. It was bright; she could see branches with green leaves and a blue sky above. She knew the man Ricky was not far away. She lay rigid pretending unconsciousness. She was in bad trouble and it could be worse if they thought she was listening. She still felt shocked but she was convinced she could stand and walk.

'All right, I've fixed it – run through the gate down into the field,' said Alex. 'Are you saying the magistrate's wife got topped?'

'Yes I did, and it was none of my doing. It was that Jayvy, he's a nutter.'

'What happened?'

'Is that Jew bitch listening?'

'No, she's out cold.'

'We'll move away a bit in case.'

Hannah heard footsteps as the two men moved but little more than ten metres into the wood. She had to take the chance. Hoping the wind in the trees would cover her sound she rolled into a dry ditch and began to crawl towards the voices. Painful as it was, she blocked that out, blessing the tough training she had received in that desert camp. She heard a match strike and then gritted her teeth as the still burning ember fell on her hand.

'We were opening up the place on the hill when this snooty cow rides up on a bloody great horse,' said Ricky.

'Did she see it?'

'She might have – nosy bitch. She had a plum in her mouth, all lahdiddah – bloody lady muck. Then she got off the horse and began to go in the wood telling us we were trespassers. So Jayvy walks up to her and breaks her neck, just like that – evil bastard. I wanted to run for it but he said he'd do the same to me.'

'What happened then?'

'We took her on the horse, down the bridle way to the steep bit. Then Jayvy pitches her over the edge into the trees and we let the horse go.'

'Seems it worked.'

'He got away with murder, but they say he's good at that – bloody Yanks – I hate 'em.' The man belched. 'I'm going into those trees I want a piss.'

'You're bloody modest.' Alex laughed.

Hannah waited for no more. Very slowly she wriggled round in the ditch and slithered back to the spot she had vacated. She was sick, in pain and exhausted.

The footsteps were returning. She caught the odour of the spent cigarette as it was stamped into the dirt. She knew the two men were looking down at her.

'Jew or not, she's a beautiful woman.' It was Ricky.

'You're getting soft.'

'We'll leave her – she may die anyway. The worst that could happen is a hit and run charge. Another year in the nick wouldn't hurt you.'

'Oh yeah – it's all right for you.'

'I wasn't the one driving.'

'Sod that…'

'Tell you what we'll do. Carry her down to her car. We'll torch it and leave her nearby. That'll keep everyone guessing.'

'What about our motor?'

'You can hide it at the back of the workshops.'

Hannah almost vomited again at the stench of Alex's body odour. She knew she had to act lifeless; a helpless rag doll. Her captor slipped and swore as he carried her down a sloping pasture. Without warning he dropped her on the ground, an impact that shook the last breath from her body.

'Hannah, are you hurt, can you hear me?'

The voice broke through her defensive cocoon. She knew that voice but couldn't assimilate the words – if only she didn't feel so cold. She opened her eyes. Two faces looked down at her both spinning in half focus. One was an elderly man, with grizzled cheeks and a flat cap. And the other one … of course, it was Tom, that was his voice. She remembered it now in the bungalow a long time ago.

CHAPTER 34

Tom peeped round the door of the spare bedroom; Hannah lay sleeping. The swelling on the bruised face had subsided, but it remained as a desecration of a lovely young woman. Politically incorrect thinking perhaps, but he wished that Hannah had been born in another time and place. It seemed wasteful that she should be so serious; so joyless in her obsession with her personal war.

Hannah had been fully conscious when they brought her into the house. She had refused to let them call an ambulance with such vehemence that it seemed she might give herself further injury. Tom had left Lucy to get on with it while she put the woman to bed and treated the injuries. He could hear Hannah's voice. Her tone was too soft for him to assimilate the words, but she sounded tense. Seconds later, without a word to him, Lucy had stormed from the bedroom and careered downstairs, seizing her car keys from the table. He heard her outside shouting for Al Otford. She drove away, tyres screaming, with Al in the passenger seat.

Tom did not like her attitude and he worried about Lucy's mental state. The anguish on her face just now was real and he could think of no reason for it. It seemed his little girl was breaking under the strain of events. Once again he railed against fate, cursing the day he'd met Gustav Fjortoft.

'Doctor, will you slow down – cool it!'

Otford was shouting. Lucy didn't care that she was hurling the car around corners, courting the sort of head on collision that had done for Hannah.

'Lady, if you wanna' kill yourself, OK, but I don't deserve you kill me – 'specially after you've saved my life.'

Al was gaping nervously as the hedgerows flashed past in the glittering light beams. Lucy slowed; he was right, she must calm herself; she had a mission to accomplish. Seconds later Al's premonition came true. She stood hard on the brakes as a tractor and trailer filled the road ahead. The other driver saw her and braked on the wet surface. The trailer jack-knifed and the whole unit slid on the wet surface ending in the ditch.

Lucy knew the tractor man; it was Lonny the estate foreman. He was waving a fist and yelling incoherently.

'Sorry, Lonny, but I'm in a hurry and I could use your help.'

Lonny, the sixteen stone black rugby player was more a friend than an employee. Like all the estate staff he was devoted to Lucy's mother and had taken her death badly.

'Listen, Lonny, my mum never died accidentally. She found trespassers at Bechams Wood; they killed her and threw her over the hill. Alex Cornbinder's been boasting about it. I'm on my way to find him and get the truth. Are you with us?'

Lonny blinked and shook his head as if Lucy had landed a boxer's punch. He walked across and looked in the car.

'Mr Otford, I thought it was you – is this on the level?'

'The Doctor says so and I believe her. She's talked to an eye-witness.'

Lonny pulled open the rear door; Lucy felt the car lurch as he settled his weight inside.

'I'm with you. Alex doesn't like black guys and I don't like him. What d'you want me to do – give him a hiding?'

'We'll have a little chat with Alex and see what he has to say – no instant justice.'

Lucy put the car in gear and drove on. The madness had left her to be replaced by that same horrible void she felt when her mother died. Now she must suffer it all again and God knew what it would do to Dad.

The approaches to Taraton brought Lucy into slow rush hour traffic. She silently fumed as she came up behind a line of slow moving coaches. Lonny muttered a string of expletives.

'Look at that,' he muttered. 'Read the sign on the back of that bus.'

Lucy was not really interested but she looked. 'RON, South of England Rally.'

'Racist bastards – could be trouble tonight,' said Lonny. 'Police banned them from Portsmouth. Rumour is they're making for Warrior Down.'

'On top of the hill?'

'Sure, it's a public open space. I've heard that little turd Gannemeade is going to speak to them.'

Lucy could not take this in. She was looking for the turning into the Lime Tree estate, a sprawl of local authority housing on the eastern side of town.

'Where's the lime trees?' asked Al.

'They always name places after the trees they've cut down,' replied

Lonny.

Lucy found the turning that ended in Robins Close, a cul-de-sac of twenty houses in the shabbiest area. She knew it from her rounds as a place of dysfunctional families and shy intimidated elderly folk. Alex lived in number nine, which Lucy recalled as a jungle garden filled with empty beer cans.

The front door was a mess of peeling paint and the frosted glass window was cracked and patched with a square of cardboard. Lonny thumped the door with a clenched fist and gave it a hearty kick.

'Go round the back,' shouted a voice within.

'That's Alex,' said Lonny.

Lucy led round to the kitchen door, a walk requiring them to scramble over piles of rubble. She tried the door; it was open so she pushed it aside and walked in. The kitchen was filthy; Lucy grimaced with disgust – of Alex there was neither sight nor sound.

'Alex, come out here – I'm Doctor O'Malley – I want a word with you.'

No reply.

'He's in here somewhere,' said Lonny. 'I'll go find him.'

Lonny and Otford disappeared into the house; Lucy stood in the hallway and waited. Al began to search the ground floor rooms while Lonny ran upstairs.

From above came a thump and a shout. 'Found him – the bastard's hiding in the loft.'

'Fuck off, coon.' Alex sounded nervous.

'Alex,' Lucy called. 'I want to talk to you.'

'Sod off too – fuckin' bitch…' The voice ended in a grunt of pain.

Alex came slowly downstairs with Lonny holding his arm in a wrestling hold. He looked venomous and scared in equal proportions.

'Hello, Alex.' Lucy started back as the man spat in her face.

Lonny swung Alex round and punched him hard in the stomach. He doubled up gasping and retching.

'Sit him down,' said Lucy.

She surprised herself with her calm. She remained unmoving never bothering to wipe the foul spittle from her face.

'Tell me who killed my mother.'

'How should I know? I was in the nick when that happened.'

'All right, if it wasn't you then who was it?'

'I tell you, I wasn't there.'

'But you don't seem surprised that it was murder.'

Alex didn't like that. Lucy could detect a shifty gleam in his eyes.

‘I’m not saying nothing.’

‘Was it the man you were with today? Unwise of you to sound off in front of a witness.’

‘That Jew bitch – I thought she was as good as dead.’

Lucy marvelled at the stupidity of this man.

‘Having said this much it’ll be in your interest to be truthful. Co-operate and it’ll stand you in good stead with a jury.’

‘I tell you I wasn’t there. You ask Ricky – he knows.’

‘Ricky who?’

‘I’m not saying nothing. Anyways, it wasn’t Ricky as topped her.’

What a garrulous idiot, Lucy thought, as she looked at the figure in front of her with his thin unhealthy face and stubble chin. She would have the truth now and nothing would stand in her way.

‘If this Ricky didn’t kill my mother and you were in prison, you’ve nothing to fear.’

‘That’s what you think. I know who did it, and you’ll never prove it. I ain’t telling – he’d kill me too.’

‘Mr Otford,’ said Lonny. ‘I’ll hold him – you pull his trousers off.’

He gave Lucy a surreptitious wink.

Alex struggled and kicked but Lonny only tightened his hold. Otford pulled down Alex’s oil stained jeans to reveal a grubby pair of boxer shorts.

‘Can you hold him?’ Lonny asked.

‘Sure, no problem.’

Lonny released the grip, as Otford took hold of Alex and lifted him off the ground. Lonny fumbled in his pockets and produced a small leather case. To Lucy’s horror it contained a surgical scalpel with a folding handle.

‘Lonny…’ she began to speak.

Once more he half turned and winked.

‘My castrating knife,’ he stroked it lovingly. ‘Have to use it for bull calves. Nothing quiets the stroppy male so much as a loss of balls – eh, Alex.’

Alex screamed, lashing out with his legs as Lonny walked towards him. ‘Stop him, stop him – the fuckin’ coon – you’re a fuckin’ doctor – stop him!’

Lucy ignored him; her mother was murdered and she wanted the truth.

‘Please, please,’ Alex snivelled. ‘I’ll talk.’

Sweat was pouring down his face and into his filthy T-shirt. He was wild eyed – on the edge of hysteria. Lucy suppressed a pang of sympathy: she wanted the truth.

'It was Jayvy; I don't know his other name but Ricky says Jayvy broke your mum's neck, tied her to the horse and then threw her over the hanger – he'd do that – he's a psycho. Please, I don't know any more – I tell you I wasn't there.'

'Who is Ricky?'

There was no reply as Alex looked nervously around the room.

'Lonny,' Lucy inclined her head.

Lonny advanced on Alex knife poised.

'Ricky's my brother – he never had nothing to do with it. Couldn't have stopped it if he'd tried; most likely Jayvy'd top him as well.'

Lucy stared intensely at him. Yes, this was the truth; Alex was too frightened to lie or bluff.

'All right, Lonny, that'll do.'

Lonny grinned, kissed the flat of his knife, and replaced it in its case. Otford lowered Alex to the chair.

'One more question – who is Jayvy?'

'I told you, I don't know his other name, only that he's a Yank.'

'American – how old – description?'

'Skinny weasel, might be my age, older maybe.'

'How do you come to know him?'

'I don't know him personal, and I don't want to. He was with that bloke last year – property developer – the one with the helicopter.'

'Tallisment?'

'Yes, that's him, some sort of Aussie he sounded like.'

'He's South African. Thank you Alex – well done.'

Lucy turned and walked from the house. Suddenly she felt cold, giddy, and desperately tired.

Chief Inspector Oats rang at half past seven.

'Mr O'Malley, I have an official request.'

'What do you mean official? Man, I'm up to my neck in trouble; we sent a message hours ago. Where the hell are your people?'

'Something to do with Miss Berkovic?'

'Yes.'

'Believe me we will deal with the matter but I cannot make it a priority. Listen, we talked about the Reclaim Our Nation movement – remember?'

'Yes.'

'They're holding a big rally on Warrior Down right now. Could you come with us in your official capacity as an observer. We've asked two of your colleagues as well.'

'Observe what? I can't read the Riot Act, those days have gone.'

'Yes I know, but we're in a very difficult position legally. I don't have the powers to ban the meeting. We can only observe and make arrests if there is a breach of the law.'

'Are they likely to misbehave?'

'No, I don't think they'll be violent, but there's more of them than we expected. Worse, it's our Mr Gannemeade who's the speaker, and some high-powered American. We've got to tread warily. I've all my uniform officers at Warrior Down along with two bus loads from outside the division. There'll be villains rubbing their hands for miles.'

Tom groaned audibly. 'All right, I'll meet you there in half an hour.'

Warrior Down lay a mile south of Taraton and was the highest point locally. This hilltop with two hundred acres of open grassland had stunning views towards London and southward to the Isle of Wight. At the summit stood the beacon, a metal post topped with an iron fire basket; part of a chain lit to commemorate royal occasions.

The car park was full but he managed to find a space on a roadside verge. Tom spotted four police mini-buses, their occupants sitting inside. A growing stream of people moved towards the beacon; Tom joined them observing the crowd as he went. He felt surprised and almost disappointed by the dullness of the gathering. Most were male, young teens and twenties, with a substantial percentage of middle-aged and a couple of elderly men wearing war medals. Tom wished he could accost these; make them see they were conniving with everything they had fought against. All these people seemed poor-white, socially disadvantaged city dwellers. The accents were predominantly London, but included many from the south coast ports. No one here fulfilled his vision of a Nazi. He remembered his father speaking of the Blackshirts in nineteen-thirties London dockland. This gathering seemed drab by comparison.

He spun round in alarm as a hand gripped his arm; it was only Oats; his uniform concealed below a dark civilian overcoat.

'Glad you could make it. All's quiet at the moment. I've two plainclothes officers near the platform to record everything that's said. I imagine Gannemeade will have anticipated that; he won't step over the line into incitement.'

'How do you define incitement?'

'Incitement to racial hatred is a criminal offence. I surmise Gannemeade will be careful but we'll watch this American who's speaking.'

Tom came to a decision. 'Did you know that Gannemeade attempted to rape a woman in America?'

'Really?'

'Yes really; the lady told me so herself. She wounded him and he backed off.'

'No charges?'

'No, the victim is satisfied with her own vengeance and Gannemeade has enough pull to cover things up.'

'In America you say? There would be nothing we could do in that case.'

Oats left him and vanished into the crowd.

Tom could smell frying food. Two mobile canteen vans were doing a roaring trade selling burgers and kebabs. The queues were orderly and quiet; the whole affair seemed mundane and rather sad. A public address system began to blast music, heavy rock music, black in origin: an odd choice for a neo-fascist rally. The sound came from loud speakers, positioned beside an articulated lorry trailer on the gravel in front of the beacon. A row of chairs stood on this platform with a microphone and a long canvas banner. At ground level stood a row of men. Tom was amazed how alike they were: shaven heads, stubble chins, tattooed skin. With stern faces and linked arms they made a formidable guard. The audience began to pack around this stage where a foulmouthed comedian was performing a warm-up act. Tom tried to make an estimate of the numbers – at least a thousand – about the size of a minor league football crowd.

Tom found a place on the outside fringe with a clear view of the platform. The music had re-started, it was Elgar now; *Pomp and Circumstance*: not *Land of Hope*, but the other one. A collective murmur swelled through the crowd culminating in a mighty roar as the platform party appeared. Tom knew only one of them. There in the glare of the floodlight stood Roland Gannemeade, dapper-suited, milking the applause of this motley audience.

The noise faded and he spoke. It was the expected line: the democratic system had failed and the political parties were corrupt. He, Gannemeade, was quitting the system because he alone could lead the people. The man was an indifferent orator; he did not have the stamp of a populist dictator. Tom wondered what these devoted followers would think if they knew that this self-appointed leader was a rapist. Tom noted with satisfaction that Gannemeade's right arm was bandaged and in a sling. The speech finished amidst warm, if not wild, applause. This vast crowd had not travelled miles to hear Gannemeade; they were restless. Tom could feel the collective excitement and expectation. A new figure had mounted the stage and now stood, arms outstretched, face upturned into the light. A man that Tom had met but once, and wished profoundly that he had not. It was crazy, unbelievable, but…

'My friends,' announced Gannemeade. 'Our guest and most distinguished visitor – the Reverend Randell Mulgrum.'

The rest of the words were drowned in a reverberating cheer that seemed interminable. Cold sweat might be a cliché but that was how Tom felt. It seemed Mulgrum's reputation had crossed the Atlantic in advance. A month ago Tom had never heard of him and yet this crowd was doting on Mulgrum like a pop star. He remembered that awful moment when Van Zyl had killed a wounded man; less murder, more a cold-blooded execution. It was only now as he spoke that Tom began to understand Mulgrum's sinister power. The man was mad, as Hitler was mad; both had the ability to move a multitude. That gift, so often tainted that could compel simple people to follow them into fire and death.

Mulgrum spoke of the isolation of the white race, the source of Western civilisation; a tiny minority in a world of other races united in their hatred. There was nothing here that the police could interpret as incitement, indeed Mulgrum was careful to say he wished no harm to the world's coloured peoples. Indeed these peoples also suffered; as pawns in the game of the one evil race. By allowing themselves to be infiltrated into the white nations they too were victims of the great conspiracy. Mulgrum did not name the conspirators but everyone present knew to whom he referred. He called for a joyful world of separated races, each pursuing its culture without contamination or cross breeding with others.

Such was Mulgrum's power, hypnotic almost, that Tom was spellbound although his reasoned mind knew he was hearing garbage. Tom had travelled widely and had always found the peoples of any continent, particularly farming people, much the same everywhere. Hardly anyone had shown him hostility for his skin colour or nationality. This crowd was awed by Mulgrums's words, not because they felt superior, but because they were afraid. Irrational fear, that most corrosive force, made the Reverend Mulgrum's message the more dangerous.

The speech concluded and the crowd yelled and swayed with

emotion. The speaker had struck the chord he intended, tapping into all their insecurities and yet never extending beyond his democratic rights. Tom looked up and saw a man silhouetted against the rising moon climbing a ladder to reach the top of the beacon. With a stab of fire and a smell of paraffin the basket exploded. Flames roared as the fire spluttered and cracked with tiny explosions. A hot gust blew back over the assembly. Now the crowd was ecstatic as one by one other points of fire answered on distant hills. The ancient tribal calls arousing a beleaguered people to defend their land.

Tom had seen and heard enough to make him temporarily forget his own troubles – not for long though. Two more figures had appeared on the platform and Tom knew them both. One was Hellmunt, the man who had abducted Gus in Oregon. The other was shouting in Mulgrum's ear. He was tall, with blond hair and an eye patch. It was John Van Zyl.

CHAPTER 35

Tom needed to find Inspector Oats. Two of the men on that platform were wanted for abduction and murder. If they were not arrested now they would slip through the net and vanish. He looked wildly around trying to spot Oats or any other police officer. The crowd blocked the way in every direction. No longer were they a disparate collection of individuals, they had become a mob; a single coherent mass, emotionally drugged and motivated by a charismatic leader. This crowd was developing its own momentum and hysteria. It would not be long before it surged over the surrounding landscape looking for mischief.

Tom sought for a way round but there was none short of plunging into a thorn thicket. He looked back at the speaker's platform. Mulgrum was still there, standing in silhouette against the light of the beacon, looking smug and self-satisfied, as he surveyed the scene. The skinheads stood grouped around the leaders in a daunting human barrier; there was no sign of either Hellmunt or Van Zyl. He watched Mulgrum leave the platform and join Gannemeade. The two of them began to walk through the crowd ringed around by the bodyguards. Tom stepped back into the shadows; he did not wish to be seen by either. The crowd began to yell as the skinheads forced a passage, viciously pushing and shoving their own supporters. No one seemed to mind; all eyes were on the two leaders. A space in the car park had been roped off. Standing in it looking wholly absurd was a white, Hollywood style, stretch-limo. Now he could see the police. They were helping to control the crowd; forming an avenue through which Mulgrum's party could pass. He spotted Van Zyl; how he arrived at this point unseen was a mystery, until he remembered that man's ability to melt into shadow. Tom cast around trying to find Hellmunt with no success. He gave up and started to elbow his way through the crowd. He reached within feet of Mulgrum before a skinhead threw a punch in his chest that nearly sent him sprawling. Recovering breath he was in time to see Mulgrum, Gannemeade and Van Zyl climb into the limo. It drove away to tumultuous applause. Tom grabbed a policeman by the arm. The officer swung round his face alight with hostility.

'Please, where is Inspector Oats?'

'Who's asking?'

'I'm Tom O'Malley, I'm a Taraton JP; Mr Oats asked me to

observe this meeting. I've just seen a murder suspect escaping in that car – can you stop it?'

'I don't know anything about Taraton, it's not our division.'

He called to another officer. To Tom's chagrin he recognised the man; it was PC Witherrick. He tried to reach him but was again pushed backwards, this time by yet another constable he didn't know. The first one called back to Tom.

'PC Witherrick is a Taraton officer. He says Mr Oats left twenty minutes ago.'

'Why?'

'I suggest that is his business and not yours.' The man turned away.

'I've recognised a man wanted for murder in the United States,' Tom shouted.

'And I've just seen Mickey Mouse. Please, sir, we've potential trouble with this lot. I advise you to go home. Talk to Mr Oats in the morning.'

Tom, seething with rage, knew he could do nothing. His only option was to go home and try and raise the alarm from there. At least Mulgrum had chosen transport that would be unmissable anywhere in the county. He pulled out his mobile phone and dialled emergency. The police lines were jammed. He rang Oats's home number and leaving a hopefully coherent message, drove home.

Tom swore out loud and gripped the steering wheel as his suppressed rage boiled over. Two miles from home and here was the lane blocked with this slow moving convoy. Two concrete mixing lorries, four ballast trucks and a tanker wagon, moving at a steady fifteen miles an hour; it made overtaking impossible with no passing place before they reached the village. He sent three loud blasts on his horn, all ignored. With resignation he tucked in behind the last lorry and waited. Relief came quickly as, without warning or so much as a signal, the whole chain turned onto the site where the council stored grit for road repair. Well that at least made sense. Tom forgot the incident and raced the remaining distance to Boxtree.

Lucy was home, standing in the lighted front door with an expression on her face that made him stop in his tracks.

'Dad, come into the study, we need to talk alone.'

He followed her and sat down in his chair behind the desk. Then she told him.

It was eleven o'clock before Tom finally reached Inspector Oats. He had been ringing the wretched man's police and home numbers for an hour. When he finally connected with Oats's mobile phone the inspector was audibly harassed and bad tempered. Contrary to his hopes the RON supporters were ranging around Taraton and surrounding villages. They had been called to sort trouble in several pubs and an Indian restaurant in the town had been set on fire. To cap it all his radio had just reported two children missing. And he'd taken the Taraton posting because his wife had demanded a quieter life.

'Anyway, what d'you want?'

'I have fresh information on the Fjortoft case and I'm afraid it won't wait. Secondly the American, Mulgrum, has a man with him who is wanted for murder in the United States. More important to me is that my wife did not die in an accident – she was murdered. Lucy, my daughter obtained a witness statement tonight.'

A strange growling noise came down the line. 'Mr O'Malley, if this was anyone else but you I'd call that a wind-up and I'd do you for wasting police time. All right, I cannot handle your matter at this exact moment, but I will call DS Chilvers – he's still scene of crime officer for Crossfield Manor. Whether he'll get to you tonight I don't know, but frankly that is all I can do.' The line went dead.

'I've rung Andy,' said Lucy. 'He's on his way here now.'

She rested her hands on his neck and began to work her fingers on the tense muscles. It was soothing and he began to relax.

'With all this rioting, shouldn't you be on duty?

'They know where I am,' she replied. 'Anything serious will go to casualty. At this moment family comes first.'

It was odd, and so very wrong, that he should be feeling relieved. Tricia's death had left that terrible grief-filled void, made so much worse for being inexplicable. Tricia was a superb horseman riding her own champion mount. It made no sense that she should have fallen and died on the smooth bridleway she rode every week of the year. Tom had driven himself near to breakdown with guilt. Now at last he had the explanation; closure would come when he could find and name the killer. Tricia would have justice and that would start the healing process for them all, including Gina.

'I think it's time I talked to Hannah. I want to know exactly what she heard.'

'You'll have to wait another hour or so – I sedated her.'

Tom sighed. 'I can see why you irritate the police. Every time there's a vital witness you stick a needle in them.'

Lucy looked defensive. 'She was badly shaken – genuinely. But I really didn't want her saying anything to you until I'd beaten the truth out of Alex.'

'And did you – beat Alex that is?'

'Of course I didn't, but Lonny scared the man rigid. He threatened to castrate him, and I'm not wholly sure he was bluffing.'

'Natalie, come out here,' Francesca shouted. 'What's happening on the hill?'

Natalie came into the garden and stood beside her. They both stared as a glow on the downs burst into a vivid flame. Over the countryside came a sound like the sea beating on shingle culminating in a mighty roar.

'What's that?'

'It sounds like a football crowd,' said Natalie. 'Like the noise they make when Pompey score a goal.'

Never having been to a football match in her life, Francesca bowed to Natalie's superior knowledge.

'It's not football,' said Natalie, 'it's the RON and their sodding rally. I hate them – why do they have to come here?'

Alan Cunningham was away on business and Marjorie was at a committee meeting. The police were supposed to be keeping a surreptitious eye on Francesca. This meant an occasional patrol car stopping, then an officer knocking on the door. Marjorie had left a meal for them in the microwave but neither girl had an appetite for it.

'Let's go round the corner to Sami's place,' suggested Natalie.

Francesca was dubious; this was a defiance of Marjorie's grounding penalty. "Sami's place" meant: the *Spirit of India Quality Eastern Cuisine and Takeaway*. This was a misnomer insofar as the shop's owners were not Indian but Bangladeshi. Sami, the teenage son of the family, attended the college and was one of the of Natalie's circle of admirers.

Most days the takeaway remained active until ten o'clock. Tonight the shop was open but a metal blind shielded the windows.

The girls went to the counter to place their order. Francesca, unused to curry, found the smells overwhelming.

'Sami, what's going on?' asked Natalie.

'We're closing in twenty minutes; before the fascists get here.'

'That's an old fashioned word. Is that why it's so quiet?'

'That's it – most people are staying off the streets 'til it's over.'

Francesa did not care for this. Taraton had seemed unusually deserted: few cars on the road and fewer than usual parked by kerbs. The curry shop was almost empty with only one other customer. One she knew, it was Curly Tong from Crossfield.

'Hi there, sweetheart,' Curly leered at Francesca.

She shrank back in disgust. She could never forgive this man for blurting out her name in court. Curly was not looking at her, no one was looking at her – all were silent, tense and anxious. Engines raced on the street; speeding cars, horns blending with the screech of hot tyres.

'You'd better close up now, Sami,' said Natalie as she glanced outside. 'That's the RON and they're looking for trouble.'

Francesca knew fear now; her sheltered life had never prepared her for this. Why was Natalie so bloody calm?

'I'll bolt the door,' said Sami. He turned to the back of the shop and shouted something in Bengali.

It was Curly who reached the door first but he was five seconds too late. A heavy boot crashed through the glass showering him with fragments. In burst four new arrivals all male. Three of them were strangers and the fourth was Alex Cornbinder. Alex stared around the shop, took in the two girls, turned and walked back into the night.

Every corner of this room was lit. Francesca could see nowhere to hide; nowhere she could shrink into her natural anonymity. These newcomers were smartly dressed, clean-shaven, with cropped hair. Their body language spelt contempt and aggression. None of them seemed to notice her; all their eyes were on Natalie and Sami.

'Oi you, Blondie, why are you talking to a Paki – ain't an Englishman good enough for you?' The accent was London, the tone vicious.

'Sod off out of our town – arsehole,' Natalie sneered.

Francesca was appalled. This was so typical of Natalie; her impetuous ways were likely to put them both in real trouble. She began to edge towards the door. Too late, three more youths and a girl had blocked the exit, standing in poses from arrogant to downright threatening.

'Alex says that one's a fucking gyppo,' the girl pointed at Curly.

Curly reacted as Francesca had dreaded. He seized a long meat knife from the counter and held it with practised ease.

'That's right, I'm a traveller, want to make something of it?'

His white knuckles gripped the handle, the knife pointing upwards at the accuser; the yobs backed off. Two formidable men had joined

Sami – his father and his uncle. The uncle wielded a baseball bat, the father held twelve bore shotgun.

'I have telephoned the police,' said father. 'Now, all you trash go!'

The RON followers backed towards the door – for the first time they seemed uncertain.

'You won't use that gun, Paki,' jeered one of them.

The others muttered in support; an impasse had been reached. Natalie heard shouting in the street and the distant sound of a police siren. The RON supporters left, scrambling through the door. The last man stopped, another hand passed him a bottle with a strip of cloth poking from the top. There was a snap from a cigarette lighter and the bottle arced through the air trailing an oily flame. It shattered on the floor behind the counter and exploded with a thump. Flames rose and hot air gushed into the room. Sami screamed, as his white overall coat caught fire. His uncle seized the boy and hurled him to the floor away from the blaze, rolling him over, beating the flames with his bare hands. Curly threw down the knife and grabbed the fire extinguisher. He doused the men on the floor at close range and then turned to the main blaze. Too late – the woodwork of the wall was well alight and flames were licking at the ceiling above. Francesca began to choke in the fumes. Simultaneously Sami's father fired both barrels of his gun. The shots smashed into the ceiling above the door where the London yobs were grinning and jeering. It was enough, they vanished, their shouting gradually submerged in the roar and crackle of the blazing house.

'Fran, this way – move it!' Natalie grabbed at her arm.

She followed through the door into the women's toilets. Natalie pulled off a shoe and smashed the frosted window, hitting it again and again until the frame was clear.

'Let's out of here,' she called and began to climb through the gap.

Francesca came out of her trance. 'Wait!'

There were splinters of glass everywhere and Natalie wore only thin jeans and a halter top. She would cut herself to bits. Francesca pulled off her denim jacket and laid it over the jagged edges. This time she took the lead and squeezed through, dropping the four feet to the outside. Seconds later Natalie was with her. They clung to each other, tearful and trembling, breathing the clean air.

Francesca was confused: half of her wanted to run and half of her worried about Sami and his family. Standing in this narrow alleyway between two housing blocks, they could no longer smell the fire but there was uproar in the main street. The girls peered around the building. A jeering throng surrounded a stationary police car. Two officers were confronting the mob with little effect. A fire appliance, all siren and flashing lights, swept down the road halting next to the burning shop. The RON crowd seized bricks from a nearby pile and began to pelt the fire fighters as they tried to deploy their hoses. There began an ugly raucous chant. 'Burn Paki burn.'

The police and firemen were clearly losing the battle. One constable was sitting on the pavement holding a bloodstained handkerchief to his head. The smoke pouring from the upper floors exploded into orange flame; a horrible acrid smell filled the street. Thank God another police car had now come. Something was happening. The RON supporters were losing interest in the fire and were looking up the street towards the market square. The road was filled with running figures and Francesca knew them. Most were farm lads, several from Crossfield, with Curly Tong in the forefront. The Taraton boys seemed to be prepared, with pickaxe handles and lumps of wood. They tore into the Londoners. The police protecting the fire fighters made no attempt to intervene. The affray was short lived before the RON supporters broke and fled.

Natalie let go of Francesca and sprinted towards the police.

'Sami,' she screamed.

Horrified, Francesca watched her turn as if she intended to run into the burning shop. A policeman caught her and lifted her screaming and struggling. He put her down and pointed to a woebegone group by an ambulance. Sami was being lifted into the back surrounded by his family.

Natalie ran back. 'Come on,' she gasped. 'Get home, Mum will be back in twenty minutes.'

'You won't fool her, the police will want statements.'

'We'll face that when it happens, come on.' She set off jogging down the alleyway.

Someone was shouting. Francesca turned round and to her horror she saw Alex running behind.

'It's them,' Alex yelled. 'They're the ones.'

Francesca ran as she never had in her life and Natalie ran with her. Alex was dropping back; they could hear his wheezing breath and blundering footsteps. This alleyway ended in the central car park: another few yards and they would be there and minutes from home.

'Jayvy, it's them – towards you now!'

Alex had stopped running and was yelling over their heads. Two men stood at the end of the alley. They would have to run past them to escape. One was very old; with him was another younger man, with fair hair half concealed below a bandage and a black eye patch. Both girls stopped running. If Francesca had felt fear before that was as nothing to the terror that consumed her now. This man had an aura that was the only word she could think of and it smelt death. She would never have termed herself a psychic, but this gut feeling washed through her. She knew for a certainty that the eye patch man had been her father's killer.

Francesca felt a pleasing languor. She was in that half-world between waking and sleeping. Her bed felt wrong. She reached out a hand and felt the soft spongy surface she was lying on, but feel no sheets or duvet. Another thing was wrong; somebody was sitting on her left foot. She tried to pull it away but her muscles would not respond. She remembered who she was; remembered the burning restaurant – then what? She opened her eyes. Above her was a dirty cobweb-infested ceiling lit by a single dim light bulb. Francesca shut her eyes in disgust; she detested spiders.

CHAPTER 36

It was midnight when the telephone rang. Tom hoped it was the police; but the caller was Gina. Could Gus talk to Tom and Lucy now?

'Gina, for heaven's sake, it's the middle of the night. I've had one hell of a day and I've still got to work tomorrow.'

'It's tomorrow now, but Tom, I think you should hear Gus. He's discovered something we can't handle – we need your advice.'

'Can't it keep to the morning?'

'Sorry, Tom, but no it can't.'

'All right come on over, as it happens I've some pretty dramatic news for you too,'

Gina sat beside Gus as he drove the Mercedes through the familiar lanes to Boxtree Farm. Gus seemed controlled but deep in thought. The hedgerows rolled by fresh and green in the headlights. An owl flitted across the road before veering into the trees. They were approaching the junction with Buttons's Lane, the rough track that led out of the hanger, the place where Tom and Lucy had found her horse that dreadful night. On the left was a piece of rough pasture; all that remained of Crossfield Common. She could see headlights on the road coming towards them. A heavy vehicle was turning onto the track to the Common. Gus slowed and switched the lights to full beam; they revealed a high-sided truck.

'What the hell's going on?' he muttered.

Gina stared at the lorry but it was impossible to make out details.

'Seems odd in the middle of the night,' said Gus. 'If it's travellers Tom'll go ballistic.'

'Is it our land?'

'Yes, but it's common ground. I've no legal right to move anyone unless they break the law.'

At half past twelve a noisy motorbike drove into the yard. The Mormon guards leapt on its rider and pulled him kicking and struggling towards the house. Lucy, who had heard the commotion, ran across to them.

'Let him go,' she shouted. 'He's my brother.'

Andrew collected his fallen bike and parked it in the barn. Lucy walked with him to the door where their father stood.

'Dad,' said Andy. 'She's told me about Mum.'

Tom studied his son's face. He was unshaven but there was a healthier tinge to his complexion and his eyes were no longer lack-lustre and sunken.

'I never bought the accident theory,' Andy tucked his gloves into his helmet. 'No way would she have fallen there – no way.'

'But it's so motiveless,' said Lucy. 'Why kill her – Mum hadn't an enemy in the world?'

'She says you've an idea who the killer is.'

'I think I know who did it and I will have justice for your mother even if I die in the attempt.'

He turned and walked to his study and shut the door. He wanted space to think: to be alone.

He heard a light tap on the door. 'Tom, listen, it's me.' The voice was Gina's.

Reluctantly, he called her to enter. Poor Gina, she was the last person he wanted to see in his present mood. She put her arms round him and gave him a hug. It was a gesture of consolation with no sexual content.

'Lucy's told me about Tricia.'

'At least we've an answer now,' he sighed.

'I blamed myself.'

'I never blamed you – I thought it was my fault and all the time...'

'It was murder?'

'We know that now.'

She stood holding both his hands. 'Tom, Gus is here – we must talk.'

'Can Andy and Lucy sit in on this?'

'Of course, it's for all of you.'

'This is going to be hard for me, Tom. You'll probably tell me I'm crazy.'

They were all sitting around the kitchen table. In front of Gus was a little leather attaché case. Its contents, strewn over the table, were fading typescripts and bundles of monochrome photographs.

Gus picked up another item, a videotape. 'I'll deal with this last because you're going to take some convincing. These pictures are the ones you know about – the record of Gostanyn. Alan Cunningham recovered them for me this morning. Poor Matthew, he never knew the contents and they killed him.'

Gus picked up the photographs. 'These are the pictures the SS man took – there's fifty of them.' He began to hand them around. The prints showed groups of children in shabby clothing against a background of wooden huts. One was a winter scene with children pushing a giant snowball. Further photographs were indoor shots of a dormitory and rows of bunks with children staring woodenly at the camera. Tom didn't want to see more, he could sense the hopelessness in their faces. They knew too well what their fate would be.

'I wonder which of these is Magda's mother?' said Lucy.

'The girl that died trying to implicate me with Gostanyn?'

'She worked on the farm here,' said Tom. 'And yes, I think she was investigating you, but even Hannah now accepts you're innocent.'

'Yes,' said a voice behind them, 'even Hannah, who does not seem to have been invited to this gathering.'

She stood behind him in the doorway. Wrapped in one of Tricia's old dressing gowns she looked fragile and deathly pale; her head still swathed in a bandage.

'Mr and Mrs Fjortoft, this is Ms Hannah Berkovic.'

'I know that,' said Gus. 'My brother Max told me about you.'

'I'm only trying to find the truth,' she said.

'And I have the right to exclude my secrets from those who would destroy me.'

'I'm only trying to find the guilty. If you, Mr Fjortoft, had no part in these crimes then I have no interest in you.'

'Lucy,' said Tom. 'I didn't involve Hannah in these discussions because I assumed she was too ill to play a meaningful part. What's your opinion?'

'She ought to be resting, but in the circumstances I wouldn't expect her to stay upstairs.'

Tom looked at Gus. 'I don't believe you've anything to fear. I'd say it was in your interest for her to hear your story.'

'She's welcome.'

Tom passed Hannah the photographs.

'What are these?' she asked.

'They're part of the dossier you tried to steal from Woolbarrow Farm, only it was never there. That's what you were after that night?'

'A source told us Mr Rowridge was holding documents damaging to Brown. I intended to find them before he did.'

'He'd already failed, but not before he killed Matthew.'

'No he didn't,' said Gus. 'Hellmunt killed Matthew with Van Zyl as his sidekick. Will was at my house, remember; earlier he'd been in

London plying his new trade.'

'What new trade?'

'Be patient – I'm coming to that. Anyway, I read young Tong's testimony; there's only Hellmunt and Van Zyl that fit his description.'

'Gus,' said Tom. 'Are you really any nearer to finding Wilhelm Brown?'

'Oh yes, I've found him. He's playing the part of someone else but then he was always an actor.'

'I want to see the rest of these pictures,' said Hannah.

Gus pushed them towards her.

She started to flip through them. 'There's Greta Little, and yes, here we are,' she released a gasp of triumph. 'Look at him, little Doctor Death!'

The picture showed a small boy holding an old fashioned glass hypodermic. An odd little bundle lay on a sheeted table. Tom looked closer and then turned away. The bundle was another child held horizontally on the table with webbing straps.

'Very well, Mr Fjortoft; even so long ago I can see this is not you – so?'

'It's my half-brother, Wilhelm.'

'And you would swear to that?'

'If needs be yes, but I cannot see how you could bring this to a court.'

'Perhaps not, but then exposure to the wide world might be the greater punishment. To risk a cliché, he could run all he liked but there would be no hiding.'

'Gus,' said Tom. 'You say you know where this man is?'

'Yes, Ms Berkovic talks of hiding; I'll quote a cliché as well. They say the best concealment is under the glare of the light.'

'Come on, man,' Tom was just beginning to be annoyed. 'For God's sake explain.'

The telephone was ringing.

'Lucy, could you answer that, it's probably the police.'

When she returned, Tom could see by her face that here was more bad news.

'That was Marjorie Cunningham; Francesca and Natalie are missing. She wanted to know if they were here.'

Francesca opened her eyes and shut them again. The light bulb dazzled her so that her head hurt and she felt sick. With an effort, she rolled on her side and tried again. She could see a wall and grime covered bricks that must once have been white. With an effort she extended a hand and felt the floor on which she lay. It was wooden and smelt of mould. Very slowly she rolled on her back and opened her eyes. This time it seemed easier; the light was not so bright after all. Next she tried to sit up but lay back again. She felt giddy and sick. Her body seemed to fill the entire space of this tiny room.

What was happening and where was Natalie? Vague recollections returned; a voice in the darkness; a voice of authority to be obeyed. She thought she remembered her own voice answering but she wasn't sure of that either.

'Fran – are you there?'

'Natalie…' her voice was a hollow croak. She tried again. 'Where are you?'

'Over here.'

Natalie's voice was near but Francesca couldn't see her. She rolled over again and tried to focus. Her eyes hurt and never had she known such head pain. The far wall was not brickwork; it was a curtain of sacking.

'Fran, can you move?'

'Not sure –I feel ill.'

'Fran we've been kidnapped – this place feels like a grave.'

'Don't say that,' Francesca's eyes filled with tears.

Now she was frightened, her mind spiralling into panic.

'Fran, I'm coming to find you.'

She heard a scrabbling noise and Natalie emerged from under the sacking, crawling on all fours. A moment later the girls were clinging together sobbing in each other's arms. Once more Francesca lapsed into semi-consciousness.

She was awake again; something was different. She realised she still had her wristwatch. It read four-thirty, but was that morning or afternoon? Once more she felt that gut-twisting fear. They would die; snatched children always died. She pictured Marjorie and Alan at a police press conference; Marjorie tearfully pleading for their safe return, while all the time they were long dead. Natalie was still there, half sitting, staring across the room. Francesca heard her intake of breath and frightened squeal. Someone else was in the room; she heard a shuffle of feet and then beside her she saw a pair of legs clad in jeans and trainers. Standing looking down on them was a giant of a man. So tall was he that he stooped beneath the ceiling. Francesca's whole body went rigid; she felt like some traumatised rabbit dazzled in a shooter's spotlight – waiting passively for death. This man's head was covered in a black hood with tiny slits for eyes and mouth; it was a spectre from a nightmare.

'What exactly did Marjorie tell you?' asked Tom.

'Those two little idiots went into the town while the RON thugs were there. They'd both been grounded and the police were supposed to watching out for Francesca.'

'Oats told me two kids were missing but he didn't specify.'

'They've only just cleared the RON from the town centre. Marjorie thinks the girls were going to a curry takeaway. The RON set the place on fire and it's gutted. The girls were seen there, but now they've vanished.'

'Do the police think they're dead?'

'They don't think they were inside the shop. The fire fighters are certain everyone got out.'

'They could have taken cover until the riot was over.'

'Marjorie doesn't think so, they could only go home – it's just round the corner.'

Gina looked grim. 'If some creepy pervert's snatched them – it don't bear thinking about.'

'God,' Gus muttered, 'I go on about my troubles, but imagine what it must be like for a family whose kids are missing.'

Tom pushed his chair back and walked around the room. He couldn't keep still. He wasn't sure how much more he could take.

'Gus,' he said at last. 'Go on with your story. You say you know where your brother is.'

Suddenly Gus smiled. 'I'll tell you what I know and then you will tell me I am crazy. It'll make no difference because I know I'm right.'

'We'll be the judges of that; just tell us.'

'Wilhelm Brown reinvented himself as Liam Roland Rhys: bit part actor, illegal diamond broker and mercenary soldier. Rhys died in the Congo in nineteen-sixty, only to be miraculously reincarnated as the South African property speculator who returned to the land of his fathers and entered politics as Member of Parliament for Taraton.'

'If you are about to say what I think you are,' said Tom, 'then you are definitely delusional – I mean I detest the man but…'

'No Dad, I know he's right,' Andy spoke. 'It's Gannemeade isn't it?'

'Andrew,' Gus was clearly astonished. 'What would you know about it?'

Andy had pushed back his chair; he stood white-faced and agitated.

'Son,' Tom spoke quietly, 'please sit down, try to relax, and say what you mean.'

Andy slumped into his chair. 'It's about Jessica Gannemeade – something happened that time, the night she died. It's worried me since and I nearly spoke, but then I thought you'd say I was either crazy, or it's some coincidence.'

'Take your time,' said Tom. 'I'll explain,' he looked at the others. 'Jessica was Gannemeade's daughter and a friend of Andy's.'

He looked his son in the eye. 'Andy, I don't hold children responsible for their father's sins. You can apply that to me when it suits you,' he smiled.

Andy returned the grin. 'That night Jessica died something happened that's wholly trivial, but it stuck in my mind. Two of the other guys wanted to play snooker but we couldn't find the balls. I went with Jessica to a junk room upstairs. She pulled open a cupboard and out fell a picture. It was an oils portrait of a doctor. He was wearing an old fashioned suit but on the table in front of him was a stethoscope and other medical gear. It had a sort of Victorian feel to it and on the frame was a metal plate. The words were in German but it said something like: *presentation to Doctor Brown from his students. Heidelberg. 1929.* I asked Jessica who it was and she went crazy – that's why I remember. She just snapped, "that's my grandfather – he's dead, thank God – bloody murderer". It was such an odd thing to say that it stuck in my mind.'

'Did anyone overhear this?' asked Lucy.

'Yes, that bastard McCann the drug dealer. He'd been following us around all evening.'

'And the next morning Jessica was dead?'

'Yes,' Andy gaped at his sister. 'Oh my God, I see where you're coming from.'

'True,' said Gus. 'The young lady said enough to kill her, and I can confirm that Doctor Brown taught at Heidelberg.'

'Gus,' said Tom. 'When did you discover all this? I know he called on you the night Matthew died.'

'He had disguised himself so cleverly I wouldn't have known him at first; especially as I thought him dead.'

'What point the disguise?' asked Lucy.

'That's obvious; he didn't want me connecting him with his reinvented persona.'

'The politician?'

'Exactly, it explains why your Member of Parliament wouldn't meet me. His local party here complained that he would never even canvass or speak in Crossfield. They asked me to invite him – so there's an irony.'

'Did you?' Tom asked.

'I told them no; I'm a US citizen, I've no interest in British politics.'

'I'm still not convinced,' Tom muttered. 'Gannemeade ... it's unbelievable.'

'It's logical,' said Gus. 'My mother was Welsh: Margaret Rhys, born in Carmarthen. When the war ended she was destitute. Her husband was in jail awaiting trial, and my father had been killed in the Pacific. Both Max and I were in the States. She needed to make a new life with her eldest son Wilhelm. She went to South Africa, a safe place for fringe Nazis. There was a lot of sympathy for Germany among Afrikaans speakers, not to the point of agreeing to the Holocaust, but latent support. I've found out that my family trust, unknown to me, gave her money on condition she stayed in SA. I think my trustees were embarrassed by the connection with Margaret and wanted her out of the way. I only made the final links a few weeks ago.'

'It all goes back to that night in April, am I right?' asked Tom.

'Almost, I had a call the day I arrived from Rudi Kolkinnen in Edinburgh. He's the man who calls himself Tallisment.'

'He's the bloke who frightened our horses with his helicopter,' said Lucy.

Gus smiled. 'Max tells me you demolished Rudi in thirty seconds – says you were magnificent.'

'Who is he?' asked Lucy. 'Where does he fit in all this?'

'He's Rudi Kolkinnen. His father was a Finnish SS man in the guard at Gostanyn. Rudi had kidney failure and he was going to die anyway. His father pleaded with Dr Brown to try a transplant – it was desperation. Brown agreed and they killed a little pure blooded German girl and switched the kidney.'

'Wait a minute,' said Lucy. 'He couldn't control rejection – I thought all his victims died.'

'True, but by some miracle, Rudi's transplant worked or at least it did partially. He was a sick man until he had a proper transplant in the nineteen-seventies. He was on dialysis before that. I can't give you a medical explanation because I haven't got one.

'Rudi came to Britain from South Africa in nineteen-eighty and started his real estate business. It was a good time for it and he had unlimited funds. I saw pictures of him in the press here and in the States. He was interviewed on TV and I recognised him instantly. Then I got wind that he was investigating my past. So I took the decision to confront Kolkinnen and warn him I was around and knew who he was.'

'That was when you went to Edinburgh,' said Tom.

'He laughed at me; said he was a victim of Brown just like any of the other kids. Then he said I'd taken part in the killings and there was photographic evidence to prove it. True of course, but the pictures were in Matthew's bank.'

'He's a blackmailer,' said Gina.

'That's what it amounts to. He said he'd been watching my film career and maybe I'd like to invest in his companies.'

'Demanding money with menaces?' said Tom.

'Oh yes, but miscalculated. You see it had gotten to the point where I'd had enough. I was prepared to go public voluntarily. I told him just that and then he turned nasty.'

'I can imagine,' said Lucy.

'He said he'd swear on oath that he'd seen me commit every brutality you could name including cannibalism. Of course he didn't know brother Max was still living. Then he said I was responsible for the slaying of a girl employee on the farm here.' Gus looked up. 'Sorry, Tom, but he said my farm manager had tried to dispose of her body in the sea.'

'Bloody hell,' Tom's temper simmering all evening spilled over into outright fury. 'I'll sue him … I'll…'

'Tom, cool it, of course I told him it was bullshit. I told him to do whatever he liked – no deal. Then I walked out.'

Tom had calmed; now he was thinking hard.

'Magdalena Sherakova was murdered forty-eight hours before your trip to Edinburgh and the break in at the Manor was the day after I found her body.'

Tom addressed Hannah. 'Why did Magda go to Chichester that day?'

'She'd agreed to be at a specific place to contact a source. Magda wasn't formally part of my organisation; she always played it close – never told anyone anything. I talked to her in Brighton that morning; she was upbeat, excited.'

Tom looked at Gus. 'How did you finally rumble Gannemeade?'

'The night Matthew died I had a guy to see me who wouldn't give his name. Remember please; I hadn't seen Wilhelm for years and I'd never met Gannemeade – never even seen a picture of him.

'I go to the front door and there's this overweight bald guy who I would swear I'd never met in my life. He produces a note of introduction from Kolkinnen – not a good move because I told him to go to hell. It's then that he tells me he's my brother. I couldn't take that – it was crazy…' Gus faltered into silence.

'But presumably he convinced you?' Tom spoke quietly.

'Yes, he could answer all the right questions and he had a birth mark about the size of a postage stamp on his neck – looks like a map of Australia.'

'Yes,' said Tom, 'Gannemeade's got that – I've seen it.'

'He disguised his voice of course; spoke with a South African accent but he had little tricks of speech that took me right back.'

'And he clashed with Gina?'

Gina bristled. 'He was horseshit – I didn't hide what I thought. I reckon that's one reason he went for me in Seattle.'

Tom looked at Gus. 'Can we ask what he wanted?'

'He wanted me to sell all my property here to Kolkinnen.'

'That explains Tallisment's attitude when he barged in here,' said Lucy.

'Gus,' said Tom. 'I hope you told him to get stuffed.'

'Indeed I did and the rest.'

'What did he say to that?'

'He told me I was the world's youngest war criminal and if that came out I'd be finished in films. Told me I'd be fine as long as I got out of England. At that point I told him to leave and I haven't seen him since.'

'Is that why you took off for the States next day?'

'Lew Gungenhorn warned me there was a story about to break; saying I was bankrolling Mulgrum.'

'Would anyone believe that?'

'Some might; you see I don't bankroll Mulgrum, but he rents the Uplands Lodge from Benson Shipping. Benson owns property all along the West Coast, but I'd never heard of that place.'

'And now Mulgrum's in England stirring hate. Gus, I heard the man speak tonight – he's charismatic and bloody dangerous. It was only after hearing him that the mob went crazy.'

'I can believe that.'

Tom wanted an answer. 'Why did you summon me all that way and nearly get me killed?'

'Selfish of me but I needed someone I could trust, a beam of light – a sane person in that madhouse. I'll never cease to be grateful – it was you got Gina out of that place.'

'All right; now let's get to the point. How do you know for certain that Gannemeade is Wilhelm Brown?'

Gus stood up; in his hand was the videotape. 'Lead me to your TV – I'd like to play you this.'

'So, you two found each other.' The man spoke. 'No need to be scared. Nobody's going to hurt you – I've brought you something to eat.'

The voice had no menace; it was friendly with authority: a school-teacher's voice. Francesca had sometimes fantasised about an imaginary elder brother. This was an elder brother's voice: warm and very English. He had a tray in his hands, with two plastic cups, and a plate with some biscuits.

'How d'you feel?'

'What d'you think?' replied Natalie, 'lousy of course – what's it to you and where are we?'

'All right, little girl. You've got yourself mixed in business you'd have done better to keep out of.'

Francesca looked up at him; she could see a flicker of light on the dark eyes peering through the hood slits.

'Just be good, behave yourselves and I'll look out for you – bye.'

With scarcely a sound he was gone.

'Who is he?' Francesca whispered.

'Dunno, I don't trust him, but he's sort of good vibes; I think they'll let us go.'

'Why?'

'He's got that hood on – so he doesn't want us to see his face.'

Tom stood with Andy and Lucy as the Mercedes turned from the yard and into the road. None of them felt inclined to say anything. He went to the study and rang the police offering to help in the search for the missing children. He received polite thanks but the offer was declined. He had scarcely put the receiver down when the phone rang again.

'May I speak to Hannah?' It was a male voice, definitely English.

'Who are you?' Tom was wary. 'I'm not sure I know a Hannah.'

'I think you do – she's staying with you. Tell her it's Joel.'

'And who might Joel be?'

'Magdalena Sherakova was my girlfriend.'

'All right, I'll take it.' Hannah was standing behind him.

She took the phone. 'Joel, where are you and what are you up to?'

She listened, face deadpan.

'I don't want to know your plans and you are not to come to this house. We are on the way to a legal result and I will not have you fouling it up.'

She listened some more and Tom could see she was angry.

'Yes, you're right – my ways are not your ways, thank God. Keep your noses out.'

She slammed the receiver down. Tom was startled; this was the first time he had seen her display anger.

'Was that Magda's boyfriend – the one we saw at her funeral?'

'Yes, she had a funny taste in men. He's a rich playboy; we dropped him as soon as we found he was a Redemptionist.'

'A what?'

'Redemption 1945. They style themselves as a direct action force, but you would call them terrorists. They're the ones who tried to snatch Hellmunt in Oregon and stalked Mrs Fjortoft in Seattle.'

'As terrorists they seemed about as efficient as the Keystone Cops.'

'Don't underrate them, they've killed and very efficiently. I'm worried – Joel is up to something and I've no idea what.'

CHAPTER 37

Tom started ringing the police at six o'clock the next morning. There had been no further contact from the Cunninghams and Tom had not wanted to call them. After twenty minutes of blocked lines and frustrating delays he was put through to Inspector Oats.

'Oh, it's you,' Oats sounded tired and disgruntled. 'Sorry – I've been up all night.'

'Any news of those missing kids?'

'No, and it doesn't look good.'

'How so?'

'Witness saw them get in a car by Bakery Alley. Witness reports they were under duress.'

'Hell! Is this connected with the RON?'

'What makes you think that?'

'Just a hunch. They were in the shop the RON set on fire.'

'In that case I almost hope you're right. You see, that little girl Natalie Cunningham turns out to be a bit of a flyer, if you get my meaning.'

'I know, but all the same I'd say she was streetwise. I doubt she'd be conned by a pervert.'

Oats grunted something that Tom didn't catch. He left it there and went to work without breakfast – he simply could not face a plate of food. His night had been a troubled one. The moment sleep began to take him he would be swamped by visions of Gannemeade.

Gus had played his video; a local news program recorded some months before and viewed again by pure chance. Gannemeade was shown pontificating to an empty Commons chamber, waffling about some by-pass scheme. Gus had become excited pointing out little mannerisms and body language then jabbing at the screen to show the birth mark standing proud above the collar of Gannemeade's pinstripe suit. Tom's scepticism began to change to a conviction that Gus was right. Apart from Andy's evidence, Gus should be able to identify his own brother. This morning all that was unimportant compared to the abduction of the two girls.

Tom took the Land Rover along the track to the common. The rough pasture was churned with tyre tracks. At least five heavy vehicles had occupied this land in the night and they weren't travellers. These were heavy commercial vehicles and Tom was not pleased. He became aware of a lone figure watching him; it was Curly Tong.

'What's going on here?'

Tom fully expected Curly to run but the man stood his ground.

'Lorries, Mr O'Malley – big 'uns, concrete lorries. Mixers, ballast trucks, one with cement and an elevator.'

'Elevator?'

'Feeds the mixers.'

'Any idea whose?'

'They be plant hire trucks – ain't local neither and they've scraped off the logos.'

'No writing at all.'

'No, but they couldn't scrub it all out – there's traces like.' Curly looked shiftily around. 'What's it worth?'

'You want to sell the information – you've got a bloody nerve.'

This was typical Curly but the man had a point – he didn't miss much, and right now he could be useful.

'All right, I'll give you ten pounds for what you know about those trucks and another twenty if you'll keep an eye out for them and anything else that doesn't fit in this village.'

'Done, Mr O'Malley. Those trucks come from Milton ken something…'

'Milton Keynes?' Tom spelt if out although he doubted if spelling was Curly's forte.

'That was it, never heard of such a place – not round here. Tells you summat else, I reckon they could be RON men.'

'Really – what makes you think that?'

'Saw 'em in the lay-by with the burger van, about six o'clock. Hears 'em talking, I'd swear they was RON. Mr O'Malley, did you hear how we duffed up them London boys in the town?'

'Curly, I'm still a magistrate; the less you say about that the better. Keep watch and I'll pay you if you're straight with me – all right?'

Tom resumed his journey as far as the Manor. Gus was downstairs.

'Couldn't sleep a wink for thinking of those kids – any news?'

'Not a thing.' Tom repeated what Oats had told him.

'Those poor people – after all young Francesca's been through. This wouldn't have been but for me…'

'Gus, you can't say that – we don't know what happened. Let's try and not lose hope.'

Gus led the way into the house and then unexpectedly he turned down the kitchen passage.

'I'll make us some coffee – afraid Gina's not so well today.'

'I'm sorry to hear that – what's the problem?'

'Bit of gut trouble. She was sick first thing and I've made her stay in bed.'

'Is this whole business getting to her?'

'Yes and no; she's upbeat about my problems, but she went a bit quiet when she heard the truth about Tricia and she's mighty stressed about those kids.'

'What do we do about Gannemeade? I feel like going to his house and confronting him.'

Gus put down his cup. 'My concern is Mulgrum; I don't want him spreading poison lies in this country. Wilhelm's the least of our problems; I deal with him myself in my own good time.'

Natalie felt dizzy; she still had a headache but she could stand again without falling over. She bit her lip, looked around, and then set out to explore their prison. In the far wall was a metal door; it had no handle and seemed immovable. She discovered a single ventilator in the centre of the ceiling with sunlight filtering through from high above. So the eight o'clock on her watch meant morning, but what day of the week, and how long had they been unconscious? She had a distant detached memory of being questioned by an adult male voice and her own droning in reply.

Natalie laid her right ear against the door and almost at once jumped back; someone was moving on the far side and now she could hear a key inserted in the lock. Like a frightened rabbit she scuttled back to the mattress and Francesca.

'Stand up,' the order was blunt and the voice American. 'Face me and stand still.'

The man was tall and slim with a face hidden behind a hood; unlike their last visitor he wore a smart grey suit. A second figure stood behind him and to Natalie's relief he was the earlier man with the kindly voice. This time he was silent as he moved behind them. Natalie gasped as he caught her wrists and pinned them together. Now she screamed with alarm as he bound her hands with a plastic parcel tie and then slipped a hood over her head.

'All right, little girl. Behave we're going to set you free.'

He spun her round and held her. 'Now walk.'

She shuffled forward into the unknown.

'Three steps ahead of you.'

Cautiously she made her way up to another level with her captor's grip beneath her armpits.

'Ladder in front; I'll hold you – just work your feet on the rungs then climb – it's not far.'

She reached out slowly with her face forward and felt a hard wall and then, yes, her mouth touched the iron rungs of a fixed ladder. Fantastic, even through the hood she could breath fresh flower scented air. Hands reached down while her guide lifted her from below. There came a scrabbling sound and she knew Francesca was beside her.

'You can sit down,' said the kind voice. 'The ground's dry.'

Natalie knelt then rolled onto her side. The surface was dry but uncomfortable and covered with woody twigs that bit into her bare shoulder. She struggled against disorientation and her wrists hurt where the plastic strap bit into them.

'You,' it was the cold-voiced American. 'What's your home telephone number?'

Natalie could not stop her tears; it was stifling under the hood and this other voice frightened her.

She still had some spirit. 'Why d'you want it – are you going to hurt my mum and dad?'

'Calm down, little girl,' it was the nice voice. 'We're negotiating for your release.'

Tom walked through his own front door as the call came.

'Tom,' it was Marjorie. 'We've had a call from Natalie.'

'Where are they?'

'I don't know, she only spoke for a few seconds and then this man cut in…' her voice broke. 'He said he'd kill them if we go to the police.'

Tom could hear her distress – he paused before quietly asking.

'Did he say what he wanted?'

'It's something to do with Gustav Fjortoft.'

'Any instructions?'

'Alan and me are to come to your house and also Mr and Mrs Fjortoft. You are to order your security men to leave. They will make contact when you've done that.'

'How are the girls?'

'Francesca was quiet but Natalie sounded OK.'

'Did you trace the call?'

'Withheld number.'

It would be of course.

'Do what they say and come here. I'll send the guards down to the Manor.'

Tom tried to sound confident and reassuring as he said goodbye.

'I heard all of that.' It was Hannah. 'You've an extension on the landing.'

'Bloody cheek – who's behind this – you bloody Jews?'

'Do I detect a trace of public school anti-Semitism?' she smiled sweetly.

'Two children are in danger. So you tell me what you know.'

'Believe me I know nothing about it. I'm not going to make wild guesses but it's certainly not the Redemptionists.'

'Very well, you will go upstairs to your room and you will stay there. You will not contact the police or talk to anyone.'

Hannah had not the slightest intention of staying where she was. Nine months work was coming to a head, but not in the ways she had intended. She must take the initiative or it would be Tom and his family who would be destroyed and not her enemies. In the meantime she would watch. The Fjortofts had arrived with Max Jiffers. All three had gone indoors and she could hear the mutter of nervous conversation. Ten minutes later the Cunninghams drove into the yard followed almost immediately by Lucy. For once that arrogant woman looked hot and flustered as she ran into the house, forgetting to shut her car door.

The final act had not been long in coming. A white transit van appeared and parked with its rear to the front door. Hannah peered through a chink of curtain as all seven occupants of the house were ushered into the van by an anonymous hooded figure. She aimed her tiny digital camera and took two quick shots. She watched the van leave but failed to see if it turned left or right. She had a clear record of its registration but that would almost certainly be false.

She picked up her mobile phone and called a number.

'Joel, things are developing too fast. I suggest for today we suspend our differences – we've work to do.'

Tom could see nothing outside the van. The driver was concealed behind a plywood screen and the rear windows were covered. He tried to read the motion but all it told him was country lanes. For a while there came the steady rhythm of a motorway, then the stop-start of town traffic, and now they were in country lanes again. Their guard sat facing them dressed in black overalls and full-face balaclava. He was taciturn to the point of being robotic. He had not uttered a single word but had communicated by a series of printed cards. It occurred to Tom that the man might fear his voice being recognised.

From a plastic shopping bag he produced some strips of black cloth, which he threw to each prisoner; crude blindfolds with elastic straps.

PUT ON THE BLINDFOLDS
NO DANGER IF YOU DO WHAT YOU ARE TOLD

Tom looked at the others. 'Best do what he says. They've no interest in hurting us at this stage.'

This seemed to reassure them. Lucy was the first to comply and one by one the others followed. Tom slipped the thing over his own eyes. At least he still had his other senses.

A blessed breeze of country air wafted into the van dispelling the stench of body odour and fear.

'Hold onto me, mate,' said a voice almost in his ear: a voice resonant of London. A hand caught his sleeve.

'Close up the rest of you and hold onto each other.'

They shuffled collectively along a hard surface, then onto soft ground like a lawn. Marjorie clung to him sobbing. Tom began to find her irritating but knew that was uncharitable; with a missing child she must be in a state of distress beyond knowing.

'Doorway,' the cheerful voice called. 'Straight ahead one step up.'

Tom felt a wooden doorframe.

'Straight ahead now.'

He followed along a passage until he bumped into something, a stair banister.

'Door straight ahead.'

The floor was hard; probably tiles.

'Right, folks, blindfolds off.'

Tom uncovered his eyes; as he did so the door slammed and a key turned.

All stood blinking and uncertain in the middle of a large square room: a shabby place, dusty and empty. Lucy grimaced in disgust at a large spider scuttling across his web.

'Where are my girls?' Marjorie shouted.

She seemed rejuvenated with a new light in her eyes.

'These people are too cocky – fancy driving us all around the country to end up here.'

'How so?' Tom was puzzled.

'I know where we are; I was born in this house.'

She went to an empty shelf and began to brush away the dust.

'I'm right – look.'

Burnt into the wood were letters. *M.R. Age 14.*

'I did that with a red-hot poker on my birthday. We're in the storeroom of Woolbarrow Farm.'

CHAPTER 38

The helicopter gave Andy one of the worst shocks of his brief life. Encased in his helmet and immersed in the roar of his bike he was in his own world. The helicopter passed over him with a deafening howl and a blast of downdraught from its rotors. For a split second he knew what it must be like to be a rabbit in the sights of a diving buzzard. He froze, failed to brake for the oncoming corner and slid sideways into a freshly dug ditch.

He felt shaken and angry as he stumbled to his feet and pushed the bike back onto the tarmac. He pulled off his helmet and listened. The helicopter was still close, seemingly hovering just over the brow of the hill. Andy brushed the dirt from his leathers and resumed his ride; he would put the incident down to experience.

The yard at Boxtree was crowded with parked cars: Lucy's, Dad's Land Rover, a Mercedes he didn't know and oddly, Gus Fjortoft's customised jeep. He went indoors to a deserted house. He was mystified and for the first time uneasy. He heard the helicopter take off again, over the hill in the direction of Woolbarrow. Where was everybody; he called but without reply. Where were the guards and that snooty Hannah? He ran upstairs and peeped round the corner of Hannah's door; she was gone, just as everyone else was gone. It was in the study that he found the note. A sheet of A4 paper lay under a weight on the desk.

Andy
We're in contact with the kidnappers of those girls. Stay in the house and await events. DO NOT contact the police before 6pm. Stay near the phone and no acts of initiative.
We'll be in touch first opportunity.
Dad. 9.45am.

This was crazy, what on earth had happened and why no police? No way would he sit in this house while his father and sister were in the hands of terrorist nutters. They must be Hannah's people. He still held a festering grievance against Hannah and she was an Israeli: a number one baddie in student political demonology. The Israelis had a vendetta against Fjortoft; Hannah had vanished – the whole scenario stood clear in his tortured mind. He had to take some action or go mad. He picked up the paperweight and hurled it across the room.

For a while he paced around the house muttering incoherently. He walked into the garden and stood in the middle of the lawn, forcing himself to breathe gulps of air. It was then that he caught a movement in the far side copse.

'Hey, you, come out of there!'

The half-concealed figure rose and set off through the trees in a loping run. Oblivious to danger, Andy sprinted in pursuit; in his own words he was up for a confrontation. He had already recognised this intruder; it was Curly Tong. He doubted if Curly's presence had any connection with his problems, but the sight of this local layabout spying on him was enough to tip Andy over the edge into blind fury.

He was lighter and smaller than Curly, who was finding it hard going between the tightly spaced ash trees. Andy caught his quarry as Curly tried to climb a stock fence. At this point he began to regret his impulsiveness. He knew the man to be an accomplished brawler who'd been known to pull a knife. Curly offered no resistance but stood facing Andy grinning.

'What were you doing in our garden?'

'Just watching.'

'Casing the house while it's empty?'

'No I weren't – I wouldn't touch Mr O'Malley's house, I got some sense.'

'What were you up to?'

'You wanna know where your Dad is?'

'Yes, I do.'

'I been watching – your Dad paid me to watch – so there.'

'Go on.'

'At Woolbarrow, all of 'em – your Dad, that Lucy and Mr and Mrs Fjortoft. They didn't go there willing neither. Lot of villains had 'em – RON men I'd guess – 'spect they want a ransom like.'

'You'd better tell the police.'

'Oh yeah and have 'em tell me I was part of it – no thanks.'

'All right, Curly; tell exactly what you've seen and anything else you know.'

Marjorie hammered on the door smashing it with her fist until her knuckles were sore.

'I want my girls!'

Gina knelt on the floor white faced and shivering.

'Are you all right, honey?' Gus looked concerned.

'No, I'm going to be sick.'

'She's not been too well lately,' said Gus, 'but she insisted on coming with me.'

Lucy walked across and sat down by Gina. She felt her forehead and stared into her eyes.

'I don't think you're running a temperature. How long have you felt ill?'

'Just these last few days,' Gina forced a smile. 'I'll be OK – guess this whole thing's got to me.'

Gina rose unsteadily and looked wildly around. The one object on the floor was an old galvanised bucket. She staggered to it, knelt down, and retched for a solid two minutes. Gus and Lucy stood in front to screen her from the others who had already turned away embarrassed. With a wan smile she wiped her face and sat down in her place next to Gus. There followed a long silence when nobody spoke.

Lucy broke the silence. 'Listen – helicopter.'

They could all hear it; the high-pitched whine of the approaching aircraft, hugging the hilltops.

'That settles it,' said Tom. 'If it lands here it's Tallisment's – so we know where we stand.'

'Could be an army chopper,' said Gus.

'I think Dad's right,' said Lucy. 'It sounds like Tallisment's. I wish we could see out of here.'

She looked up at the tiny windows high in the wall.

'Stand on my shoulders,' said Tom.

Lucy nodded and ran to him. Tom bent down while she climbed on his back.

'You're a sight heavier since I last did this.'

He grunted as he rose to his full height while Lucy scrabbled upright until she stood with her body balanced by her hands against the wall.

'It's landing somewhere in that field behind the house. Any people will have to come through the garden.'

Tom was sweating; Lucy had failed to remove her walking shoes and they were biting into his shoulders.

'I'm right, here they come,' she wiped more grime from the window pane. 'It's Tallisment and two I don't know.'

'Description?'

'One's a funny little chap, forty something, smart suit – sort of mousy brown hair going a bit grey. The other's old, seventies at least, but walks younger – smart suit too.'

'Stay up for a minute,' Tom braced himself.

'Gus, are these the two I think they are?'

'Mulgrum and Hellmunt for a guess.'

'Who is Hellmunt, where does he fit in all this?'

'I know him and I know what he did. Let's leave it for now – it's kinda personal.'

That meant Gostanyn again.

'All right, Lucy, I'll let you down.'

Andy rode his motorbike with Curly sitting pillion. Curly pointed him to a gap in the hedge; a short run over grass to the woods ended with the bike concealed in an old chalk working. Andy calculated that they were on Woolbarrow land where the woods sloped upwards to the field adjacent to the farmhouse. Hannah had hidden just inside this wood the night they caught her in the house. Andy would not forget his humiliation at her hands; this was pay back time.

'Stay here,' said Curly, 'I'll take a look.'

He scrambled over the lip of the dell and vanished. Andy was happy to let him go; Curly's ability to fade into the landscape was legendary. Ten minutes later he was back.

'They're all in the house and guess what?'

'What?'

'That helicopter's the one Jayvy uses – belongs to some Yank.'

'They're nothing to do with it – it's the Israelis – they're out to get Fjortoft.'

'No – it's RON men up there. I knows 'em – Alex Cornbinder and that Witherrick the copper.'

'You mean the police are already there?'

'No, Witherrick's a RON man; he's as bent a copper as ever walked. He's up there guarding the outside.'

Andy remembered PC Witherrick. That man had stopped him, just a week after his mother's death and accused him of stealing his own motorbike. After that he could believe almost anything of the officious prat. Colluding in kidnap though, that took some swallowing. It also looked as if his satisfying theory about Israelis was collapsing.

'Perhaps it's time I called the law.'

'Not yet, mate; let's see some more. Come with me, I can get us nice and close. We won't be seen – promise.'

Andy followed along the line of a gully that led to the top of the ridge. As they reached the field fence Curly dropped prone and Andy joined him. They wriggled forward to where they had a clear view of the house. The helicopter was parked unattended, its tail towards them.

'Shall I nobble 'im?' Curley grinned

'How d'you mean?'

'Get a sledge hammer and smash the tail rotor – they'd go nowhere then.'

'For God's sake – these are terrorists – my Dad and sister are in there. I won't provoke them.'

Andy lost count of minutes, nothing happened. The little farmhouse lay bathed in sunshine. A few cars drove past on the road, their occupants oblivious to the drama within. Then a man came from the house. He stopped, looked around, and began to walk towards them. There was something strange and rather furtive about him, before he began to run.

Curly chuckled. 'Him and me are going to have a talk.'

'For God's sake they'll see us!'

Andy made a grab at Curly but too late; the man had crawled under the fence.

'Stay there, I knows 'im, Alex Cornbinder – I'll make 'im talk.'

Both men were out of sight now and Andy could only wait. There came a muffled shout and sounds of a scuffle. Curly reappeared dragging Alex in a vicious neck lock so tight that the man was purple faced and slobbering.

'Here, take it easy,' Andy hissed.

Curly grinned and eased his grip then signalled Alex to crawl under the wire.

'I wanna' get away,' Alex mumbled. 'I'm finished with 'em.'

'Finished with who?' said Andy.

'Them Yanks; Jayvy's over the hill there – same place he killed the magistrate's wife.'

'What's that?' Andy blazed the question forgetting to keep his voice down. 'She was my mother.'

Alex stared at him. 'You're O'Malley's son – your Dad's in the house there.'

'We know that – and my sister?'

'Yeah, she's there. Look, I'm sorry about your mum, but Jayvy's a psycho, he killed old Parky Partridge, just because he knew about the wood over there.' Alex seemed wholly deflated almost plaintive. 'They're going to kill another man and I don't want no part in it.'

'Who are they killing?' Andy snapped.
'Big fat bastard – you knows him.'

Footsteps sounded in the passage and the door was unlocked. Two men stared into the room. One was the hooded guard, the other was Hellmunt. His glance settled on Gina.

'Mrs Fjortoft, would you come with us please?' Hellmunt spoke with courtesy.

'Why should I?' Instinctively she moved closer to Gus.

'Mrs Fjortoft, you have my word we mean you no harm, but there is a matter where you have a grievance and we think we should help you.'

Gina glanced nervously around at her companions.

'Can you assure me you'll bring my wife back to this room unharmed?' asked Gus.

'You have my word. Mr Fjortoft, whatever you may think of me I do not break my word.'

Gus squeezed her hand. 'I think he means that – best go with him, Honey.'

She climbed unsteadily to her feet; she felt better now and her natural defiance was beginning to warm her.

'OK, I'll go listen, but that's all.'

She followed the two men into the passage. She had never been in this part of the house. Whenever she had called with village business she had been ushered into the Rowridge's dreary lounge. This time she was led past the door of that room and into the farm office. For the first time her resolution almost failed her as she found herself face to face with her own and her husband's enemies.

Mulgrum was there; he stood and courteously pointed her to a high-backed chair of dark carved wood, as uncomfortable as it was sinister. Hellmunt sat down beside Mulgrum with another man who must be Tallisment. Thank God there was no sign of Van Zyl.

'What's going on?' She had to say something. 'We came here to win the release of those poor kids – so, what's this about?'

'The children are safe – they have fulfilled their purpose. If you co-operate with us they will be released,' said Mulgrum.

She glared at him; she was no longer frightened; she was very angry.

'Mrs Fjortoft,' Mulgrum spread his hands. 'We suspect you have suffered a grievous injury at the hands of a colleague of ours.'

This was so unexpected that Gina was bewildered.

'In Seattle you had a confrontation with Mr Gannemeade?'

'You mean the asshole tried to rape me.'

'Tried?'

'But he didn't succeed – I shot him. OK, what did he tell you?'

'A somewhat different account. However we had other information and we know the man in question too well to accept a word he says.'

'Is that supposed to make me feel better – what did he tell you?'

'Initially he told us he was rescuing you from an unknown assailant.'

'Jesus Christ!'

'No, definitely not. If I may continue. Mr van Zyl had a conversation with Mr Gannemeade in which he persuaded him to a different version. Mr Gannemeade now claims you were a willing partner – "gagging for it", is his phrase.'

'Why, the lying sonofabitch,' Gina forgot everything else in her rage. 'OK, Mr Mulgrum, how come I shot him – you answer that?'

'He claims it was an – an unrelated accident.'

'I shot the bastard with my own gun – I'd no choice.'

'Why did you not report this to the city police?'

'Simple, I was being held a prisoner in that darned hotel. They were my husband's people but I didn't trust them. I got out of there, and back to England fast as I could.'

'You have no thoughts of justice – vengeance?'

'No, Mr Mulgrum, I do not. I shot the bastard. I won – that's closure.'

'No,' Mulgrum shook his head. 'As a Christian minister I cannot condone such a crime, nor can I condone your attitude, however generous.'

'Don't Christian ministers preach forgiveness?'

'Mrs Fjortoft, can you in the depths of your heart, tell me you have forgiven this man?'

He had subtly put her on the spot. 'No, I haven't.'

'Thank you, ma'am, you may rejoin your husband and friends.'

'Just a minute, Mister, tell me why you've snatched those kids?'

'Simple, they are the lure that brings you all to us. As I said, they've fulfilled that function and we have no more quarrel with them.'

Gina felt detached and dreamlike as she followed the hooded guard back to the storeroom. Now a happy surprise, Francesca and Natalie were in the centre of the room.

She ran across to Gus. 'What's happened?'

'They brought the kids in here five minutes ago. Young Natalie hasn't stopped talking since.'

Half an hour later the guards came. They called out the names of Tom and the two Fjortofts and ordered them to follow. Lucy demanded to be included and the guards merely shrugged and beckoned her to follow. Tom didn't like this, but was powerless to stop his impulsive daughter. All four of them were blindfolded and helped into the back of, presumably, the same van. The journey was a mere ten minutes before the door opened. They climbed out unsteadily and heard the van drive away.

This time they were led over rough earthy ground strewn with twigs and bushes that clung at their ankles. Gina gasped as she tripped and fell.

'I'm through – OK, shoot me, but this thing comes off.'

'All right, folks, you can uncover.' This guard was definitely English.

Tom pulled off the blindfold and stood blinking in the bright sun. He had half expected this would be their destination. They stood on the outskirts of Bechams Wood. A second car was driving onto the site; from it emerged Hellmunt and Tallisment.

'Follow me please,' said Hellmunt.

They hesitated; the guards closed behind them with a tangible menace.

'Better do what he says,' said Tom.

Hellmunt led them deep into the centre of the wood. They followed, stumbling among the brambles and the fresh spring growth. Tom could hear the distant mooing of the Home Farm cows. He was immersed in overwhelming regret as he wondered what their fate would be and whether he would live to know these simple joys again. This wood held a secret. Tom had refused to take Rufus seriously, just as Rufus had been overly cagey about his discoveries. It had cost Rufus his life; Tom was all too aware of that.

Someone had been digging, leaving a pile of loose earth mixed with bits of brush and tree root. Beside it was a square hole.

'I'm not going down that,' said Gina. 'This is as far as I go.'

'Please, Mrs Fjortoft,' Hellmunt shook his head. 'Things are not what they seem. We mean you no harm – there is someone here we want you to meet and we would be gratified if your husband and friends would witness.'

'Do you give us your word?' asked Gus.

'I give you my word.'

Gus turned and walked to the hole. Tom followed; the hole was a metal hatch frame with the concrete lid lying to one side. Incredibly a glow of light was visible from whatever depths lay below.

Gus swung a foot onto the ladder and descended. Gina and Lucy followed with Tom last. Hellmunt climbed down with Tallisment following. The latter was breathing heavily and his perspiring face had a purple tinge.

They stood in a brick-clad chamber some fifteen feet in length with an arched roof and full standing room. The place smelt well ventilated and seemed surprisingly dry. The interior was bare apart from three rusting steel lockers and a gun rack. Against the wall stood an army-style trestle table and two wooden benches. Those car batteries wired to an ancient circuit breaker were presumably the source of the dim lighting. So this was the secret: the command bunker for Freddie Reade-Coke's resistance cell. Tom had worked this land for over twelve years and had never had an inkling of such a place.

A doorway covered with a curtain of sacking filled the end of the chamber. Behind it Tom could hear voices; angry voices, and one of them he recognised as Gannemeade's. Hellmunt pulled aside the sacking and beckoned them to enter. This second chamber was larger than the entry room and filled with people in every space apart from the far-left corner, where stood an object covered in plastic sheeting. Gannemeade slumped in a chair centre stage; the others stood around him, including three hooded guards and one other. He was tall, with a black eye patch: Van Zyl.

Gannemeade tried to stand but the two guards pulled him down into the chair. He stared wildly at Gus.

'You know who I am?'

'You're Wilhelm. Don't think I'm real glad to see you 'cos I'm not.'

All Gannemeade's bluster had gone; the man was terrified.

'Gustav, you are still my brother; you must intervene.'

'Why?'

'Help me!' he wailed.

'What's going on?' Tom asked.

Hellmunt ignored him and addressed the room.

'We have examined the case of Wilhelm Roland Brown who now calls himself Roland Gannemeade. In the Gostanyn Medical Research

Facility, Wilhelm Brown showed a callous and sadistic attitude that could well bring the true race into disrepute. In South Africa he stole diamonds and precious metals and shot dead two local men, both Afrikaans speakers of good race. Finally, he attempts to rape a woman of pure Nordic blood. We cannot put our movement at risk from the activities of this individual.'

Tom tried to get to grips with this man's logic. Three hundred children had been exterminated at Gostanyn. Hellmunt talked as if this was a legitimate act that Brown could bring into disrepute because he enjoyed the killing.

Hellmunt continued. 'Wilhelm Brown, the Reverend Mulgrum suggests that you be given a short period to make your peace with God.' He looked at Gus. 'Mr Fjortoft, I understand Wilhelm Brown forced you to take part in his Gostanyn activities – were you under duress?'

'He forced me to kill a child.'

'Mr Van Zyl, please explain the procedure.'

Van Zyl pointed at a table with display of bottles, some glass flexible tubing and two hypodermic syringes.

'Execution by lethal injection – takes place in two stages. Mr and Mrs Fjortoft I invite you to complete the second stage.'

'Wait,' Tom felt compelled to intervene. 'Gannemeade's a high profile figure around here. Kill him and all hell will break loose. If you can prove the South African murders Gannemeade will be dealt with by legitimate justice.'

'Mr O'Malley, I hear what you say but this court has made a decision. J-V, please proceed.'

Tom could feel his ears singing and his heart pounding. He could no longer restrain his grief and fury.

'John Van Zyl – Jayvy your friends call you around here. You killed my wife – murdered her – for nothing – for no reason!'

Andy recovered his bike, opened the throttle wide and set off for home in a cloud of dust and gravel chippings. He must reach a phone – he cursed himself for leaving his mobile in the farm kitchen.
He must talk to the police and convince them to act instantly. His father's written instructions meant nothing now.

He had left Curly behind in the woods keeping an eye on Alex. Andy didn't entirely trust Curly and he certainly didn't trust a habitual violent criminal like Alex. With apprehension bordering on panic Andy swept into the Boxtree yard, scattering a group of people whom he saw too late to stop. He stood on his brake pedal, skidded and parted with the bike. Bruised and humiliated he sat up, removed his helmet and hurled it against the barn door. Somebody was standing over him; it was Hannah.

'So, you're back,' he said. 'Is it you people who are holding my father?'

'On the contrary I am taking steps to rescue him.'

CHAPTER 39

Francesca looked at her watch – it was only mid-afternoon yet she felt she had been trapped here for an eternity. She was feeling acute and embarrassing discomfort. She kicked the door and yelled until she heard footsteps.

'I wanna' go to the toilet.'

'Use the bucket,' came a gruff reply.

'I won't – somebody's puked in it.'

The door opened and the man stood there: PC Witherrick. Francesca was not surprised but she could sense the shock among the others.

'You scoundrel!' Alan was outraged.

'Constable, how could you?' Marjorie added her indignation.

'There is nothing worse than a corrupt police officer,' Alan added.

Natalie stared open mouthed; reduced for the first time in her life to stunned silence. Francesca had different feelings; she remembered the voices in the wood; one the American and the other that of the man who stood before her: PC Witherrick who'd frightened her with his recent threats.

'Listen to Taraton's finest,' sneered Witherrick. 'One dodgy accountant, one half-daft little girl, and one bit o' jailbait.'

'I'm seventeen,' Natalie shouted, 'nearly eighteen.'

Witherrick pointed at the open door.

'You people scram – get out of this house, run for the woods and don't stop running.'

He turned and walked away. The door remained open.

The silence in that room lasted for a full minute.

'What the hell is going on?' Alan muttered.

He walked to the doorway and stood listening.

'Is it a trick?' Marjorie asked.

She crossed the room to stand with him.

'Come on,' said Alan, 'we'll try it. You girls, walk behind us – close as you can.'

Francesca clung to Marjorie as they tiptoed through the familiar house. The hall was deserted, the front door wide open revealed a sunlit countryside. It seemed so peaceful, just like any other spring day on the farm. She could hear a tractor moving, see sun glinting on an airliner high in the clear sky, hear the call of a collared dove. She wanted to wake from this silly dream, or she wanted to cry, or she wanted to do both.

Alan had left them and was standing in front of the porch, alert and listening.

He turned and spoke quietly. 'I think he's gone – they've all gone. I think we'll chance it and move.'

Francesca was aware once more of her physical misery.

'I must go to the toilet!' she stamped her foot and instantly regretted it.

'In the woods,' said Marjorie. 'You can have all the privacy you like but let's get there.'

'Keep with me,' said Alan, 'and run like hell.'

'Yes, that's right – run…' A hooded guard stood in the doorway with a handgun pointed skywards. 'Go on, you stupid idiots – run!' The man pointed the gun over the roof of the house and fired three shots.

Francesca ran, her discomfort forgotten, her whole body driven by panic. With every stride she expected to hear more shots and the pounding footsteps of pursuers. The un-mown grass was ankle high and beginning to tire her, but nothing happened. Marjorie was lagging, gasping for air; Alan slowed the pace, grouped them together, and then hustled them under the sagging wire of the field fence.

'Keep moving,' he called.

They were in the woods of the steep hanger, sliding down the hillside towards the road far below. Francesca knew this place; it had been her favourite spot: just above the little green valley, the abandoned watercress beds, with the pool and the dam. In past times this was where she would escape from home tensions and enter her own dream world. Now she could hear voices and engines running. They slipped down the last few feet and stood watching from the edge of the trees.

The rough track was crowded with massive lorries and surrounded by men hard at work. An elevator was moving gravel into a concrete delivery lorry and a pumping engine was drawing water from the pool. Francesca didn't care who these workmen were; she was alive and safe. She slunk behind a thorn bush and relieved herself.

Alan had walked into the sunshine; Francesca could see him talking to one of the men. She felt a little shimmer of unease; this builder's body language looked none too friendly. The man shouted something and a slim figure walked from behind a truck; a young woman and beautiful were it not for the plaster dressings on her face.

With her she recognised Lucy's brother Andrew. Marjorie and Natalie had joined Alan; all three stood in animated talk with the dark woman. Francesca ran to them.

The woman turned and smiled a welcome and it washed away the last of her fears.

'You must be Francesca – I'm Hannah.' She turned and faced them all. 'This is Joel.' She indicated the man they had first seen.

He was tall, of athletic build, with a gaunt face and hair flowing into a ponytail. There was something about him that stirred Francesca inwardly in a way that was both pleasurable and oddly disturbing.

Hannah spoke to him. 'I have no idea what you intend here but I think we should walk away and leave you to it.'

'Mr O'Malley, would you kindly explain?' Hellmunt looked at Tom.

'Last July my wife died supposedly in a riding accident. I now have an eyewitness to say that an American, described as Jayvy, murdered her without motive. I failed to connect this with the initials JV. Last month in Oregon I personally saw Van Zyl kill a wounded man.'

'Is this true?' Hellmunt looked at Van Zyl.

'He means that horse-riding woman. Sure, I eliminated her – she was asking questions.'

'You had instructions not to molest or involve local people – you know what that means?'

'Who cares? Lets find the hymies, bring 'em down here and the job's done.'

'You know perfectly well that the elimination of those Jews is planned for four days time. Where are they now?'

'The Berkovic woman's at Boxtree Farm; the others I don't know.' For the first time Van Zyl looked defensive.

'Then you will go and find them!'

'Not so, Mister, I give the orders.' Van Zyl smiled.

Tom caught the look and it was chilling. He also had a crumb of hope; these mad people were dividing among themselves.

'Arrest him,' Hellmunt addressed the guards.

The two hooded men looked at each other.

'No chance, mate,' said one.

'You Yanks sort your own troubles – nowt to do with us,' the other agreed.

Tom glanced at Gannemeade; the man was slumped in the chair seemingly in a state of collapse.

'Doctor Hellmunt,' said Gus. 'I think you were also in Gostanyn. I think I know why you are so keen for Wilhelm Brown to die. When he killed those kids he was a child himself. We can expose him to the world, discredit and humiliate him – make him a pariah.'

Hellmunt shrugged. 'So?'

Gus continued. 'Wilhelm made me kill the little girl by using another man to hold me down while he broke my fingers. Did you think I would ever forget a moment of that day? I can tell you every detail is imprinted on my mind.'

'Aw, spare the tear jerk,' Van Zyl jeered.

Gus ignored him. 'Hellmunt, I have been puzzled about your interest in me. I wondered who you were and I knew I had seen you before. Last night it came to me – you are Corporal Schreiber, the very one who held me down while Wilhelm laughed. You are a hypocrite and you are as guilty as the man you are planning to kill now.'

'You're raving – you've no witness.'

'You're wrong,' said Jiffers, for the first time Tom became aware of him. 'I didn't witness the killing, but Gustav is right, you're Schreiber; I named you the moment I saw you.'

Tom listened to this conversation with mounting alarm. Couldn't Gus and Max have waited, while they found a way out of here? A new figure pushed his way past the sacking. A tall man he overawed everyone in the tiny space; as with the other guards his head was concealed in a balaclava. He sounded agitated as he addressed Van Zyl.

'Jayvy, there's been shooting over at the farm – that stupid sod's eliminating the hostages – trying to save his own skin I guess.'

'Where's my Dad?' Andy rushed at the Cunninghams.

'All right, calm down,' replied Alan. 'He was removed with the Fjortofts about an hour ago and we don't know where.'

'And my sister?'

'She went as well. But they were given an assurance of safe conduct. The man in charge said he wanted them as witnesses.'

'Of what!' Andy knew he was wild eyed and aggressive but he must know.

'I don't know – I wish I did.'

'Are these friends of yours?' Marjorie asked Hannah.

She pointed at the first concrete lorry that was moving slowly off the site.

‘No they are not,’ said Hannah. ‘I’m being forced to co-operate with them through lack of choice. Joel has just told me what’s going on in Bechams wood.’

‘Tell us then,’ Andy demanded.

He’d had enough of this bloody woman with her posh accent and irritating self-assurance. She knew how desperate he was; yet all morning she’d made him follow her around like an obedient Labrador.

‘Explanations later,’ she said. ‘Andrew, would you take these people to Boxtree Farm and look after them?’

‘Where are you going?’

She didn’t answer; she had swung round and was looking into the trees. Andy could hear it too, clumsy footsteps racing towards them. Then he saw the two men: Alex Cornbinder and Curly.

‘They’re killing people, up at Woolbarrow,’ Alex cried. ‘It’s nothing to do with me – I’m not part of it.’

Curly grinned. ‘It’s true, there’s shooting up at the farm there, but nobody’s dead.’

‘How d’you know?’

‘I know’s guns– some nutter was firing into the air – dunno why.’

Andy didn’t know what to think. He was watching the last of the cavalcade of building wagons rolling down the track to the Crossfield lane. Above the trees he could hear a new sound; the helicopter was flying again. He couldn’t see it but he knew it was moving at treetop height away from them. For barely a minute he heard it and then the sound died; somewhere not far away it had landed again.

Tom determined to stay controlled; panic now would destroy them for certain. He refused to accept the worst. So, there was shooting at Woolbarrow, why and by whom, was not known. The guards were all British, RON men certainly, co-opted into something much more sinister than they had expected. The reaction of this new arrival said it all; in no way would they stomach even a suggestion of killing defenceless women. Perhaps Van Zyl did not realise this.

The fat guard, who’d been with them all along, answered Tom’s question.

He faced Hellmunt. ‘You said no killings.’ His fists were clenched.

‘Maybe we kill you instead,’ replied Van Zyl.

He had a gun, another clumsy Magnum. The guard shied away. They had reached an impasse; Van Zyl was taking over. In the silence they heard a fresh sound from the outside world; the helicopter was overhead.

'He's early – who ordered that?' Van Zyl glared at Tallisment.

'I don't know – maybe something's happened.'

'Sure, things are going to happen. I say we move the stuff right now.'

Van Zyl beckoned the guards and began to strip away the plastic covers from the stack in the corner. Tom craned to have a look. He saw four small wooden boxes and more of the wrapped parcels of bank notes – another division of the Winchester robbery and a much larger pile than the one guarded by the decomposing body of Vanessa Rowridge.

'That's RON money – ours,' said the fat guard.

Van Zyl drove the gunpoint into the man's chest. Then he pointed it at Tom.

'You too, Mister, and you Fjortoft, that broad of yours can help. You too, Missy.' He pointed at Lucy.

'It was you that grabbed me in the hospital,' she said.

'Shuddup and move it.' He swung the gun towards Tallisment. 'You too, Buster.'

'Don't be a fool – I can't – it would kill me.'

'Either way, if you don't help, sure as hell I'll kill you anyway.'

Tom couldn't help noticing that Van Zyl's usual smooth East Coast speech was breaking down into cruder language. Could he be nervous?

Tallisment shuffled painfully forward and tried to lift a parcel. His face was puffed, and his breathing noisy.

'He's not bluffing,' said Lucy. 'Look at him.'

Van Zyl laughed. 'When I want your opinion I'll ask – so shut your mouth, bitch.'

Tom had moved as close to Lucy as he dared. 'Co-operate – at least we'll get outside this place.'

'What about the Cunninghams and the girls?'

'Shuddup, and get lifting,' said Van Zyl.

Gus and Gina were already shifting bags up to the guards on the surface. Van Zyl had moved to the bottom of the ladder, alternately pointing the gun at those in the bunker and then upwards at the guards. Tom hardly dared to feel hope, but it was clear that Van Zyl was isolated. Everyone, villains and victims alike were his enemies now. He counted ten money parcels; how much value in each one Tom didn't care. Given the chance he would set fire to the lot rather than let this maniac escape with it.

‘You there, farmer,’ Van Zyl was looking at him. ‘Shift your ass and help with the boxes.’

The nearest box had a rope handle; Tom caught hold of it heaved and let go. It was too heavy for him.

‘Help him,’ Van Zyl waved the gun again this time at the tall guard.

The man shrugged, walked to the box and lifted it as if it was nothing.

‘You too, Schreiber – help the farmer.’

Hellmunt bristled. ‘This isn’t our property – I don’t know where it came from, but it’ll be too hot without authority.’

‘This is my authority,’ Van Zyl slashed the gun barrel across Hellmunt’s face.

Hellmunt was muttering in German as he caught hold of a rope. He tried to lift the box but dropped it.

‘Old age, Van Zyl,’ said Tom. ‘You’ll have to use your RON friends.’

‘You just shut that yap. Don’t think I’ve forgotten what happened in Oregon.’

‘I’ll take the boxes,’ said the tall man as he returned empty handed. He gently pushed Tom aside and as he did so he turned the palm of his hand towards him. There was a message written on the skin in neat capital letters.

Stay cool – help near.

No eye contact, no indication whatever, as the man lifted a second box and carried it to the entrance. There was something about the way he moved, and his cultured voice, that was at odds with the RON men.

‘Doctor O’Malley,’ called a voice from the surface. ‘Come quick, Rudi’s collapsed.’

‘Ask Doctor Hellmunt,’ she replied.

‘I have a doctorate in chemistry and that does not help us,’ said Hellmunt. ‘Please, Mr O’Malley, persuade her.’

‘All right,’ said Lucy. ‘Of course I’ll go. I would like Doctor Jiffers to come too – he’s more experienced than me.’

Ignoring Van Zyl and his gun she climbed the ladder to the outside.

‘Goddam,’ he muttered half raising the gun.

‘Come on,’ said the tall man as he shouldered the fourth and last box.

Tom followed him knowing he was gambling on Van Zyl not loosing off his clumsy gun in the confines of the bunker where a ricochet bullet could as easily hit himself.

Tallisment had collapsed and was lying on his back on the edge of the wood. His mouth was open and flecked with foam. His legs twitched and his face was an awful tinge of mauve and yellow. Tom felt sickened; the sight reminded him of Matthew Rowridge. Nearby Gus and Gina sat on the pile of money sacks. Lucy and Max Jiffers were already kneeling beside the body. Fifty yards away parked in the field was the helicopter – Tom could see the pilot sitting at the controls.

Van Zyl cupped his hands and yelled. 'Say, Gerry, I'm needing help here.'

Evidently the man heard nothing. Van Zyl swore and kicked the ground.

Lucy stood up and walked to Van Zyl. 'We need that helicopter. The only chance that man has is to get him to hospital now.'

'Isn't that too bad.'

'It's as good as murder if you leave him to die.'

'And you'll be dead if you don't shut that mouth.'

'Lucy, don't provoke him – leave it.'

'Best advice of the day, Mister,' grinned Van Zyl.

Lucy walked back to the body.

Jiffers spoke. 'It's too late – he's gone.' He shook his head. 'He's been living on borrowed time for fifty years – Gostanyn claims another victim.'

Lucy sat down her head slumped forwards. Tom felt for her but could do nothing. They were both in the presence of her mother's murderer and were impotent to stop the man escaping.

For some minutes Tom had been aware of a new sound. A heavy tractor was climbing the hill from the village. It was the big John Deere with the bale trailer carrying feed for the Woolbarrow pedigree Sussex herd. Tom had intended to move the cattle to fresh grass but these unforeseen events had always been in the way. He heard the tractor change gear as it climbed the last slope and turned into the track that led to Bechams Wood.

'Get down the hole,' Van Zyl swept the barrel of his gun around the whole group.

Tom heard him but had already taken his decision. He would not go tamely down that bunker. He would prefer to die here.

'You heard me – underground!'

Tom, staring at Van Zyl, missed Gus's move. He swung round at the sounds of commotion. Fjortoft caught Hellmunt from behind and with a bear-like hug lifted him from the ground so that his legs dangled like a rag doll.

'Nobody's going anywhere – I've grown a bit these last few years – it's my turn now, Schreiber.'

'Put him down, or I'll kill your wife.' Van Zyl's voice was deadpan.

'And would the Reverend Mulgrum like that?' Gina began to walk towards Van Zyl. 'I don't think so. Maybe I blind you in the other eye and then you don't shoot so well.'

Tom felt transfixed, unable to move or speak. This woman who he had always known as an agreeable simpleton had transformed – it was as if a light shone from her. If ever there was a confrontation between evil and simple goodness, this was it.

'Don't try me, bitch. I owe you for that eye.'

'Oh, what d'you know?' she laughed. 'I thought you told the Sheriff it was Tom who did the damage. Now you're blaming little girly me; you great macho guy.'

Gina walked within a foot of Van Zyl's gun. No, it must not happen; Tom would not allow it. He ran to stand beside her.

'Gina, please don't do this. We love you – I love you.'

The silence that followed could only have been seconds but to Tom it seemed eternity.

'Hide the gun,' called the tall man. 'Here's that tractor.'

Tom looked up. He saw the agonised expression on Lucy's face. Gus dropped Hellmunt who seemed about to collapse. The tractor was upon them, the trailer stacked high with hay bales. In the driver's cab was the reassuring figure of Lonny. He saw Tom and waved, clearly he had no idea that anything was amiss. All he could have seen was the boss and Mr Fjortoft with a group of strangers. Van Zyl held the gun behind his back and the hooded guards had dived into cover. What happened next was the stuff of nightmares. It was a deliverance, the memory of which was to haunt Tom until the end of his days.

Lonny stopped the tractor five yards short of the field gate, opened the cab door and dropped to the ground. Tow saw him yawn and stretch his arms. Then with a leisurely walk he went to the gate and opened it. The cows and their calves surged through the opening and surrounded the trailer trying to reach the tasty hay. There was nothing unusual here; Tom knew the cattle would follow the moving trailer back into the field. He was thankful for the diversion, but wondered whether he should try and attract Lonny's attention. The first of the animals had reached them and Tom instinctively put out a hand to touch the nose of the red-brown Sussex cow. Her calf nuzzled her trying to extract the last drop of milk.

Tom smiled. 'Go on – get your grub.'

His words were lost in a scream of intense fear. Van Zyl was flinching away from the cattle in abject terror. Tom knew that phobic fear of cows was not uncommon among city dwellers, but he had never seen one as frightened as this. The cow was still licking Tom's hand when she stiffened; blood and brains spurted from a round hole in her forehead only inches from Tom's arm. The great beast died before she crashed to the ground. The calf scampered away a few feet and stood looking at the wreckage of its mother. More shooting; Tom saw a second cow fall, then a third. Horrified he saw the bull, *Woolbarrow Majestic,* pride of the herd, crumple and die. He wanted to reach Van Zyl; forgetting fear, forgetting the gun, forgetting everything except the need to stop this slaughter; this vandalism that offended everything central to Tom's life. He reached Van Zyl and grappled for his throat; saw him turn and raise the gun.

'Guvnor, stand back!' It was Lonny.

The voice was not the slow-spoken countryman. It had a timbre and a crackle of command. Lonny was standing on the trailer, a giant silhouetted against the skyline. His right arm held a pitchfork flexed above his head; a long handled shaft and two steel points. Lonny had changed; in that split second, he had reached back to another dimension; perhaps retrieved a deep ancestral memory. Tom heard the whistle and felt the flutter of the wind as the fork passed him and buried itself to the hilt in Van Zyl's chest. Van Zyl fell; he twitched, and a spume of blood and froth vomited from his mouth.

Tom could see new people running from the trees and more from the track. In front of him stood Gina swaying unsteadily her eyes tight shut. Gus was running towards her his face twisted in horror. Van Zyl, ashen faced, was clasping the wooden shaft of the fork between his blooded palms. Then slowly and painfully he picked up his gun, raised it with both hands and aimed at Gina. Tom launched a kick at the gun and missed. He grabbed Van Zyl's shoulder as the gun fired. The bullet missed Gina but it took Gustav Fjortoft full in the face. Gina screamed, an awful wail of unrestrained grief as she knelt and clung to the lifeless corpse of her man. A sweet aroma of spent cordite wafted across the scene.

Strangers surrounded them. Tom had no idea who they were and he didn't care. His limbs wouldn't respond properly; his life was meaningless, his friend dead, and he could feel nothing. Through a mist he could see Lucy kneeling beside Van Zyl. Andy was there, and Hannah – why? Andy moved to pull the pitchfork from the prone body; Lucy shouted at him and shook her head. Lonny was slumped against the tractor, weeping without restraint. Tom went to him.

'Lonny,' he spoke gently. 'Well played – good man.'

'God, what have I done?' He was shaking. 'I've killed him – what'll happen to me – to my kids?'

'Nothing will happen to you if I have anything to do with it – you saved us. That man was Tricia's killer.'

Lonny showed no sign that he had heard; Tom looked into the glazed eyes.

'Lonny, get into that tractor. Finish the job – feed those cattle.'

Very slowly Lonny moved, zombie like, and climbed into the cab. He drove through the gate; the cows and calves followed leaving trampled ground and dead bodies, animal and human.

CHAPTER 40

'Hannah, who are all these people?' Tom heard Lucy's voice.

'They're nothing to do with me, but they're dangerous. You people are not out of the wood yet.'

'I must have an ambulance,' Lucy pointed at Van Zyl. 'This man will bleed to death if I don't do something.'

She looked at Andy. 'Take off that T-shirt.'

'Why?'

'I need a wound dressing.'

'Forget it.'

'Andy!'

'Nothing doing, I know who he is – that's McCann the drug dealer who killed Jessica.'

'Are you sure?'

'Of course I am – sorry – can't help you.'

Van Zyl also killed the boy's mother, though Andy didn't know that yet. Tom pulled off his sweater and removed his shirt.

'You'd better use this,' he passed the shirt to Lucy.

'Dad, could you see to Gina?'

Tom walked across to where she crouched on the ground beside her husband's lifeless body. He didn't want to look at the bloody ruin of his friend but he couldn't help himself. Gus lay on his side, right arm outstretched. The purple hole in his forehead became a ghastly bloody mess where the exit wound showed in the back of the skull.

Slowly he bent down and lifted Gina to her feet; she made no resistance. Someone was laughing; one of the new arrivals was standing over Gus's body pointing and laughing. How any sane person could do such a thing was beyond comprehension. Hannah turned on the man, berating him angrily in some foreign language.

'They still think Mr Fjortoft was a killer,' she said.

'Who are they – explain?'

'They're the Redemption 45 – that's 1945 of course – they work to their own agenda. I don't approve of them and I suggest we keep out of their way.'

Gina stood without support but Tom was not sure she registered anything.

'Let me take her away from here,' said Max.

Tom nodded, he couldn't trust himself to speak. He released Gina and Max led her away, stumbling at his side, towards the edge of the field. The terrorists made no move to stop them.

Van Zyl was still moaning. Lucy shrugged her shoulders and spread her hands in despair.

'There's nothing I can do. He'll die if we don't get him into hospital.'

Frankly Tom didn't care; were it not for Lonny's predicament, it would be better Van Zyl was dead. The world would be a cleaner place and the taxpayer would be saved the cost of locking him up for life. Four men comprised this new grouping. The one apparently in command seemed familiar. He carried a small handgun, which he held with a practised assurance. The man was mustering his captives towards the entrance to the bunker. Of the original groups only Hellmunt and the three RON men remained. Tallisment's body lay nearby; Van Zyl was expiring on the edge of the track. Gannemeade was presumably still underground. Tom saw that the mysterious tall guard had taken off his hood to reveal a head of long straggling dark hair. Tom watched him exchange words with the terrorist's leader, then he turned and walked away. So, this man was an infiltrator, which explained his earlier written message.

A heavy vehicle was climbing the long hill from the village. Tom beckoned to Hannah.

'I can't just stand here and do nothing.'

'You've no choice. I suggest we be patient and wait for the cavalry.'

The lorry moving behind the hedgerow on the road was one of a convoy turning into the track for the wood.

'Them's the concrete wagons, the same that was at Buttons End.'

Tom spun round to see Curly Tong.

'Where did you spring from?'

'I been watching.' He looked around and bent nearer to Tom. 'Mr Fjortoft's men's at Woolbarrow.'

'It'd be more use if they were here.'

Curly looked at Gus's body. 'Who done that?'

'The man over there with the pitchfork in his guts.'

Curly sighed. 'We liked Mr Fjortoft, the village'll take this hard.'

Tom could see Lucy pacing towards him; Curly saw her and scuttled away. Lonny was walking slowly up the track his face a picture of misery. He knelt beside the fallen Sussex bull and stroked his head.

The concrete truck rumbled cautiously down the track to the edge of the wood where the leader waved it onwards. With its four wheels spinning it reached the door of the bunker, its front wheel over the entrance lid. Two men unrolled a rubber hose and attached it to the truck's exhaust. Two more were attacking a point in the wood, an ancient oak stump, with picks and shovels.

'That's the air vent,' said Hannah.

Tom remembered that he was a magistrate with a duty in his own parish.

'What are these people intending? I will not stand by and watch murder.'

Hannah grabbed his arm; he jumped at the strength of her grip.

'Tom, you will do nothing. I've watched you these last few weeks and I'm going to say my piece. I couldn't before, it wouldn't have been right and it might have compromised my mission.' She paused as she squeezed his arm.

'Everyone in this place thinks the world of you. Gina Fjortoft adores you and so do your children. There are a lot of people around here who are very fond of you,' she turned and looked up into his face. 'Me too.'

She meant that, he could see that; this time there was no deceit.

'Tom, your duty is to be a witness. You observe and report. You will not get yourself killed for these people – they're not worth it.'

'Hannah, would you at least talk to them. The three RON men are English. They are racist bigots, but they resisted Van Zyl and refused to help him; I was there, I saw it.'

Hannah showed no response, no sign that she had even heard him. He took her arm and shook it until he saw her wince.

'These people are not wartime Nazis. They're all young; I expect they've wives and small children. Vengeance may sometimes be just, but you gain honour if you mix it with compassion.'

'My God, Tom, you've a way with words. Very well, I will try.'

She released his grip and ran to where the leader was standing. Tom saw her speak; the man shook his head. Hannah seized the front of his jacket; Tom could hear her voice, angry and high-pitched. The leader pushed her away, turned and walked to the lorry door. Tom saw the truck move slowly away from the bunker lid. One by one the RON men were brought out blinking in the late afternoon sun. The leader spoke a few words to them; his body language told of deep disdain. The three men crossed the wood, picked up Tallisment's body, carried it across and pitched it down the hole. A hand appeared clutching the hatch rim; the leader screamed and stamped on it. The hand vanished and the terrorists slammed down the lid. The rubber hose now stretched all the way to the vent. The men were piling earth around the stump sealing every aperture.

Hannah and the man were walking towards him. Tom remembered him: the man at the Chichester funeral – Magda's boyfriend,

'This is Joel,' said Hannah.

'It's what they did to my grandparents, my aunts and uncles, and all their children.' He looked Tom in the eye. 'Retribution and atonement.'

Joel walked away; the lorry driver gunned his engine. For ten minutes the truck poured its carbon monoxide poison into the bunker, more than enough to kill every living creature within. The lorry pulled forward until its tail was over the entry hatch. Two men swung the discharge chute and the concrete poured into the reopened hole. More lorries were moving onto the site pulling slowly up the wooded slope. As the first lorry reversed away the next shot its cargo into the bunker. Then the third repeated the process.

'Why,' said Tom? 'What's the point?'

'Quick setting concrete,' said Hannah. 'Bodies sealed for eternity – no stench, no trace.'

Tom felt the stirring of alarm. If that were to work Joel would need to eliminate every witness. He said so to Hannah.

'Remember,' she replied, 'that includes me – stay calm and stop worrying.'

Tom was not impressed. 'You know something don't you. What did you mean – wait for the cavalry?'

Hannah did not reply; she walked away to where the tall man from the bunker was standing watching.

Tom could see Lonny still wandering among the dead cattle. All those town dwellers that claim farmers have no love for their stock should see Lonny now. Something would have to be done for him. He would be bound to face charges, even if it was as clear a case of justifiable homicide as Tom could imagine. He wondered if he should try and comfort the man but he could think of nothing helpful to say. Lonny never saw him as he walked past and took the folded tarpaulin from the trailer. Tom carried it to Gus, and laid it over the body. He felt utterly drained with grief.

'Where are the police?' Tom muttered to Andy. 'I thought they'd been alerted.'

'They have been, but we told them the two kids were at

Woolbarrow and I guess that's where they've gone. The Fjortoft men are there as well.'

Andy explained about the Cunningham's escape.

'They're all at Boxtree at the moment.'

'So, the police have no idea what was happening here, but they must have heard that shooting.'

He could see Hannah and Joel striding back towards them. Joel was an impressive character with his flashy dark looks and black ponytail. Tom could feel the madness that the man exuded.

'Mr O'Malley, our mission is over, we're leaving.' Joel held out his hand,

Tom ignoring it stared back unsmiling.

'What are you going to do with us?' he asked.

'Do with you?' Joel looked surprised. 'We're not going to do anything – you're free to go.'

The helicopter's engine fired and the rotor began to turn, the noise making conversation difficult.

Hannah shouted to Joel. 'He's worried because we're all witnesses to your killings.'

'But we want witnesses – tell the world.' Joel's eyes gleamed.

'You want us to tell the police you killed Roland Gannemeade?' Tom asked.

Joel grinned. 'In the last eighteen months my organisation has carried out fifteen retributions. Half the police of the world are looking for us.'

'That's true,' said Hannah.

Tom stared at the helicopter. A pilot was busy within the cockpit, but it was definitely Tallisment's machine. He watched as Joel's men crossed the field and clambered aboard.

'I really must be going,' said Joel. 'I think I see flashing blue lights and overzealous policemen.'

It was true Tom could see them now on the outskirts of the village and heading their way.

'May I ask a favour?' Joel asked. 'The concrete lorries belong to a legitimate firm. Unknown to the owners our enemies planned to do to us exactly what we have just done to them.'

'How do you know that?'

'A friend warned us – she was a brave and lovely lady, Magdalena Sherakova. She learned much about our enemies, enough for them to kill her. As for the lorries, we took them over. Mr Tong, I think his name is, has offered to wash them out; there is a hose and water tank on each unit. Perhaps you could inform the owners where they are.'

'What about the original drivers?'

'You can help us there as well. They're locked in your empty grain silo.'

'You've got a bloody nerve.'

'Yes, I know,' Joel threw back his head and laughed. 'That's why I succeed. Goodbye, Mr O'Malley – tell the world what you have seen – spare no detail. Goodbye Ms Berkovic – I think you are well meaning but deluded.'

Joel bowed courteously, turned and ran to the helicopter. It lifted into the air and swept away over the first of the police cars speeding along the road to the track for Bechams Wood.

Tom sat on the grass at the edge of the field. Around him lay the chaos of that whole traumatic hour. The concrete lorries silhouetted against the skyline; the money parcels and the boxes; the dead cattle already bloated and grotesque. Gina sitting a few yards away with Lucy's arms around her: old antagonists united in grief. Max Jiffers staring dumbly at the covered shape of his murdered brother. The unconscious distorted body of Van Zyl. From nowhere came a memory. It was exactly eight weeks since he had walked by the harbour shore and found the tide lapping at the body of a girl.

CHAPTER 41

'Alex Cornbinder's been most co-operative, he's hardly drawn breath – we had to fit a new tape to the recorder.' Inspector Oats looked both smug and relieved.

'May I be let into the secret?'

Tom was too tired to even try and suppress the sarcasm. He still felt woozy from the concoction that Lucy had forced on him along with a lot of psychobabble about posttraumatic stress. A fat lot of good the police had been. The Armed Response Unit had crashed onto the scene at Bechams Wood with a swagger more appropriate to Hollywood. A pompous officer had bawled at them through a loud hailer ordering all present to lie on the ground. For some it had been too much. Lucy had finally given way and lain sobbing her heart out. Gina had refused point blank to lie down. Tom was afraid she'd temporarily found a death wish. The whole scene had dissolved into a babble of shouts and screams.

The regular police, who had arrived next, restored some sort of normality. They insisted in splitting everyone into groups for questioning. Tom tried to explain about the helicopter but was ignored, though by now he was past caring. Van Zyl had been removed by air ambulance to hospital.

Oats was looking at him oddly. 'Don't you want to know what happened the night Vanessa Rowridge died?'

Tom shook himself back to the present. 'Yes please.'

'One of the men we've arrested is Vanessa's fancy man; he's an ex-jockey, O'Dolgan. Alex set up the bank raid from jail, but it was Vanessa's idea. She had some crazy scheme to pay off Matthew's creditors. Nice of her, considering she was two-timing the poor sod. She'd intended hiding the money at Woolbarrow, but then she remembered the old Home Guard armoury at the Manor. Brilliant idea, except that instead of the house being empty along comes Gina Fjortoft and her minder.'

'Alan Otford.'

'Correct; but what they didn't know was that Van Zyl was in this country watching. We're not sure, but we suspect he chatted up Vanessa and she dropped it that Matthew was hiding documents for the Fjortofts. That was enough to kill both her and her husband. Vanessa fell right into Van Zyl's hands that night. He had disposed of the Sherakova girl the day before. He knew Sherakova had been getting inside information from Otford, and Otford confirmed it. When Van Zyl heard that Otford was a diabetic he planned to kill him with insulin – make it seem an accident. Then it all went wrong for him. Vanessa and O'Dolgan were stashing the money; it was Vanessa who let the horse out to distract Mrs Fjortoft's attention. Neither party reckoned on you and Doctor Lucy rolling up when you did. We think Van Zyl bolted for the cellars, found Vanessa, cracked her on the head and locked her in the cellar room with the money. We found her key when we searched his clothing. Certainly O'Dolgan waited for Vanessa and she never came out of the house. He ran when the police and ambulance came and he never saw Vanessa again. He's only just learned she's dead and that makes him willing to testify anything against Van Zyl.'

'It was Van Zyl I saw in the kitchen?'

'Yes, after he'd committed the murder, and you can call yourself the luckiest man around. If the light had been on and you'd seen him…' Oats shrugged.

'Van Zyl is still alive?'

'He's in intensive care; in the same hospital where he and Hellmunt killed poor Partridge.'

'And tried to kill Lucy.'

'Exactly. You know he bled from his eye wound while he was there that night. It gave us a perfect DNA match for that murder, and for material from the killing of Matthew Rowridge.'

'If he survives, whose murder will you charge him with?'

'That's up to the Crown Prosecution Service and they're spoilt for choice. We'd like to charge him for Mrs O'Malley, but there's others, and the Americans may apply for extradition.'

'That could mean the electric chair?'

'Very possible – you'd hardly object.'

'No I wouldn't, but Tricia was adamant against the death penalty – it was something she felt very strongly about. In the American case I would be the prime witness.'

'I take your point.'

'How did any of these people know about the bunker in Bechams wood? I've worked in these parts for twenty years and I never knew about it.'

'Vanessa did and that old gamekeeper's son.'

'I can't see Charlie Marrington's speaking out of turn.'

'That's right, but it was Vanessa who blabbed. Apparently her old father was one of the army sappers who built the place in nineteen-forty. They sealed off the whole area for forty-eight hours while they built it, with the anti-aircraft post on top as a cover. Vanessa was involved with Partridge's amateur theatre. We suspect she told him about the bunker, and when you produced that old paperwork it set him off.'

'Who sabotaged his car?'

'Alex's brother Ricky – same day as he tried to knock your daughter off her horse. He's got some grudge against Lucy going back to schooldays. We think it was him that drove her car off the road and daubed slogans on your barn. Seems Ricky worked on the car's steering and brakes while he knew Rufus was deep underground in the bunker. I don't think he was working for anyone; Van Zyl was still flying in from the States. My guess is that Ricky knew Rufus would find that money and would be on his way to talk to us.'

'Did Rufus phone you?'

'No, I suspect the silly old bugger never even noticed the money. According to young Natalie the stack was still sealed under sheeting – Rufus never touched it.'

'Who put it there?'

'Ricky did, it was meant to finance RON in this region.'

'And the wooden boxes?'

'Total mystery how they got there. It's Spanish, believe it or not – part of a hoard of church plate, solid gold and silver; all stuff that went AWOL in their civil war – sixty years ago.'

Tom said nothing – he had a fleeting vision of the ailing Freddie Reade-Coke in his wheel chair. He wondered if Clarry knew. Well, Oats could solve that puzzle for himself.

'What are you doing about Mulgrum?'

'The Home Office withdrew his visa; the Reverend was put on an airliner for New York this morning. After that it's up to the Yanks.'

'And Hannah Berkovic?'

'I know what Rufus Partridge would say. Quote: *much suspected of me – nothing proved can be*. Queen Elizabeth the First, another forceful lady. I think the Home Office will suggest Ms Berkovic takes a holiday in her own country. We can't expel her, she was born here – educated at Roedean, would you believe it.'

'Who burnt her house and killed that boy Anton?'

'Neo Nazi thugs – set up by Hellmunt and Tallisment. They were after Berkovic of course.'

'What about Gannemeade?'

Oats grimaced. 'There's a man working at the crime scene at Bechams Wood; he wants to see you. I said I'd pass on the message.'

'He's there now?'

'Yes, I think you should keep the appointment,'

'All right, after I've seen Mrs Fjortoft. Now, what do you intend to do with Lonny Horton?'

'Your pitchfork man; he should take up the javelin – must be Olympic standard already.'

'Don't mess about – are you charging him?'

'That's for the Crown Prosecution Service; the matter's out of our hands, but we're releasing him on police bail – he can go home with you now. We've already released the helicopter pilot.'

Tom had heard that Tallisment's pilot had been snatched from his machine by Joel's men and locked in a Woolbarrow outhouse. It appeared the man was a genuine innocent in the wrong place at the wrong time.

Tom had one last question. 'PC Witherrick, what are you doing with him?'

Oats laughed. 'PC Witherrick is a long-standing member of our awkward squad.'

'He's a bent copper! He threatened young Francesca.'

'She's not the first local kid he's bullied. He's bad tempered and he's a racist. His only disciplinary offence was to covertly join the RON. To his credit when he found what was going on below the surface he reported it to CID and they tipped off MI5. They suspended judgement and told him to carry on which he did. The miserable sod acted his part brilliantly. Van Zyl actually took him to Bechams Wood and hinted they had a place to bury their enemies. The Home Office never told us, and nor did Mr Witherrick, who has taken retirement with a nice golden handshake. He won't be back on the beat in Taraton.'

'For that at least we can be grateful.' Tom replied although he had severe doubts. He remembered Francesca's testimony.

Lonny's wife, Diane and children, were standing by the gate of their house on the village council estate. Their faces spelt utter bewilderment and misery. Lonny hugged each of them and stumbled up the garden path to the front door. Tom tried to reassure Diane. Lucy would shortly call to see Lonny, and he needn't return to work until he was ready.

'Mr O'Malley, we'll cope, but if that man dies, will Lonny be done for murder?'

'Not if my word counts for anything. I saw it all and so did the others. We'll testify for him loud and long.'

He drove to the Manor. The sun was bright on the old stonework of the house. He heard the sound of a lawn mower and smelt the scent of roses and cut grass.

Gina sat in the drawing room. She wore jeans an old shirt and was barefoot. Her eyes were hollow and her face lined with lack of sleep.

'Have you seen a doctor?' Tom asked.

'Sure, he came an hour back – Lucy's young man.'

There was a catch in her voice and she was barely audible.

'Tom, Van Zyl killed my Gustav and you said he was the one who murdered Tricia.'

'He killed her with his bare hands and threw her over the hill. I saw him kill Gus, but the bullet was meant for you.'

'Will he live?'

'I don't know.'

'Tom, I've gotta talk to the newsmen – what do I say?'

He was surprised. 'I'm sure you don't have to do that.'

'Max says I ought to say a few words. Tell them it was a hunting accident – get it over and they'll go away.'

Tom remembered Max Jiffers. Yesterday he'd stood firm while all around had been death and mayhem. The last of the three brothers was an impressive man. Gina slid off the sofa and walked to a table by the door. She picked up a plain white envelope.

'I found this on Gus's desk. It had this note pinned to it.'

The envelope was addressed to him. Tom unfolded the note.

Should misfortune strike me this day, please see that this letter is given to Tom O'Malley.

He put both items in his pocket without comment; something in the familiar writing brought a lump to his throat. This was a letter he would open when he was alone and could summon the resolve. Gina walked with Tom to the front door. She said nothing but raised a hand and touched him lightly on the cheek. He could see her still standing there as he drove away.

He called on all his strength to drive the short mile to Bechams Wood. The place swarmed with uniformed police but he was not prepared for the machinery. A mechanical digger was stripping away the bushes and small trees to reveal the upper structure of the bunker.

Tom had authorised none of this and he was not pleased. He ducked under the police tape and was instantly apprehended by an officious officer who demanded his identity.

'I'm the estate manager and I haven't given permission for all this digging.'

The policeman ignored him and began to speak into his radio. Two civilians joined them a minute later, one of whom Tom knew; the tall man from the bunker who'd written the message on his hand. The other seemed an older sallow-complexioned individual and Tom didn't like him. He couldn't really say why but the man made him uneasy.

Tom spoke to the tall one. 'I must thank you for yesterday. I take it you're Special Branch or something?'

'Hardly,' he smiled. The voice this time was educated, cultured almost.

'What are you then?'

'A humble civil servant.'

'I've never met a humble one yet.' Tom glared.

The man laughed. 'How are Natalie and Francesca?'

'They've made remarkable recoveries; the counselling people have more or less given up on them.'

'Yes, they're brave kids – very British.'

Tom looked at the older man. 'I suspect that you also are a civil servant.'

'Correct.'

This was a cold fish, exactly what Tom would expect from his shadowy trade.

'I notice you've buried the dead cattle but I take it you're not from the Ministry of Agriculture.'

Tom's sarcasm had no effect.

'I am a Government servant.' The voice was flat with a trace of North Country.

'All right, why do you want to see me?'

'Mr O'Malley, we have a problem. I believe you know that the late Mr Gannemeade MP had a dual identity.'

'Yes, he was a war criminal and he murdered children at Gostanyn in Poland.'

'Please accept that none of this was known to us prior to ten days ago. Do you see our problem?'

'No I don't; he's dead and good riddance.'

'It's not that easy. The Second World War finished fifty-five years ago. Mr Gannemeade had rehabilitated himself. He was a wealthy man and a Member of Parliament.'

'So what, you should have vetted him before you put him there.'

'He was the people's choice, not mine. Mr Gannemeade also leaves behind a wife and family.'

'His daughter's dead – choked on her own vomit with drugs supplied by Van Zyl.'

'How did you know that?' The questioner's voice was without emotion.

'My son, Andrew, was a friend of the girl Jessica.'

Tom did not mention that Andy had been present at the drugs session, not that that would be likely to bother these spooks.

'I didn't know that – I'm sorry.' He didn't sound particularly sorry. 'Mr Gannemeade still leaves a son and a wife. The son David is a cadet at Sandhurst. He knows little of his father's origins and his instructors think highly of him. There is talk of his receiving the sword of honour.'

Tom sighed. He was in a corner, being squeezed of his beliefs and scruples by an inquisitor who had none. He stared back, conscious that this man was probably an expert poker player.

'Mr Gannemeade's wife also deserves some consideration. She is a lady of birth and distinction; are you aware she is the daughter of...?' The man mentioned a familiar name.

'You want me to keep my mouth shut?'

'I would ask you to be discreet; there is nothing to be served by persecuting the living for misdeeds committed by others before they were born.'

'I may keep quiet and I may persuade my children. The Americans may put pressure on Mrs Fjortoft and Doctor Jiffers, but Miss Berkovic saw it all – she's your loose cannon.'

For the first time he revealed a wintry smile.

'Redemption 45 never talk about their victims, they leave that to others. As for Ms Berkovic, she is a fellow professional, we think highly of her. Let us just say that the Israeli government are being most understanding.'

'Nice of them, but what about Van Zyl?'

'Mr Van Zyl took a turn for the worse.' The man studied his watch. 'He died ten minutes ago.'

'How d'you know that?'

'We know – so no problem.' The eyes were cold.

'You killed him!' Tom was shocked. 'In hospital; just like he tried to kill my daughter.'

'He killed your wife and many others. He also killed a respected schoolteacher there. Perhaps it was a case of the biter being himself bit.'

'You're going to let Lonny Horton go down for a murder you ordered? The hell you won't – I'm sorry; the deal's off.' He turned to walk away.

'Mr O'Malley, please do not prejudge. Mr Horton did nothing but protect himself. I understand Van Zyl stumbled and fell on a sharp object – isn't that so?' He turned to his companion.

'Quite right; I witnessed it all. He couldn't see so well with one eye, but he should have been more careful.'

Lucy was hammering on the roof of the Land Rover. Tom was home in the yard at Boxtree. He remembered nothing of the journey; he must have driven home on autopilot.

'Dad, look at this – I simply do not believe it.' Her face was red as she waved a newspaper.

Tom stepped out; he held onto the bodywork of the car feeling sick as his head throbbed. Lucy thrust the paper at him. She jabbed a finger at the headline: *MP dead in horror crash* and a picture of a wrecked car, a Jaguar, which had apparently left the road and hit a brick wall somewhere near Godalming.

The sole occupant, Mr Roland Gannemeade MP, appears to have died instantly.

The report ended with an unsubtle hint about drink driving.

'It's a cover up!' Lucy was furious.

'Yes, love,' Tom handed back the paper. 'But it's an imperfect world. I wonder who the real body was?'

EPILOGUE

The sun shone down on the Gloucestershire countryside to create a perfect summer's day. The wedding party was in full swing as a tasteful chamber quartet sawed away at equally tasteful melodies. In contrast, in the depths of the house, came the pounding beat of a disco. Through the veranda doors Tom could see the bridesmaids and some of the younger male sparks cavorting to the music. Tom cradled his empty glass and leaned against the stone balustrade that surrounded the terrace of Lansbury Hall.

The bride and groom stood by the fountain. How stunning Lucy looked as Mike put his arm around her and whispered something in her ear; they both turned and looked across to the terrace. Lucy gave him a wave; Tom grinned and waved back. He felt a twinge of regret and loss. This house had been Tricia's childhood home, but he had never been particularly welcome here. The Lansburys had been slow to accept a son-in-law descended from an Irish quarryman who had long ago worked in their own mines. Tricia's murder and the subsequent events had swept away any remaining animosity. Tom's expertise and advice had helped the declining Lansbury farming empire, while Lucy was firmly established as favourite grandchild.

Tom caught sight of Andy. The boy had divested himself of the embarrassing morning coat that his sister had forced him to wear. He was in deep conversation with Mike's best man, talking motorbikes for certain. He could see Lonny at the far end of the garden with the Lansbury son and heir, happily passing a rugby ball. His own parents were admiring the rose garden.

'Tom, let me fill your glass.'

He turned to see his father-in-law, Colonel Lansbury, champagne bottle in hand.

'Look at that little minx,' the Colonel pointed.

Through the glass doors Tom saw Natalie Cunningham; she had divested herself of her "uncool" bridesmaid's dress and replaced it with a flimsy shift that left nothing to the boys' imaginations.

'Another ten minutes and she'll be dragging that lad upstairs,' the Colonel laughed.

Francesca, in contrast, was swaying shyly to the music, appearing puzzled but happy.

'Well, Tom, this has been a triumph, don't you agree?'

'You've surpassed yourself, Gerald.'

They stood watching the scene looking across the landscape to the distant outline of the Forest of Dean. Into view came a large motorcar rolling slowly up the avenue from the main road. It swept majestically onto the gravel in front of the house and halted by the front door. Tom recognised the Crossfield Manor Mercedes. Charlie Marrington, wearing his chauffeur's cap opened the passenger door. Gina alighted, dressed in a cream designer outfit, with a matching flamboyant hat.

'Good heavens,' said the Colonel. 'Looks like a scene from the Great Gatsby – who is the lady?'

'She's Gina Fjortoft.'

'Wonderful, gives us a touch of Hollywood.'

The Lansburys could no longer afford a butler so the manager of the catering firm announced Gina's arrival in ringing tones. For a few seconds this hushed the gathering. Very few of them knew the truth. Gustav Fjortoft had not died in – *a shooting accident* – just as few people questioned the restrained obituary for Roland Gannemeade, dead in – *a road accident.* Tom worried about the breathtaking scope of the cover up. Gus had been buried in Seattle amidst a frenzy of showbiz hype. Tom had not been there, he preferred the dignified memorial service in Crossfield parish church. Gina had written to him from America several times; she would, she said, be returning to England to make Crossfield her permanent home. Tom felt in the inner pocket of his jacket for the sealed envelope that had been Gus's last message to him. He had never opened that envelope afraid that its contents would drag him back to that dreadful day. The lonely nights had been bad, the visitations had returned. Tricia's death had merged into the bloody carnage of Bechams Wood. Lucy had pressured him further, advising counselling, against which he was adamant. Gradually life had returned; time really did heal and the preparations for Lucy's wedding had helped.

Lonny had escaped charges over the death of Van Zyl. Now they were being told that no such person as Van Zyl existed. It seemed no records of his birth education or parentage could be found. The Reverend Mulgrum, whose visa to Britain had been revoked, had no comment whatever. An accidental death had been recorded, but that was of John McCann, photographer and suspected drug dealer. Inspector Oats thought the impetus for all this was coming from the United States. His sympathies were with Lonny, but he hated seeing the security services manipulate justice. The three RON men were in

Parkhurst along with Vanessa's ex-lover, O'Dolgan. Their involvement in the bank robbery had been the end for Reclaim Our Nation; that organisation had fractured into a dozen feuding splinters.

Tom awoke to the present; the Colonel was greeting Gina with an old-world bow. Lucy and Mike had run across hand in hand to welcome her. Lucy's old suspicions of Gina seemed over and Tom was glad of that. The trek in Oregon had forged an unshakeable bond. Once in his darker moments he had blamed her for Tricia's death. The facts had exonerated Gina and he could not disguise the truth that he was very fond of her.

Tom walked down the steps onto the front lawn; all around him he could hear the happy buzz of the wedding party. Gina ran to him and planted a kiss full on his lips releasing him at once before he could become embarrassed.

'Tom – isn't this just great?'

'How are you?' a banal question but he meant it.

'Fine, just fine,' there was a strange wan smile on her face.

'Tom, I've news, can we talk kinda private?' She glanced at the house.

'Not in there,' he said. 'It's full of kids – complete mayhem. Let's take a walk.'

He led her from the garden, past the tennis court and along the path that ended in the little colonnaded folly. They sat down on the stone benches in the cool interior.

'I like this place,' she said, 'it's cute.'

They sat silently listening to the birdsong in the ivy and the distant sounds of the party.

'Tom, you've never mentioned Gus's letter,' she looked at him half-accusing.

'It's true,' he hesitated. 'I still haven't read it.' He pulled the envelope from his pocket. 'Call it cowardice if you like.'

'He printed two copies. I've the other one; it was meant for us both.'

'I've been frightened of what it might say.'

'It's OK, Tom, Gus wanted out; I don't think life meant much to him and he'd had a sort of premonition.'

'Then I'll read it now.'

'No, wait, I've something to tell you, something you maybe won't believe. I'm going to have a baby.'

Tom was startled; as he understood it Gina was barren, congenitally unable to bear children.

'Are you sure?'

'I'm damn sure. I had a second scan ten days ago. I'm sixteen weeks pregnant and all's going well – the gynos are really upbeat.'

'But I thought…?'

'So did I, and so did all the medics – I'm a miracle.'

'Well done, Gina, it's what you've always wanted – it's sad Gus will never know.'

'Tom, it was never Gus's doing; I promise you. It sounds disloyal but Gus lost his drive two years back; it was torture for him and me too.'

'He as good as told me he knew about us. It made me feel so guilty.'

'Don't say that – don't ever think that. Sure Gus knew but he wanted the best for me. He was never jealous he was too big a guy.'

'How come the baby?'

'Oh darling Tom,' she buried her face in his chest. 'Don't act so dumb – the baby's yours – ours.'

'What! … but how – when?'

'Remember that night in Oregon; we made love to keep warm.'

Tom remembered. 'That kid who mocked us!'

'Mitch, he said we were making a baby, and he knew only too well. I'll tell you something. Two weeks back I went to Oregon and I stayed with Lisa and Don. That rock where we made love, it's called the birth rock in Indian language. Luke Johnson says the Klamath have a tradition. A couple making love and drinking the water from the spring will conceive. Lisa said it worked for them after they'd tried for years.'

Gina was laughing but she had tears in her eyes. Tom wasn't sure what to think. It was so easy to mock but strange things did happen.

Very slowly he tore open the envelope and took out the letter. It had been typed hurriedly on a word processor with a few ink correct-ions.

Tom,

I'm writing this for you with a copy for Gina.

I have spent a lifetime running from my past but it won't do. Today will settle matters. If Schreiber, Kolkinnen and Wilhelm want me I'll confront them.

You see I am not the innocent you tell me I am. I know you mean well but it won't do. That kid didn't know what was happening, thank God, but she smiled. She looked me straight in the eye and she smiled so sweet. I only know I should have let Schreiber and Wilhelm break every bone in my body before I pushed that plunger. I was weak, I killed her and Miss Berkovic is right. I killed a child in the Holocaust. For that I must answer to God and I believe that day may have come.

I've spoken to my lawyers and I've signed documents. Gina is to have the Crossfield estate, all hers, no strings. I love Crossfield and all its people. I ask you, my friend, to look after Gina and to watch over the land. In return I leave substantial bequests for you and your two children.

Farewell, Tom, my friend. Don't think badly of me.

Gus.

Tom sat silently; he wondered how he would have reacted to torture at the age of eight. He didn't know, it was all beyond comprehension.

Gina was watching him. 'Gus wanted out. Much as I grieve for him, I know what happened was kinda meant.'

'But why this cover up, why are the Americans and our people so keen to hide the truth?'

'I can tell you that,' she sounded bitter. 'It's hard to believe but Van Zyl was flesh and blood – he had parents.'

'So have we all, but I gather his are lost without trace.'

'It's his father they're protecting.' Gina's expression was inscrutable.

'Why?'

She leant forward and whispered the name.

'Good God! That explains everything – his son a racist, a serial murderer, and a drug dealer. There'd be hell to pay if it ever came out in the open.'

'He'd never be president that's for sure; it'd be the scandal of the decade. Best forget it, we've been through enough.'

'Agreed, it's none of my business anyway.' He turned to face her.

'Gina, this has all been a shock, I mean the baby, the farm, you and me – everything.'

'Tom,' she caught his eye with an odd wistful look. 'That day by Bechams wood, that time Van Zyl pointed the gun at me because I wouldn't do what he told me. Right then I wanted to die.'

'Yes, I remember.'

'You pleaded with me, you said, "I love you", it's what you'd never said before – not in all the times we've known each other.'